I0594181

Moorin
Gracita
Kusmerk
N
W E
S

Thick as Blood

Beatrice B. Morgan

AUTHORS 4 AUTHORS PUBLISHING
Marysville, WA, USA

Published by Authors 4 Authors Publishing
1214 6th St
Marysville, WA 98270
www.authors4authorspublishing.com

E-book ISBN: 978-1-64477-134-1
Paperback ISBN: 978-1-64477-135-8

Edited by Rebecca Mikkelson
Copyedited by Brandi Spencer

Authors 4 Authors branding is set in Bavire. Headings are set in IM FELL English Pro. All other text is set in Garamond.

Hard as Stone Book 2

Thick as Blood

Beatrice B. Morgan

Authors 4 Authors Content Rating

This title has been rated 17+, appropriate for older teens and adults, and contains:

- strong language
- graphic violence
- brief implied sex
- mild alcohol use
- mild positive fantasy drug use

Please, keep the following in mind when using our rating system:

1. A content rating is not a measure of quality.

Great stories can be found for every audience. One book with many content warnings and another with none at all may be of equal depth and sophistication. Our ratings can work both ways: to avoid content or to find it.

2. Ratings are merely a tool.

For our young adult (YA) and children's titles, age ratings are generalized suggestions. For parents, our descriptive ratings can help you make informed decisions, but at the end of the day, only you know what kinds of content are appropriate for your individual child. This is why we provide details in addition to the general age rating.

For more information on our rating system, please, visit our Content Guide at: www.authors4authorspublishing.com/books/ratings

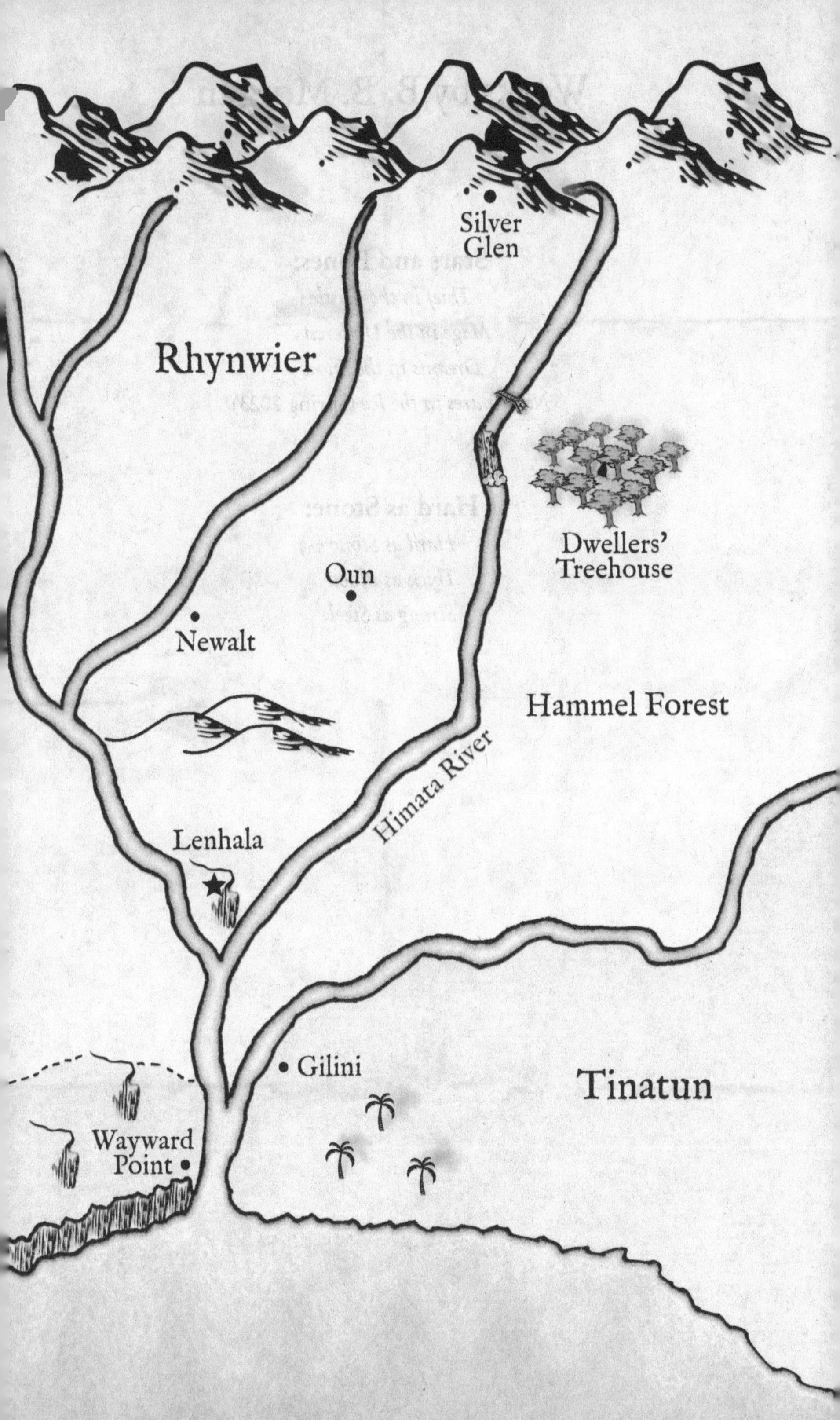

Rhynwier
Silver Glen
Dwellers' Treehouse
Oun
Newalt
Hammel Forest
Himata River
Lenhala
Gilini
Tinatun
Wayward Point

Works by B. B. Morgan

Stars and Bones:
Thief in the Castle
Mage in the Undercity
Dreams in the Snow
Nightmares in the Ice (Spring 2023)

Hard as Stone:
Hard as Stone
Thick as Blood
Strong as Steel

Table of Contents

Table of Contents

"Your stance is wrong," Thalame said, pointing his wooden practice dagger at Raven's legs. Sweat glistened along his dark hair and neck. "Your feet are too close together, and you need to bend your knees a little more."

Raven adjusted her stance.

Thalame considered it silently while catching his breath. "Not the best," he said at last, "but better."

Raven held in her irritation; she half wanted to throw her practice dagger at him. They had been practicing combat basics since dawn. Her stomach growled. Her head hurt. Her muscles ached from the strange new use. She had the beginnings of calluses from the wooden daggers and swords. But she couldn't quit. She had to be stronger.

So she adjusted her stance a bit more.

Thalame let her catch her breath while tossing his wooden dagger into the air. He caught it effortlessly, like he had been handling weapons since he could walk. Knowing him, he might have. He'd told her that he liked the stealth of a dagger but preferred the surprise of a well-timed grenade.

Of all the Dwellers Raven had come to know in the past two weeks, she knew the least about Thalame. He didn't talk about himself or his past, except in dodgy answers. According to Ivy, he had an unhappy past, but she didn't elaborate. Thalame didn't move like a soldier; he moved like an assassin, and his mysterious and unhappy past made him all the more interesting to Raven.

Despite his bulky build, he moved with grace and lethality. He had tawny skin, neither northern pale nor southern brown—a mixture, she had decided. When she had asked Thalame where he had come from, he had shrugged and said, "A town not worth mentioning."

All the Dwellers had come from somewhere else, and she loved the sheer diversity of them all. Some came from the north, some from the south, some from the far southern islands, and some from the far east. Everyone had different stories of how they had ended up with the Dwellers. It was so unlike her home of Silver Glen, where everyone looked the same and thought the same and knew the same stories.

She rolled her neck, and a few strands of her light brown hair fell into her face; her braid had loosened. She whisked the leather strap from the end and quickly braided it back. Raven had turned seventeen a few months prior, but she felt so much older than the little naïve girl who had left Silver Glen. She had seen and survived much. In those days of travel, her pale northern skin had turned a shade of peach. According to Ivy, she no longer looked as though she lived underground.

"Ready?" Thalame asked, catching his dagger by the hilt without looking.

She tossed her braid over her shoulder. "Ready."

Thalame shifted gracefully from his leisurely stance into a fighter's stance. She had only a heartbeat to see it—he came at her. Raven met his wooden dagger with her own, and the wood thunked as she defended and attacked. Thalame moved slower than he would have in a real fight, mostly for her benefit. She had gotten better, but Thalame met every attack she threw like he could sense her movements before she did.

He moved like he hadn't been injured a few weeks ago when part of a tunnel had collapsed on him. He healed remarkably fast thanks to his healing magic, bouncing back from that night faster than anyone else. Zander still winced from time to time, although with Thalame's magic, his injuries had healed remarkably fast too.

Raven ducked to dodge Thalame's attack that would have sliced her throat open in a real fight. She thought herself safe, aimed to counterattack, but his foot came around the back of her knee—down she went.

Thalame was on her in a blink, blade to her throat. "Gotcha," he said, a wicked smile stretching out his battle-serious grimace.

Raven released a sigh of defeat. Not that it bothered her; she hadn't defeated Thalame once.

"You lasted longer than you did last time." Thalame shifted the daggers into one hand and stood. He offered his free hand to her. She took it, and he hoisted her to her feet.

"I'm still horrible," she said.

Thalame shrugged, not denying it. "You won't learn years of combat training in a few weeks."

She rolled her neck and stretched her arms above her head. She adjusted the loose-fitting blouse she had borrowed from Ivy. Raven had accumulated a few basic articles of clothing from the nearby villages, but their stock was nothing impressive. A breeze fluttered through the ceiling of the training room, hot and humid with the sun-parched stench of summer.

The Dwellers lived in a treehouse; Raven didn't know where exactly it was, other than in the middle of a dense forest. She didn't have a clear grasp on the geography of Rhynwier, but she knew it was east of the capital city of Lenhala.

The Dwellers were outsiders, not part of the Gracitan military—the Gray Elite—that ruled both the Empire of Gracita and the Kingdom of Rhynwier, nor were they part of the resistance against the Gray Elite, known as the Order of the Hawks. The Dwellers were a group unto themselves, though from what Raven had gathered, they had ties to the Wraiths, an ancient society of magicians who worked all over the continent to smuggle magicians out of the Gray Elite's clutches so they could live peacefully.

The Gray Elite had decreed magic illegal, and anyone caught using it or helping those who could use it were executed.

The Dwellers were rebels.

Raven bent down to touch her toes, stretching the back of her legs. Her locket shifted under her blouse. She straightened and felt for it, tucked under her collar and out of sight. Her locket was special for two reasons: first, it was the only thing she had of her mother's; second, it contained the centrum of Altair's Augur, a doomsday device. The machine was useless without its magical core.

No one knew she concealed the centrum, except for Zander. Even now, the locket felt strangely warm against her chest.

Thalame got a drink of water, and Raven joined him. The earthenware cup felt warm to the touch, much like everything else in the treehouse. She drank the cool water eagerly; it surged down her throat but turned warm as it met her insides.

Sisters, she was burning up. Sweat coated her skin and lined her scalp. It shimmered against Thalame's brow. Summer's heat had permeated the entire treehouse. At the peak of midday, the heat became nearly unbearable.

The Dwellers' treehouse had been built into the thick branches of the ancient trees. Many of the walls and floors were made of timber or scrap metal. On the highest level of the treehouse, the ceilings opened to the canopy, to the sky. In other places, the branches twisted so tightly together that not even the rain could squeeze through. On the good side, birds and bugs were always chirping and singing. On the bad side, it was blasted hot.

"All right, one more go," said Thalame.

He and Raven returned to the center of the room, wooden daggers in hand. She fell into her stance. Thalame considered it but didn't offer her corrections; her pride swelled.

"Watch me," he said, like he did during every one of their training sessions.

He came at her. When he moved slower, she could see how his body moved as he began an attack or a block, how his muscles shifted, how his stance changed to support his shifting weight. They danced around the floor, and he even let her get a few jabs at him. Gradually, he sped up the combat. The faster he moved, the harder his movements were to predict. How could he predict hers so fast?

Around and around they fought. Sweat slid from her temple, down her face, and into the collar of her blouse. It covered her, thick as a wool blanket. Thalame stepped to the side, preparing for an attack, and she saw it—that small window of opportunity where his other side was left open.

She moved to strike, and then the air rushed out of her lungs of its own accord. A vicious, gasping cough knocked her to her knees. Her daggers clattered to the ground beside her. She gasped for breath—panic rose like bile in her throat, stealing what breath she managed to hang onto. Her skin went clammy.

"Sisters," Thalame gasped and knelt in front of her with the same lethal grace with which he fought, his own daggers laid forgotten on the floor. He pressed his bare hand against her collarbone, his calloused fingers against her throat. His face fell into a deep concentration—to detect any illness.

Gradually, her panic lessened, and her breath returned to normal. The sweat had chilled, but it came as a welcome relief in the heat.

"Hmm. Your fever is small but there," Thalame said, frowning. "I'm not feeling any obvious, known illness." And it worried him. She knew it did. She could see the frustration in his eyes.

She'd had a strange, mild fever since they'd returned from Lenhala. She hadn't said anything about it to the others. A fever was nothing serious, and most took care of themselves.

"The heat's not helping either." He frowned at the ceiling. The branches did not grow as tightly in the training room, and bits of pale blue sky peeked between the leaves. "Take it easy for the rest of the day, Raven. You've been training hard, and your body needs rest."

"I can do it." She jumped to her feet. The floor shifted—it took a moment to realize that *she* had shifted. She steadied herself.

Thalame stood and crossed his arms. "I have no doubt you can, but not today. You're trying too hard to learn too much in a very short time."

She started to argue, but a headache started somewhere behind her eyes. Thalame put his hand on her arm, and the headache dulled.

Pain flashed briefly across his face. He, like the magicians she had met, had evaded the Gray Elite's magic-hunting automatons by tattooing a rune on his back. When he used his magic, the rune burned off the magic that would normally escape into the air.

"Thank you," she said because she knew it hurt him a little to do so.

Healing the others had taken a lot out of him. He had used his magic enough in the past few weeks that Ivy had to hunt down aloe to ease the burns the rune caused to the skin around it.

"Your exhaustion is making you sicker," he said sternly. "You're pushing yourself too hard when you should be resting. You're running yourself ragged."

Raven heaved a sigh. She wanted to argue and keep going, but she also wanted to lie down for a while until her head stopped hurting. "Maybe you're right," she admitted.

Thalame snorted. "Go get yourself a cool drink and some rest." He returned the wooden daggers to the rack by the wall and glanced up at the bits of the pale blue sky. "Maybe the Sisters will grant us rain to take the edge off this heat."

The Sisters were Wilyn, Goddess of the Forest and Keeper of the Stars; Minerva, Goddess of the Sea and Wind; and Solen, Goddess of Stone and Steel. Legends told of how the Sisters had gifted magic to the people of Rhynwier, and the people of Gracita became jealous. That jealousy fueled their desire to conquer and to prove the superiority of their machines over magic.

Raven glanced up at the sky as if Wilyn might answer with a storm cloud. She didn't. Not even a slight breeze. Raven doubted the Sisters would do anything against the heat, just as they had done nothing when Gracita invaded Rhynwier and massacred their worshipers and demolished their temples.

Sweat smothered her in places she would rather it didn't, not to mention everywhere else, and she left the training room to cool down. Thalame was right; she was overheated and working herself too hard. Whatever fever she had picked up in Lenhala needed time to get out of her body.

And working herself to death wouldn't solve anything.

When Raven had glimpsed the treehouse for the first time, she hadn't realized how extensive it was. Ivy had given her a tour, and its sheer size astounded her. The Dwellers had built their treehouse high above the forest floor, hidden among the thick branches. They had rooms for everything: weaving, herbs, stargazing, reading, leatherworking. The treehouse wound around the thick tree trunks, connecting the rooms and halls with spiraling staircases made of tied-together branches and timber, ziplines, rope bridges, and ladders. The timber floors rose and fell with the branches, around the wide trunks, over and under branches thicker than a house.

Raven retreated to one of the bathrooms higher in the treehouse. Woven walls separated the water basins from the toilets and showers, with multicolored metal pipes connecting the basins to the tanks of gathered rainwater. Planks and woven reeds formed walls between the showers, and curtains looped over the branches of the ceiling for privacy.

Raven turned the knob over one of the basins, and rainwater flowed through the pipe. She washed her hands and face in lukewarm water. The burning underneath her skin eased a little. She held her hands and forearms under the water until she no longer felt as though she might combust. She glanced at herself in the shined brass that served as a mirror. Sisters, she looked terrible: sweaty, tired, and sick. Bags hung under her eyes, and sweat plastered her hair to her temples. Her entire face was flushed pink.

She placed her wet hands against her cheeks. Hot. Too hot.

Overheated—Thalame was right. These were the hottest days of summer, and with the open canopy of the treehouse, all the humidity and heat came right inside. It was nothing like Silver Glen, where the mines remained cool, regardless of whether the surface sizzled with summer or slept under piles of snow.

What she wouldn't give for a pile of snow to lay in...

She glanced up at the pieces of the pale blue sky. A few birds tweeted.

Rest. She needed rest. But how was she to rest when it was so ungodly hot?

Ivy had shown her a lagoon by the waterfall, half-tucked inside a shallow cave, half-shaded by towering oaks. The water stayed cool, perfect for an afternoon swim.

Raven let out a sigh. Her hot breath puffed against the shined brass mirror. Ivy had returned to Lenhala a week prior to assess the damage done. Raven hadn't heard a whisper or word about her friend, and each day tightened the ball of anxiety in her chest.

She let her face air dry, which didn't take long. She meandered back to her room—the room she shared with Ivy—mind on the rest that Thalame told her to get, but she found someone already inside. A younger girl, ten or eleven, was dropping a leather satchel onto Ivy's made bed. A heavier satchel had been placed on the floor at the foot.

"Tara?" Raven asked.

The younger girl spun fast enough that her two long brown braids swung in an arc. Her sun-tanned cheeks spread in a wide smile. "Good news, Rae," said Tara. "Ivy's back. She asked me about you, and I said you were well, though I suspect she'll want to ask you herself." Raven inhaled, question poised, but Tara continued, "She's in the lounge upstairs, or she was when I saw her, waiting to discuss with the others."

Raven couldn't help the smile that stretched across her cheeks. "Thank you, Tara!" she said as she ran down the hallway and toward the lounge.

The Dwellers scattered themselves throughout the kingdom as informants, ambassadors, and spies. They bartered in information. Ivy wasn't a Hawk or Gray Elite or a magician; she was a spy. She lived two lives: one as Ivy, the free spirited girl in the woods—her true self—and one as Ivaline Pemberton, an uppercrust girl with a sickly disposition, who stayed inside for long periods of time. Ivaline was the cover while Ivy gathered information.

Raven stumbled through the doorway and found Ivy reclining on a wicker chaise. Thalame was sitting on a wooden stool beside her.

A fragment of movement, so quick she nearly missed it—and in Raven's mind she completed the image—Thalame and Ivy's interlaced hands quickly coming apart. Thalame glanced away, and Ivy's face brightened at Raven, though pink highlighted her pale cheeks. Raven decided not to mention it.

"Raven!" Ivy said cheerfully.

"Shouldn't you be resting?" Thalame asked, one brow higher than the other.

Ivy started to speak, then glanced at Thalame. Worry creased her brow. "Resting?" She turned her gaze to Raven. "Are you still feeling under the weather?"

"A little," Raven said. "But it's nothing I can't stand."

"That's good to hear," said Ivy. "But just in case, I'll hug you and kiss your cheek when you're feeling well again. I'd rather not catch whatever it is you've got."

Raven nodded, sitting in one of the wicker chairs that circled the lounge for meetings. "I will hold you to that."

Being in one of the highest points in the treehouse, they had an unobstructed view of the pale blue sky. Currently, a wispy cloud inched along.

"When did you get back?" Raven asked.

"Not long ago." Ivy still wore pigments of Ivaline's pale makeup and dark kohl, though it looked as though she'd tried to wash it off. She wore trousers and a blouse, rather than the dresses and corsets they wore in the city. Dust stuck to her boots. "I've just had time to grab a cup of tea and put my feet up."

Footsteps sounded outside the lounge, and Zander Winchester appeared. The sunlight had brought a healthy glow to his bronze skin, though standing in the shade of the doorway, he looked gaunt. He had left the top few buttons of his shirt undone, and sweat glistened along his collarbone. He wore knives on his suspenders and guns on his hips—he had named his favorite gun Birdie. Zander's sapphire eyes flickered between Ivy and Raven, and his straight-line mouth twisted into a scowl. "Ivy," Zander greeted. He sounded irritated, like he had been interrupted.

"Most people say 'hello' in a greeting," Ivy said playfully, "particularly when greeting a lady."

"Hello," he said through gritted teeth.

Ivy pretended not to notice and fanned herself with a piece of lace strung between wooden sticks.

Zander sulked into the lounge and sat beside Raven, though he didn't speak. He didn't even glance in her direction. She didn't have time to tease him about his mood before Niall—tinker, mechanic, spy—appeared. The dark braids that usually hung to his shoulders had been twisted up in a hasty yet somehow elaborate style. Sweat glistened along the brown of Niall's neck and face; the heat in the workshop, she figured.

Niall sank into the chair beside Zander, and the two boys shared a short, knowing glance. Raven frowned. Secrets had passed between them, she knew it. Zander met her gaze, and his frown deepened.

Zander and his many secrets, she thought bitterly. Had they not promised to be more honest with one another?

More Dwellers filed into the lounge; some she knew by name, and some she knew by face only. They all looked bogged by the heat. After a time, Ivy cleared her throat—a lady's signal to attention. The chatter silenced.

"Well?" asked Tay, the unspoken leader of the Dwellers. A hulking mass of a man, his intimidation contrasted greatly with his gentle demeanor—most of the time. He motioned toward Ivy. "Fill us in, girl, before winter sets in."

"Well…" Ivy started. With all eyes on her, she sat up a little straighter. If the attention bothered her, she didn't show it. "Lenhala is still in shock. Everyone is talking about the murders at the Summer Solstice Ball. The following attack on Deacon's life is fueling the Gray Elite's story that the Hawks were behind the whole thing. According to Father, they used the murders as their reasoning for storming the Hawks' headquarters. He told me that the Hawks are holding." Ivy looked to Zander. "Unfortunately, both the Hawks and the Gray Elite consider you a traitor. Father knows you're alive and well, but he's promised not to give your whereabouts away."

A few spat curses, including Zander.

Guilt weighed on Raven's shoulders. She knew, deeper down than she could think, that the murders and the attack on the Hawks hadn't been her fault, but it didn't stop her from feeling like it had been. The events of that night had been started by her, and so they felt like her fault. And as a result, Zander had been barred from his home by his own family.

"And," Ivy said, looking at Raven, "because General Deacon has framed Raven as his attempted assassin, she is the most wanted person in the city, possibly the kingdom. Regent Dunel has officially declared that the automatons are to seize you on sight. Alive."

A chill went through her bones at that word. Alive.

They wanted the centrum. Had Deacon figured out that the box she'd given him was empty? When he did, he would be furious. He would know that she'd lied.

"On the bright side, bards have already composed songs about you," Ivy said, waving her fan at Raven, her eyes glittering. "Some are rather endearing. Everyone loves a good antihero, you know."

Thalame scoffed. "That means the automatons will be looking for you with intent," he said to Raven.

"The general also claims Raven wrongly accused and planted evidence against Brigadier General Winchester," Ivy said dryly, looking at Zander with her head cocked to the side.

His brooding gaze widened.

"However, Deacon assures the public that Brigadier General Winchester and his wife are clean of dealings with the Hawks and that the accusation was a ruse."

Raven and Zander laughed, she scornfully and he bitterly.

"My father is a master of lies," Zander said, each word sharp as a dagger. "He's been spinning lies to the Gray Elite for years, and the general has fallen for it. My father has done well to make sure the public sees him campaign against the Hawks, and he's even staged fake missions with the Hawks so that the Gray Elite thinks he's on their side. He's a clever bastard, I'll give him that."

Raven held in her words. Had Zander inherited his father's knack for deception? He had fooled her and the people of Silver Glen. He had hidden his identity as Gray Elite, as a Hawk, and as a magician.

Zander leaned forward, elbows on his knees, the same look of disgust twisting his features that he wore whenever he spoke of his father—the father who had accused him of treason, thrown him in the dungeon, and tortured him for information. Raven wasn't fond of the man either. He had smacked her to the floor when she had refused him information.

Zander glanced at her as if he could sense her thoughts. A flurry of butterflies intertwined with her agitation, mixing into an uncomfortable anxiety. She averted her gaze from him and sought out Ivy instead.

"But," Ivy said, "the good news is that while Lenhala is ripe with petty politics, they aren't paying attention to us."

"Good," said Thalame. "There's a lot riding on this rescue mission. We can't afford to have any more Gray Elite attention than we've already got."

The air in the room tensed. For the past two weeks, they had been healing and training and planning, all in preparation for their upcoming mission: to rescue Princess Rosaria from her imprisonment in Moorin, the capital city of Gracita and center of the Gray Elite's military power. Rosaria was the rightful monarch of Rhynwier, and with her on their side, they could dismantle Altair's Augur for good.

"Speaking of that mission," piped up Tay, his booming voice taking up as much space as his shoulders, "how's that coming along?" He looked at Zander.

"Niall and I have been working on getting the maps together," said Zander. "We want one master map, not dozens of them. We've got maps of city streets, waterways, and surrounding villages, a few of the major buildings."

"I'm working on finding anything that might give us an advantage," added Niall.

"Good," said Tay. "Keep at it. We can't afford for this mission to go wrong or to let the Hawks or the Gray Elite know what we're up to."

Raven held her shoulders straighter. The mission was also why she had been training. She didn't want to be useless, not like she had been in Lenhala.

"I doubt the Gray Elite will be nice about it this time," said Zander, an edge to his voice—the same edge he got whenever they spoke about Rosaria. "If they think we're after her, they'll either get rid of her or put her somewhere we can't reach."

"They already think she's unreachable," Thalame reminded him. "And, generally speaking, anyone inside the Tombs is."

Thalame and Zander shared a prolonged glance. More secrets, more unsaid things.

Raven fought the urge to say something. Was she the only one in the treehouse who didn't have a mound of secrets? Even after she and Zander had told them everything—well, most things—everyone else still had secrets.

Sweat broke out over her skin, along her scalp, down her back, cold and hot all at once. The fever returned. Hot. Too hot. Burning. The edges of the world blurred; the lounge swayed. She gripped the arms of the wicker chair to remind herself that she had balance.

Thalame spoke, but his words were muffled. Zander spoke, muffled.

Neither were speaking to her.

Then, everyone stood—meeting adjourned. She stood too, and the blurriness faded enough that she could walk straight. It faded a little more with every step. She passed into the hall, and Zander brushed against her shoulder. His sapphire eyes briefly met hers, and then he continued down the hall and out of sight.

Raven kept walking. Her feet took her toward the cool lagoon where she could drown this burning fever.

Zander acted like he hadn't kissed her during their harrowing escape from the city. He talked only about Rosaria, about the mission, about the importance of saving the princess. She understood him being busy with all the preparations, but did he not have a spare breath for her? A heartbeat to spare for a good morning or a goodnight? He had said few words to her since their return. He'd been busy, she reasoned, as had she.

She would rather take his worry than his indifference. He likely didn't have room to think about her between his thoughts of Rosaria, his darling princess, the precious key to saving the kingdom.

The fever burned sudden and hot, blurring her vision. She careened into the wall, the side of a tree trunk, and rested against the bark until her legs could support her again. Luckily, she was alone in the hall. She didn't feel like listening to anyone else talk about resting or her health.

She heaved a slow breath. The lagoon. The cool water.

That was what she needed.

Raven meandered to a ladder concealed within a fake tree that led to the forest floor. She found purchase on the ladder's rungs and started to descend, already feeling a coolness from the shade of the tunnel. At the bottom, a door led to the forest floor. The door and the fake tree had been so cleverly hidden with bark and vines that if she hadn't already known where they were, she wouldn't have spotted the difference.

Between the treehouse and the impossibly thick tree trunks, the forest floor received little sunlight. Few plants grew in the thick shade, and it smelled strongly of tilled dirt and damp. It resembled a perpetual twilight—a nightmarish version of daytime—but it had a peacefulness to it. Birds chittered in the canopy, and cicadas sang incessantly.

Raven started toward the lagoon, and soon sunlight dappled through the canopy as she left the treehouse behind. The summer heat turned blistering in the direct sun, and by the time Raven came to the lagoon, the humidity had risen. It would rain soon.

She found the lagoon deserted, and she eagerly undressed and stepped into the cool water. It covered the overheated skin of her legs. She walked to the deeper end of the pool and submerged herself, staying under as long as her lungs would allow. The coolness of the water, the shade of the shallow cave—her fever relaxed. It did not relent, but it calmed. An underground river fed the lagoon, and the water continuously flowed to meet the aboveground river—the lagoon was always cool.

She closed her eyes and reclined against the water-smoothed side of the lagoon, a calm blue-gray stone. With the cooling, soothing, relaxing water, her mind didn't feel so cluttered. Her anxiety ebbed.

Why did it matter if Zander worried about Princess Rosaria? He was supposed to be on the princess's side in this war, the war their kingdom had lost. Raven should feel the same stubborn pride when it came to Rhynwier, but she didn't. Not really. She did want to see the Gray Elite fall. And, if they succeeded in this impossible mission, if they saved the princess, they would still have to put her on the throne and banish the Gray Elite from the kingdom.

That sounded more impossible than saving the princess.

"I thought you'd be here," came Ivy's chime.

Raven opened an eye to see the blonde girl walking toward the pool. She stopped by the rocks where Raven had left her clothes, and added her own to them. She joined Raven in the water. She dunked herself, coming up with a sigh of relief, her flaxen hair flattened against her head.

"I'm glad you're back," Raven said as Ivy settled against the stone beside her. "I missed you. The others aren't nearly as pleasant to talk to."

Ivy chuckled. "I don't suppose they would be. Everyone is all in a tizzy about this mission. They want to get it done as fast as possible but also as efficiently as possible, and I see those two things as counterintuitive. Personally, I vote we rest for a good two or three weeks more before plunging into something that could very well get us all killed."

"I second that," said Raven.

They rested for a while in silence. Raven had missed Ivy. She had missed having a friend to talk to.

"Zander is worried about the princess," Raven whispered at last, her words sharper than she intended.

"Does that bother you?"

Raven didn't answer. Her gaze drifted to the dark gray of the rocky ceiling. *Yes*, was the correct answer. "No," she said.

Ivy hummed in disbelief. She eyed Raven suspiciously, urging Raven to admit the truth.

Raven sighed through her nose. "A little," she whispered. "That's all he talks about, all he thinks about, and he hasn't said more than a few words to me since we've been back, and when he does, he glares. It's like he doesn't want me to be here." Saying it all out loud made it sound foolish. Raven's cheeks warmed.

Ivy didn't say anything for a moment. All the world was the trickling of the water through the rocks, the cascading of the underground river along the rockface and into the lagoon, and the thousands of birds chirping amidst the summer's heat.

Then Ivy said softly, "Zander feels responsible for Rosaria's capture. A few weeks before he fled, she was captured by the Gray Elite. It wasn't his fault, not entirely. Rosaria can be...willfully ignorant of risks. That's how my father put it. She and Zander went out one night, and, well, they got separated, and then she was captured. Zander knew only of his mission the night the Hawks were going to rescue her," Ivy said grimly.

An assassination, Raven remembered.

"He didn't know it was connected to Rosaria. When he didn't eliminate his target, the overall mission was exposed. No one knew what had happened. Zander was just gone."

Escaped. Zander had learned of his father's plan to use Altair's Augur. He'd stolen the centrum and fled as far from Lenhala as he could.

"The Gray Elite had Rosaria moved," Ivy said. "Until recently, we didn't know where. Zander didn't know about Rosaria until his father told him about it. Now he blames himself twice over."

Raven had seen his face when his father had told him. Shock, disbelief, shame. "And now Zander thinks it's his responsibility to get her back," Raven said.

"Yes."

Raven sighed. "He must care about her a great deal," she whispered. The words left a bitter taste on her tongue. Raven knew she was fishing for information—she had seen Ivy do it as Ivaline, and she had seen her own stepmother do it to her plenty, asking seemingly simple questions, only to dig through the answers.

"He does," Ivy said, her voice reserved. "But not in the way you're thinking. When the king and queen were killed, Brigadier General Winchester smuggled Rosaria out of the palace. He took her in, raised her in secret. She and Zander are the same age, and they grew up as siblings. So, yes, he cares about Rosaria, but not like he cares about you."

Raven let out a bitter laugh, guilt and anger and jealousy all mixed together.

"I'm being serious," said Ivy, smacking Raven's shoulder playfully.

"His father said he planned for Zander to marry Rosaria," Raven said. Which would make him king of Rhynwier, should they succeed and put Rosaria on the throne. *King.* Raven's stomach collapsed at the very thought.

Ivy didn't respond. Her silence and lack of comforting information confirmed that she had known. After a lengthy pause, she said, her voice full of its usual charm, "Well, Brigadier General Winchester isn't in charge of them now. If we get to Rosaria first, it will be her will against the Hawks, and I'm fairly certain her opinion outweighs theirs."

"And having her on our side will change things?" Raven asked.

"It will give us an advantage," said Ivy. "With Rosaria, we can start plotting the downfall of the Gray Elite and push them out of our kingdom. She's got a mind for political juggling, I've heard. And, she's royal by blood, so our chances of her having that royal magic is high."

"Royal magic?" Raven asked, turning her head to Ivy.

She nodded. The hair at her temples had begun to dry, and it curled like fishhooks around her face. "Yeah, they say that the royal magic was stronger than any other, passed down through the bloodlines, having been gifted from the gods to the first king of Rhynwier. Something about the ruler being tied to the land, or whatever. Who knows?"

So not only was Rosaria a princess and future queen, she was a powerful magician too.

"I only met her a few times. I'm not officially a Hawk," Ivy said, sighing through her nose, "but everyone tells me she's a clever girl with a good head on her shoulders. If only they said that about me." She chuckled.

Raven offered Ivy a smile and returned her stare to the rocky ceiling of the lagoon. Logically, she should want the best for her kingdom, her home, her princess, but where that sense of pride should have been, she felt a numb bitterness.

Even her sense of adventure had depleted.

Maybe Thalame had been right about the fever. It was making her sicker than she realized.

Ivy nudged her arm. "Don't worry about Zander. He's just being protective and vengeful. You'll see. We'll go on this mission, save our princess, and then you'll see how it is."

"Okay," Raven said because she could fathom no other response. "I'll take your word for it."

Because she wanted to believe Ivy.

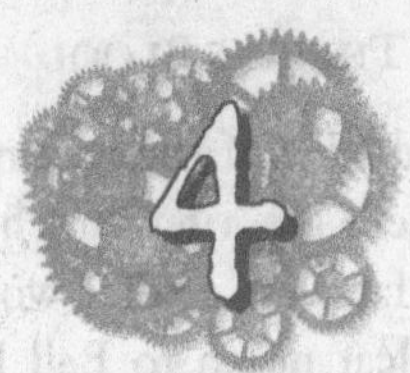

A week passed, and Raven spent her days in a stupor. With all the planning, no one had much time for anything else. Raven's fever didn't recede. She slept sometimes for ten or twelve hours. The heat of the summer intensified, and it made her fever all the more prominent.

She kept her training sessions with Thalame light and short, her meals small and controlled, and her fluid intake high. Most of the Dwellers were too busy to notice anything amiss; only Ivy and Thalame seemed concerned.

When asked, Raven blamed the heat. Thalame didn't like that answer, but he never pushed for more information.

Raven escaped to the lagoon every day—sometimes with Ivy, sometimes without.

At the end of the week, the Dwellers gathered in one of the lower chambers. Bark and tight branches formed the ceiling and walls, and no natural sunlight lit the space. Instead, lanterns hung from the branches. Raven sank into a chair beside Ivy. The chamber was far too stuffy for her liking.

Niall and Zander stood beside a wooden table on which they had arranged a number of maps and diagrams. When everyone had gathered, Niall spoke first.

"We've gone over various ways we won't be able to get in," Niall said, motioning to a large map of Gracita. "Automaton patrols have increased on the main roads, waterways, and ports into Gracita. Air traffic is tighter than the roads."

"And there are no tunnels or cave systems leading under the border," Zander added. In the shadowy light, his exhaustion showed. Bruises hugged his eyes, and his skin looked pale. "That we know of, at least."

"We've few options for entry," said Niall. He pulled another map from the pile. It was an air traffic map; all the ports were marked by red and blue dots. "First, we can go by air. It's the quickest route, but also the riskiest. To avoid alarming Air Patrol, we would have to find a ship with clearance over the border. We would have to buy or threaten our way on board."

"And finding one that won't turn us in is going to be near impossible," said Zander, his distaste for the plan obvious. He pointed to the northern border of Gracita. The jagged edge of the mountains had been drawn with sharp points, like teeth. "There are a few uncharted airways into Gracita. They're to the far north and far west. Either would take us weeks to get to, although if we took the Hellcat north to Bell Falls, we could shave a few days off that."

Raven scanned the map for Bell Falls. It wasn't terribly far from Silver Glen—just to the southwest.

"It would take longer," Zander said, "but it would be safer."

"Either way, our chances of being caught or seen or reported are high," said Niall grimly.

Thalame shifted from his place against the wall. He uncrossed his arms to motion to the map. "What about to the south?"

"The south is heavily guarded," Niall said, looking as though he expected Thalame to have known that. "It's the main airway for the ports. Automatons and Gray Elite would be everywhere."

"Which would be the last place they'd expect us to come in through," said Thalame, raising a brow.

"Because it's near impossible," added Zander dryly.

"Maybe for us," Thalame said. "It wouldn't be hard to slip into Tinatun's western territory to see if our old friends won't help us out. If I remember right, Malik owes me a favor. He's got connections to the sky and to the Crusaders."

Silence drifted into the room and landed thickly. That silence quickly became uncomfortable. Thalame and Zander stared at one another, unsaid words passing between them.

"Who are the Crusaders?" Raven asked, her voice slicing through the silence.

"They're pirates," Zander spat. "They stayed out of the war and kept to themselves. They've made it clear they want nothing to do with our problems. What makes you think they would even hear us out?"

"Like I said, Malik owes me a favor," Thalame repeated. "And if he can't help us out, there's always the Wraiths."

Zander glared daggers. "No."

Raven glanced between the two boys. Zander's eyes were predatory, filled with warnings and threats. Thalame remained unfazed by it.

Thalame continued, ignoring Zander's silent but obvious objections, "The Crusaders will know every crack in the border patrols, and getting us through won't be a problem for them. Malik knows the ports; he might be able to get us on a cargo ship. Either way, we can slip into Gracita, maybe even into Moorin."

Zander heaved a sigh of displeasure. "We can find another way in."

"By trudging across the kingdom? By the time we get to Rosaria, we'll all be gray-haired," Thalame argued. "The Crusaders are the best chance we've got."

Niall rubbed the back of his neck, dark eyes moving cautiously between Thalame and Zander. "As much as I hate to admit it," he said, wincing as Zander turned his glare to him, "Thalame might be right."

A rumble of the room signified that most agreed with Niall. Zander released a long, agitated sigh.

"The only problem will be getting to Wayward Point without automaton interference," said Thalame. He strolled to the table and pointed to the southern border of Rhynwier where it met the kingdom of Tinatun. "While the borders aren't patrolled as heavily, they're still patrolled, and I'd rather not run into any wandering raiders."

Raven blinked at the mention of Wayward Point; she had met a thief who had told her to go there if she wanted out, and that thief had given her a wooden coin and instructions. Her lips parted, and as if hearing her thoughts, Zander shot her a steep warning glare not to interrupt.

She pulled her lips closed and met his glare with one of her own.

"If we take down an automaton, the Gray Elite will notice when it fails to return after its patrol," Niall said. "The Hellcat could take us most of the way, but we'd still have to get across the border."

"And because someone is the most wanted person in the kingdom," Thalame added, nudging his elbow toward Raven, "we'll have to be careful."

Raven felt a surge of gratefulness toward Thalame, but also the desire to kick him. He winked at her like he knew.

"Raven's not going," Zander said flatly.

Her heart jumped into her throat. "What?" she stammered. "What do you mean I'm not going?"

Zander looked up from the map and met her glare with his own. "It will be dangerous, and this mission is critical," he said, his tone low. "And you will only be a hindrance."

Thalame opened his mouth, but Raven cut him off, "A *hindrance?*" Her voice squeaked on the word. The fever burned underneath her skin, heating with the embarrassment that flooded her cheeks. "I would not."

Zander crossed his arms; he did not believe her.

She huffed. "Without me, you would still be rotting in the Hawk's dungeon."

Zander scoffed. "Even if you hadn't come to get me out, the Hawks wouldn't have killed me, and the Wraiths would have sent someone sooner or later."

She fumed. She opened her mouth to argue, but he spoke first.

"And, if it weren't for you, I wouldn't have been in that damned prison in the first place."

She balled her fists. If she had been paying attention during her watch duty, the thief wouldn't have slipped into the mines, wouldn't have stolen the centrum, and they wouldn't have had to chase him down. None of it would have happened.

Her fault. Her fault. Her fault.

Her cheeks burned, and she knew he was right. She held her tongue, and the subtle smirk that came over Zander's lips made her want to throw something hard and sharp at him.

Niall cleared his throat, and Raven became aware of the dozen other people in the room, all of whom had witnessed their disagreement, and her embarrassment turned to something poisonous. Her stomach weakened, her knees threatened to give, and she wanted nothing more than to be out of the meeting room and far away from them all, Zander especially.

"And...we will continue this discussion tomorrow." Niall started to gather his maps. "I'll have something on the borders of Tinatun and Gracita to present."

Raven stormed out of the meeting room first, pushing past Thálame to get out of there as quickly as possible. She headed straight for the outside, toward the lagoon, toward some semblance of peace between her uselessness and her fever. By the time she arrived at the mouth of the shallow cave, she was breathless, sweaty, and felt as though the fever would burn the skin off her body. She tore at her clothes to rid herself of them, and half fell and half jumped into the cool waters.

A *hindrance.*

How dare he! Why did he have to remind her how useless she was?

She submerged herself as long as she could, until her lungs felt like they might burst, and she let herself float to the surface.

A hindrance. That's what she was to him. A problem. She had let the thief slip into the mines; she had gotten them caught; she had gotten Zander accused and thrown into the Hawk's dungeons. Everything had been her fault! And he loved to remind her about it.

Without anyone in the lagoon to hear or see, she let her frustrations out—she screamed. It echoed off the cavern walls, frightened unsuspecting birds, and for a heartbeat, stilled the forest around her.

And then it felt like something had been lifted, removed. She sank against the lagoon's smooth sides. The birds resumed their chirping as if nothing had happened.

Raven soaked until the fever retreated. By then, the sun had sunk to the west and gilded the humid forest in blazing golds and pinks, setting the summer haze aflame. Cicadas sang, thousands of them, overshadowing the birds. She stood in the dying sunlight to dry, and in those fleeting moments, she felt something like peace.

A piece of a memory—she stood in the afternoon sun in the northernmost parts of Hammel Forest around Silver Glen. She was nine, and it was the first time she'd snuck out of the mine. Her father didn't know. Her stepmother didn't know. She'd kept out of sight from the lookout tower and slipped through the forest to the boundary fence. While she wouldn't have the guts to go beyond it that day, she stood at the fence and watched the forest fade from bright afternoon to hazy evening. At nine years old, the night forest still scared her.

An owl hooted. Raven blinked, and she stood again in the mouth of the lagoon, seventeen years old. Some days, she didn't feel any braver or smarter than she had back then.

Maybe she wasn't.

Maybe Zander was right in leaving her behind. She wasn't a spy or a magician. She had no skills that would get them out of a tight spot. She would only be a hindrance.

She dressed and left her hair loose and started back toward the treehouse. By the time she returned, the sun had gone entirely. With only the moonlight and sparse candlelight to go by, Raven guided herself with one hand on the wall as she made her way back to her room.

Her steps meandered, her mind for once restful. She needed a long sleep. She crossed an intersection of two halls, all shadowed in the clouded moonlight.

"...being overly protective," came Thalame's whispered voice from a lounge down the hall. "Her training has been going fine—well, considering."

"Fine enough to send her on this mission?" came Zander's whispered reply.

Raven stopped dead. Her heart skipped a beat. Her peace shattered like glass. They were talking about *her*.

"I wouldn't say that," Thalame said lowly.

"She doesn't need to go," Zander said, almost a plea. "It's too dangerous, and the Gray Elite will be looking for her. The automatons will be too. All the Detectors will have her face memorized. Not to mention the starving citizens who would gladly sell her or information about her to the Gray Elite for a few tokens. She doesn't know how to fight. She doesn't understand the gravity of this mission. She doesn't understand the finer elements that will be necessary in order to get in and out of Moorin without detection and without problem."

She felt her face burn with shame and embarrassment. Zander was right about those things, and though she knew it, his words stung like a sword through her chest.

Thalame scoffed. "I'm not sure If *I* have those things," he said, his words sharp. Zander started to speak, but Thalame cut him off. "And if you think you do, then you don't."

Zander grumbled something too low to hear.

"You said she did fine in Lenhala," came Niall's kind chime of a voice. "Moorin won't be much different."

"Except I don't know who to trust and who not to. In Lenhala, I had the advantage," said Zander.

Thalame mumbled something too low for her to hear. Niall's soft voice came after, but his words were lost to the blood gushing through her ears. She tiptoed closer to the door.

"...not well enough. She's nowhere near trained to survive a real fight," said Zander. "She will only slow us down or get herself killed. She's..." An exasperated sigh. "She needs to stay behind, where it's safe."

Raven heard the inflection on his tone, the half truth, the truth he wanted to tell them but couldn't. She touched the locket around her throat. The centrum, the core of Altair's Augur. Zander wanted her to stay behind and protect it, to keep it out of enemy reach, but he couldn't explain that to the others without telling them about the centrum. She and Zander had decided it would be better if no one else knew.

But she could leave it in the treehouse or bury it in the forest below.

Thalame let out a short sigh. "I know, mate. You're right on those accounts."

"But we can't just leave her here," Niall said, and Raven felt a surge of goodwill toward the tinker. "She will never speak to any of us again."

"She needs to go back to Silver Glen," said Zander. Firmly. "It's the safest place."

"That's why you wanted to go north," Niall said, at the same time as the thought passed through Raven's mind.

Her heart tumbled into her ankles. That was why Zander had been so adamant about going north; he wanted to send her back to Silver Glen.

Thalame made an argumentative sound.

"What?" asked Zander. "You don't think so?"

"Travel may not be the best thing for her right now," said Thalame. The silence thickened. "She's been fighting a fever since we got back from Lenhala."

Zander spat a curse. "Why did I not know about this sooner?"

"Because she asked me to keep quiet," said Thalame defensively. "I thought it'd go away on its own, but it hasn't." He dropped his voice. "A fever that lasts more than a week isn't a good sign; you know that. It's been three. She doesn't need to be traveling in this heat. It very well might do her in."

"But you've been training her?" Niall asked, and Raven could picture his face, one dark brow raised, his intelligent eyes searching Thalame for unspoken answers.

Thalame resigned a sigh. "Lightly. It's also how I've been monitoring her condition without her knowing. She gets defensive when I talk to her about it."

Silence fell between the boys.

"Fine," Zander said firmly, the final decision. "She stays in the treehouse for now. If she's ill, then she doesn't need to go on this mission."

No one disagreed, and Raven's lungs fell into her ankles beside her heart, yanking her breath with it.

"I'll leave it to you to break it to her, then," said Thalame.

Zander harrumphed.

The conversation ended, and before any of them could step out and see her, she tiptoed away, around the end of the hall, and darted away as quietly as she could. She didn't know what to think about first: that Thalame had told Zander about her fever, that they all wanted to leave her behind, or that she knew they were right.

She would only slow them down.

She was sick, untrained, and useless. Utterly useless.

A silent tear swelled at the corner of her eye, and with a blink, it ran down her cheek without her permission. She forced her chest calm, her breathing even, though it yearned to sob; if she started to cry, someone—everyone—would hear. It would be a scene. She couldn't handle that kind of humiliation and exposure.

The fever, the damn fever, burned like fire, and she broke out in a sweat. She walked past the hall to her bedroom. She couldn't face Ivy either. Not like this. Not until she got herself under control.

She stumbled down one of the secret ladders, her hands and feet shaking on the rungs, and half fell to the forest floor as her meager control broke. The first sob quaked through her chest, emitting a strangled cry from her throat.

They would leave her behind while they went to save the kingdom. They would leave her behind while they changed history, had an adventure, did the impossible, because she would be a hindrance.

Useless.

She meandered through the forest, away from the treehouse, and with no one to watch or listen, she let the tears fall. They rolled down her burning cheeks with vigor. Maybe the fever would burn her up, and then she wouldn't be in anyone's way. Zander could go save his precious princess and forget about her, the stupid, useless, simple girl that could do nothing and ruined everything.

A part of her hoped the princess would be dead before they got to her.

Another part of her knew how horrible of a thought it was.

Back in Silver Glen, Raven had a tree. She had carved her initials—RT—into its bark. It stood beyond the border, safe and unsafe, and had been a place where she could go without being found, without being chided for skipping chores, and just *be*. How many hours had she lounged in the tree's fork, daydreaming about sky cities and airships and all the adventure and romance and magic to be found in the sky?

Enough that her head had been without room for reality, it seemed. Strangely, Zander had been the only one to find her hiding place.

Raven wished she could run to that tree now and hide within its thick branches, imagine the world on the other side of the forest, and retain a fraction of the sense of wonder she'd felt when gazing at the horizon—of all the adventure she could imagine, there for the taking. Adventures just waiting to be had.

But there were no trees like that in this forest. She was far from Silver Glen, and she did not want to go back.

Raven walked and ran and ran and then walked. She didn't mind where she went, only that she moved. It helped, a little. She ran herself breathless and, when she could go no further, collapsed in a small clearing. The grassy, summer-baked earth barely gave under her knees. She had cried herself dry, but the trails on her cheeks felt fresh. The fever burned underneath her skin, pulsing with her heartbeat. Her vision blurred around the edges, each breath harder than the last.

She stayed a while on the forest floor, regaining her strength and breath. When she finally pushed herself to her feet, it felt as though she had been wrung out. A step—she lost her balance and leaned against a tree.

Sisters, she shouldn't have run so much. Everything hurt. She pushed sweaty hair out of her face and turned to go back to the treehouse. Sleep. She needed sleep. Her cot. Her room. Rest.

But...which way was the treehouse? She looked around the forest. The treehouse was at the thickest, oldest part of the forest. It wouldn't be too hard to find, right?

The fever pulsed, and she leaned against another tree. She closed her eyes, taking each breath as it came. All around, the night bugs and birds chirped and chittered. She willed her heart to slow, to calm; willed the fever to ease or just take her and be done with it.

It did none of those things.

Raven opened her eyes and looked up into the endless stars. Some glowed faintly blue, some yellow, some pink. Would those colors become more distinguishable if she were closer to them?

Her small reverie shattered with the sound of footsteps. Big, thunderous footsteps. Too big, too heavy, too wide a stride for a man. And then she heard the unnatural clicking of gears, the churning of belts and cogs, and the interval hissing of steam.

She froze and put her back flush against the tree. The footsteps came closer—to her left, on the other side of the tree.

Clomp, clomp, clomp.

It paused.

Raven held her breath and dared not move.

Pale red light flooded around the tree's trunk. It shone against the weeds and brush, on the stone and tree roots, throwing dangerous shadows. It was looking. Searching. *Hunting.*

The automaton took a step to the left, and she took a step to right—keeping the tree between them. It took a step; she took a step at the same time, hiding her footsteps within its. Soon, they had traded places. It took another step, and then another—away from her.

Raven dared peek around the tree. She saw the automaton's posterior, thick panels of steel, bronze, and iron. Its searching red eyes panned the forest, side to side. Its two arms ended in three prongs, made for grabbing. The thick chest resembled a barrel—a cage, she suspected. It moved further away from her, steam hissing from the shoulders. A second later, steam hissed from the hips.

Heart racing, fever pulsing, Raven let out a slow, steady breath. It hadn't seen her. She could already hear Zander's lecture of how dangerous the forest was, how she had recklessly thrown herself—and the centrum, by extension—into danger.

Raven started in the opposite direction of the automaton. She found a tall tree to climb and made it to the top easily. From the top, she spotted the thickest, tallest part of the forest with ease. That would be the treehouse. Raven climbed down and hopped to the forest floor. Before her knees straightened, pale red light flashed around her.

The light turned blood red.

"Do not resist," came the automaton's mechanical voice.

She didn't turn around. She didn't scream. She ran.

The automaton gave chase.

Raven dodged through the trees, around brushes, over tree roots, through weeds. Her breath became ragged quickly, her lungs heaved, her legs ached, the fever pulsed underneath a thick layer of sweat. Still, she ran.

Not fast enough.

The automaton closed in. Its large feet nimbly maneuvered over the forest floor, pushing weeds and bushes out of its way like they weren't there. Raven ran, ran, ran, but the fever blurred her senses. Unbalanced her.

She tripped. She fumbled along the forest floor, tree roots smacking into her arms and legs, and she fought to regain her unsure footing. She only made it a step before thick metal hands clasped around her upper arms. The automaton yanked her backward, off her feet, and the gears clanked as its chest opened.

She did the only thing she could: scream.

She screamed as the automaton lifted her, as its chest cavity opened, as it pulled her inside. She screamed to let anyone hear her, to let anyone know she needed help. The doors of its chest closed, shutting her in near total darkness, muffling her screams. She beat her fists on the door, or what she thought was the door, but it did not open.

The automaton began to walk through the forest calmly, as though it hadn't just swallowed her.

Raven beat against the thing's chest until her arms fell limp against her sides. In her current state, it didn't take long. The automaton's chest became her personal oven; the fever burned worse than it had in days, burned with her exhaustion, her anxiety, her stress. Burned. Burned. Burned. It echoed off the metal insides of the automaton like sound.

She had room to sit, and she hugged her legs to her chest.

What would happen now? What would Ivy think when she never came to bed? What would they all think?

She'd messed up. Again. She only caused problems, and this time, she couldn't get herself out of it. Zander was right. If she were to go with them to Moorin, she would get them caught or worse.

Useless.

Why had she gone into the forest like that? She deserved whatever happened next.

She thought she'd cried all her tears, but as she sat there, a new wave pushed against her eyes. Before the first tear fell, a creak came from above her. Metal sliding against metal. A hiss—Raven felt something cool touch her skin, featherlight, like fog. Then she smelled it. Acidic and sweet. Sickly.

She coughed and coughed and panicked as the strange odor coursed through her nose, down her throat, and into her lungs.

It pulled her down. She tried to fight it, but couldn't. The darkness came, and she went under.

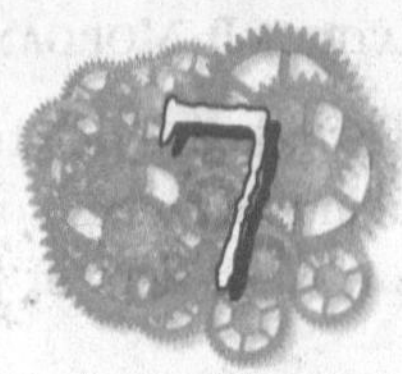

Raven woke to a thump and a crash, then stillness.

All around her, darkness and groaning gears. The automaton's insides clicked desperately, but with each hiss of steam, lost force. Her heart sped up as her mind woke, as the drug wore off, and the past several events returned to her. Captured. She'd been taken by an automaton.

Outside, she heard male voices, muffled and quiet. Her heart jumped—Zander had come before it was too late.

The two men continued to speak as the automaton groaned and creaked and hissed to silence. It had to be Zander and Thalame and Niall; they had wondered about her absence and come to find her.

Raven pressed her hands against the metal walls around her, willing her friends to stop talking and get her out faster. She didn't like this dark, cramped cage. She opened her mouth to scold them for dallying, but she stopped. Her heart fell into her stomach. What would they think of her after this? Zander's point about her being a hindrance had been proven—by her—and they would send her back to Silver Glen or lock her in one of the rooms in the Treehouse.

Something hard hit the automaton's head, and then metal creaked and groaned and slid, piece by piece. She had heard the sounds often enough when she'd meandered into the tinker shop of Silver Glen. They were taking the automaton apart.

"Niall?" Raven called. Her tongue slurred the word, making her acutely aware of how heavy and dry it was.

The tinkering stopped.

A male voice spoke, too low for her to hear the words or make out the speaker.

"Get me out!" Raven said. She gathered her strength and beat against the chest cavity, once, twice.

Silence came from the other side. The voices spoke lowly, and then something hit the chest cavity. Slowly, groaning and creaking, they wedged the doors open. Sunlight poured in, obnoxiously bright, and Raven shielded her eyes with her hand.

Two silhouettes stood over her.

Her eyes adjusted—but it was not Zander or Thalame or Niall.

She did not know the two men standing over her. They were tall and lean and had the dark hair and skin of Tinatun. They were looking down at her with a mixture of confusion and curiosity. One of them spoke to the other, his words lilted and quick, the syllables sharp. Tinatunian, she realized. She had only heard a few words of it from Niall.

The man speaking held a crowbar over his bare shoulders, sweat glistening on his dark skin. A talisman hung around his neck on a leather cord, a fishtail made of polished stone. Around his middle was a belt of tools that looked like something Niall would wear when scavenging. The second man wore a tattered vest; it hung open, and she saw the beginning of a dark tattoo on his chest. Both wore tattered and patched trousers.

The first man pointed the crowbar at Raven and spoke in Tinatunian. She shook her head, and he repeated himself, agitation on his words and on his face. He furled his brow at her and poked at her with his crowbar. "*Lin?*" He spat that word several times, *lin, lin, lin*. He jabbed at her with the crowbar.

She swatted the end away from her and growled, "I don't understand!"

The man in the vest twisted his head to the side and shouted, "Nia!"

Someone shouted back, a female by the sound, and the two men stepped aside as a third person approached. A woman with several years on Raven's seventeen stopped in front of her. She had the same dark skin as the men, and her hair had been cut short. Tattoos ran up and down both muscular arms.

The man with the crowbar said something else to the woman, the language quick and impossible to understand.

The woman nodded, and then gave a broad, welcoming smile to Raven. "Ah," she said. "We caught one with a catch of its own."

Raven's anxiety melted at the sound of her own tongue, even as curved as the woman's accent was.

The woman held her hand down to Raven. Her nails were short, filed not bitten, and a tattoo encircled her wrist, twining vines with small lotus flowers. Raven gingerly set her hand into the stranger's. The woman hoisted Raven to her feet and out of the automaton's chest.

The two men descended on the automaton, yanking it apart one panel at a time—not like Niall did, carefully and precisely with quick fingers.

Raven glanced around. The sun was shining, meaning she had been in the automaton's chest all night and into the morning. She felt it too. Stiff back, aching legs, pinched shoulders. The forest didn't look familiar, but it didn't look strange. Still the same forest. Hammel Forest stretched over most of Rhynwier; she'd seen that much on Niall's maps.

"Nia," said the woman, drawing Raven's attention.

"I'm sorry?" Raven said.

"Name. I am Nia."

"Oh!" Raven fumbled slightly with the woman's accent. The words were tilted and short. "My name is Raven."

The two men dissected the automaton with easy efficiency. They had taken the internal workings apart, scraping the gold, silver, brass, and steel. They piled the parts into a wooden cart. The Dwellers had mentioned automatons found in the woods, strung apart and stripped—by scavengers. These people must be some of those scavengers.

"Thank you," Raven said to Nia.

Nia nodded, then said something quick to the men. One of them spat something back.

Nia half laughed. "Good thing we came along," said Nia to Raven. "This one would have taken you somewhere far, far worse. This one is called a Retriever. They go out, find prey, and take it back to the Gray Elite hold in the west. The gas—" Nia pointed to the top of the chest cavity, to a small nozzle—"knocks the prey out cold."

They stood a moment in silence as the two men pulled bits and pieces from the automaton.

"Where are we?" Raven finally asked.

"We're about a day northeast of Gilini," answered Nia.

"And...that is where?" Raven asked, feeling foolish.

Nia blinked and looked at her with pity and humor. She said something in Tinatunian, then said to Raven, "Not the best with direction, eh? You one of those sheltered girls?"

Raven crossed her arms. The way Nia said *sheltered*, it felt like an insult. "I suppose I am."

"Gilini is in Tinatun," Nia explained. "We are about a day and a half north of the coast."

The blood drained from Raven's face. "That's far from where I started," she said quietly.

"Where did you start?"

Raven opened her mouth to answer, but then realized she didn't know where the treehouse was or even what it was close to. From the maps she had seen, she knew it to be somewhere in the middle of the eastern forest.

But how to explain that? The Dwellers were supposed to be a secret. And now she was a day's journey from Tinatun? Her skin prickled. How long had she been inside the automaton's stomach knocked out by its gas? The automaton must have been running since her capture. It terrified her to think that a machine could move that fast. Then again, the Dwellers had the Hellcat which had taken them from Lenhala to Oun in a fraction of the time it would have taken on foot. Could automatons travel that fast?

"Not want to answer, then?" asked Nia, a friendly smile on her sun-warmed face.

Raven shook her head. "I don't have an answer. I don't know where I started. I was..." *Running through the forest like a fool.* "I was lost when it found me."

Nia's confusion and slight humor melted together into pity, and Raven looked away. She was smoothing the wrinkles in her blouse—or trying to—when a thought bloomed in her mind. A streak of hope in an otherwise bleak situation. A chance.

Feigning innocence, Raven hung one hand on her elbow, and asked, "How far is Gilini from Wayward Point?"

One of Nia's brows rose. "Wayward Point?" She said the name like a place she knew, and the hope in Raven's chest swelled.

Nia turned her head and said something to the other men, who were tossing the last bits of the Retriever into the cart. Raven heard what might have been Wayward Point pass her lips, but Nia spoke too quickly. The two men stopped working, both looking at Raven. Sweat dripped down their faces, shimmered on their brows and shoulders and cheekbones. Both wore varying expressions of interest.

Nia asked a question, and both men gave an affirmative answer.

Nia looked back at Raven, smiled, and said, "Good news, Raven, you can ride with us to Gilini. We'll get you to Wayward Point. But not for free."

Raven's heart sagged.

"You'll have to work for your passage."

"Okay," Raven said. Though she knew little about automatons, she knew about scavenging. She had done it plenty at Silver Glen, though the bounty had never been very good.

What, exactly, she would do in Wayward Point, she didn't know. Maybe she could use that blasted wooden coin or find someone who knew the Dwellers; Thalame said he knew people, that someone owed him a favor. Or the Crusaders might help them get over the border. She had options, she realized, and a dangerous bloom of hope-lined anxiety warmed her chest.

Raven joined the three strangers; they took turns pushing the cart over the forest floor, though Raven moved it much slower. The two men only spoke Tinatunian, and Nia didn't translate, so Raven spent much of the trek in the dark on their conversation.

Not that she minded. It saved her from having to be part of it.

They guided the cart to the bank of a wide, gentle river. Pockets of bugs swarmed over the still surface; fish swam underneath; and a mad cacophony of bugs chirped and chittered from the overgrown bushes along the banks. Trees grew wild on either side, looming over the water, some nearly halfway over the river. The muddy blue-green river ran as far as Raven could see either way, winding out of sight.

She tried to recall Niall's maps. There had been a river that ran down the southeastern side of Rhynwier, but she couldn't think of its name. Only that it passed through the eastern edge of Tinatun and ended in the ocean. The men unloaded the cart into a ramshackle skiff tied off on a stump. Raven helped Nia loosen the strange knot, and then—cargo loaded and people aboard—they were off down the river, toward the coast. The river naturally flowed south, Nia explained, and as long as they weren't in any hurry, they would go with the river.

Raven held her face into the breeze, ablaze with river mist and birdsong and the ripe scents of the river, as the two men and Nia chatted in Tinatunian. The two men lounged on the sides, looking like they had no place they'd rather be.

Had the Dwellers discovered her missing? Would they be worried? Relieved? Would Zander be glad that he didn't have to tell her that she had to stay behind?

A spiteful thought sprang. *She* had left *them* behind.

Not that she could find her way back to the Treehouse. She might as well go on to Wayward Point. Odds were, someone there knew the Dwellers. Or maybe she could take Conrad the Thief up on his offer of something new. She still had the wooden coin.

Raven had kept up the habit of keeping three things on her person at all times: her mother's locket, which held the centrum; her ebony-handled dagger; and the thief's wooden coin to freedom. She took a deep breath of the muggy river air, muddy and fishy and dank. A fresh start. Those words reverberated like a cold heartbeat, welcoming but dreadful.

She banished the worries of tomorrow. She would worry about what she would do when she got to Wayward Point. Until then, there was nothing she could do unless she planned to swim upriver until the forest looked familiar. Right now, sitting in the scavengers' boat, she had something of a plan. Get to Wayward Point, to the Destiny Show, and present her coin and see what happened. Conrad said he had friends, and she could only hope that he did.

Raven and her three new companions floated downriver toward the river city of Gilini. The two men rattled away in their tongue, and Nia offered no translation. Did everyone speak Tinatunian in Gilini? In Wayward Point? She hadn't thought of that. What if she got to Wayward Point and no one understood her?

Nia spoke to her occasionally, her grammar imperfect and her accent lilted with Tinatun's sharp syllables and quickness. She asked simple questions: where Raven had come from, how she had ended up in the forest, if she had done anything to upset the automaton.

Raven kept her answers simple. She had come from a village to the north; she had been wandering a while; she had been separated from her friends. Her non-answers caused the crease between Nia's brows to deepen.

One of the men said something, pointing to Raven, speaking to Nia. His black eyes glittered in the sunlight, his skin wrinkled from squinting and laughing.

"He wants to know why the automaton had you," said Nia flatly. "Retrievers go after people, he says, but not just anyone."

Fugitives, was what she didn't add. The two men were looking at her like they knew why, like they thought her a criminal, and Nia gazed at her with the same interest. Raven swallowed, unsure of what story to feed them, of what would appease them and not land her in trouble.

The second man spat a question at her, frowning.

"You are a magician?" Nia translated.

"No," Raven said quickly, too quickly, even though truthfully.

The men narrowed their eyes at her. They didn't believe her. Nia's steady, curious gaze never changed.

"I'm not a magician," Raven said, urging Nia to believe her. "If I were, I wouldn't have let that automaton get me. I would have blasted it to bits or something."

Nia gave a halfhearted smile.

One man said something to Nia, and she spoke back, her words low and threatening, and even though Raven couldn't understand, she knew they spoke about her. Nia exchanged a glance with the man, and he shied away. Nia obviously commanded the scavenging team.

"Take me to Wayward Point," Raven said to Nia. "Please. After that, I will be out of your hair forever."

Nia nodded, though she didn't speak.

They crossed the border between Rhynwier and Tinatun without a fuss. Gilini came into view a little before nightfall. It was a port city of mismatched wooden planks, shanties, and shacks. The forest grew around its edges, giving the impression that the weeds and the people were in a constant state of battle for dominance. Shacks had been built in the trees, accessible by rope ladders and spiraling stairs bound by twine. Lanterns hung from storefronts, porches, and trees. It gave the village an eerie glow, like stars had fallen and landed haphazardly in the forest.

It reminded Raven of the treehouse, and she felt a pang in her chest.

The two men guided their skiff into the rickety docks that spanned the river side of Gilini. They spent the next hour haggling over automaton parts. Golden piks were exchanged, the currency of Tinatun. A pik was about the size of a Gray Elite token, stamped with the image of the crescent-shaped kingdom.

They stayed at an inn that smelled of damp wood and sweat, and Raven had barely fallen asleep when Nia shook her awake to leave. The first rays of dawn had barely streaked the inky sky in pale blues and pinks. She followed Nia back to the market, which bustled as it had the night before. Raven didn't ask questions as Nia handed her a plate of cooked fish and boiled roots. She ate it, though it tasted like muddy water. Food was food, and these people had bought it for her and had offered to take her to Wayward Point.

And she was grateful.

With the sun teetering over the edge of the world, they started back downriver. According to Nia, Gilini was a stepping stone, the first city on the river past the border, whereas Wayward Point was the last city on the river before the river emptied into the Linila Sea.

The Linila Sea, thought Raven. One of her favorite stories had taken place over the Linila Sea, a young stowaway named Leon Stark boarded a pirate ship by mistake. His adventure took him to see mermaids, sea monsters, cloud dragons, and a pirate lord. Raven kept her eyes on the river as it widened, as the trees changed from forest to jungle with lush ferns and fronds as long as their boat.

The change happened gradually. The dirt became light and sandy, the trees thinner, the leaves fronds, and the air stickier and wetter. The farther south they drifted, the stickier the air and the sweeter the smells, like salt and adventure.

Their skiff passed a dozen boats before midday, some heading south, some paddling upriver with giant wooden wheels painted an assortment of colors and a pillar of steam vanishing into the sky. Several boats chimed with laughter and song, picked lutes and swift drums.

Raven leaned forward to spy a school of tiny fish as they darted underneath the boat. They moved like glinting daggers, and the ease with which they moved as one marveled her. As she watched them pass, she leaned a little farther forward, and her locket shifted under her blouse.

One of the men said something, but she had gotten used to not understanding. She paid it little mind. The fish swam away and out of sight. She leaned back into the boat and jumped at the sudden proximity of one of the men. He had crouched forward while she had been looking at the fish. His dark eyes were focused on her neck—on the locket.

Her heart thudded in her chest.

The man's warm fingers brushed her throat; he started to pull on the locket's golden chain. As he started to lift it, he spoke, but Raven only stared at him, panic hot and fluid under her skin.

She didn't want him to see it, to touch it. Not her locket. Not her mother's locket. Not the centrum. It was *hers*.

Before he could form a grip on the chain, his face contorted in pain, and he wrenched his hand away, dropping the locket as if burned. The locket fell back against her blouse, and through the fabric, it was hot to the touch. She folded her fingers around her locket, and already, the heat faded. She tucked it back underneath her blouse where he couldn't see it.

The man was staring at her, trailing his fingers in the water—the fingers that had touched the locket. The other man spoke lowly, and the man who'd tried to take the locket spoke back without taking his eyes off Raven. His words were angry and disgusted—but his eyes were afraid.

In the moment between heartbeats, she felt a burning desire to make them all afraid, to make them see that she was no fool, but that desire faded as quickly as it had appeared.

Had the man been about to demand payment for their help? Raven refused to part with her mother's locket or the centrum inside it. She would rather swim to Wayward Point.

The man said something else, and she thought she heard Minerva's name—Goddess of the Sea and Wind—cross his lips. Raven looked to Nia for explanation, but the woman gave none. She was looking at Raven with a blank stare.

Raven steeled herself. She would have to be more careful around them. No more daydreaming. No more looking away. She wouldn't let them take it.

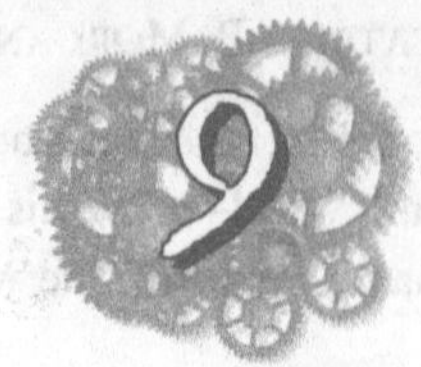

Wayward Point came into view as the sun began its downward descent. It looked a lot like Gilini and the smaller villages they had passed, with lopsided wooden shacks and ramshackle structures, all cobbled together with wooden planks, driftwood, rusting iron, and odd shaped metal sheets. The river had widened considerably, twice what it had been when she first boarded the skiff. Birds she had never heard before sang, cawed, and chirped; bugs she hadn't seen flew past in blurs of green, blue, and yellow.

They crossed into the outskirts, and docks lined both sides of the river. Bridges arched over the river, some held up with wooden poles, others with steel, and one with what looked like pink stone. As their skiff passed underneath, Raven saw that the pink stone was highly textured, almost like coral.

The sounds of the city hit them, the chattering of thousands of people—words she knew and words she didn't—singing, shouting, laughing; music made of drums, strings, and flutes; and vendors shouting prices in piks, tokens, and marks. It smelled like dead fish and the unmistakable stench of unwashed bodies.

They docked, tied off the skiff, and stepped onto the lopsided wooden dock. Raven spotted several men and women in similar armor. They wore crossbows on their backs and short swords at their sides. A few had pistols, but not all. They regarded the ships and the people lingering on the docks with matching looks of weary disdain. Raven followed Nia up a sandy stretch of beach and into the town.

Nia led the way through the busy docks. Men, women, and children worked, loading ships, unloading ships, scrubbing decks, hauling barrels and crates this way and that, shouting out wares and different fish and all manner of buyable things. She caught bits of her own tongue mixed with Tinatunian, and it created a strange harmony. They passed through a street where fisherman lined both sides, selling fish, gutting fish, selling parts of fish; the smell of fish and salt water made Raven want to hold her breath.

The gilded evening began to sink into the shadows of twilight as they started over the coral-looking bridge, the widest and grandest of the bridges. Lanterns hung from the ceiling, their light dim but enough to illuminate the timbers of the bridge and the faces of strangers.

In the center of the bridge, Raven glanced south. Through the palms and scraggy brush and sandy city that leaned over the river, the twilight gilded the Linila Sea. Raven's heart skipped a beat. It went on forever, as if the rest of the world were made of water.

Nia didn't pause, and Raven jogged a few steps to catch up to her. The streets on the other side of the bridge were only slightly more organized. They came to a vast market square of hundreds of stalls, twice as many people, and more things than Raven had ever seen. She took in as much of it as she could in passing. She saw food, sweets, drinks, tools of all metal and size, baskets in every shape and weave, bolts of fabric, stacks of books—more than one person could ever want or need.

People meandered through the market in all manner of clothing, mismatched finery from all three kingdoms, silk and canvas, velvet and burlap, leather and cotton. She spotted the gray and yellow trousers of the Gray Elite uniform, and several gray coats—stolen Gray Elite uniforms. She spotted armor made to mimic automatons and some pieces that looked to have once been pieces of automatons. One man wore a Goliath's head as a helmet.

Everywhere she looked, she found a dozen things to see.

By the time they reached the other end of the market, the lanterns had become the main source of light. The sun had gone down, the moon had risen, and millions of stars spotted the sky, with the odd dark cloud passing by.

The two men started to talk to one another, lowly, cautiously.

They passed a building with scorch marks, the scars of a fire. The torches on either side of its door were hanging loosely. A small shake, and they would tumble. The wooden shack wouldn't stand a chance.

Jokingly, Raven asked Nia, "How many times has this place burned?"

"Several," Nia answered without pause.

Raven's brows rose.

Nia shrugged. "It is not a big deal when it burns. People do like they always do. They rebuild. The market used to be over there, but the last time it burned, they decided to build it over here. The old say it used to be by the beach, but a storm washed it away, so it moved inland."

Raven nodded. It made sense, though the idea of Wayward Point burning to the ground and being rebuilt left a strange taste in her mouth.

They left the crowded, bustling market behind and walked into a calmer side of Wayward Point. Stalls became shops and stores and smiths. They passed tavern after tavern, and even a place Raven suspected was a brothel. Still, they walked. She kept her eyes open for a white brick building, the Destiny Show, as Conrad had told her. She felt the wooden coin in her pocket, though she didn't reach for it. She didn't want the men to see it or think it valuable.

They came to a side of town with streets of cobblestone. The buildings were older and made of stone and wood. She spotted fewer and fewer scorch marks. The streets had no names, no signs, and they zigzagged and crisscrossed and ended abruptly, as though the buildings had been built wherever their owners wished. It left Raven feeling lost and confused; the darkness didn't help. This side of town had fewer torches too.

Finally, as a yawn worked its way up Raven's throat, they stopped at a large building of pale yellow stone. It took up half the block and held few windows, all of which were shuttered. The two men walked to the front door, illuminated by a lantern on either side, one of brass and one of iron. Nia stood beside Raven.

The shirtless man knocked. A grunt, and then a deep male voice replied in Tinatunian. The shirtless man opened the door. He walked in, the second man followed, and Nia set a hand on Raven's shoulder and guided her inside.

The room they entered had a single lantern hanging from the ceiling. The floor, the walls, the ceiling were stone. A circular rug adorned the floor, a swirl of red and yellow and white. A wooden counter stood at the far end of the room, and a barrel-chested man stood behind it. He leered over the counter on one elbow.

The shirtless man spoke to the big man but gestured to Raven.

Her skin pricked. The barrel-chested man's black eyes looked to her, first meeting her eyes and then running over her body with a fluid, cold indifference. She did not like the man; he looked at her like a butcher looked at meat.

Without looking at her, the barrel-chested man spoke to the two men. It took a moment to recognize, but the two men were bartering. But for what? Passage? Room and board?

Raven shifted on her feet, and she felt Nia's sure grip fasten around her elbow. Behind them, a large man stepped in front of the doorway. Blocking the exit. He leaned lazily against the wall beside the door, his wide face blank, his dark hair tied behind his head. Tattoos lined both hands, and scars dotted his knuckles.

Her gut twisted. *Wrong*, said something inside her. Wrong, like the silence of the forest when the birds go quiet.

A clanking brought her attention back to the counter, to the two men. A bag of coins had been dropped. The two men gathered and counted out the coins quicker than Raven could, but she saw a mixture of golden piks, silver tokens, and copper marks. A mixed currency for a city of mixed culture.

The man behind the counter looked at the two men, then at Raven.

Get out.

Raven tried to pull her arm free of Nia's grip, but the woman held on tight. The two men gathered the coins. Talking low, they started toward the door without a glance at Raven. Nia released her, speaking low to the two men, and started to follow them out. Raven felt a bruise forming from where Nia had gripped her.

She took a step toward the door, to get out of this place, but the man leaning by the door shoved her back.

"Hey!" Raven spat at him. "I'm with them. Let me out."

"No," he said, his voice deep, his accent rough.

"Excuse me?" Raven started, but the man behind the counter spoke up.

"You stay here," he said, his accent less rough but tilted. His appraising eyes met hers.

She felt relief that he spoke her tongue, but it did little against the coiling dread in her stomach. "What? No, I have somewhere else I need to be." She opened her mouth to tell him about the Destiny Show, but he held up a hand—his hand roughly the size of her head.

Then, the man stood.

Raven paled. She thought he had been standing. He was a tower of a man in height and width. Her words grumbled in her throat and fell silent.

"You stay here. You live here now," he said.

The man standing by the door shoved her another step forward, and she shot him a glare over her shoulder.

The man behind the counter grabbed her arm and yanked her against the counter. "You belong to me now."

Her gut twisted and squirmed at his words, their meaning, and the sound they made as they left his lips—a warning, a threat, something dreadful.

The man pulled her through a door behind the counter. It had blended in so well with the darkness, she hadn't seen it. He pulled her down a hallway lined with iron-cage doors—*cells*—each no bigger than a cot and narrow window. Most held people—sad, pitiful people.

He threw Raven into a cell near the end of the hall. She stumbled to the stone floor, and not a heartbeat later, the door slammed shut. A heavy click followed. Raven fumbled to her feet and turned in time to see the man standing on the other side, holding an iron key, one of a dozen on a heavy keyring.

"No," Raven gasped. She stumbled forward to the bars, folding her shaking fingers around them. "Please, there's been a mistake. I—I need to get out, I have people I need to see."

"Who?" he asked.

Her words froze; she knew no names. Stupidly, she said, "The Crusaders."

He laughed, a single burst of wind. "No mistake. You belong to me. Paid for in full."

She paled as realization hit her. The bag of coins. It had been payment. For her. Nia had *sold* her.

A cold thought went through her: how long had they planned on selling her?

From the start, said a little voice. *You should have known better*, said another voice that sounded like Zander's. She could see his scowl at the mess she had gotten herself in, hear the exasperation in his voice.

"You stay here until someone buys you." The man crossed his thick arms and looked her up and down. "It won't take too long. Pretty young things go fast." He returned to the other room, leaving her in her cell.

She stood there, hands clutching the iron bars, for what felt like a long time. The world went in and out of focus. A dream. It had to be a dream. A nightmare.

A nightmare she'd brought onto herself.

Raven stood at the door until her legs gave out. She collapsed to the stone floor, her hands sliding down the bars.

A single lantern hung in the hallway. The flickering light striped her cell with light and darkness.

She had been sold. And she would be sold again.

Her father's voice rang in her head, fresh from the repetition, his warnings of what happened to the people the automatons found and took back to the Gray Elite. The lucky ones became slaves. He never said what happened to the unlucky ones.

She had a feeling she was going to find out, and sooner rather than later.

In the quiet of the cell, the breathing of her fellow captives grew louder. Distant and muffled chatter filtered in through the narrow, barred window. Laughter. Music. Singing.

Raven pulled herself onto the cot, nothing more than taut canvas stretched over a wooden frame. She had never felt more alone, more helpless, more useless. No one knew where she had gone. No one knew where to look.

No one would be looking for her.

She lowered her head into her hands. What had she gotten herself into?

Thalame had seen a lot in nineteen years, more than a nineteen-year-old boy should. He stood by the window in his room in the treehouse, fingering his favorite dagger. He didn't have a need for it, but the leather grip was familiar, worn by his hand, and it was that familiarity that he craved.

From his window, the forest stretched on forever. It didn't go forever; he knew that. Eventually it hit the ocean, but the wilderness between the forest and the ocean was a nightmare and a half to cross. He'd only attempted it once and swore to the Sisters he'd never do it again.

He heard footsteps on the stairs, and as he turned, Zander stalked past the doorway, past his own bedroom, and to the lounge at the end of the hall. Grumbling too. Not a good sign.

Thalame sheathed his knife and meandered down the hall to where Zander stood in the lounge. He stood at the window, hands clutching the bark-covered sill, his shoulders hunched. Even without touching him, Thalame could sense Zander's unease, the turmoil, the panic.

"Anything?" Thalame asked anyway, leaning against the doorway.

Zander didn't answer. He hung his head and let out a quick sigh.

Thalame felt his own unease rise—that tiny sliver of hope quickly diminished—but he dispelled the unease. He had always been good at casting away his own emotions. Like stones, they sank to the bottom.

Zander heaved a breath and collapsed to the floor, back against the wall. He had dressed in dark clothes, armed and ready for a fight, and he nearly vanished in the shadows. Thalame wondered if any of those shadows were his own.

"I couldn't find her," Zander said quietly.

Thalame glanced out the window, at the endless treetops.

Zander buried his hands in his hair, shaking slightly. He looked a mess, unshaven, hair tangled and unwashed, bags under his eyes. Even the blue of his eyes seemed to have faded into a pale blue-gray. Maybe it was a trick of the dark.

Raven had been at the meeting, had been irritated with Zander's decision to leave her out of the mission, had stormed out, and then vanished. Not even Ivy knew where she had gone. The Dwellers had scoured the woods for the past few days, searching farther and farther out.

But Raven had vanished.

Thalame knew what he wanted to ask, to suggest. But he kept his dark thoughts to himself. "What now?" he asked instead.

Zander let out a woeful sound, a sigh, a whine, a plea. He gazed at the ceiling, the intertwined branches and leaves. "We move forward with the plan," he said, his voice stony.

Thalame didn't argue but added in a quiet voice, "You sure, mate?"

Zander closed his eyes and stood—wobbled but stood. He hung onto the window for support. He nodded once. He met Thalame's gaze, his eyes hard. "Yes. We have one chance. We will take it. Regardless of this, we have a job to do."

Zander started back toward his room. He brushed past Thalame, and then collapsed onto his cot, daggers and boots included. Thalame lingered in the doorway, waiting, hoping like a fool for a commotion to start downstairs, to signal that Raven had come back or that she had been found.

It didn't.

"Even if we're gone," Zander said, muffled by the pillow, "the others will keep looking."

Thalame nodded, though he kept his thoughts to himself.

Zander's breathing evened, his curled fists relaxed, and Thalame silently made his way into the room. He laid his hand on his friend's back, soothing the worry, easing the panic, and trying to give him a peaceful night's rest. He would need it for the journey ahead of them.

Thalame made his way back toward his room. A shadow stood at the end of the hall. It was Ivy; the moonlight glinted off her blonde hair, turning the outline silver. Thalame walked past his room and stopped a step from her.

"Anything?" she whispered.

Thalame shook his head.

"Shit," Ivy groaned. She rubbed her face. Thalame had always liked the sound of curses on her delicate mouth. "What are we going to do?"

"Keep looking," Thalame said.

Ivy rolled her eyes. She looked exhausted. Like Zander, she had been searching for Raven nearly nonstop. She had scouts with their ears to the ground, and she had pulled the strings of her spies tight. If something happened to Raven elsewhere, their spies would carry the news. Ivy knew that. Zander knew that. They all knew that, which made the prolonged silence all the more frightening.

"Thalame, if the Gray Elite had her, we would have heard about it," Ivy whispered fearfully.

"I know, mate."

"I'm scared." Her whisper quivered.

He stepped closer.

"I'm scared I'll find her at the bottom of some ravine or half-eaten by something or floating in a lake—"

"Stop." Thalame set his hands on her bare shoulders. He stole away her fear and panic in less than a heartbeat. In a slow breath, it felt as if it had never been there to begin with. Ivy had always been easy to calm. "We'll find her."

Ivy didn't argue or agree. She shut her eyes and sighed into her hands.

"You need rest." Thalame guided Ivy toward her room, the room she had briefly shared with Raven.

With Ivy tucked away for the night and Zander lightly snoring, Thalame returned to the window in his room. The forest stretched on forever, but nothing about it had changed since he'd been gone. Was Raven still out there somewhere? Did she even want to come back? Maybe she'd taken her chance to give them the finger and escape—he knew the feeling all too well.

They would find her. He knew they would; he just didn't know when or how. The sense of such things had come with his magic. He wouldn't call it premonition, but more of an intuition. He'd never told anyone about it, mostly because he didn't know how to. But he knew Raven was out there, somewhere, and likely alive.

He just didn't know how the hell to explain it to anyone else. So he didn't.

Raven woke to the sound of the hallway door opening. She didn't move from the cot. Water and a pitiful ration of stale bread had been passed to the prisoners that morning, sating her hunger a little above starvation.

Two sets of footsteps sounded on the stone floor. They paused. They started. They paused again. "No, no," said a male voice.

Raven's chest squeezed at being able to understand him.

"None of these will do. I need strong young men. These *yenti* wouldn't last a day."

She had heard that word several times from the people who'd walked by. She didn't know its exact meaning, only that it was an insult. By the way the man spoke, she guessed that Tinatunian wasn't his native tongue. *Yenti* didn't roll as sweetly off his tongue as it did others.

"May I interest you in my latest purchase?" came the deep, slithering voice of the man who had bought her—the slaver.

The two footsteps continued down the hall and stopped in front of Raven's cell. A man appeared on the other side of the bars, his skin lighter beige, tanned by the sun. Gray streaked his brown hair. "I asked for young, capable men," said the man, narrowing his eyes at Raven. "Not whores."

The slaver chuckled. "Whores always have their purpose," he said, and Raven's skin went clammy and cold. "This one came in two days ago. Fresh."

Two days? Raven blinked. The man came into better focus. He had wrinkles around his eyes and his mouth. The slaver stood to his side, two heads taller.

Had she been in his cell that long? She didn't know; time ran together. It slurred. Her fever came and went, and she found that if she thought about nothing at all, the fever didn't bother her so badly. But the notion of being bought as a whore agitated it, and she felt the burning course underneath her skin worse than it had in days.

The potential buyer sighed, then brought his attention back to Raven. She met his gaze with her own. If he bought her, she wouldn't have to sit in the cell anymore. She might be able to find a way out of here, away from him, and to the Destiny Show. If it even existed. For all she knew, this was the Destiny Show, and that thief had planned to sell her too.

Or it might be another hell entirely.

The man leaned closer to the bars. Raven refused to look away.

"I suppose she would make a nice gift to my son," said the potential buyer as if he had a thousand other things he could buy. "How much?"

"One hundred piks," said the slaver.

The man laughed. "For this skinny rat? I'll give you seventy."

"Ninety."

"Seventy-five."

The slaver frowned. "Eighty, and she's yours."

The man nodded. "Eighty."

And the deal was made. Sold, just like that, for eighty piks.

The two men retreated down the hall to the main room, their voices low. Sometime later—how much later Raven didn't know—the slaver returned with his keyring in hand. He unlocked Raven's door—wearing the face of a man eighty piks richer—and hauled Raven to her feet. He pulled her along the hallway a second time and back into the main room where the buyer stood.

A pile of coins sat on the counter. Piks. Her payment.

"Easy on the goods," snapped the man she now belonged to. He swatted the slaver's hand from her arm and then inspected the damage. Her owner—she cringed to think of him that way—led her by the arm to the door, his grip not any gentler than the slaver's.

The sunlight blinded her, bright and unforgiving, as if the sun were closer to Tinatun than anywhere else she had ever been. It might have been. It would explain the heat.

"Please," Raven begged once her eyes adjusted.

The man led her down the street, away from the market, away from the slaver's shop.

"There's been a mistake."

The man paid her no mind. She tugged on her arm, and he tugged her a step forward. "Keep your voice down," he commanded.

Raven tried to dig her heels in, but the cobblestone gave no resistance. "No! Let me go!"

No one on the street paid mind. A few quick stares, and then their gazes averted.

They took a few more steps, and then the man yanked her down a side street, narrower and less crowded. He grabbed her by the wrists and slammed her back against the stone wall. "No one is going to help you," he sneered. "Let me inform you how it works here. You are nothing. The Gray

50

Elite aren't coming to save you. And I suggest, for your own benefit, to behave if you plan on eating for the next week."

Panic and rage pulsed underneath her skin. Tears pushed against her eyes.

"None of that," he said, his voice softer but no less comforting. His grip tightened on her arm, and he pulled her down the side street and onto another.

This side of Wayward Point felt subdued. People lounged in wide doorways, on porches, on benches. The flitting of music came and went: a harmonica, a guitar, winds that she couldn't name, strings she'd never heard before. It was beautiful; it was horrible. The buildings were made of stone, but none white.

Knowing her luck, the Destiny Show didn't exist.

Clouds were gathering overhead, shadowing the sky in grays and light blue. Somewhere in the distance, thunder rolled, low and lazy. The city went on as if nothing happened, as if she weren't walking to her life as a slave, as if she hadn't just been sold like a fish at market. No one met her eye either.

Like she truly didn't exist.

Like she was less than a person.

None of it seemed real. How could it?

She tried not to think about what would happen once this man—her owner—got to wherever he was taking her. She tried not to recount all of her father's warnings. Instead, she looked at the clouds, at the sky, at the sliver where blue met blue, where the world went on forever.

Finally, they came to a dark building on the edge of the old side of town. While mostly wooden, it had a stone foundation and several stone walls. It looked to have once been several buildings that had grown together like trees, growing upward rather than outward. Scorch marks licked along the stone foundation. Several wooden panels had been replaced recently, and several more needed to be.

Two men lounged outside a wide wooden door. As they approached, she realized that one of the men was a woman, a woman with shoulders made for crushing. She sat like a man and spoke like one, though her voice carried a feminine lilt.

Her *owner*—she cringed—spoke in Tinatunian to the two guarding the door. They snapped to attention. They nodded toward him, and the man swung forward to open the door. Raven had no choice but to follow the man through. The sudden darkness blinded her. The man pulled her forward, across what sounded like a stone floor. Distantly, she heard a roar of voices, cheering and shouting.

Her heart squeezed at the sound. Where had she been taken?

Her eyes adjusted, but she had but a moment to take in her surroundings: stone floor, stone walls, a single lantern on the ceiling, unlit. The man pulled her down a hallway wide enough for two. The cheering grew louder. They turned down a hall, and he pulled her down a staircase. The cheering grew quieter. He pulled her into a hallway—her heart sank—lined with cells. Half iron bars, half wooden panel.

Three lanterns hung from the ceiling, though only one was lit. He pushed her into one of the cells. It was twice as large as her previous one, with a bed, a table with an unlit candle, and a narrow barred window. Dulled sunlight streamed inside, catching the dust motes. The walls were stone; the ceiling, wood.

Thunder rumbled closer than it had been.

"This is your new home." The man pushed Raven a step further into the room and closed the door after her. He locked it. "You may call me Mr. Barrow."

"What?" she gasped. She turned to face him, her body feeling numb, disbelief like poison, the fever a drug.

"Your new home," Barrow repeated.

"What about your son?" Her words fell out of her mouth.

Barrow shrugged. "I haven't seen my son in ten months," he said as if it didn't matter. "He's out on the water most of the year. I'm lucky if I see him once a year. It suits me. The boy's a scumbag out for gold, just like his mother."

Her shoulders quaked, her knees gave out, and she fell back onto the bed. Softer than the cot. Not that it mattered.

"Why am I here?" she asked. Her knees twitched together.

He noticed and scoffed. "You think I bought you as a whore? I've got prettier women than you at home."

She wanted to laugh. She had never been more grateful to have a plain face.

Barrow leaned against the door, his face smug. "I've got something better in mind for you."

She swallowed, and a nervous twist stole whatever words she'd had on her tongue. "What?" she asked, though it came out as a whisper.

"You are going to win me back those eighty piks," he said, smirking.

"Win?" she repeated.

He laughed. "You think I don't know who you are?" he asked, narrowing his eyes.

She stared back at him blankly.

His smirk turned malicious. "I was in Lenhala when you tried to murder the general. Took me a week to get out. Your little face covered every bulletin board."

Oh. The blood drained from her face. Of all the horrible things she had thought about happening to her in the past few hours, being recognized hadn't been one of them.

"You're a wanted girl, you know," he said. "The bounty the Gray Elite put on your head is four times what I paid for you. That fool didn't know who you were. I'd love to see his face when he finds out." He laughed and slapped his hand against his side. "Maybe I'll invite him to the match."

"The match?" she managed to choke out.

He leaned against the bars of the door. "Yeah, the match. This is the *Chjelhu Tal*, the Kill Ring, little girl. Where anyone with guts comes to beat their opponent to a bloody pulp. Last one standing wins. Folks bet on the one they think will win. Winner gets half the coin. Since I own the place, I get the other half."

"You're going to let some pirate beat me into a bloody pulp for money?" she said, the words sounding ridiculous and dangerous. The fever pricked along her skin, behind her eyes, pulling at her mind.

"And when word spreads that I have the assassin who nearly killed General Deacon and threw the capital into chaos, these fools will pay anything to see you in action," he said, his words slithering, coiling around her throat, dampening her breath. "I'll make more than double your bounty in a single night."

"I-I'm no fighter," she said in a single breath.

"You don't have to be," he said. "One match, and you'll be paid for. If you die, you die. Besides, if you are the big bad assassin that the Gray Elite say you are, you'll have no problem fighting a few mangy pirates, right?" He grinned like he knew the truth about her.

Laughing, Barrow started back the way he came, keys jingling. Raven sank against the cool stone wall. It felt as though her heart had realized her fate; it fell silent for a long moment.

Admittedly, this was better than what she had feared would happen, but not by much.

Raven tried to sleep. She reclined on the bed, listening to the sounds of life pass by her window. Chatter in Tinatunian, mostly, but she heard bits of her own language mixed in.

A slave. Her stomach curled. Sisters, was this really what her life had come to?

Would Barrow tattle on her before he threw her into the *Chjelhu Tal*? Would the Gray Elite come stomping across the border to find her and drag her back to General Deacon? What would she do if they did?

She heaved a sigh. Her limbs ached. Her heart pounded, fever pulsing in time with her heartbeat. She closed her eyes and listened to it, her heart, the fever, beating. Behind her eyes, she saw red. She might have laid there too long, gone a little mad in the seclusion and fever, but she thought she could feel it humming through her blood, thrumming with its life-sucking force.

Why hadn't she just gone to bed that night? Why had she stopped to eavesdrop? Maybe she could have argued with Zander's decision to send her home. Now she would never see Silver Glen again.

The storm finally rolled in, shading her cell in stormy light. Lightning flashed; thunder rolled a beat later. Soon, thunder and lightning fell into perfect sync.

In Leon Stark's story, storms happened when the cloud dragons flew.

If only.

Rain smacked against the stone outside her window. An awning prevented the rain from coming inside, but stray drops streaked down the wall, leaving dark trails behind on the stone. Soon, the rain beat with force. It sounded like a horde of hooved animals parading through the streets, stomping over the cobblestones. People ran by the window, children played and laughed, though, for the most part, it sounded like Wayward Point had calmed.

The rain continued for hours, and somewhere within its blur of time, Raven found sleep—only to be interrupted by a tray landing on the bedside table. She rolled over in time to see a short woman shutting the door. The lock clicked back into place.

The tray held a chunk of bread, hard cheese, nuts, and roasted fish. A canteen rested on the table. Her stomach cramped just looking at it. She crawled out of bed and pulled the tray onto her lap. She ate all of it and then took a large gulp of water—and spit it back into the canteen.

Ale, not water.

Weak ale, but ale nonetheless.

She took another gulp, smaller this time, and then another.

Thunder rolled lazily overhead. The rain had lightened into a mist.

She returned the empty tray to the table and fiddled with the canteen's cap. Her father had kept a small flask in his desk drawer. He carried one with him too. When she was little, she had asked him once what he kept in it. He'd told her strong tea, and she had believed him. It wasn't until she saw Zander sipping a flask some years later that it dawned on her that he had lied.

Zander. What was he doing? Had he started out on his important mission to find his lost princess? Had he realized Raven's absence?

She heaved a sigh. No sense worrying about it now.

She laid an arm over her eyes; her skin felt hot to the touch. Why hadn't this sickness gone away? It worried Thalame, who had spent more time than any of the others with illnesses, and though she wouldn't admit it, because it worried him, it worried her. If he didn't know what it was, what was she to do?

As a child, she rarely got sick. Whenever the winter colds would blow into Silver Glen, she would evade them, while Lena caught ill. Raven's stepmother had said it was the difference in their constitutions. Had she somehow happened upon one of those diseases that slowly ate away at a person until they didn't know themselves or their friends and their brain gradually forgot how to breathe?

Thunder crashed into the sky, and Raven shut her eyes. She thought of Leon Stark, the brave boy who became a pirate captain. She imagined herself on the deck of an airship, sailing through the skies, looking for smaller ships to loot, empire ships to attack, and adventure within the clouds.

That daydream might have been the only thing keeping her sane.

Raven stayed in her cell that night, being led out only to use the bathroom by the same silent Tinatunian woman. If she understood Raven's questions, she didn't say anything. She didn't act like Raven had spoken at all. The next morning, the woman returned with a fresh set of clothes. Raven shut herself in the bathroom while the woman waited outside.

She washed quickly and dressed in the provided clothes—a pair of snug sand-colored pants and a sleeveless top that wrapped around her waist and tied behind her neck. It left much of her torso exposed. She secured her ebony dagger into her boot, her mother's locket around her neck, and the coin to the Destiny Show in her pants pocket.

When she returned to the cell, a tray of food had been delivered—smoked fish. While she ate, the woman combed a strange scented oil through her hair, smoothing it to a sheen. She then braided it tightly so that two identical braids started at her temples and wove together at the base of her neck.

Raven put a hand to her hair when the woman had finished.

The woman gave her a grin—she was missing several teeth—and said, "Better than shaved."

Raven nodded. Indeed, better than shaved. She thought of the slaves in Lenhala. They'd had shaved heads. Had they been tricked and sold like she had?

"You fight tonight," said the woman as she left, empty tray in hand. "You eat big meal later."

Raven nodded, though her stomach clenched. Tonight?

She sat on the bed. If she lost in the *Chjelhu Tal*, she would be dead or beaten near death. Neither of those sounded good. Or, when the truth of her came out, when they realized she was no assassin, what would happen to her then? Would her plain face be enough to save her from a life of whoring? Would they sell her half-dead to the Gray Elite?

The worry made her sick. The cell was barely big enough to pace, though she tried. The fever came in waves, and she rested for hours, hoping for it to die down, but it didn't. It ebbed but always returned. Fire under her skin. Burning.

She exhaled; her breath felt more like steam than air.

If she looked hard enough, she thought she could see white vapor leave her mouth, dissipating as it met the cooler air outside her body.

Nonsense, that logical part of her brain said.

Maybe I'm becoming an automaton, that illogical part of her brain added.

The woman returned with a hearty lunch: fish, cheese, berries, nuts, ale. Raven ate what she could.

And then, when the sun had lowered—according to the cloudy sunlight's shadow as it transitioned across the room—Barrow returned. He looked smug. "Your time to shine," he said, unlocking the door.

Barrow grabbed her by the arm and hauled her to her feet. He led her out of the basement prison, down an unfamiliar corridor, and up several narrow staircases. With each step, the roaring of a crowd grew louder. The stairs led into a windowless room with two sets of double doors, one leading forward and one leading back. The din of hundreds of restless voices came from the forward doors, talking, shouting, anticipating violence. The volume shook the wooden planks under her feet and vibrated in the walls like thunder.

Slimey anxiety and icy dread wormed underneath her skin, crawling from the base of her skull to the back of her knees. She would likely die tonight, and in front of a bloodthirsty crowd.

Barrow started toward the doors. Raven dug her heels in, but it did little. Barrow yanked her forward. He wrenched the doors open and threw her into the *Chjelhu Tal*.

It was a wooden arena built around a dirt-floored pit. Wooden benches rose all around the pit, and hundreds of people had packed into the stands. The ceiling above the pit opened, and clouded moonlight draped inside. A hundred torches lit the space in flickering yellow. She and Barrow stood on a small wooden balcony that overlooked the arena.

"They all came to see you." Barrow gripped her shoulder. "The biggest crowd we've had in years. All because they want to see the general's little assassin in action. They want to see this little girl who nearly killed one of the most powerful men in the Gray Elite."

Her hands trembled. She felt like she might burn alive before she took another step. The fever twisted the arena before her eyes, elongating it, turning it sideways. Had Barrow not been holding her shoulder, she would have fallen.

"See him?" he said, pointing to the other side of the arena. A man stood on a platform similar to the one under her feet. He wore no shirt, only dirty trousers. Scars crisscrossed over his dark chest. He was shouting, beating his chest, egging on the crowd. "He's been a crowd favorite, but the problem is, he's become unbeatable. Man's like a feral cat. He's your opponent."

She shuddered. She was going to die.

Barrow laughed like he already knew the outcome. He leaned down and said in her ear, his breath hot and rancid like cheap ale, "All you have to do is beat him. He's got to be either dead or out cold in order for you to win. If you win, you'll get your share of the winnings. If you die, then you'll be tossed to Minerva's court with the other losers."

Minerva's court lay at the deepest part of the sea. The goddess snatched the souls of those lost at sea and brought them to her underwater kingdom, a haven for sailors, pirates, and seafarers.

Raven swallowed. She tried to recount all the things that Thalame had taught her, her stance and how to read another in battle. All those sessions, but she had only learned to fight against someone moving slow, and against someone who didn't want to really hurt her. Suddenly, her sessions with him and the wooden daggers felt utterly useless.

At least, when they threw her body into the sea, she would forever protect the centrum.

But as Barrow pushed her toward a rickety metal lift in front of the platform, she realized she didn't want to die.

She wanted to live.

She wanted to see the treehouse again, to see her friends again, to see Zander's face when she returned. She wanted to tell Ivy about this strange adventure. She wanted to find those scavengers who had sold her and shove them into a pit to fend for their lives.

The lift started its descent, the gears shifting and twitching, causing the lift to sputter. Across the arena, her opponent entered an identical lift. He roared and swung his lift back and forth, much to the delight of the crowd. Raven wished for the chains of his lift to break, to fall and crush him before the fight had to begin.

But his lift made it safely to the floor, as did hers.

Her blood pounded, the fever twisted, and she felt like she might empty her stomach.

Barrow's voice boomed over the crowd. He spoke in Tinatunian, through a horn that magnified his voice a hundred times. From his safe balcony, he threw his arms out in welcome and wore a victorious grin. He pointed to her opponent, and the crowd cheered. He pointed to Raven—a pause of confusion—then the crowd erupted into a bloodthirsty roar.

People craned over heads and shoulders to see her better, and whispers churned into shouts. Fingers pointed at her. Faces turned doubtful. Barrow had announced her as the assassin.

"A lot of people don't like the Gray Elite," said a rough voice behind her.

She turned.

A tall and wide woman stood behind her, armed to the teeth, one of the arena's guards. She had one green eye and one brown eye; the difference was alarming. "Had you actually killed that Deacon bastard, you might have been a hero."

"Too bad," Raven managed to say.

"Too bad," echoed the guard.

With a final shout from Barrow, the crowd erupted. The guard opened Raven's lift at the same time another guard opened her opponent's. Raven stumbled onto the hard-packed dirt floor on wooden legs. She met her opponent's dark eyes, his stare wild and hungry. In a heartbeat, he was running toward her.

And the fight began.

Raven didn't have time to think. Her opponent came at her. She tried to dodge but couldn't. He slammed into her, knocking her to the ground. She stumbled back to her feet. The world tilted. His fist collided with her jaw. Stars burst across her vision. Another fist slammed into her stomach, knocking the air out of her lungs and almost her lunch with it.

The fever burned worse and worse, fire under her skin. Her heart sped to a frightening speed, trying to jump out of her chest and run from this.

Something hard—a foot—collided with her ribcage. She felt her insides give and threaten to snap with the impact. Her breath was already gone, and she couldn't draw another. Breathless, she collapsed to the dirt floor. Her hands and knees hit hard. The pain flared a heartbeat later: her chest, her stomach, her ribs, her entire body.

The fever's burn surged, eclipsing the pain, thrumming through her blood as fast as her heartbeat. Faster. The edges of her vision turned red.

She gasped; she would die here, either from her attacker or from the fever.

Boos and disapproving shouts sounded from the arena. She barely heard them over the pumping in her ears, the rushing, the surging, the pulsing.

She was no assassin, no fighter—simple girl, simple town, naïve enough to let herself get tricked and sold.

She wobbled to regain her footing, but something hard crashed into her side, sending her sprawling to the ground, gasping for breath. Pain seared through her middle like magma, liquid and spreading. The world blurred, the dirt shifted between her fingers. The fever burned like mad; she knew would catch fire any moment, burn up entirely.

But she wanted to live.

Her opponent appeared above her, his face doubled and hazy. He came closer, pinning her to the ground. His hands found her throat. Pressure from his hands closed her airways, silenced her gasps, pushed her into the dirt.

And something snapped.

Deeper than her bones, her breath, her heartbeat. Deeper than she thought possible. The thrum became a roar, the hum a song, the beat steady.

Somehow, she knew what to do.

Her opponent's face came into focus, and his dark eyes widened. A scar, she noticed, ran underneath his left eyebrow. She clamped down on his wrists, feeling the bones moving underneath as he tried to release her throat. His fingers loosened, but hers tightened. He let out a yelp of pain, of fear, pulling against her.

She released him. He yanked his hands away from her, stumbling back, clutching his hands to his chest.

Raven staggered to her feet. She didn't hear the fluctuation of the arena's crowd, the odd beat of silence. She heard the thrumming in her ears, the humming in her blood, and the pulsing of the fever. She saw only her opponent—the one standing in the way of her living.

He glared at her, eyes wide and furious and fearful.

Him. He tried to kill you, would have killed you, will still try.

"I won't let him," Raven whispered so faintly, no one but the man heard her.

Because she would live.

"*Aggi?*" the man spat. The fear did not vanish, but he grew enraged. He came at her again.

This time, she did not cower. She threw herself at him, grabbing at his neck like he had grabbed hers. He dodged, and her hands slid instead to his bulky arm.

Good enough—she gathered the fever and pushed it into him, as fast and hard as she could. She felt it leaving her body and flooding into his. The man let out a bloodied scream, shrill and piercing, painful—it filled the arena—and then silenced. His eyes dulled, his stance wobbled, his mouth fell open, and his dark skin turned gray.

He started to collapse. Before his body could hit the dirt, he disintegrated. His body and bones fell apart, crumbling into dark ashes at her feet. No bones, no clothes—just ash.

Burned.

Raven took a gasping breath as if she hadn't been breathing; the fever subsided. The red clouds on the edge of her vision shrank. The arena reappeared. The stench of ash reached her nose: burned cloth and hair and flesh. The stunned crowd erupted into wild cheers.

Her heart beat once, twice, and then—she stumbled backward away from the ash.

All around her was the roar of drunken applause, boots stomping on wooden floors, sloshing ale. Several wooden mugs crashed to the arena floor, spilling their contents onto the thirsty dirt.

Raven swallowed. Her senses returned.

She... She just killed him. *Killed* him. With her hands. With a touch. Dead. The man, her opponent, dead. Turned to ash.

Burned, she realized, by the fever. It had burned him alive from the inside out. She didn't even have a face to look into, no lightless eyes to save for her own guilt. She blinked and looked away. She didn't want to see the ash any more than a body. She looked into the crowd instead, the joyous, riotous, nearly hysterical crowd.

All cheered and shouted, except for one.

Near the middle of the stands stood a man in hooded robes. He did not cheer. He did not clap. He stood with his arms crossed, dark eyes gazing down at her—his straight-line mouth tilted to one side in a carefree smirk, but something dangerous lay beneath it.

Heavy footsteps sounded beside her. The guardswoman with one brown eye and one green eye appeared at her side, a broad grin on her face. She guided Raven back to the lift. Raven glanced back to where the hooded man had been, but he was gone. The lift started up, and she got a better look at the arena, but she still didn't see the hooded man.

The guardswoman guided her back onto the platform and back into the windowless room. Raven wanted nothing more than to sink to her knees and curl up somewhere dark and quiet.

"Assassin indeed," barked Barrow. He wore a vicious grin. He dabbed the sweat from his brow with a patterned handkerchief. "And you said you weren't a fighter. Ha! I'd say you earned yourself a warm meal and a cold drink."

The far door burst open, and a little woman with a dozen braids in her hair threw an accusative finger at Barrow. "What are you thinking?" snapped the woman. She glared at Raven. "You bring this *aggi* here?" She spat something in Tinatunian that made the guardswoman tighten her grip on Raven's elbow. "I don't want any freaks on my doorstep."

"It's fine," said Barrow. He spoke low and fast in Tinatunian, but the woman didn't look convinced. She kept glaring at Raven like she had insulted her.

Finally, the woman stormed back the way she'd come, and Barrow laughed halfheartedly.

"Freaks?" Raven asked, feeling a little insulted. Had the woman called her a freak? In truth, she felt a little like one. Was that what *aggi* meant? Her opponent had called her that too.

Barrow waved his hand toward the door. "Don't worry about what the old bat says, my little champion. She's superstitious. Nothing for you to worry about. Now, come on, let's see about that drink!"

Barrow guided Raven into another part of the arena, talking all the while about the match, how nervous he had been, how fantastic of an end—she tuned him out. Rather than underground, he took her up a staircase and to a room at the end. It had a single window that overlooked the street. She could see a sliver of midnight blue beyond the city and a smaller sliver of the Lanila Sea. At night, even under clouds, it shimmered as if made of diamonds and onyx.

The rest of the room was far better than her cell. A narrow bed had been pushed into one corner, a desk in the other, and a table in the middle with three chairs. The table held a tray of roasted fish, melon, hard cheese, and sliced bread. It smelled delicious, though she wasn't sure she could eat. She sat down at the table anyway; the green bottle of what she assumed to be ale called to her more than anything.

"I hope you like your new accommodations," said Barrow with a tone of parting.

"It's nice," Raven said absently.

She reached for the bottle, and Barrow left. He locked the door with an obvious click. She poured herself a glass. The deep red and sweet smell indicated it was wine, not ale. She took a drink. It didn't taste that different from the wines she'd tried at Silver Glen, tangy and a bit bitter but drinkable.

A heavy set of feet stopped outside her door—a guard.

Not a cell but still a prison. She stared down at her glass of wine. Now what? Would she have to fight someone every night?

She was far too exhausted for thinking. She drained her wine in a single gulp, then collapsed onto the bed.

Raven woke up to a scratchy female voice speaking Tinatunian. She pulled her groggy self off the bed and sat up just as the speaker left. The food of the night before had been cleared away, and a small porcelain teapot and a plate of buttered toast had replaced it. Raven scooted off the bed and gladly made herself a cup of tea. She relished the sweet, warm, and soothing taste.

The city had come alive with the morning. Laughter and playful chatter filtered in through the window. Gulls sang to each other, flaunting their freedom. Raven plopped into the chair. Sleep and food had cleared her mind, and the reality of the night before settled on her bones like lead.

She looked at her hands. It didn't seem real. How had she burned the man alive? There hadn't even been a fire, just...heat and then ash. The whole fight had a blurriness to it, like a dream, like she hadn't been herself. In truth, she didn't feel like herself.

Somehow, she had given her fever to him, and it had burned him alive like she thought it would do to her. She flattened her hands against the wooden tabletop. She tried to burn it, to turn it to ash, but nothing happened. It wasn't even warm.

Freak indeed.

She poured another cup of tea. She remembered wanting to live, and then...something happened—not a rage, but something feral, something not herself. It hurt her head to think about.

Footsteps sounded in the hall.

"Good morning, Guardswoman," came a charming, joyful male voice. He added something in Tinatunian. He spoke both tongues elegantly.

Her guard spat something in Tinatunian. Raven didn't have to understand it to feel the threat in her words.

"Off limits?" said the charmed voice. He scoffed.

Something about the voice sounded familiar, but she couldn't place it.

The guard said something in Tinatunian.

He answered with, "Well that's not very nice, is it?"

The guard grumbled and shifted. The next few moments happened fast: a scuffle, grunts, clothing swishing, blades colliding with flesh. A thump. A scoff.

"Let's see here," said the joyful man. He hummed a few notes of a song she had heard fluting through the city near dusk. "Ah, found you."

Raven set her cup to the side and slid to her feet. A key slid into the lock, turned, and the door swung open. She froze. Standing in the doorway was the hooded man from the arena. He had the dark, rich skin of Tinatun and coal-like eyes that quickly took her in. He wore dark blue robes made for adventure, with plenty of places for blades to hide. Several leather belts hugged his torso, holding all manner of things: a flask, a dagger, a compass. A saber hung from his waist.

He glided into the room with feline ease. "Well, well, what do we have here?" he said in a simpering, playful tone. He closed the door behind him. He sauntered a few steps closer, keeping the table between them. "A lost kitten?"

"What do you want?" Raven asked, trying to uphold an image of the strong girl who'd killed a man only hours ago.

Humor danced in his black eyes. "I saw what you did out there," he said, his velvet voice calm and sure. "And that poor bastard thought he stood a chance." His eyes narrowed slightly.

"So?" She straightened her shoulders. The woman's voice resounded: *freaks*. "Want me to do it to you?"

He chuckled and took a step around the table. "You could try, little bird, but I would rather talk first." He took another step, and then he stood on her side of the table. "What is a little bird like you doing all the way down here? Hmm?"

"I was kidnapped and sold," she spat. The spite came easy.

"Ah," he said, as though it explained everything. "Happens more often than it should."

A sound came from somewhere within the arena, a crash, a groan of wood, then a shout.

"Since we don't have much time before someone comes looking for you, I'll be quick." He stepped closer, close enough she could hit him, but she didn't.

She held her hand away from herself and tried to draw on the fever like she had before, but she couldn't. She couldn't feel the fever at all.

His eyes narrowed at her hand, then at her. "Can't use your magic now?"

"Magic?" she gasped, her heart skipping every other beat. "What are you talking about?"

He raised a brow. "What do you think you did out there? You turned a man to ash," he said, his lilting voice humorous but deadly serious. He took another step toward her, and all humor dropped from his words. "I am a seeker for a society that strives to keep magic alive as humanity and its machines insist on ending it. I'll give you a choice, little bird. Come with me, or stay here and live out however many days you have left before someone gets tired of you."

A choice: here or somewhere else.

The seeker extended his hand toward her, his dark skin laced with thin scars and calluses.

She swallowed. "What—"

Footsteps started down the hallway, toward her room. Whistling.

"Can you take me to the Crusaders?" she asked, her voice low.

The seeker's eyes widened a bit. "How do you know about them?"

Footsteps came closer.

The seeker glanced toward the door, then at her. He shook his head. "It doesn't matter," he said quickly. "Stay here, or leave with me." He wiggled the fingers of his extended hand.

The whistling stopped. A man shouted in Tinatunian. Footsteps stomped toward her door.

She slapped her hand into the seeker's.

The seeker twisted his body. In a single smooth motion, his heel came down on the door handle. With a crunch of metal and a crack of wood, the handle broke. A breath later, the person standing on the other side spat a curse, then threw his weight into the door. He shouted in Tinatunian.

The seeker wasted no time. He threw open the shutters and lifted Raven into his arms. She let out a shriek as he started toward the window. Her heart sank as she realized his mad plan. She curled her face into his neck, squeezing her eyes shut. He jumped, and for a sickening moment she felt nothing. Her heart skipped a beat and then jumped into her throat.

They landed, but she dared not open her eyes. He ran and jumped, his feet landing on something that sounded like wood. Another short run and a jump, and then they landed on solid ground. He started running, the cobblestone underneath his feet, and she dared to open her eyes.

They had landed on a narrow street between rows of red and gray stone buildings. People continued on their business, most of them. Some stopped to look to where the seeker had jumped from. Her heart sank a little—he'd jumped from roof to roof.

Shouting came from down the road, behind them. As the seeker slid down a side street, guards from the arena ran around the far corner. The crowd looked only mildly bewildered.

The seeker turned down an alley, down another side street, across a short bridge, and soon Raven had lost her sense of direction. Too many streets and alleys and bridges. The arena guards didn't seem to be following anymore either. He ducked into an alley and set her back on her own feet.

"How was that for a daring rescue?" he asked, a hum on his breath. Barely breathless. The morning sunlight darkened the hood's shadow over his face, but she caught the flash of his teeth. A wide smile curved, brightening his entire face.

"Thank you," Raven said because he had, however audaciously, gotten her out of the ring.

And now she was standing in Wayward Point, friendless and lost. The muggy air pressed in all around her, a second skin. Her sleeveless shirt now made sense. She would hate to wear the long-sleeve and high collared dresses she had worn in Silver Glen.

The seeker straightened, eyes on her. He adjusted his feet to take up more room in the alley, blocking her way past him while angling himself to see if anyone approached from the street.

"What?" she asked, as breathless as if she had run instead of him.

He tilted his head. He was looking at her, but not at *her*—all around her. "Interesting," he said.

And it hit her; she stood in an alley with a stranger. She had her dagger, but would it matter? She had one; he had at least five that she could see. He had proven his fitness with the rescue. She took a single step back. She might—if she were fast enough and lucky—outrun him.

The seeker pivoted toward her faster than she could move. The palm of his hand rested firmly against her cheek. She jumped at the contact.

"You're burning up." His smirk tilted downward.

She pulled her cheek away from his hand. "It's just...a fever," she said. And the thoughts came together. The fever had burned like fire with her panic, and after she had pushed it into the man, he had burned. Then the fever had gone. Now, it returned. It pulsed under her skin, though not as powerfully as it had before.

The seeker's hand hovered in the air for a heartbeat, then he returned it to his side. "A fever indeed."

A woman in a white shawl walked by the mouth of the ally. Two children, each no more than ten, held onto her hands. Raven met the eyes of the child closest to the ally. The boy pointed to the seeker and spoke in Tinatunian. The seeker casually rolled his head over his shoulder to look at the boy.

The woman looked once at the seeker, and her scowl vanished. Her mouth straightened, her dark eyes widened, and her skin paled to a sickly ashen gray. She forced her gaze away and started to walk faster, yanking the children with her. The boy spoke again, but the woman cut his words off.

The seeker looked lost between humor and distaste.

"Why did she look at you like that?" Raven stopped herself before she asked if he was one of the freaks she had heard about.

He shrugged. "I might have something of a reputation. Not all good."

"Clearly," Raven mumbled.

He glanced to the street. "It doesn't sound like we were followed. Good." He took a step onto the street. He motioned for her to follow.

She stayed still.

The seeker paused in the mouth of the alley. "Is something wrong with your feet?"

"Why should I follow you?" She wanted to reach down for her dagger, if only to show him that she was armed. "How do I know that you're not going to sell me to someone else or lead to somewhere worse than where I came from?"

He shrugged. If only she felt as calm as he looked. "You don't," he said. "That's one of the great mysteries of life. Trust is one of those fickle things that can hurt you far worse than it can help. But sometimes it's worth it." He extended his hand, not for her own, but for her trust.

A shout in Tinatunian came from the street, and the seeker's brows rose. His calm expression didn't crack. He leaned back to look and then leaned forward. "Well, I was wrong. Looks like your friends from the arena did follow us."

"What?"

"That doesn't leave much of a choice, does it?" The seeker stepped toward her, grabbed her hand, and pulled her down the alley.

They crisscrossed a dozen alleys, passed doors of wood and doors of cloth and doorways without doors.

He let go of her hand. "Follow me or make your own way. Pick fast." He didn't stop.

In the span of a single heartbeat, she had to choose. She didn't have the time! Face the strange city alone or with a stranger. She felt the tug, somewhere deeper than she understood, and she jogged after the seeker.

"This way," he whispered.

They walked through a building's backroom—a bakery. Barrels were stacked three high; crates of vegetables and fruit were stacked on the stone counters; bags of flour and sugar turned one corner into a white, powdery mess. From the front, the smell of fresh bread wafted through the air. Quick and silent as a breeze, she and the seeker were on the other side.

He led her through alleys and down streets and through a few more hidden passages that went behind and through businesses and homes. She noticed the way people—at least those who dared notice him—looked as the seeker's presence registered. Their faces paled, expressions turned to something between shock and fear. Everyone else pretended as though he didn't exist and, by extension, that she didn't exist.

She didn't mind, considering that the arena guards chased them, but she minded that she didn't know why.

Freaks.

They worked their way through the sprawling city. She heard the calls of the market square, the smells of sizzling fish and mystery meat, the vendors in their mixed languages, hagglers, and a dozen different songs. The cobblestone turned to dirty sand, packed by generations of feet. They passed barefoot children in scraggly clothes, who laughed as they played. It seemed to be mostly residential; older adults lounged on front steps and on porches, smoking or speaking to one another, sipping from coral-colored cups.

This part of Wayward Point felt older. The buildings were of a lighter stone, sun-bleached and well-used. The people didn't turn in fear of the seeker. Many waved, and he waved back without slowing down.

A ballgame played by older children stopped when the seeker walked onto the street, the children all gawking in mixtures of disbelief and awe. Several spoke in Tinatunian, at which the seeker answered. The children all smiled.

Revered.

On these streets, Raven did not go unnoticed. The people looked to her with the same revered awe as they looked at the seeker. It made her stomach plummet at the same time her heart skipped a beat. What did it mean?

When someone waved to her, she waved back.

A group of smaller children halted their walk and surrounded the seeker, dark eyes wide, faces brushed with sand and dirt. They all spoke rapidly, some looking to her, but most to the seeker.

He laughed, glanced at Raven, and spoke in Tinatunian to the children. They giggled.

"What did you say?" she asked when they had passed.

"That you didn't speak their language," he said. "It's true, isn't it?"

She nodded. They walked a little further in silence. She was about to say something else when they walked onto an old wooden bridge that stretched over a small canal. The water dribbled down the sandy stones and stretched out to—

She gasped at the view.

The beach stretched on from the bridge to the sea. The sea stretched endlessly to the horizon, glittering sapphire and aquamarine. She lingered a heartbeat too long. The seeker was waiting at the far end of the bridge, a curious smile on his face. She jogged to catch up.

He led her to a small clearing where palms and ferns grew between sandy shacks. They all seemed to be empty. Before them, the view of the ocean hadn't changed. He let out a sigh and leaned against one of the palms.

"Why are you helping me?" Raven blurted.

"Mostly because you needed helping," he said simply. "And because you have magic. Are you warded?"

"Warded? What does that mean?"

"I'll take that as a no." He cleared his throat. "I'll start from the top." He flattened his hand against his chest. "I am a seeker. I took an oath to protect magicians. You, a magician, were being held against your will. The rest is self-explanatory."

"I've never heard of a seeker."

"Not many have," he said, "seeing as how we're from a fairly private society—not to mention rare."

"What society is that?"

"It's a secret. I can't tell you out in the open, in case you scamper off and tell the world where we are. We wouldn't want the enemy to come flooding through the gates, now would we?" He tilted his head.

"The enemy? You mean the Gray Elite?"

He shrugged, a non-answer.

She sighed through her nose. "And I don't scamper."

He chuckled. He started to say something else, but she cut him off. "Can you help me find the Crusaders?"

His expression didn't change. "Why do you want to find them?"

"They might know people that I know, and they might be able to contact them or help me get back to where I was," she said, avoiding all names.

"They're a rowdy bunch of pirates," he said. "I'm not sure they're in the market of helping strays." He looked her up and down. "Unless you've got a few hundred extra piks in that outfit."

She blushed and held her tongue.

"Hmm, broke?" he asked. When she didn't answer, he added, "That's what I thought."

If the Crusaders wouldn't help her, then... "Can you help me with something else?" She pulled out the wooden coin but held it in her fist. "I want to go to the Destiny Show."

The seeker's smile faded. "Why would you want to go there?"

"It's where I wanted to go in the first place," she said bitterly. She tightened her hand around the coin. "Before the people I thought were helping me sold me."

"Why," he said, not a question. His smile flattened into a straight line, and he studied her face with such an intensity that she wanted to take a step back.

She held her ground. She wouldn't let someone else push her around. "Someone told me to go there," she said, though the memory had fogged. She could remember the dark outline of the thief, the smell of the musty inn, and the feel of the wood coin as he'd pressed it into her hand.

"It's not a fun place to go," said the seeker. "Security is tight."

She opened her hand and showed him the coin. "He gave me a coin to get in."

He pushed off the tree with surprising lethality, and her body tensed. His dark eyes pierced her hand, the coin, then her eyes. "Who gave it to you? Do you remember?"

She swallowed; the sudden change in the seeker had stolen the breath from her throat.

"*Who?*" he whispered.

"He said his name was Conrad," she managed to say.

The seeker took a step back, and the predatorial gait fell away. He put a hand against his chest, over his heart, and looked at her as though he hadn't seen her before.

Had the name been a code? A message of passage?

The wind—cool from the sea—pushed against her, ticking her nose with salt and adventure. It smelled like Leon Stark had described it: dirty with silt, ripe with stone and sand that never dried, and full of the unknown, of endless horizons and bottomless seas.

Then the seeker laughed. He doubled over in laughter, and she felt her cheeks go hot, the sense of adventure from the sea breeze shattered. She turned to go, but he grabbed her arm. His eyes were shimmering with tears.

"Wait," he said, laughter still on his words.

"Why? So you can make fun of me some more?"

"No, no," he said, straightening. He cleared his throat and repeated firmly, "No. I'm not laughing at you, little bird. I'm laughing at fate."

She huffed, not in the mood. "What does that even mean? You think my situation funny?"

He let out a sound, half laugh, half groan. Then he leaned toward her. "You don't recognize me?"

She looked deeper into his coal-dark eyes, his plump cheekbones, his joyful smile. She shook her head. "Should I?"

He pulled back his dark blue hood. "I suppose not; it was dark, after all, and I didn't know you at first either."

She started to speak, but then she stopped. The seeker wasn't that much older than her. His black hair fell halfway to his waist, done in dozens of braids. Gold and bronze beads clicked together as his hair fell free of his hood. He smiled, and his entire face lit up. A gold bead studded one ear, and she spotted gold necklaces beneath his robes.

"You," she whispered, disbelief curving her words, her thoughts.

The seeker was the thief, the very thief who had given her the wooden coin.

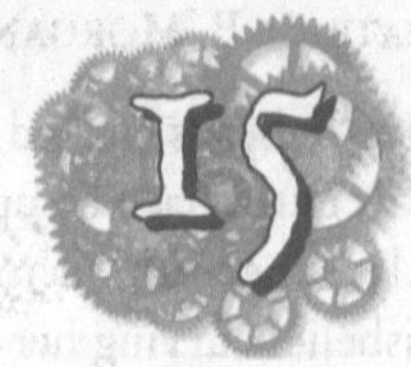

Conrad, thief and seeker, leaned against the palm. He kept his coal-dark eyes pinned on Raven, his smile wide. "Took you long enough," he said.

"You," Raven breathed.

"You," Conrad repeated, gesturing to her. "It looks like you took my advice to heart after all."

Conrad had been the one who had stolen the centrum from the Temple of the Three Sisters in Silver Glen. He had been the one she and Zander had chased to Lenhala. He had been the one Zander's father, Brigadier General Winchester, had hired to recover the centrum. He had been the one she had stolen the centrum back from.

She swallowed the urge to reach for her locket. Conrad knew how much the Hawks would be willing to pay for the centrum's return.

"So what happened, little bird?" Conrad asked. "You finally fly away from that windbag?"

He meant Zander. He and Raven had disguised themselves as traveling lovers. When they had met in that shabby inn, Zander had been distracting the people so that she could sneak into their rooms and search for the centrum. Conrad had found her on the stairs, listening while Zander sang lewd songs of mermaids, and had given her the coin. He had told her that if she wanted to leave Zander and start a new life, she should seek out the Destiny Show at Wayward Point.

Raven looked down at the wooden coin, the diamond and circle insignia engraved in its surface. The same insignia engraved on the inside of her mother's locket.

In a way, she had left Zander. Just not entirely on purpose.

"I..." She looked up to see Conrad patiently listening. "He was planning on going somewhere" —she twisted her fingers over the coin— "without me. He said I would be a hindrance. So I left him before he could leave me."

She decided to leave it at that because the truth of it would sound cowardly and stupid.

The slight humor in Conrad's face vanished. In its place, sincerity. "You did the right thing. I've met plenty of scoundrels in my life—trust me—and he was one of them. Men don't change, contrary to what some girls think. You are better off without that worthless excuse for a man."

She nodded. A part of her thought the same. Another part of her shuddered.

"If we're trading sob stories," said Conrad, bitterness in his words, "I'll offer you mine to make you feel better. I had a girl, and I loved her. I thought she loved me. I took a job that required time and travel—that's when I met you—and by the time I got back home, she'd already found someone to replace me."

Conrad let out a short, lighthearted sigh. He looked out toward the sea, toward the breeze of salt, mildew, and adventure. The bitterness in his eyes became a shadow of heartbreak, of betrayal. She thought she understood, but the grief in Conrad's eyes went deeper than his tone implied.

"I'm sorry to hear that." She meant every word.

He shrugged, and the bitterness fell away. His good humor returned, along with his grin. "Oh well. What's done is done, and my life has gotten easier to manage with just me to worry about." He laughed. "I had a mercenary threaten her life not a week ago, and I told him to go ahead and do it. He looked at me like I'd gone mad."

"Did he...?" Raven asked.

Conrad heaved a sigh. "No. Bitch is still alive." He took a step and clapped his hands together. "So, as I was saying earlier, before we were rudely interrupted, I am a seeker. You've got magic. It's my obligation to take you to see some people about that."

She tensed. "People? Who?"

"It's a secret."

She frowned. "Your secret society?"

"Yes."

"I refuse."

"Why?"

"Because I don't know who they are, what they are, or what their goals are. For all I know, they're slavers. And I have had enough of slavers," she said, her words sure and steady. She crossed her arms for emphasis.

"You won't even stop by and say hello?"

"The last people I said hello to sold me as a slave."

He nodded. "That is as fair a point as any," he said with a sigh. "In that case, the people I want to introduce you to are not slavers, on my honor, whatever it's worth these days. They are in the business of preserving magic. That includes people. Like you."

"They help magicians," she said.

Conrad nodded. "Most of the associates are magicians, and they are interested in finding more magicians before the Gray Elite gets to them."

Just like the Hawks, she thought. "What about the Destiny Show? You told me to go there."

"That is our first stop, should you agree," he said. "Even if you were not a magician, had you presented the coin and my name, someone would have offered something of help, be it a job at the docks or cleaning stalls."

"But..." She thought about it. "Is that where this society of yours is?"

"It's their office here in Wayward Point," he said. "I can't tell you where they are beyond that. That is a guarded secret. But I can take you to the Destiny Show. Do you still want to go?"

"Yes," she said without hesitation.

"Good." He nodded, his smile widening. "Then let's not waste any more time growing old."

Conrad started along a grassy path that hugged the beach, and Raven followed a step behind, the coin clutched in her hand.

Conrad guided her to the far side of Wayward Point, away from the arena, away from the market. He led her across the mouth of the river and across the coral bridge and past the fish-smelling docks. He weaved through sandy alleys and narrow streets of ancient cobble. The city gradually shrank to single-story wooden shacks and lean-tos, dotted with palms and scraggly bushes and leafy vines. They passed wooden shacks with fronds for roofs and doors, shells pressed into the stone around the doors and windows. The hard-packed dirt became loose sand, the houses vanished, and the wild nature took over. Palms clustered together, weeds and harsh grass grew in the sand, and dark gray rocks punctuated it like scattered bones.

The Destiny Show stood on the edge of Wayward Point, an old white stone building with no other discernible features. No sign announced its name. A vine had taken over a large portion of the roof, dangling off lazily and swaying in the breeze. Conrad stopped before a plain wooden door, the only entrance she could see.

He winked at her, then knocked three times.

No response came.

Conrad let out an agitated sigh and knocked three times more.

Heavy footsteps approached, and the door opened. The doorman stood tall and wide, built like a bodyguard, like the doorman of the arena.

Raven caught the tendrils of thick gray smoke hovering near the ceiling behind the man, twirling slowly. It looked as though the smoke itself formed the ceiling.

The doorman grunted; he looked at Conrad, then at Raven.

"I've a client who would like to speak with Madam Mallori about the stars," said Conrad.

The doorman frowned, and Conrad repeated his words in Tinatunian—not without a bit of spite, Raven noticed.

The doorman spoke only a few words. His voice was deep and unsettling.

"Out?" Conrad snapped. He raised an eyebrow. "If Mallori is *out*, then who is *in*?"

The doorman frowned. Conrad repeated himself in Tinatunian. A heartbeat later, the doorman grumbled, "Malik."

Conrad sighed, no small amount of irritation on his breath. "Fine, we'll talk stars with dear Malik instead."

The doorman waited a beat, then stepped aside. Conrad guided Raven into the dark space, and when the doorman shut the door, what little sunlight had been with them vanished. Candles burned on a sidebar, each in a strange glass globe that funneled the smoke up, up, up, through a series of tubes, where it puddled on the ceiling in shades of gray and dark blue and green. The candles flickered and gave the room an eerie sense of shadows. Raven did not like it. It felt too small and cramped. The doorman showed them to the back of the room, where a curtain hung in place of a door, its edges frayed.

The doorman stepped halfway through the curtain and spoke in Tinatunian. A second voice answered him in the same language, a calm, smooth, tenor male voice.

Was she to have this conversation in Tinatunian? Would Conrad have to translate? Her skin prickled at the idea, at the memory of all the conversations the scavengers had had about her, right in front of her, about their plans for her.

The doorman stepped back, holding the curtain for them.

Conrad hesitated, and Raven wasn't about to walk into a new space first.

"Well?" came the voice from the room, with barely a hint of an accent. "Are you going to show your face?"

Raven tensed at the change of tone; where the voice had been somber a heartbeat before, it now spoke in maliciousness. Conrad clenched his fists, then relaxed. He inhaled, straightened his shoulders, and took the first step through the curtain. Raven followed a step behind. The curtain *whooshed* back behind her. The doorman's heavy steps retreated.

They stood in a dimly lit room. A few clouded globes flickered, blue and green and gray, all sitting on a small round table in the middle of the room. Cushions of different sizes and colors lay around the table, and resting on the largest pillow was a young man in dark robes. Undoubtedly, he was one of the most beautiful people she had ever seen. He had khaki skin, high cheekbones, and sharp eyes a honeyed shade of brown. He wore a dozen necklaces around his slender throat, beads, golden and silver chains, and three pendants at varying lengths. Raven counted three rings on each of his dark hands.

In the flickering candlelight, though Malik sat still, his jewelry glinted and shimmered.

Conrad took a step forward, opened his arms wide, and said happily, "Malik!"

Malik moved faster than she could blink. In less than a heartbeat, he pulled a knife from his billowing sleeves and hurled it straight at Conrad.

16

Raven gasped as the knife whisked through the air. Conrad dodged; the knife *thunked* into the wall behind him. She glanced over her shoulder to where the knife had embedded itself an inch into the wooden wall.

"Glad to see your aim has improved," Conrad said, hand on his cheek. He brought his hand away, and to Raven's surprise, red glimmered on his fingers. Not a lot, but enough to make her heart flip flop in her chest.

"I was aiming for your throat," growled Malik.

"Oh," said Conrad, wiping the blood off on his sleeve. "I suppose it gives you something else to work on, then."

"What do you want?" Malik sank back into the largest cushion with the grace of a bird landing on a branch. He draped one arm over the side and set the other on the table. The candlelight caught on his jeweled rings.

Conrad meandered to the table and sank into one of the smaller cushions, as calm as if Malik hadn't just tried to kill him. Raven tried to follow his calm lead, but her heart still thudded against her chest. She sat beside him, the cushion pulling her down. Getting up wouldn't be easy. Or graceful.

Malik looked between the two of them. His gaze lingered on Raven's.

"I've brought you a new friend," said Conrad, gesturing to her.

Malik's expression didn't change.

"I found her in the arena, of all places. Turned a pirate into a pile of ash with her bare hands."

Malik's brows rose. "This is her?" he asked, gesturing to her with a wave of his slender fingers. "I heard about the incident. The girl sucked the soul right out of the flesh, and the body withered in mere seconds."

"I don't recall soul-sucking," Raven said quietly.

Malik's gaze roamed over her. "I don't sense anything."

"I don't either, not right now," said Conrad. "But I saw it with my own eyes. I felt it then, strong as any, but by the time I got to her, it had vanished. That pirate didn't just wither away, he disintegrated to ash. No blood, no bones, no nothing. *Ash.*"

Malik looked again at Raven, his honey eyes searching hers like Conrad had done, looking at her, but not at *her*. Several long, slightly uncomfortable moments passed.

"What is this place?" she asked, looking at Malik, though she directed her question to Conrad.

"The Destiny Show," he said plainly. He motioned to Malik. "He's a seeker."

"You're both seekers?"

Conrad opened his mouth and inhaled to speak, but Malik spat, "This fool isn't a seeker. Not anymore." Malik's eyes narrowed. "His greed got the better of him. He's nothing but a scoundrel and a pirate."

Conrad shrugged, not denying it. "But, despite that, here I am, fulfilling my sacred obligation."

"You are bargaining for your redemption," countered Malik.

"Bargaining," Raven repeated. She turned her sharp glare onto Conrad. "I'm a bargaining chip?"

Conrad shifted, his joyful smile faltering into one of nervousness. A cat, cornered. "Yes and no. I did save you from the arena, and you wanted to go to the Destiny Show."

"But she doesn't have magic," said Malik, almost bored. "Is this another joke, Conrad?"

"No," Conrad said firmly. "I saw her turn that man to ash. I felt it in the air."

Malik leaned forward, eyes on Raven. "Why don't you explain what happened in the arena?"

She swallowed, and then she recounted being attacked by the Retriever, saved by the three scavengers, sold, and thrown into the arena. All the while, Malik's honey eyes never left hers. He barely blinked. When she finished with being broken out of the arena by Conrad, she felt winded and relieved.

"This fever," Malik said, "how long have you had it?"

How long had it been since they had left Lenhala? She didn't know. "About four weeks," she guessed. "Maybe more."

"Hmm. And you haven't shown signs of magic before it?"

Raven shook her head.

Malik leaned back in his cushion. "That is strange."

"What do you think it is?" Conrad asked. "I've never heard of magic coming and going like that."

"Because it doesn't," said Malik.

A strange weight of guilt fell on her shoulders. Raven tore her eyes from Malik and focused on the silk tablecloth. The threads frayed at the edges. Magic. She didn't have magic; she never had. Yet she felt the fever under her skin. It had been calm since she had killed that man. The fever had killed him, the fever that she had somehow pushed into him, through touch.

"What happened?" Malik asked, softer.

She glanced back at him.

Malik leaned onto the table. "When did this fever first appear? What were you doing when you first noticed? Did you meet anyone strange or go somewhere you hadn't been before? Had something strange happened in the days before it?"

The locket around her throat felt heavy and hot against her skin. Conrad and Malik both held their waiting stares on her. She couldn't tell them about Lenhala, the Hawks, or the centrum. Her skin prickled, she started to sweat, and her heart skipped every other beat.

"Is that when you left him?" Conrad asked.

Raven blinked.

"Left who?" Malik asked.

Lies, lies, lies. "My husband," Raven whispered.

Malik raised a brow.

"A rat of a man," Conrad said darkly. "A drunk and a bastard. Talked about women like a farmer talks about cuts of beef."

"You met him?" Malik glanced at Conrad.

"We stayed at the same inn not that long ago," Conrad said. "I met Raven, looking like a forlorn turtledove on the stairs while her husband sang unsavory songs about mermaids in the barroom. I told her about the Destiny Show."

"Hmm," hummed Malik. "Tell me about this fever."

She swallowed against the lump in her throat. She looked down at her hands, the hands she had latched onto her opponent with, the hands that had given him the fever, the hands that had held on when he crumbled to nothing.

"It's there," she said. "I can feel it. Not like it was. It feels like something squirming, like a second skin underneath mine." She ran a hand over her arm. "When I think about it, I can feel it more. I get overheated so easily now, breathless, like I'm burning up from the inside. And when I thought that man was going to kill me, I just...I don't know what happened. It's blurry. Like I wasn't myself."

Conrad and Malik both frowned.

"What?" she asked them.

"I've never heard of someone catching magic like a cold," Malik said.

"You think that's what it is?" her voice came out a wisp.

"What else could turn a man to ash?" came Conrad's voice.

Malik stared at her, his eyes hard. "Tell me about your husband, the one you bravely left."

"Scum," Conrad hissed under his breath. "The whole lot of them."

Malik didn't seem to hear, or if he had, he ignored it. But the word caught Raven's interest. She looked to Conrad and repeated, "The lot of them?"

Conrad's face went slack. Caught. He looked between Raven and Malik. He swallowed.

"Conrad?" Malik said, a warning.

"I may have come into contact with her husband's relation," Conrad said carefully.

Raven tensed. He *had* met Zander's father. It was a detail she hadn't considered until now.

"Our encounter was brief, but he was every bit as much of a pompous scumbag as his son. Shady fellow, but they looked strikingly similar."

Malik looked between Raven and Conrad, eyes searching.

"You know his father?" Raven asked. Her voice came out shakier than she anticipated. Conrad had met Zander at a tavern, though she didn't know how or to what extent that brief contact went.

Conrad scratched his chin, looking elsewhere. When no one else spoke, he let out a grievous sigh. "Fine, you caught me." He held up both hands. "His father hired me to find something. I lost it. That scumbag son probably stole it back." Conrad cast a wary gaze back to Raven.

She curled her fingers into her palms to keep from touching the centrum. Did he suspect her? She could cast the blame on Zander if she had to.

Malik released a resigned sigh.

"I didn't complete the contract," Conrad argued.

"It doesn't matter," Malik said, rubbing his temples.

Conrad glanced at Raven, his smile wide. "What can I say? I'm a pirate at heart."

"Raven," said Malik, "If you were staying at an inn, that implies travel. Were you and your husband going somewhere? Had you been somewhere odd? Sisters only know what affairs this fool is involved in." He gestured to Conrad, who took pretend offense.

"There's also the matter of how you ended up down here," Conrad added.

Malik didn't brush the comment off. He stared at her with curious intent.

She bit her lip. A lie. She needed a lie, a cover story. In a quick second, she chose a thin version of the truth. Under Malik's sharp gaze, she knew that a total lie wouldn't be good enough.

"My husband," she started. "He was—or he is—involved in plots to overthrow the Gray Elite."

A crease formed between Malik's brows. His lips moved, but no sound came out.

"He kept it secret from me," Raven said quickly. "He told me we were chasing a thief." She glanced at Conrad, who didn't look surprised. "But his brother found us. He talked us into going to the capital. His father knew that he had whatever it was that he'd wanted stolen, the thing that Conrad had been hired to find, and he wanted it. So did General Deacon."

Malik's eyes narrowed. "Wait. You...you're talking about the Hawks."

The blood rushed from her face at the mention.

Malik let out a groan. "And that means you're talking about Zander Winchester."

Her breath escaped her faster than she could think about keeping herself composed.

"Zander Winchester?" Conrad repeated. "Even his name sounds pompous."

Malik leaned onto the little table and rubbed his eyes. The candles flickered with the motion. "The bastard," he muttered. He looked to Raven again. "I heard he brought a girl back with him, but I didn't realize he had married."

Raven bit her lip, the truth written all over her face.

Malik noticed. His frown deepened, and he said, "You're not married."

She shook her head.

Conrad leaned forward, looking between the two of them. "Should this name ring a bell?" he asked.

"You'd already gotten kicked out by the time Zander came along," Malik said. "He was here less than two years, and he left to play the Hawks's game of resistance."

"You know Zander?" Raven asked Malik.

He looked back at her, and she saw the hesitation in his eyes. She put the pieces together herself. The mixed look that people gave Conrad, terror and awe, reverence and distrust. The woman's fear of freaks coming to the arena. The secret society that helped magicians.

"You're Wraiths," she whispered, and Malik's eyes narrowed.

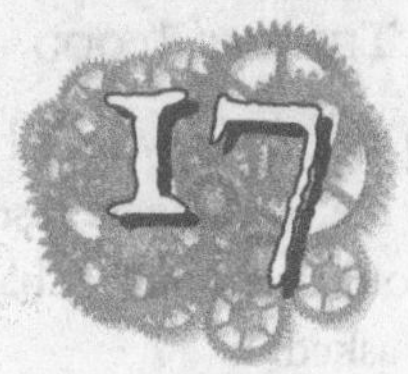

Raven's heart shuddered. *Wraiths*.

Conrad blinked. "You know about us?" He frowned at Malik. "Zander's a Wraith? He didn't look like one when I saw him."

"He's also a Hawk," Malik said with distaste. He looked to Raven. "You're not surprised. You knew he was a Wraith."

"It's one of the things I learned about him in the past few months," she said. Not a lie. "And you're a Wraith too?"

Malik held her stare for several breaths. "I am," he said at last. "Tell me, Raven, what he told you about the Wraiths."

"You're magicians," she said. "You smuggle other magicians out of the Gray Elite's clutches."

He nodded. "Those things are both true. We are not assassins, thieves," —he shot a pointed look in Conrad's direction— "or mercenaries. The Hawks have stolen Wraiths and turned them into assassins, sullying the name of the Wraiths."

"You saw how people looked at me out there," Conrad added. "People fear the Wraiths now. But the older neighborhoods, the people who have been here longer know better. They know what the Wraiths really are."

"Which is?" asked Raven.

"*Ulinta*. Protectors," said Malik. "We are a society dedicated to keeping the tradition of the Sisters alive. We protect magicians from their deaths, or worse, at the hands of Gray Elite."

"We also tend to be shadowy and sneaky," added Conrad with a smile. "So the jump to assassins and pirates isn't that far."

Malik glared at Conrad and said, "Indeed. As you would clearly know."

Conrad shrugged. "Some would prefer the name privateer."

Malik hummed his disapproval. He returned his gaze to Raven and said, "And you've left Zander because he's a bastard, and then you ended up down here."

"And I brought her straight to you," Conrad said.

"But as of right now, she is not a magician," Malik countered. "Raven, tell me what really happened."

"The rest of the story is exactly how I told you," she said. "I was in the woods, an automaton caught me, scavengers rescued me and then sold me. I thought the Destiny Show would help me get back there or something."

"Where is *there*?" Malik asked.

"That's also a problem," she said. "I don't really remember. But...I could find my way from the town of Oun." There was a Hellcat platform underneath it, and one of the Dweller scouts worked at the blacksmith.

"Ah," said Conrad. "Is that why you were looking for the Crusaders? A free lift?"

"The Crusaders?" Malik asked. "They're pirates. Who told you about them?"

"Zander mentioned them," Raven lied quietly. She didn't like how much Malik and Conrad already knew, and she didn't entirely trust either one.

Malik studied her a while longer. "He is still traveling," he said, never breaking his eye contact, "and...the Crusaders."

Raven's pulse beat harder.

Malik rapped his ringed fingers on the table. "Zander wants to get somewhere without anyone noticing. And the only place he would need to get without being noticed would be Gracita."

Raven didn't have a lie; she hadn't anticipated him figuring that out so quickly.

Conrad leaned onto the table, his eyes burning with curiosity.

"Why?" Malik whispered, more to himself than anyone else.

Raven didn't give him an answer.

Then his honey brown eyes blinked, softened. "He wants to get Rosaria out."

A pang of jealousy shot upward from her toes.

"The dead princess?" Conrad asked.

"There are rumors she is alive," Malik said. "It doesn't matter. It's a fool's errand. Even if Rosaria is alive, she has no military or political power. She is a figurehead. It would change nothing. That, and she would be well-guarded, or poised as a trap for any would-be rescuers. Even if she retains a fraction of the royal magic, she would not be able to take on an empire."

Raven didn't argue. A part of her thrived on Malik's distrust of the Dwellers' plan and his denouncement of the princess's importance. Another part of her worried for her friends' safety as they attempted that fool's errand.

The centrum hanging around her throat pulsed, and she fought the powerful urge to reach for it. Malik didn't know about Altair's Augur or its missing part. If he did, he held it in well. No one knew Zander's real mission had been to get the centrum far away from his father and the Hawks.

And it would stay that way.

Let everyone think the worst of Zander. Let them think him a deserting bastard. That way, no one would look any closer at his actions. The centrum would remain safe, Altair's Augur would remain silent, and no one would die from its use. It hurt to toss him to the vultures, but what choice did she have? She couldn't tell Malik and Conrad about the centrum, and if she tried to make light of Zander's actions, they would ask questions.

"But there's still the matter of our little bird," Conrad said, motioning with a graceful wave of his hand to Raven. "Magic or not, she turned a man to ash. Surely, that counts something toward my redemption."

"She's not a magician," Malik said with finality. "And your redemption lies with the Sisters, not with me. Of course, that doesn't mean you can't grovel at my feet."

Conrad heaved a dramatic sigh and turned to Raven. "I apologize for wasting your time."

"If you want help getting out of your mess, I will offer a hand," Malik said to Raven. "I can find you work if you are interested."

"What kind of work?" Raven asked. She hadn't intended to say it with as much bite as she did. Her first thoughts had gone to a job as a whore, then as a slave, and then as a fighter in the arena. "I'm not good at anything."

"Doesn't mean you can't learn," added Conrad lightheartedly.

"At the docks," Malik said.

"The docks?"

"He means air docks," said Conrad. "Not the sea docks."

Her heart skipped a beat. "Air docks? As in airships?"

Malik nodded.

Her thoughts scattered. "On an airship?"

"If that is what you want," he said. "I know a captain willing to accept a stranger onto his crew. You can work as long as you'd like. Seeing as you have no coin for boarding or food, I suggest taking a job."

Raven blinked at him. Her, work on an airship? The thought sent a nervous tremor down her spine and into her toes. She thought of her friends, of Zander and Ivy and Thalame. What would they think if she never returned? A mean little voice reminded her that her friends had wanted to send her back to Silver Glen. Zander hadn't wanted her along on his mission to save the princess; he had called her a hindrance.

Still, the idea of working on an airship in the meantime gave her a fluttery feeling. She couldn't tell if it was the good or bad kind of fluttery.

It took her a moment to realize Conrad and Malik were waiting for an answer. She swallowed and said as firmly as she could, "Yes. I'll work."

"It's hard work at times but better than fighting or whoring for your supper," Malik said. He shifted, and his beads shifted with him, clinking. He looked to Conrad and added, "And you."

Conrad waved off the concern. "I don't need a job, but I'm flattered you thought of me."

"If you're bent on redemption, our brothers and sisters in Moorin have had a string of bad luck. The Gray Elite are coming down hard on them. I'm sending you there to help."

Conrad let out a grunt of refusal.

"Moorin?" Raven asked without thinking.

"The capital of Gracita," explained Conrad. "The least friendly city to magicians. Filled with Gray Elite patrols and automaton soldiers."

"And," added Malik with a smirk, "I believe there is a ship leaving for Moorin tonight."

"Fantastic," Conrad mumbled, his humor gone.

Conrad led Raven back to the street. The sun seemed much too bright, and she shielded her eyes with her hands. The air felt just as sticky, though. She glanced to where the ocean met the horizon, the impossible blue on blue that stretched forever. How would it look from the deck of an airship? She imagined Zander's face when she told him about all of this. A rock fell into her stomach as a mean little voice reminded her that she might not see him or any of her friends again. If something happened to her or if something happened to them while they attempted the impossible... No, she couldn't think that way.

"A pik for your thoughts?" said Conrad. He was leaning against the white stone of the building.

She had no desire to talk about her growing mess of problems. "Malik said you were a pirate."

Conrad shrugged, but didn't deny it.

"How far have you gone?"

He followed her line of sight to the ocean. "Far but not that far. I've gone three days out in an airship. I've seen the southeastern half of Tinatun, the Islands of Ninulia, the Monilo Province. I've glimpsed the Gold Castle from the sky."

"The Gold Castle?" she asked. "It's real?"

"Oh, it's real," he said. "It's not as impressive as I thought. Spires of gold sure, and it gleams in the sun, but it's just a castle."

"Just a castle." She half laughed. "A castle is still a castle."

He nodded. They stood for a moment in silence. They were waiting on Malik to take them to the air docks. Raven hadn't gotten to stand still much since she had left the treehouse, and now that she had a moment, her thoughts churned, and her anxiety worsened until she thought she might be sick.

"So this friend of yours, Zander, was following me?" Conrad asked.

She nodded.

"And he took back that little box?"

She felt her skin prickle.

"And yet it was there when I left the room, and he was in the barroom the entire time, and you weren't. When I went to get it, it had mysteriously vanished."

He knew.

She swallowed and met his gaze.

"You stole it back, didn't you?"

She didn't deny it.

To her surprise and relief, Conrad laughed. "I'm lucky that old man of his didn't flay me on the spot for not having the damn thing. Tell me, little bird, what was in it that caused such a fuss?"

"I don't know. He never told me."

A lie, but not one that Conrad questioned. "The old man wouldn't tell me either. If you ask me, those Hawks are up to something."

"They're resistance," Raven said. "Of course they are."

Conrad chuckled.

The front door of the Destiny Show opened, and Malik walked out. He had left his dark robes in favor of leathers and robes similar to what Conrad wore. He had taken off his rings and necklaces, save for one ring and one silver chain with a pendant the color of the sun. He had a frightening number of knives and daggers. As he stepped toward them, he pulled his hood over his short brown hair.

"Let's be on our way." Malik fell into step beside Conrad.

Raven walked a step behind. She thought of Wayward Point—where would they have room for air docks? The air docks in Lenhala had been a towering structure of steel and glass with room for the hundreds of airships moving in and out. She surely would have seen such a building in Wayward Point.

They rounded the corner, and both Malik and Conrad halted. Raven nearly walked into them. Both stood still as stone. A feverish panic ran along her spine.

And then she saw what they had seen.

Men stood abreast in the street, armed with short swords, daggers, and clubs.

"There she is," one of the men drawled. Another man spoke in Tinatunian. A half dozen men spilled from an alley on their right, and more came from their left, surrounding them.

"Whatever do you gentlemen need?" asked Conrad. "There are nicer ways of asking for directions."

"The girl," said one of them, pointing his sword at Raven. "Boss is looking for her. He don't like you freaks stealing his things."

Raven tensed. Boss must be Barrow. The man who had bought her, from whom Conrad had stolen her.

"Ah," said Conrad. "He knows he lives in a city built on piracy, yes?"

"She belongs to him," another spat.

Another grumbled in Tinatunian.

"I belong to no one," Raven spat, earning herself a raised brow from Malik and an approving nod from Conrad.

"Nicely said, little bird," said Conrad. "I like the venom."

The thugs surged toward them, swords and clubs raised. Raven gasped, but Conrad stepped in front of her, and Malik stepped behind; both had drawn daggers. Conrad's blade found its mark on the first pirate's throat, and then a second and third. The two Wraiths moved with the lethal grace of a seasoned predator and a trained fighter, faster than wind, fierce as lightning.

And then the fight ended. The few wounded pirates who were left sulked and limped away. Most stayed on the ground, out cold or dead.

"Sisters," Raven breathed. She pressed a hand over her pounding heart. Served them right.

Conrad cleaned his bloodied blades off on a dead pirate's shirt. Malik did the same and then slid the daggers back into their sheaths. One fit on a belt that hugged his torso; another vanished into his robes.

"Glad to see you're not rusty," Malik said to Conrad.

"Me?" Conrad gasped, hand on his chest in exaggerated shock. "Even the idea is absurd. If anything, I've improved."

"You're pale," Malik said to Raven. His honeyed eyes looked her up and down. "Are you all right?"

She nodded. She glanced around at the bodies. It was worse than looking into a pile of ash. The ash didn't bleed. These bodies slowly leaked onto the dirt street, staining it dark, seeping into the packed dirt and sand.

"They're dead," Malik confirmed. "And they would have done worse to you if we hadn't. This is a message to their boss that he no longer owns you, and if he wants to argue, he will have to take it up with the Wraiths. Few in this town are foolish enough, and those who are don't last long."

"One thing I always liked about the Wraiths," Conrad said to Raven with a nudge. "Not afraid to bully the bullies."

"I thought you weren't assassins," she said, her voice wobbly.

"We're not," Malik said. "We did not accept payment for these deaths. We were defending you. They attacked first. We reacted in defense."

It made sense, logically. Conrad nudged her arm again and offered her a calming smile. That he could be so calm after killing someone... She didn't know what to think about it.

"Come on," Malik said. He put a steady hand on Raven's back and guided her down the street, around and away from the dead pirates.

She didn't want to think about them or the man she had turned to ash or the stranger she had stabbed in Ivy's garden back in Lenhala. She turned her gaze to the ocean instead, the endless blue that whispered of adventure. What would it be like to sail on an airship toward the horizon? What would she find on the other side?

She trained her thoughts on adventure as Malik and Conrad walked with her toward the air docks. She imagined herself in one of her old storybooks, a world where the magical core of a deadly machine didn't hang around her neck.

The air docks of Wayward Point were cleverly hidden inside a large cavern that opened to the ocean. A rickety wooden staircase, half smothered in sand, led down to the rocky shore and to a small platform floating on pontoons made from heavy balloons that looked to have once been in use by an airship. As they walked across the platform, Raven thought she spotted a pirate insignia inked on the side of one of the pontoons, worn by time and the salt water.

The platform wrapped one side of the cavern's wide mouth and led into the shaded cove. Blue-green water rushed through the cavern mouth, between the teeth-like rocks that jutted upward from the shallows. A waterfall cascaded down one side of the cavern, echoing over the stone. The docks themselves started just above the waterline and rose all around the cavern—a clutter of steel, brass, and copper attached to the walls. Catwalks and ladders connected the ports to each other, all supported by steel cables. Laughter ricocheted off the cavern walls. The space had a strong stench of brine and fish. Underneath it all, she sniffed grease and the heat of engines.

Malik started up narrow metal stairs; they wrapped around the cavern, stuck into the rock with pitons and thick steel cables. With every step, the metal groaned like it might give way, yet it held. Without a rail to hold onto, Raven trailed her hand along the rocky wall.

"How high are my odds of these stairs collapsing and sending me to my death?" Raven asked casually, though her voice trembled.

"Low," Malik answered. He didn't even glance back. "Sailors come up and down these steps several times a day. They're worn, not rusty."

Raven glanced down; indeed, she didn't see a bit of rust. Magic? For in a cavern of humid air and saltwater, rust would be impossible to keep away.

They made it to the main platform of the air docks, a thick floor of steel that formed a semicircle around the cavern. Raven glanced down; the floor was not solid but a lattice, and she could see down to the water below. Malik paused beyond the door of what appeared to be a tavern. Laughter and unharmonious chatter flooded from within, voices harshened by years of breathing exhaust and shouting over the engines. Inside, men and women in working clothes drank and talked.

Malik led them not inside but to a patio beside it. Fewer people lingered there. One man had fallen asleep on a table, drool soaking into his beard, while two others were speaking quietly over a hand-drawn map.

"I've got to find my contacts," Malik said. "You two, wait out here. Don't get into any fights you can't win."

Raven blinked, then realized that Malik had spoken to Conrad, not to her. Malik walked away, toward a building on the other side of the platform.

"Do you often get into fights you can't win?" Raven asked.

"Trouble likes me," he said, stuffing his hands into his pockets.

Raven meandered to sit at one of the tables, and Conrad followed her. He sat where he could see the ocean beyond the cavern, and his dark eyes settled on the horizon. Raven thought she saw the thirst for adventure there, maybe a longing for what he once had seen, the desire to see it all again.

"I've heard that a man can sail the world until he's old and blind and deaf, and never see the same thing twice," she said.

"Who said that?"

"I read it in a book."

Conrad laughed. "Reading fairy tales?"

"They're not fairy tales," she said. "They're adventure novels."

He shrugged. "Life out there isn't always as neat and adventurous as people make it out to be. It's hard work, constant work, and if you're...not operating on a strictly legal account, you're paranoid." He let out a sigh of defeat.

Raven let her mind drift. She imagined Conrad as a Wraith, then as a pirate, then as the thief. He'd done more than she had, more than she might ever do. No, she told herself. She would do more than what she had. She would see what the horizon held.

And there, sitting outside the tavern in the hidden air docks of Wayward Point, she decided that she would have her own adventures. Yet, in her mind, when she imagined adventure, she also imagined a blue-eyed, dark-haired boy beside her. She reminded herself that he wanted to send her back to Silver Glen while he played hero; he clearly hadn't imagined the same of her.

Shaking off the surge of bitterness, she asked, "What are you going to do?"

Conrad let out another sigh, this one deliberate. "I suppose I could go to Moorin and see what adventure is to be had there. I've never been to the city itself, you know. I've been to smaller outlying cities around Moorin, but I've never been in the heart of the Gray Elite empire. Might be fun."

"You could leave now," she whispered.

Malik hadn't returned. The path to the stairs, to the town, to the ocean, was clear.

Conrad seemed to read her thoughts. "I could. But I would rather the Wraiths not be any madder at me than they already are."

"What did you do to make them mad?"

He shrugged and leaned onto the table. It tilted slightly. Resting his cheek on his hand, he said, "Like Malik said, I'm a greedy bastard. I like shiny things. I became a Wraith when I was eleven. Thought it was what magic folk like me were supposed to do. Turns out, I'm a pirate at heart. I found a map in the Wraiths' archives. I borrowed said map without permission, and they kicked me out not two years later."

"Did it lead anywhere?"

Conrad blinked as though that hadn't been the response he had expected. "It did. An island about three days from the southeastern Tinatunian coast, abandoned. Found good loot there." He sighed with longing and sank a little further onto the table. "The Wraiths didn't see it like that. They took the map and burned it, something about desecration or something sacrilegious."

"What did you do after?" Raven asked, building the story of Conrad in her head. Wraith, pirate, thief, seeking redemption for his crimes—she would read that book.

Conrad straightened. "Why so interested in my life?"

"Because it sounds like an adventure," she said.

Conrad gave her a half smile. "I suppose it does. Though isn't every life an adventure?" He looked toward the ships that lined the docks. There weren't very many, and most were small. "Besides, I could do with a vacation from this place. The beach is nice, and the people are entertaining, and I can sleep without worrying about my throat being sliced at night, but I've been here too long for my own liking. I'm starting to get anxious. And they say if you want to broaden your horizons, the best thing to do is go toward one."

She liked that advice. She liked it a lot.

"But what about you, little bird?" Conrad tilted his head toward her, dark eyes glinting in the lantern light. "I don't know if you know what you're getting into by jumping aboard one of these...fine vessels." He eyed the array of airships. None were shiny and none were new; most were patched and ramshackle. "You might fall in love with it and never want to get off."

"I don't know," she affirmed.

Conrad lifted his brows.

"I've never been on an airship or worked on one, but I've always wanted to." She looked into the sliver of sky she could see, where it met the sea. She felt a ping of longing, the urge to go toward it. Just to see. She thought of the airships and sky cities that she had carved into the stone ceiling of her bedroom in Silver Glen, of the dreams she had nurtured while trying to fall asleep. "I've always wanted to see the world from the sky, to just go wherever I wanted, see the world, see what's out there."

Conrad hummed. He set both elbows on the table and leaned toward her. His dark eyes searched hers.

"What?" she asked.

"I'm looking to see if there's a pirate in there somewhere," he said, looking down his nose at her, exaggerating a squint.

She let the comment roll off her shoulders. "I'm not a pirate."

"Yet," he said. "I wasn't a pirate either until I walked the gangplank onto the deck. Then I was."

"I wouldn't be good at it," she said. "Pillaging and stealing."

"Ah, got one of those pesky consciences?"

She nodded.

He let out a grievous sigh. "Well, I suppose someone in this world needs one. Thank the Sisters it's not me." He shifted in his chair. The wood groaned. "I sailed for a while, but I came back to Wayward Point because I had someone to come back to." Something dark passed over his eyes. "But, that string has been cut, and I can head toward whatever horizon I damn please. I don't have to come back here anytime soon—or ever."

She suspected he meant his lover, his girl, who had left him for another. She didn't know if the bitter pain she felt when she thought of Zander was the same or something different. Zander had not outright left her for someone else, though they hadn't been together in order for him to have left her in the first place. Yet it felt like it. A wound inside, as her stepmother had put it, that phantom pain of loss, grief, and heartbreak.

In a blink, that pain vanished from Conrad's face, and a smile replaced it. He glanced at Raven, then at the ocean. "I hear the west coast of Gracita is lined with white sand beaches," he said dreamily, "mermaid lagoons and sunken pirate ships, hundreds of islands waiting to be explored."

"Sounds exciting," she said.

"When I'm done in Moorin, I think I'll head west, see what's over there," Conrad said with certainty. "What about you, little bird?"

"I'd like to see as much of the world as possible before I'm blind and deaf and too old," she said. "I think I'll start with whatever Malik has lined up for me."

His grin widened, and he laughed—not a teasing laugh but one full of joy. Raven tried to picture him as a ruthless pirate, out there pillaging and sinking ships. He had made the decision to have adventure, and she had too.

While Zander was out rescuing his princess, Raven would have her own adventure. Maybe a job on an airship was what she really needed. She would only have been a bother to him and the others, a hindrance. Raven had always wanted to ride an airship and see the world, and now she had nothing stopping her.

Malik returned with good news; he had found a ship that would take Raven on as crew. It happened to be the same ship that would be taking Conrad to Moorin. Malik took them to the ship, docked on the first tier. It was a plain ship of dull steel and bronze, its bow and stern both pointed, its balloons a reddish brown. On the side, *Marianne* had been painted in a darling silver script.

Marianne, Raven quickly learned, was a cargo vessel that specialized in rum—a special rum only made in Vinitula, a city in the southern half of Tinatun, and according to Conrad, gold in a bottle.

"Goes down like liquid sunshine," he said with a coy smile and a wink at Malik, who scowled.

Raven sensed a story in that scowl, and she wanted to ask about it. Later, she told herself, when Malik couldn't frown.

Malik introduced them to Captain Warren, a narrow man with charcoal hair and a full beard to match. He wore a battered tricorn hat with a gold rim to signify him as captain.

"This the new meat?" asked Captain Warren in a gruff, jolly tone that sounded like it belonged to a much broader man. He looked Raven up and down. "She'll do. I've trained plenty of kids to sail. You won't be trouble, will ya?"

"No," Raven said. She quickly added, "Captain."

He nodded. Then he turned his attention to Conrad, who had been examining the lettering of *Marianne*.

"And you want me to transport this pirate into Moorin?" asked Warren. Every word dripped skepticism.

Conrad acted as though he hadn't heard.

"Yes," Malik said, drawing out the word, scowling at Conrad. "With full payment for passage."

Warren harrumphed. He looked none too enthused about Conrad.

"You have my permission to lock him in the cargo hold for the duration of the trip," Malik said.

That got Conrad's attention. He frowned at Malik.

"Keep him away from the rum and out of trouble."

"I'll consider it," said Warren, looking at Conrad like a piece of contraband that he didn't want aboard his ship. "Might make the crew feel more secure. And if we're stopped by the Gray Elite, we can claim him a stowaway, and then he'll be their problem."

Conrad's scowl deepened.

Raven swallowed. If they were stopped by the Gray Elite, they would recognize her. If they found her, she doubted they would care about a stowaway pirate.

Malik cleared his throat. "It would be best if the Gray Elite didn't know she was on board either."

Warren's eyes narrowed.

"It would be best if they didn't see her," Malik added lowly.

Warren frowned at Malik. "You're giving me some risk, boy," he said, though not maliciously. "You're going to owe me after this one."

"Of course," Malik said, nodding.

Conrad rolled his neck. "Don't worry about the Gray Elite, Captain," he said confidently. "They won't find me."

"Not if I tie you to the bow," Warren countered, his mouth a straight line.

Raven didn't know if the captain joked or not, and by the looks, neither did Conrad.

Warren turned back to Malik. "I forgot to mention," he said, his voice low. "There's no official word, but we heard rumors that Luckett's scouting ship went missing. They suspect it went down somewhere to the north. The crew's gone—captured, most likely."

Malik didn't respond, but his lips tilted downward. His fingers flinched like he wanted to make fists, but he didn't. He held himself remarkably still. "Thank you for the news, Captain," he said, his voice strained. "Keep me informed."

Warren nodded. "All right you two," he said to Raven and Conrad, "Let's get you settled in. We leave tomorrow at first light."

The captain led them up the gangplank and onto the *Marianne*. A U-shaped passageway went around the main deck, skipping over the back of the ship where the engines were. The interior mirrored the outside, all ramshackle steel and bronze, patched and welded, but it did not dull Raven's anticipation—a real airship!

He led them through a bulkhead and into the bridge. The pilot's raised seat faced an expanse of angled windows, giving the best view of the sky. Right now, those windows held a marvelous view of the cavernous air docks. The navigator sat to the left of the pilot, as noted by the mess of maps and charts, air traffic maps, patrol routes, no-fly zones; land, sea, city, and sky. The area to the right of the pilot held a number of gauges, speaking tubes, levers, and dials. Behind it all, a raised platform overlooked the entire bridge—the helm. Beside the brassy railing, a dozen speaking tubes surrounded the captain's chair.

From the bridge, Warren started the official tour of the ship. The passageways were barely wide enough for two average people to pass. Ladders connected the various decks: main deck, middeck, and the lower deck, also known as the cargo hold. The cargo hold took up the most space, though not much larger than a small tavern. The engine was a tangled mess of pipes, gears, gauges, and pots. It was silent now, but Raven could imagine all the parts moving with efficiency, just like an automaton.

The quarters were located on the middeck, along with the galley. The rooms weren't much bigger than her old room at Silver Glen. Rather than doors, sage green curtains hung in each doorway. Each room held four cots and four footlockers. There were two small washrooms at the end of the quarters—no bath, no shower, just a copper basin and a small toilet.

Warren led Raven to one of the rooms and pulled aside the curtain. "You'll be in here. You're sharing with two others, both women." He looked Raven dead in the eye, and all humor faded from his face. "If any of the men on my ship give you grief, you let me know. I don't tolerate such behavior."

Raven blinked, but the captain didn't relent his stare.

Conrad leaned closer to her and whispered, loud enough for the captain to hear, "I think he's serious."

"I am," said Warren. "When you meet Lewis, ask her what happened to the man who gave her grief."

Raven nodded. Where had Captain Warren's sense of justice been when she'd been in the arena?

"Do I get bunkmates?" asked Conrad.

"No," Warren said flatly. "I have a special room set aside for you."

Conrad's grin fell into a frown. "It's not a cell, is it?"

Warren chuckled, and Conrad's frown deepened.

"Can I stay in Raven's room?" Conrad whined. "I promise Raven will keep me in line."

It was Raven's turn to laugh. The bubble in her chest felt unnatural—when had she last laughed?

She thought of how easily Conrad and Malik had dispatched those pirates. Neither had gotten so much as a scratch. Conrad didn't need her, or anyone, to keep him in line. He knew it too, and Raven envied that about him. How easily he moved through life, knowing he could survive a fight. Then again, Malik seemed adept at keeping Conrad in line.

"No," Warren said firmly. "You want to sleep in that room, you ask the girls. If they say no, it's a no."

Conrad deflated a little.

Conrad's room turned out to be behind a secret door near the end of the quarters. A steel panel that blended in near perfectly with the rest of the wall—save for the natural-looking dent that served as a handle—turned out to be a door. The room beyond held a narrow cot, nothing more.

Conrad stuck his head in, examining the space. He hummed in disapproval. "I suppose it's not the worst. I was imagining something with a bit more footroom and color. Maybe a window."

"I'll inform the maintenance crew," Warren said dryly.

Raven glanced into another of the rooms. In the one across from Conrad's closet, each of the four bunks had a pillow. Every locker had a piece of fabric sticking out of it. One had a picture of a little girl taped to the front.

A crew. She would be in very close quarters with this crew. The rooms had barely enough room for one person to stand, let alone four. She imagined they had to get into bed one at a time and get up in the same manner.

Her gut trembled, but she didn't think it was from making a bad choice. No, it had the trademarks of newness, the anticipation of the unknown, of taking a risk.

"That's about it for right now," said Captain Warren. "The crew will help you learn the ropes. Best to learn by doing, in my opinion. Let's head back. Most of the crew is staying at the inn here, though a few have wandered into town for their dose of depravity, but we'll be meeting back here tonight to be ready to launch tomorrow."

With that, he led them back to the main deck and down the gangplank to the air docks. Warren headed to the inn—the tallest building in the cavern—while Conrad and Raven meandered to the tavern. Conrad went to buy himself an ale; he offered to buy one for her, but she declined. She had had enough ale for a while.

She leaned against the table and absently pulled the chain of her locket, pulling the locket into her fingers. The metal felt warm. She ran her thumb across the engraved front, thinking of the engraving inside. What did it mean that the Destiny Show's emblem was inside her mother's locket? Had her mother left her a message to go there? Had her mother been to the

Destiny Show? To Wayward Point? Was there something here Raven was supposed to find? A clue in some scavenger hunt?

Or maybe the real answer was simple. Maybe her mother had bought the locket here—or stolen it, given the town's reputation—although the idea that her mother had stolen the locket didn't settle well. It took some of the magic of it away, and she didn't like it.

"That's a nice locket," came Malik's smooth voice.

Raven jumped and clutched the locket in her fist, hiding it from view. Malik stood a few feet away; she hadn't even heard him approach. Part of being a Wraith, she supposed. Malik's eyes were intent on her closed fist, the one that held the locket. He held a bundle of fabric in his arm.

"I haven't seen much jewelry like that around here." His eyes moved up to her face, searching. "Where did you get it?"

She thought for a moment to lie but, after a hesitation, didn't see the point. "It was my mother's," she told him.

She thought about asking him if the Destiny Show emblem had significance, but he might ask why. He might ask to see the emblem inside the locket. She couldn't open it. She couldn't let him see the centrum.

Malik wore an unreadable expression. "Your mother? She is..."

"Dead, I suppose," Raven said. "I never knew her. This locket is all I have of her."

"Oh," Malik said, with neither pity or sympathy. He handed her the bundle. "I found you a few changes of clothes. That outfit is fine here in the heat, but it's cooler inland, and you know how stingy people can be when it comes to skin."

The bundle looked to be a few simple shirts, a corset of brown leather and brass grommets, and simple trousers.

"Thank you," she said.

Malik started to say something else, but at that moment, Conrad sauntered around the corner. He wore a wide grin and held a tankard of ale. When he spotted Malik and Raven, his smile flickered into a frown, but quickly recovered. He walked up and threw an arm around Malik's slender shoulders.

"I could feel the seriousness ten feet away," Conrad said, mostly to Malik. "Has anyone ever told you to lighten up?"

"You have," Malik said, his mouth a straight line. "Several times."

"And you still don't take my advice to heart," said Conrad, sipping his ale loudly.

Malik gave a halfhearted chuckle and pushed Conrad's arm off his shoulders. With the distraction, Raven slipped the locket back under her shirt.

Raven spent her last moments in Wayward Point at the tavern. To keep her mind off her own anxiety, she picked Conrad's mind for stories, including the one that cast him out of the Wraiths' good graces.

"I'll find that island again," Conrad said, no doubt in his voice or in his eyes. "There was more to be found there, I know it."

After a meal at the tavern, they returned to the *Marianne*. As did the rest of the crew. They were fewer than she imagined, though on a ship as small as the *Marianne*, it wouldn't need that many hands. They all met in the galley—the only space big enough for all of them, minus the cargo hold, which was full—and Warren introduced Raven as the newest crew member, and Conrad as living cargo.

Lewis greeted her eagerly. She had olive skin and short dark hair. Lewis radiated warmth, and she reminded Raven of Lena—always happy, always smiling. Her other roommate, Jetta, stood a head taller than Lewis and held herself with authority. Jetta had dark red hair that she kept braided down her back, and a well-tanned complexion. Tattoos covered both arms, her neck, and most of the exposed skin Raven could see, mostly of tinker tools, blades, and fish. Lewis greeted Raven with a warm hug; Jetta greeted her with a handshake.

Conrad tried to say hello, but Jetta glared down her nose at him. "Cargo doesn't talk," Jetta said, her words accented with Tinatunian.

"The door locks from the outside, you know," Lewis added, winking at him.

Conrad frowned. "I will keep that in mind."

"See that you do," Jetta said, patting him on the shoulder. Conrad's knees buckled under the force, but he quickly recovered.

Night fell, and the lantern light of the docks and the reflection of moonlight on the bottom of the cavern combined to cast an eerie glow. Standing on the sundeck—the walkway on the top of the ship—Raven leaned over the railing to see the undulating reflection of moonlight, ever shifting, ever moving, casting a ghostly light over the cavern walls. The distance made her knees weak, and she tightened her hands around the railing.

A wild thought stuck: she could set sail and never come back. She could leave all her mess behind and start new in the skies. She could—

She couldn't walk away from her friends. She couldn't just leave Zander and Ivy, even if they might have done it to her.

A warm breeze blew into the cavern, brushing against her cheeks. It pulsed underneath her skin, and for a sickening moment, she stood in the arena, burning alive, fighting for her life—

She gasped, hands clutching the metal rail, and the vision faded.

But the heat did not. She put a hand against her neck. Warm. Too warm. Feverish.

Panic started at the base of her neck, along with a dull throb, and as she started back to her bunk, she convinced herself that it had been a long, stressful day. Pirates, escapes, and magic—too much for one girl. Too much for her. She needed to sleep it off.

Lewis reclined on the bottom bunk on the right, and Jetta had the bottom bunk on the left.

"There's the new kid," said Jetta, grinning. She fingered a dagger that had seen better days. "Don't be alarmed if you hear what sounds like a dragon trying to get in, that's just Lewis snoring."

"I don't sound that bad!"

"How would you know? You're asleep."

The comradery between the two women felt more welcoming than her introduction had. Raven tucked her boots into one of the empty footlockers beside her few articles of clothing and climbed onto the bunk over Jetta. Something about the woman's presence felt comforting.

"This is your last chance to jump ship and land on solid ground," Lewis said to Raven.

"I'm not giving up so soon," Raven said.

"Good," Jetta said. "You're going to need that spirit. The boys don't think they need to wash when they're in the sky."

"What's wrong with the privy?"

"Nothing," Lewis added. "But boys are boys, and whoever smells the worst gets bragging rights."

"That's disgusting."

"That's men for you," Jetta said, half laughing.

Raven rolled onto her side so that she could see Lewis. "The captain told me to ask you about the guy who gave you grief."

Lewis chuckled. Jetta snorted with bitter laughter.

"I hadn't been on the crew very long," Lewis said. "One of the crew kept making lewd comments to me, but I didn't take it seriously. I grew up in Wayward Point, so I'm used to stupid men and messy rules, you know? Then one afternoon, I was working the deck with a few others after a rainstorm, and the guy smacked my ass. Hard too. The guys all stopped like they'd been slapped, and the next thing I knew, they grabbed this guy and heaved him overboard."

"Oh," Raven said.

"We were over the ocean, a day out from the closest land," said Jetta. "The bastard either died on impact or drowned."

"I always imagined that he had survived the fall, floated on a piece of driftwood for days, dying of thirst, burning under the sun, going mad with hunger, and then, just when he thought he couldn't make it, he spots land, glorious land! And then a shark takes him under in a spreading pool of blood," said Lewis without a speck of malice in her voice.

Jetta laughed.

Raven offered her a smile. "That's a vivid picture."

Lewis grinned at her, the pale light from the window glinting off her eyes.

Raven didn't fall asleep immediately. She laid on her back, listening to the calm breathing of her bunkmates, breathing in the scents of steel, leather, and salt. An airship. All that daydreaming, and she had made it. It didn't feel real.

She lifted her hand to the cool metal of the ceiling. In the dim light, she could barely see the outline.

And she could feel it.

It might have been the humidity, the stale air of the airship, the stressful day, but she felt it. The fever, snaking underneath her skin like something alive. It wasn't as strong as it had been, a ghost of itself. Since she had burned that man in the arena, it had felt repressed, calmed.

Could Conrad be right? Had it been magic? But how?

She put a hand to her throat, where the chain of her locket rested. She hadn't taken it off; she didn't want anyone else to find it. The locket rested against her chest, warm.

Magic or fever—she didn't know which she would rather it be.

The next morning, Raven worked alongside Lewis. She gave Raven tips and advice almost constantly, but Raven didn't complain. She had never known how much work there was in readying an airship—tanks to check, supplies to organize and load, locks to secure, procedures to follow, and a tremendous amount of up and down ladders, shouting jargon, and checking things. And finally, finally, the engine rumbled to life.

Lewis took Raven to the sundeck, and from there, she watched the airship nimbly maneuver out of port, away from the dock, and through the cavern opening. The engines growled, then purred, and the *Marianne* started its ascension to the cloudy sky. The rocky shore fell away, the specks of Wayward Point shrank, and the ocean stretched on forever. Her eyes followed the gentle curve of Tinatun's coast, shrinking until it vanished into the horizon.

The ship rose through low clouds, and Raven held her breath—chilled mist graced her skin. She blinked, and the clouds were below them.

She had touched a cloud!

Lewis laughed. "It gets old after a while." She leaned onto the rail beside Raven. The wind rustled her short hair. "Or so they say. It hasn't for me yet." She winked. "And the view is always nice."

The view—Raven gasped. The *Marianne* rose high enough for her to see the expanse of Tinatun, beaches as far as she could see, spotted with cliffs and thatch-colored villages. The blue-gray of the sea became deep blue, light blues, and shadows, every bit of it glimmering. The ship started north, and they left the sea behind. Below, Tinatun passed at alarming speed, and soon they had crossed the border into Rhynwier.

"Should we go back inside?" Raven asked Lewis when the ocean was a speck on the horizon.

Lewis shrugged. "The captain said you might want to see the view your first time around. Says it keeps the new kids from wandering away from their work. This way, everyone knows you're up here and not down there, or assuming you're working when you're not. Clarity and communication are key to life. Keeps people alive."

Raven nodded, but a guilt settled on her shoulders.

"Don't worry about it," Lewis said. "The ship won't fall out of the sky because we're up here."

Raven meandered to the bow of the ship. The countryside stretched on forever to the north. The green became blue, then blurry blue-gray. What had happened in Silver Glen since she had left? Had her father cursed her out of his family? Had Mel told him what happened? What did they all think now that she and Zander had been gone all this time? Did her father assume her a failure, dead and enslaved in the city?

Maybe, if she got a chance, she would send him a letter, just to let him know she was alive and well.

And somewhere else, the treehouse stood hidden. Had they left to rescue the princess yet?

It didn't matter. She wouldn't worry about Zander or his princess. She had her own adventure to have, her own future to plan out. Raven turned her attention to the world as it passed below. The airship passed over numerous little villages and farms, so many people going about their days, doing chores, living.

Lewis came to stand beside her.

"Makes the world feel smaller," Raven said.

"Up here, yeah, it does." Lewis propped a thin leg on the lowest rung of the railing. "But once you're down there again, the world feels just as big as it did before."

"Does it?"

Lewis nodded. "I've been working for Captain Warren for seven years, and I haven't tired of it yet. I've seen places I never thought I'd see, places I didn't know existed, and met people whose lives were so different from mine, I thought I'd gone into another world. I didn't have any family to speak of when I joined, but the crew has become the family that I chose." Lewis turned to Raven. "It can be yours too, if you want. I'm not so sure about that friend of yours, but you are welcome."

Raven laughed, but the wind stole her breath. She coughed, and Lewis laughed.

Raven returned inside to work. With the minimal crew, something always needed to be watched or fixed. Raven spent the day with Lewis and Jetta. Lewis worked odd jobs. Jetta worked in the engine, the best damn pair of hands it had seen in a long time—according to Jetta. She spent the majority of her time in the engine room or in the tank room, shouting orders to the other mechanics, who listened without hesitation.

"That's the trick." Jetta nudged Raven's arm. "You got to let them know you're no pushover."

Raven nodded, though she doubted anyone would ever listen to her like they did Jetta.

The crew took meals in turns, and while Raven dreaded it being the slop she had read about in her books, the food turned out to be jerky, water, ale, and dried fruit and nuts. Conrad joined her for meals. He worked in the cargo hold, the least troublesome part of the ship.

Throughout the day, Raven kept busy, but she couldn't forget her fever.

When her attention slipped, when her mind wandered, she felt it, under her skin, burning a little hotter when she thought about it.

By sunset, she couldn't ignore it any longer. It burned when she thought about it; it burned when she didn't think about it. Lewis took her and Conrad to the sundeck to watch the day fade into night, and Raven relished the cool air on her face and neck, the mist of the low clouds, like tiny little drops of ice.

Raven glanced over the railing and spotted the mass of metal and glass behind them, sparking in the evening light, a blur on the horizon. In front of them, the countryside was green and speckled with small villages, rolling hills and curving rivers.

"We'll be crossing into Gracita around midday tomorrow," Lewis said, nodding toward the west. "We've got clearance, so they don't have a reason to search us at the border, but if they do, you know the signal."

So Conrad and Raven could hide.

Raven leaned against the cool railing of the bow, letting the chill leech some of the heat from her skin. It didn't last long. Soon, the metal under her hands was hot. She moved her body a little further down it, where the metal was still cool.

It didn't last long either.

"Raven?" purred Conrad. He appeared at her side without a sound. He tilted his head toward her, his eyes knowing more than he said. He searched her, around her, seeing more than most could.

She couldn't hide it anymore. She opened her mouth to tell him, to explain, but the words were lost. A sudden, violent upheaval of heat sent her sprawling onto the sundeck. She gasped for breath, the fever burning her alive, turning her to ash just like it had the pirate. She couldn't think, she couldn't breathe. The heat. Blinding, suffocating heat.

Conrad appeared and rolled her onto her back, but he quickly pulled his hands away, shaking them as if burned. His coal-dark eyes had gone wide. On her other side, Lewis bent over; she was speaking—her lips moved—but Raven couldn't hear her. All she heard was the rushing pulse of her blood; all she felt was the surge of heat through her skin.

Darkness ebbed on the edge of her vision.

Closer, farther. Closer, farther. Pulsing with the fever. Beating with her heart.

Every time she opened her eyes, Conrad met her gaze. She was still on the deck. Then stars blinked all around them, brighter and closer than she had ever seen them, almost close enough to touch. Were they made of mist too?

The darkness receded a little with every heartbeat.

"Sisters," Conrad breathed.

He sat beside her. Someone had put a pillow underneath her head. Something cold rested against her throat and her forehead. She tried to reach for them, but her leaden arms didn't respond.

"What happened?" she managed to ask, her voice hoarse, like someone who had been screaming.

"I was going to ask you," Conrad said, his smile gone. "Is this the fever you talked about?"

She tried to nod but couldn't. "Yes."

"I can feel it," he whispered. "The magic, it's there—unstable and violent, but it's there. No doubt about it now. It's unlike anything I've felt before." A crease formed between his brows. "Before, the magic was weak and fluctuating, but this... I don't know." He ran a hand through his braids, throwing them over his shoulder. The beads clinked. "The crew thinks you're sick, which is why you're still up here. That, and we couldn't touch you without burning ourselves."

"Am I?" she asked weakly. "Sick?"

Conrad met her gaze but didn't answer. His coal-dark eyes wore worry, and she didn't like it on him.

Raven slept on and off during the night. Clouds rolled in—cooling clouds and blessed mist—and blocked out the stars. The lantern on the deck went cold. Raven thought she had died, that she had crossed over to the other side or become something new entirely. The certainty of her death shattered when the first glow of dawn appeared, brightening the inky darkness with light blues and golds.

Conrad stayed with her. Lewis brought food and cold packs for Raven's head, though nothing worked. The fever consumed, and it would consume her. She knew it. Her bones knew it.

She closed her eyes, pushing away the thoughts of people she would never see again, the places she would never get to see. She didn't want to die, not yet, not until she had seen everything—

Conrad sat beside her—humming—and pulled her out of her sullen thoughts. He held an ink bottle and a fine-tipped brush.

"What's that?" she asked, her voice weak and wobbly.

"Protection." His lips formed a straight line that reminded her of Malik. "I'm worried you might attract the wrong sort of attention at the border. The automatons there can detect magic, and this is a temporary solution to get us into Gracita."

He uncorked the ink bottle, and the pungent smell carried more than simple ink.

She coughed. "What is that?"

"Tampered ink." He met her gaze. "I'm going to draw a rune on you. It will hide your magic from the automaton's detection. It won't last long, but it will be enough for a time."

"Like the tattoos?" She thought of the rune-like tattoo that Zander, Marie, and Thalame shared, for burning off the extra magic when they used their powers, to hide them from detection.

Conrad met her gaze. If he wondered how she knew, he didn't ask. "Yeah, like the tattoos."

With permission, he pulled up her loose fitting-shirt to reveal her stomach. Then the cool, wet stroke of ink brushed against her burning skin. The coolness lasted only a few seconds. The brush traced a complicated round whorl over her stomach. She tried to create the image in her mind as Conrad painted it, but she got lost in the sprawling, curving, spiderweb-like rune.

It relaxed her. The more of the rune he painted, the calmer the fever became. Something pulled the fever back, down and in, blocking it, sheltering it, hiding it somewhere deep within. Locking it away. A wet blanket over a smoldering fire.

Conrad set the ink bottle aside. "There. That ought to work for a while." He sighed and mumbled something in Tinatunian. Though she couldn't speak the language, it sounded something like a prayer or a mantra—practiced words.

"What did you say?" she asked.

He repeated himself in Tinatunian, "*Gua a ihignni ninun*. It's an old pirate saying: 'May the sea be kind,' or in this case, the sky. There's no word in your tongue for *ihiginni*, but it means the journey, the ride, the voyage. It's how we ask Minerva to guide the ship and keep it from crashing or capsizing or any those nasty things."

"I can feel it," she whispered.

"I can as well. The magic isn't as wild or tangled," he said. "The rune is old, far older than the Wraiths, one of the few things left over from the old world. It might be the only thing capable of hiding a magician these days."

"Old world?"

He shrugged. "No one knows much about the world before Gracita and Rhynwier, before magic and machines. It existed, but its ruins are scattered. I think of it like a mystery waiting to be solved." He looked down at her face and offered her a small smile. "You look better, less on the verge of death."

More like self-combustion, she thought. She said, "Zander has a tattoo."

"Most of the Wraiths who travel beyond Wayward Point do," Conrad said. "It's a safety precaution. If they didn't have it, the automatons would be able to detect them and hunt them down."

"It burns?"

He blinked, then nodded. "A side effect of the rune. It blocks detection, but it also blocks a bit of the magic, making it harder to use." He lifted a brow. "I take it you've seen Wraiths in action?"

"I have." She thought of Marie, the blood-binder, and Thalame, the healer. Their tattoos had burned when they used their magic.

"Ah, yes, my mysterious little bird," Conrad said, a smile in his words and in his eyes. "You've got quite the mystery behind you. Hawks, Wraiths, Gray Elite, and a bounty the size of a small bank vault." He hummed his approval. "Is this what you thought about when you wanted adventure?"

"I'd rather have mermaids and sunken treasure," she said.

Conrad laughed, a warming, heartful laugh. "I accept that answer. Though, in fair warning, mermaids are as temperamental as the sea: calm one minute; the next, a storm to rip unsuspecting vessels to shreds—not unlike a woman."

They sat for a while in silence. The sky warmed gradually, the clouds streaking with orange and purple and blue. The stars wavered, blinking out.

"Conrad," she whispered.

"Hmm?"

"What's happening to me?"

He didn't answer right away. "I can't say, little bird. I've never seen anything like what you've got. It's magic, that is for certain now, but it acts more like a sickness."

A magical sickness, which was why Thalame couldn't identify or heal it and why it hadn't gone away on its own. She wanted to ask if it would ever go away, if she would get better, but she feared his answer.

"I'm no expert when it comes to magic," he said darkly, "but when we get to Moorin, I know someone who is. The Wraiths there will be able to help. Because you're a magician, they are obligated by sacred oath to help you. I don't remember the exact words, but it's something about assisting the magically gifted regardless of risk to themselves."

She let out a long breath. A terrifying thought occurred—she had turned that pirate to ash, had burned him alive from the inside out. The fever had consumed him in a matter of seconds. What if it was consuming her, only slower? Would she fall asleep as a person and become a pile of ash in the night? Or wake up with her bottom half ash?

With that thought stuck in her mind, she couldn't find comfort. When sleep pulled, she fought it. Not even the cooling sensation of the rune could help.

When they came closer to the border, Conrad helped Raven into the ship and into the closet space. Her limbs were wobbly, her vision filled with shadows, her awareness numbed. She leaned heavily on Conrad. She didn't know how long they stayed hidden. She closed her eyes, and then Lewis stood in the doorway.

"All clear," she said, her voice distant, as though from underwater. "They didn't find reason to board."

"Good," came Conrad's voice from behind her.

And then Conrad half carried and half pulled her back to the sundeck where they wouldn't be in the way. As she sat down on the bow, a cloud passed over the ship and swathed her in cooling mist. Too soon, it left.

"Another day, and we'll be in Moorin," said Conrad, sitting beside her.

Raven didn't have it in her to respond. Would she make it another day?

The fever came and went in waves. She thought of rain. She imagined it would feel delightful against her skin, like the mist of the clouds, only better.

Conrad and Lewis exchanged positions beside her, one then the other, but always someone stood or sat nearby. Watching her, she realized. She felt guilty about not being able to work after Malik had gone through the trouble of securing this job for her. If she ever saw him again, she would have to apologize.

Gradually, the sky changed from bright blue to dim blue, and then streaks of yellow and orange made their way across the clouds. It was one of the most marvelous sights that Raven had ever seen, but the fever refused to allow her enjoyment. She could barely move, and so she had to witness the splendor while lying down.

Lewis left, and a second later, Conrad appeared.

He crouched with feline ease and folded his legs underneath him. He set the bottle of ink between them. "Let's see about that rune." He pulled up her shirt, and then gasped. "Sisters."

"What?" she asked, fear twisting her words in pleas.

"It's gone," he said, his dark eyes searching her stomach. "It's not been rubbed off or smeared. It's just gone."

"I haven't..." she started, but then she didn't really know. She might have moved too much and made the ink flake off.

"Not tempered ink." He frowned. His cool fingertips touched the skin just above her navel. "You're warm to the touch. Too warm. And the magic..." His gaze took her in, looking at her, but not at *her*. She realized then that he looked at the magic. "It's like the magic ate through the rune. I've never seen it happen that fast."

The color drained from his face, and her own panic flared at the sight.

Conrad painted another rune where the first had been. The initial strokes of the brush felt cool as ice, refreshing, but the feeling didn't last more than a few seconds. She could almost feel it working, feel the rune pushing down the magic, but at the same time, she could feel it working the opposite direction—the magic pushing back.

The sun sank lower as he worked, painting the delicate strokes and whorls. She set her sights on the changing colors of the clouds, from bright orange, to lush pink, to deep purple, to the stars as they blinked awake, one by one.

If she survived, she would come back to watch the sunset properly, standing with a mind ready to take in the beauty of it.

Only when the sun had gone completely did she notice that Conrad hadn't moved. He sat beside her, still as stone, his gaze on her stomach, on the rune. No emotion played across his face.

"That's what I thought," Conrad said after a long moment. "The magic is slowly pushing through the rune, devouring it, and it's dissolving. It's the same process that happens to the tattoos over time. The use of magic will deteriorate the rune. I've had mine done twice because of it."

She felt the cool touch of the brush, the coolness of the ink, as Conrad touched the rune up in places.

She released a slow breath, trying to keep her stomach steady as he worked.

With the rune fixed—for now—she sat up in her temporary lull to drink from a canteen. She hadn't eaten or drunk anything that day, and her thirst magnified at the sight of the canteen. She held the steel bottle with both hands, drinking eagerly, greedily.

Conrad held his hands over her, moving up and down her body. Searching the magic; he wore the same serious look. His hands hesitated over her chest. He frowned. "What's that?" he asked, his voice a rasp.

She pulled the canteen from her lips. Her hands shook as she twisted the cap back in place. His hand hovered above the locket.

When she didn't answer, he took the initiative and pulled it out of her shirt by the chain. Something in her bones snapped. The idea that someone else had their hands on her locket, her mother's locket, the centrum, turned her insides into something molten and furious. He turned it over in his hands, and then Raven yanked it out of his grasp.

"It's mine," she said firmly.

Conrad scowled, but underneath it, she saw something she hadn't yet seen in his features: fear. "What is in it?" he asked carefully.

"Nothing."

"Bullshit." Conrad grimaced. "I can feel it, Raven," he said, his whisper urgent. "There is something in there. I can see the magic around it. I couldn't see it before because it was cloaked in your own. Whatever is in that locket, it's the same magic that's killing you."

Raven spent the night slipping in and out of consciousness. Conrad repainted the rune on her stomach five times. He asked no more about the locket. He didn't speak much, but when he did, his words came out pleasant but forced. He was nervous about landing in Moorin—that much she could tell from the way his eyes flickered to the horizon, toward their destination, and the way his calm smile would fade into a straight line.

Moorin, capital city of Gracita, was the beating heart of the Gray Elite empire and the most dangerous place on the continent for a magician. She would be more worried about Moorin if she didn't feel like she might fall asleep and become a pile of ashes, never to wake up again.

Raven was somewhere between asleep and awake when she first heard the distant hum. She opened her eyes. From the sundeck of the *Marianne*, she could see airships in the distance. With every blink, they came closer. They glinted in the midmorning light, gold and silver and bronze and an array of other colors; balloons painted like clouds, like lightning, like bluebird eggs, like automaton heads; hulls sleek for speed, hulls wide for accommodating passengers and cargo.

Her breath tumbled from her lips.

"We're approaching Moorin," Conrad said, crouching beside her. "We need to get below before we land."

Though she knew Conrad was right, she wanted to stay and watch the airships fly. Conrad helped her to her feet and half carried her back into the airship. The buzz of the airships muffled into a dull roar. The commotion of their airship met them instead, the organized crew shouting jargon through the speaking tubes, preparing for landing, communicating with the air patrol in Moorin.

Conrad helped Raven to the galley instead of the closet. The cook put a canteen between her hands, and she drank the cool water eagerly.

"Attention," came Warren's voice over the speaking tubes, "prepare to land."

Relief and dread zapped through Raven. Relief to be off the ship, dread at what she might find waiting for her in the city of automatons and Gray Elite.

Lewis found her in the galley; she had assembled a disguise for her of men's clothes. Lewis helped her into their room to change; she didn't ask about the rune on her stomach. Raven quickly pulled the undershirt over her head to hide it. She didn't bother with a corset.

"It's all right," Lewis said softly. "You two aren't the first guests we've transported."

Lewis winked, and Raven got her meaning. If the captain and Malik knew one another, then this ship had likely smuggled magicians out of the city before.

Raven tucked her brown hair into a shipyard cap—a popular style in Moorin, according to Lewis, and thus inconspicuous. The brim extended along the front, shadowing her eyes. A loose-fitting vest hid her feminine frame, as did the trousers.

From the portholes in the galley, she and Conrad watched as they entered the city of Moorin, a sprawling metropolis of steel, bronze, and copper. The city sprawled farther than Lenhala. The buildings rose tall at the heart of the city, each building boasting a different color of metal, shining like a kaleidoscope in the sunlight, spotted with the vibrant greens of parks and gardens. The outskirts rose and fell along the rolling hills that surrounded the city. Several rivers intersected underneath grand bridges of white and beige stone, designed with gold and blue.

The *Marianne* approached the air docks, a massive stadium that rose above the shipyard, a dozen stories of docks arranged on a circular structure of steel and brick. Each dock opened with a copper-lined archway. Ships came and went from the air docks, the sounds a deafening roar of engines hissing and churning. Bigger ships docked on the highest levels, where the archways were wider and taller to accommodate size. The smaller ships docked on the lower levels. Raven craned her neck to see more as the ship slowed, as the engine purred lower and lower, but then the *Marianne* entered the air docks.

The crew busied themselves with docking; a Gray Elite met the first mate at the gangplank, a clipboard in his hand, asking for clearance permits; and Raven and Conrad slipped out of the cargo hold with the others and then into the air docks.

"Walk like a man," Conrad whispered to her.

Raven frowned but tried to mimic his saunter. She pictured how Zander walked, long legs first, hips still, shoulders tense.

"Better," Conrad whispered. "Might want to leer at a girl or two, for the ruse."

She didn't, mostly because the girls she saw on the dock were workers who looked like they could crush her throat with one fist.

Conrad guided her to the center of the air docks, where a dozen lifts carried cargo and crew and passengers up and down in gilded brass cages. Above, a glass dome protected them from the weather. Conrad chose a less crowded lift of passengers, and they started down to the street level.

Raven couldn't take in the sights fast enough. Every level buzzed with activity, boarding and unloading, people going every which way. The crowd was threaded with Gray Elite, but none paid any mind to her. Their lift landed on the street level, and she kept her eyes on Conrad as he weaved through the crowd toward the street.

Gray Elite guarded the exits, crossbows on their backs, pistols on one hip, a saber on the other. None of the guards looked enthused; most looked bored out of their minds.

They approached the gate, and one of the Gray Elite shifted. His green eyes met Raven's. Her heart thumped against her chest. She looked from him and to the city she approached. Across the street, a café declared the daily specials on a large blackboard, the letters neon and glittering. Beside it, a tavern advertised vacancies, three tokens a night. Somewhere, a bard sang about the Tinatunian girls and white sand beaches.

She focused on her saunter, on Conrad's back, and on the archway that would lead them onto the street. And just like that, they walked through without trouble. Her feet hit the stone of the sidewalk, and she released a calming breath of relief. Conrad didn't slow, and she sped up her pace to keep up with him. The city blurred to shades of steel and copper and stone. The voices, the singing, the roaring and the airships—it all echoed.

Conrad turned down one street and then another and then turned into an alley. He caught Raven's arm and pulled her in with him. They walked down the alley and into another alley, blocking all view from the street.

"Are you doing all right?" he asked.

"A little flushed," she said. "But otherwise I'm...fine." Her breath left her. She felt the fever there, under her skin. She had been so focused on the arrival that she hadn't noticed it.

"Show me," Conrad said, motioning to her stomach. She lifted her shirt to the bottom of her ribs, and he clicked his tongue. "It's barely there. We don't have a lot of time before you'll need it redone. Come on."

Raven followed Conrad back onto the wide streets of Moorin. With every step, she felt the rune give a little more, felt the fever return a little hotter. She kept her eyes on Conrad, on the glints of sunlight off the beads in his braids.

They walked for a long time, or so it felt to her, with each step a chore, each breath a hammer in her lungs, each heartbeat a wave of burning heat. She stopped looking at the city around her. She stopped caring if someone recognized her.

"Hey," came Conrad's urgent voice. He appeared at her side.

She leaned on him; she had to. Her strength faded with each breath.

"Hold on," Conrad whispered. "It won't be long."

She forced her legs to move. To keep going.

Finally, when the darkness ebbed and flowed on the edges of her vision, when her legs no longer felt like her own, they arrived at a shoddy little inn tucked away on a side street. A plain wooden sign hanging above the door welcomed them to the Wooden Goblet Inn and Tavern. Conrad ushered her through the door and into the lantern-lit tavern.

"What can I get for you, gents?" came a pleasant woman's voice, though her words came out raspy and irritated. "Ah, drunk already?"

"No time for that," Conrad said. "I've got a problem for Engor. Immediately."

"He's in the back," said the woman, the irritation gone from her voice.

Conrad paused just long enough to hoist Raven into his arms. Relief swam through her limbs, and she gladly dropped her head against his shoulder. She heard the muttering of voices, quick and desperate; she felt the rumble of Conrad's chest as he spoke; she heard the telltale squeak of wooden stairs; and in the next moment, her back touched down on a hard mattress.

Through her swimming vision, she saw a room with dull plaster walls, no bigger than her room on the ship, just big enough for a narrow bed, a nightstand, and a washing basin.

Conrad stood at the bedside, and beside him stood a man with graying black hair and olive skin. His dark brown eyes beheld her with worry and jaded curiosity. The older man flattened the back of his hand against her cheek, her neck, her forehead. It took her a moment to register Conrad's voice—he was explaining the situation to the other man, the fever, the magic, the rune on her stomach.

"I didn't know what else to do with her," Conrad said. "I was hoping you would know something or someone who might."

"Caroline is your best bet," said the older man, his voice raspy and rough, not unlike his face. "Woman's got an eye for magical maladies, but getting to her is the problem. She doesn't leave her cave often. You might have to take this girl to her."

"Can we arrange a meeting?" Conrad asked, a bit of his joyful humor leaking into his words. "I would hate to drag Raven all the way there only to find she had stepped out for the evening."

The older man nodded. "I can arrange something. In the meantime, keep her cooled down. She's burning up. I'll find some iced cider or tea."

"I'll need ink," Conrad said.

"We've got plenty."

The older man left, and Conrad took his place beside the bed. He leaned against the wall and crossed his arms.

After a moment, he slid down the wall and folded his legs to his chest. He leaned forward on his knees and looked more like a child hiding than a grown man. "That's Engor. He's a retired Wraith. He no longer participates in the action, but he runs this little inn and tavern as a shelter and waypoint for magicians and Wraiths. It's something like a headquarters, though they have several other places like this in the city." He sighed. "I can't say what will happen now. You might have to stay here until the captain brings the ship back around."

Raven hadn't the space in her mind for such thoughts of her future. First she needed to survive. Then she could worry about Captain Warren and her job aboard his ship.

Engor returned with a pitcher of iced cider and a bottle of ink. He poured a small amount of the cider into a glass, and she drank it eagerly. Each sip cooled her, making it farther down her throat before her body heat warmed it. She drank three glasses of it before Engor set the pitcher and the glass on the nightstand.

Conrad took the bottle of ink and the brush and causally lifted Raven's shirt to show her stomach. He again drew the rune. This time, the ink felt like ice, and it took longer for the cooling sensation to fade.

"I was just telling Raven here how you are one of the few Wraiths who grow old in Moorin," Conrad said, a smile on his lips as he watched the older man's reaction.

Engor huffed. "Old? I hardly count forty-seven as old."

"For a Wraith living in Moorin, that's ancient," Conrad said.

"I won't argue that." Engor's gaze fell on Raven. "Life here is dangerous for magicians. One mistake means death. Like that Revenant. No one's heard from or seen him in months, which means he's probably dead."

Raven gasped. "The Revenant? He's real?"

Engor blinked in surprise; then the expression faded. "Of course he's real. He's a Wraith. Or was."

"I thought it was just a ghost story?"

"He's an assassin," Conrad added darkly in his storyteller's voice. "Deadly and accurate. The only people who see the Revenant are the ones he kills."

"If he kills anyone who sees him, then where do the stories come from?" Engor lifted an eyebrow, wrinkling his forehead even more so.

"That's an unimportant detail," Conrad said, his smile fading. He finished the rune, corked the ink bottle, and set it on the nightstand beside the pitcher.

"The Revenant is a Wraith, but he acts on his own," said Engor. "Some magicians do. He wore a copper mask when meeting with clients. That's how he kept himself hidden. I met him once. Creepy fellow. Silent. Still like stone. Let one of his fellows do the talking." Engor's frown deepened.

Raven pictured the Revenant in the dark blue and black robes like the Wraiths wore—the hidden daggers, belts and buckles, steel plates, and hardened leather. She imagined the copper mask, blank of expression, only the eyes visible, and the eyes her mind painted were entirely black, lid to lid.

She shivered.

Engor leaned against the wall, arms crossed. "But the real question is: what are we going to do with you? There's nothing more I can do without consulting Caroline. I've never heard of magic coming and going like this. Until we can get ahold of her, the only thing we can do is keep you alive."

Raven nodded as best she could. The rune helped to push down the burning fever and pull the darkness from her vision, from her mind.

Survive, she told herself.

Engor left, but Conrad lingered behind. When Raven glanced at him, she found his eyes pinned on the locket hidden beneath her shirt. Sensing her gaze, he looked up. A frown pulled his lips downward. She wished he would smile, tease, or joke, anything—he didn't.

Conrad touched up the rune—Raven had lost track of how many times he'd done it. The ink he used here lasted longer than the tempered ink on the ship, but even it succumbed to the fever. She drank continuously, iced cider, iced wine, near-frozen juice. It helped a little. She tried to sleep, but her worry of waking up as ash kept her awake.

Conrad vanished for periods of time, and she listened to the chatter coming from below. According to Conrad, the Wraiths met in the kitchen of the tavern. They talked about recon missions, interrupted automaton captures, and commandeered Moths, whatever that meant. They also shared patrol stories, jokes, and gossip. They spoke lowly, but with nothing else to listen to, Raven caught most of it.

"Hear anything more about Captain Luckett?" came one voice, and Raven's ears perked at that name. Warren had mentioned her to Malik.

"Captured," said another. "Found the reports. The Gray Elite wanted her alive, so she's not dead yet, but they're planning her trial and subsequent execution."

"Where's she being held?"

"The reports said East Wing in Doven Prison, but a guard we interrogated confirmed she's really being held in the Tombs."

"Then the reports about her being in Doven are a trap," said Engor.

"Most likely."

"We should do something if we can."

"The tombs won't be easy to get into or out of."

"Can we work her rescue into Project Demo? According to the maps, there's a way into the plant through the Tombs."

"It would be a suicide mission," said Engor. "The Tombs are impenetrable. No one escapes."

"So we let her sit down there until the Gray Elite execute her?" asked Conrad. "Or are you planning some daring rescue during that execution?"

Engor mumbled something under his breath.

"We've got scouts trying to pinpoint her exact location," came another voice.

"Project Demo is still being finalized, and we might be able to find a way in through the Tombs," said a mousy girl's voice. "Maps of the Tombs are harder to come by than maps of the emperor's house."

Raven took all the information in. What she would do with it, she didn't know. Captain Luckett had been taken into the Tombs, the prison where the Gray Elite had taken Princess Rosaria. If these Wraiths and the Dwellers could work together, they might be able to save them both.

What was Zander doing? Were he and the Dwellers on their way into Gracita right now looking for ways to save their princess?

Raven released a slow sigh.

The door to the room opened, and she sat up to see Conrad close it behind him.

"I hate meetings," he said as he sat on the floor beside the bed, back against the wall. He leaned his head against it. "So much talking, so little action. This is why I left. I hate all this waiting around and planning and talking and discussing and trying to keep everyone happy. It's a waste of time when I could be out there doing something. It's what I like about pirates, they're impatient. Never been the planning or debating kind."

The girl who ran the kitchens—Gretchen—brought up bread and hard cheese. "I made stew, but it's hot, and I didn't think you'd like it."

Raven accepted the plate of bread and cheese with gratitude. Gretchen was right—the idea of warm stew churned her stomach and agitated the fever under her skin.

She took a bite from the bread, despite her hunger's nonexistence. When Gretchen had left, Raven asked Conrad, "Who's Captain Luckett?"

"She's a retired Wraith. She does more piracy and smuggling nowadays," Conrad said. "She's been captured by the Gray Elite. The Wraiths here are working on getting her out, but they don't know how. It's a work in progress."

"Everyone is planning," Raven said more to herself.

"Are *you* planning?"

"It's hard to plan anything when I might not wake up tomorrow," she said grimly.

He frowned. "That's no way to look at things." He hummed, tilting his head. He lowered his voice. "Think about this instead: did you hear them talk about Project Demo?"

She nodded.

"It's an upcoming mission, bigger than anything they've done in ten years." Conrad's eyes glittered with mischief. "They are planning to blow up one of the automaton factories."

She blinked, unmoved by the plan.

Conrad leaned closer. "The big plant where they manufacture their magic hunters," he whispered. "It would put a serious dent in production, bruise the Gray Elite's ego, and make it easier to sneak a large number of magicians that the Wraiths have been hiding for months out of the city."

"That sounds more exciting," she said. She noted his frown. "You don't like the plan?"

Conrad waved away her concern. "I don't have a problem with the plan. It's big and dangerous. I love both those things, though I'd rather be on the beach somewhere or on a ship bound for an island I've never been to, but if this will grant me redemption with the Wraiths and the Sisters, then I'm here to help."

And he didn't like it. Conrad the pirate needed wide open skies and never ending seas, not the planning and scheming of the Wraiths. Raven would rather be elsewhere too.

He let out a sigh and leaned back against the wall. "In other news, Engor secured a visit with Caroline for you tomorrow night."

"Who?"

"Caroline," Conrad said. "I don't know if she has a last name or not. Never asked. She's not a Wraith, but the woman knows more about magic than anyone else alive today. It will be a harrowing trip across town, but the Wraiths are also planning a surprise on the Gray Elite to draw their attention elsewhere. That way, no one will pay attention to us. And we might have our answer as to what is happening to you."

She hoped so.

He stood and dusted off his trousers. "Now, if you will excuse me, I've got to see about a payment. Caroline won't be free. I could ask the Wraiths, but I'd rather not be in their debt."

Instead, she would be in his debt. She already was, more than she could repay. "Payment? How are you going to... You're going to steal it."

Conrad didn't deny it. "I won't be back until late. I've got a friend I want to stop and see. Don't you worry, little bird. I'll see if Gretchen won't sit up here with you." He flashed her a grin, then left.

Raven reclined. She draped an arm over her eyes, dousing her world in darkness. Even the shadows on the backs of her eyelids were tinted crimson.

The fever worsened. Raven drifted in and out of awareness. She drank cold teas and ciders and herbal water. Someone set ice wrapped in cloth against her face and throat and chest.

Despite the rune, she felt herself deteriorating, turning to ash.

People came and went from the room: Engor, the barmaid who never stayed too long, Gretchen the cook, and Conrad. He drew the rune anew every few hours.

Even now, the Wraith's ink wasn't enough.

No one wanted to say it, but she knew. She heard it in their calm, soothing words, the false hope. She would die. Raven focused on her breathing. In, out. In, out.

Between it all, the fever burned constant and harsh, stealing her breath, pulling on nerves. It wove vicious daydreams of her father's anger at her disappearance, her stepmother's frown of disapproval, Zander's scowl that she had gotten herself into so much trouble, and a man in a copper mask, blades drawn, gazing at her through blackened eyes.

She woke with a hand on her shoulder; the daydreams dissolved into the plaster room at the Wooden Goblet.

Conrad knelt by the bed. "Good morning, sunshine. You've slept the day away," he said, his smile undermined by worry. "You think you're up for a trip to see Caroline?"

She didn't think so, but she didn't want to tell him. Instead, she nodded. She tried to sit up, but her arms and legs refused to move. Her back felt leaden, and her stomach clenched. Conrad grabbed her hands and pulled her up; the world spun. Her muscles protested as if they had already turned to ash. Her bones felt like water.

Slowly, carefully, she sat her feet on the floor. The barmaid came and helped her wash her face and hands, helped her dress in dark clothes, and then Conrad carried her down the stairs. He carried her through the backroom and into the alley. The balmy air brushed against her cheeks. All around, the city settled for the night, with evening fading to inky gold in the low western horizon. Twilight stained the world in golden shadows.

Three Wraiths were making the journey to Caroline's with her and Conrad, and they had procured four automaton horses. Conrad helped her onto the back of one, and he climbed up after her. He secured one arm around her waist. The Wraiths set out down the alley, toward Caroline's, and Raven had a seed of hope that this mysterious woman would be able to stop the spread of the fever.

"She'll ask you about that locket," Conrad whispered. "She can see magic like I can, and she'll know that you're hiding something."

Raven tensed. She started to protest, to lie, but her words faded on a gasp—the fever stole her breath.

How could she explain the centrum to anyone? If anyone found out she carried the centrum of Altair's Augur, they would want it. They might sell the information to the Gray Elite. Anyone else who knew about it would be a liability.

But...if the centrum was poisoning her like Conrad had said, what option did she have?

She should have buried it in the woods when she had the chance.

As if tuned to her thoughts, the centrum's heat pulsed through the locket and against her chest.

No, she silently told it.

And it listened; the heat lessened but did not go away. The fever remained, wild and untamed, pulsing under her skin. She felt it burning through the rune on her stomach, burning the ink away. The steel horse she rode on blurred. Conrad's arm tightened around her, and she leaned into him.

"Just a little further," Conrad whispered. "Don't die on me now."

Zander wouldn't know what happened. Ivy wouldn't know what happened. Her father and stepmother wouldn't know what happened. They would wonder for the rest of their lives where Raven had gone, never knowing the full truth. Never knowing that she had turned to ash in the backstreets of Moorin, lost to the wind.

Maybe, if she were ashes, she could travel the world on the wind.

She didn't want to die. Not in Moorin. Not for a long while. Not until she had seen it all. So she fought against the magical fever, fought to keep her body alive, fought to keep it from swallowing her whole like it had the pirate, like it did the ink.

No, she told it.

Maybe Caroline would help her. Maybe she would know how the centrum was doing whatever it was doing to her and be able to stop it. Caroline might also tell her she only had a few days to live.

Raven closed her eyes. She missed her bed back at the inn. She missed the cool tea, the still air that smelled of cooking dinner, the feeling of the cool ink across her skin. The air of Moorin felt too balmy and warm, suffocating.

Someone ahead of them hissed; Conrad stilled and brought their horse to a halt.

Raven kept her eyes closed.

And then the night air shook with a violent wave of hot wind and bright light. Conrad's grip on her tightened; he gasped and curled his body around hers, shielding her eyes from the bright blast that lit the night like day. Then she heard the explosion. Thunder on the ground, shattering the air.

The automaton horses did not kick and nicker. They remained perfectly still.

The light faded, and Conrad shifted.

Raven opened her eyes. A plume of red and orange rose into the night several streets away, consuming the shadows with flickering, vengeful light. Fire.

"Sisters," Conrad breathed.

Two of the Wraiths in their procession jumped to stand on the backs of their automaton horses, and then jumped in unison onto the nearest building, effortlessly making their way to the rooftop. They moved like water given form, like shadows.

"What is it?" the Wraith ahead of Raven called up, his voice a loud whisper.

The Wraiths didn't get the chance to answer—the screaming started. Steel hit steel. Automaton gears hissed. Bullets seared through the air. Automation feet clomped against the stone street.

"Raid!" one of the Wraiths shouted.

"Gray Elite," spat another.

The screams grew louder, and several of them ended abruptly. A siren started—a vicious, high-pitched undulating wail.

"Get her out of here," said the first wraith, but Conrad was already directing his horse in the opposite direction of the flames.

Over his shoulder, she saw the chaos behind them. The flames grew. More sirens joined the first. Raven saw shadows running through the night, over rooftops, silent. She saw people on the other side of the alleys, shadowed by the flames, running.

A raid, one of the Wraiths had warned.

A man stumbled into the alley, screaming, pleading, his clothes on fire. An automaton chased him, its slender body twice as tall as a human, each of its arms ending in a blade. The flames flickered off the bronze and steel plating, its too-human-like face, and its glowing red eyes. Steam hissed from its shoulders and elbows as its arms moved in an effortless arc—slicing through the burning man. The two halves thumped to the alley's floor.

The automaton lifted its eyes to Conrad's fleeting back.

Raven grasped his sleeve. "It sees us," she gasped.

The automaton started for them, its long legs sprinting, gears silent, steam hissing out from its hips. Conrad urged the horse into a gallop. The automaton gained on them, its legs moving it twice the distance that the horse could.

It's slender arms stretched toward them, one blade bloodied, the other clean.

The blades came down.

Raven screamed.

A shadow appeared between them, landing on the automaton's shoulders. A Wraith. In a shower of sparks, the Wraith ripped the head from the automaton—a flash of lightning crashed through the automaton's body, electrifying the metal and overpowering the machine. It staggered and jerked, and then the Wraith dropped something into the body and vanished as quickly as he had appeared.

The automaton horse carried her and Conrad away. They turned down an alley, and a heartbeat later, an explosion shook the alley they had just left. Pieces of the slender automaton scattered the alley, raining down on the rooftops, the stone ground, clattering and clanking.

Raven wanted to bury her head in Conrad's shoulder, but her fear kept her alert. She watched their backs for any other automaton threat. In the distance, the raging fire grew smaller and smaller.

Conrad abandoned the horse in an alley and carried Raven the rest of the way to the Wooden Goblet. He entered through the kitchen and paused on the other side. Engor and a handful of others stood around the meeting table, looking devastated, anxious, and angry.

"What in Minerva's name happened out there?" asked one of the cooks—he wore a stained apron.

"A raid," Conrad said, his voice thin with panic. "On Caroline's street."

"Barely made it out," said a Wraith entering the kitchen. She whisked off her hood. It was Gretchen, the cook. In the better light, she didn't look much older than Raven. Her dark brown hair had been elaborately braided, and a faint scar crossed one of her pale golden cheeks. "They were waiting for us. Caroline's cave is gone. Smithereens." She demonstrated an explosion with her hands. "There's nothing left. Half of each building on either side is gone too. Those Gray Elite weren't messing around with this one. They wanted it gone, and it's gone. Pulled out half a dozen Slenders too."

Slenders must have been those automatons. The name fit.

"They would have been planning this for a while," Engor said grimly. "The Gray Elite don't blow up buildings on a whim."

"We didn't have time or the people to take care of it," reported Gretchen. "We barely made it out ourselves."

"I don't like it," Conrad said, frowning deeply. He looked to Engor and motioned to Raven with a nod. "They knew she would be there."

Engor frowned. "Why?"

"Don't you recognize her?" Conrad asked, a playful lilt in his voice. Engor's frown deepened. Gretchen put her hands on her hips. "She's the assassin General Deacon's so worried about."

Engor spat a curse. Gretchen spat a dirtier one.

"And she's got a bounty to kill for," said Engor.

"A bounty worth betrayal," said Gretchen, her tone like a blade ready to slice through flesh. She turned her deadly gaze onto the other cook. "Where's Merril?"

"She's been gone since this morning," said the cook.

"She's been bitching about money for months," said Gretchen. "My token's on her slipping information to the Gray Elite in exchange for a slice of the bounty."

Engor growled under his breath, though he didn't object.

Raven squeezed her eyes shut and flattened her palms against her eyes to block out as much light as possible. Her fault. Her fault. Someone had been looking for her, and they had blown up Caroline's cave—likely Caroline with it. All in an effort to find her.

Entirely, inexcusably, her fault.

She thought of the man on fire whom the automaton had cut down without hesitation. His death had also been her fault, along with anyone else hurt tonight.

"We will wait on word before we assume Caroline's fate," said Engor. "The old woman isn't a pushover."

His tone said what he didn't—Caroline was missing, and she couldn't help Raven.

Conrad carried her back upstairs. He sat her on the bed, and he sat against the wall, resignation on his face. She wanted to apologize, to take the blame for the failure, to tell him that it would be all right, but she couldn't form the words.

She trembled. The seed of hope of finding help shriveled and died, and she would likely follow.

The following day went by in a heavy blur. The crease between Conrad's brows never went away. The Wraiths didn't know what else to do for her, beyond iced cider and the rune. Conrad drew a new rune every hour. Ice melted against her skin.

Raven had the thought to ask Engor to keep a message for Zander, to use the Wraiths to somehow get it to him, so that he knew what had happened. Maybe Zander would tell her father and stepmother. But thinking about leaving a final message pitted her stomach, and she didn't want to think about it.

The door to her room opened, and by the time she worked her eyelids to move, Conrad sat on the edge of the bed. He held a few large splinters of wood. Fire kindling.

"I have an idea." Conrad set a splinter on her palm. "You had this fever, and then you used it to turn that pirate to ash, and then you were fine for a few days before the fever came back. So, I want you to try and turn these slivers of wood to ash."

She closed her fingers around the splinter as much as she could. Her fingers didn't want to grip; she hadn't the strength.

Raven tried to turn the splinter to ash, but she didn't know how. She didn't understand how she had given the pirate her fever. She tried to push the fever into the splinter, but it didn't move. It stayed with her. The wood remained wood.

Conrad held his face neutral. He watched her hand, the wood, waiting. After a while, he took the splinter from her.

"Warm," he said. "But not ash." He let out a grievous sigh.

"I'm trying," she said weakly.

"I know," he said. *Not enough*, was what he didn't say.

That evening, Conrad came to her room. He wore common clothes, a thin summer tunic the color of spring leaves and beige trousers. He redrew the rune, then sat on the bedside.

"The Wraiths are planning a counterattack on the Gray Elite." His coal-dark eyes were on the wall ahead of him. "I volunteered to stay behind with you. If Merril did sell information about you to the Gray Elite, then the Wooden Goblet isn't safe anymore."

She didn't know what to say, so she said, "Thank you."

Conrad looked down at his hands. "I don't know what to do about your condition. The magic you've got is beyond what I know or anything I've seen. Sooner or later, the Gray Elite will find you if you stay here." His words sank in, but he refused to look at her.

"Conrad?" she asked, the trembling in her stomach working its way through her limbs. "What—"

Conrad took a deep breath and released it; then he fixed his gaze on her. Nothing of his humor remained. "I have a friend here in the city. He might be our last hope at saving your life. The Wraiths don't know about him."

Raven stared back at him, unsure of what to say. She didn't have much of a choice. She could barely move on her own. So she nodded. "Okay."

Conrad didn't say who, and Raven wasn't sure she cared enough to ask.

"When they go," he whispered, "we'll sneak out. If my friend doesn't know what to do, then at least he can provide us a safe location where the automatons won't be a threat."

She nodded. She had reached the point where nothing mattered. Anything that might offer a sliver of hope, of help, she would take. Risk or not.

The air in the Wooden Goblet was tense. Whispers echoed through the floor, low enough that Raven couldn't make out what they said. They worried about a traitor. Conrad slipped into the meetings, but he didn't tell her their plans.

No one had caught up with Merril either. Her tiny apartment was empty—she'd fled in a hurry. None of her neighbors knew a thing.

The evening fell into night, as signified by the sounds of the kitchen, of the pots and pans being cleaned. Raven slept a few minutes at a time; the fever never let her rest long.

Conrad came to her room dressed in dark clothes not of the Wraiths. His braids were pulled behind his head by a black ribbon. He wore a dark half-cloak with a silver brooch over his heart that caught the candlelight. He held a second half-cloak over his arm.

"Come on," he whispered urgently. He pulled her into a sitting position and quickly fastened the cloak over her shoulders. He fastened a silver brooch—identical to his own—over her heart. He pulled the hood over her head. He then lifted her into his arms and carried her down the stairs.

The Wooden Goblet had gone frighteningly quiet.

Raven leaned against him as if part of her body had already died. He darted through the kitchen's side door, and the night banished the light. An automaton horse waited for them. The horse pulled forward at a trot, and she closed her eyes. The repetitive motion of the horse lulled her into a calmness, the balmy air kissed her cheeks, and the warmth outside mixed with the warmth inside. They trotted through the dark streets. Lights passed by on the other side of her eyelids.

She took one breath at a time.

The city buzzed around her, a metronomic beat underneath it all, like the city itself ran on gears. She heard the mechanical steps of automatons, their movements fluid and graceful. She heard the canter of automaton-drawn coaches.

The horse slowed. Its hooves beat against the stone, and then they didn't; the sounds softened like it walked on grass. The air became warm and humid. She smelled dankness, like soil and stone that never dried, and the ripeness of vegetation. The horse stopped, and Conrad lifted her from it.

"Good," breathed Conrad. "I didn't know if you'd gotten my message."

Her back met something cool and hard.

"This is her? She doesn't look good," whispered someone to her right.

"I know she doesn't," said Conrad on her left.

A sharp inhale. "Sisters," the person to the right gasped. "Raven?"

That voice. She fought to open her eyes, and through the blurry, dark daze, she spotted a pleasant face and blond hair. She knew him.

Her breath came out ragged, "Ezra?"

Captain Ezra Deacon blinked at her and brought a pale hand to his hair. He wore it down and loose, not slicked back in the Gray Elite fashion as the last time she had seen him. Rather than his Gray Elite uniform, he wore a dark tunic and trousers.

Her heart sped at his presence—Ezra was the son of General Deacon, the man who had claimed her an assassin and demanded her head.

"What happened?" Ezra asked.

It took a moment to realize Ezra directed his question at Conrad, not her. The pieces came together slowly: his friend, the one the Wraiths didn't know about, the one who could provide a safe place from the automatons—Ezra.

The fever flared, and she closed her eyes. She hadn't the energy to ponder the connection between Ezra and Conrad. If she made it through the night without burning alive, maybe she would ask one of them.

"The runes fade within an hour," Conrad said.

Somewhere close by, a bird chirped. She opened her eyes; she glimpsed darkness and green. Leaves and potted plants. Flowers and budding fruit. She blinked. She lay on a worktable inside a greenhouse. Tinted glass shielded them from the city beyond. A hand lifted her shirt to reveal her stomach. The rune. Ezra and Conrad stood on either side of her, eyeing her flesh, and the vulnerability sent a tremor down her spine. Neither man wore hunger or lust. They looked at her with clinical astonishment.

"I drew this one with Wraiths' ink this evening."

Ezra gaped. "It looks months old."

"But it's not."

"The magic is eating through it that fast?" Ezra ran a hand through his hair, confused and worried.

"Every hour," Conrad said darkly.

"Sisters," Ezra breathed. "I've never heard of magic working so fast."

"Neither have I, nor have the Wraiths." Conrad replaced Raven's shirt. "The only one who might have got blown up by the Gray Elite."

Ezra flushed. "I had no hand in it; you know that."

"Still, you're the only one I could think of who might be able to do something about it."

Ezra met Raven's gaze. He doubled in her vision, became one again, and then doubled. "I have a solution," Ezra said. "But you might not approve."

Conrad chuckled. "I'm a pirate, friend. There's little that I turn my nose up at." He cracked a smile, and Raven's spirit lifted slightly. Right now, she would try anything.

"Ruby powder," Ezra said.

Conrad's brow rose. "You want to drug her?"

Ezra shook his head. "No, ruby powder gives regular humans a high, but in a magician, it will eat through the magic. It's why magicians can't get high off it, because their magic prevents it. For Raven, it might eat through the magic that's eating through her. A counterattack."

"It's better than letting her die," Conrad said. "I assume you have a plan on getting ahold of ruby powder?"

Ezra turned sheepish. He reached into the satchel at his side and withdrew a canteen. "I came prepared."

"You carry some around with you all the time?" Conrad asked, not judging, but surprised. "And here I thought you more straightlaced."

Ezra blushed and frowned. "You mentioned out of control magic, so I came prepared."

The fever surged; Raven released a low sigh. Everything hurt.

Ezra pressed the mouth of the canteen to her lips, the metal cool and then not. "Drink, Raven," he said softly.

She parted her lips, and a tangy liquid flowed into her mouth. It tasted like flowers and too-strong tea. It registered in her mind as something red—the color red, as if it had a flavor.

The drink flowed down her throat, into her stomach, and, by the Sisters, it *worked*. She felt it tug the fever back, devour it, cooling her body, pulling the darkness from her vision, and coursing through the magic that had been about to devour her whole.

She drank until Ezra pulled the canteen away.

"That should do for now," he said, corking it.

The relief spread through her bones, through her blood. Hope surged in her chest and spread her lips in a smile. In the place where that incessant worry and panic and fear had been for so long, an exhaustion stole into her. Conrad and Ezra started talking, but she didn't listen. She wouldn't burn up in her sleep. She wouldn't turn into a pile of ash in the night.

With that sweet hope on her mind, she drifted into sleep, the first peaceful sleep she had gotten for weeks.

When Raven came to, she found herself in a strange room. It was not the wooden-walled room at the Wooden Goblet. In her sleepy haze, she saw scores of white, vivid sky blue, and shades of gold. The more she woke, the more she saw.

She was lying in a four-poster bed as soft as a cloud and four times her size. The posts were copper; sheer blue and gold silk draped from post to post and formed a canopy. The copper ceiling had been carved with a masterpiece of whorls and diamonds. The room beyond was white with golden trim. A handful of scenery paintings hung on the walls, sunrises and sunsets over countryside rivers and lakes. High, narrow windows of leaded glass let in copious sunlight. The curtains matched the bed drapes, shades of gold and blue. Leaded-glass doors led out onto a balcony, to a bright blue sky. She could see the tops of buildings on the other side. A fern hung from the ceiling on either side of the balcony doors, the chain bright and glittering gold in the daylight. The fronds nearly touched the floor. On the far other side of the room, a set of oak doors—meticulously carved—led elsewhere.

It was perhaps the most beautiful room she had ever seen. But...where was she?

She continued to breathe, so she lived. That she knew for certain—unless she had woken up in the Underworld, but it looked surprisingly like the living world, but then again, who would know what the Underworld looked like?

She continued to breathe—in, out.

Raven sat up, and an aching pain seared through her body. A yelp escaped her throat, and she collapsed back onto the silken sheets.

Not the Underworld. There wasn't supposed to be pain in the Underworld.

She gasped for breath; her lungs felt like she had inhaled fire. Burning. The fever. It raged through her blood like teeth, razor sharp and everywhere.

The oak doors opened, and quick footsteps approached. "I take that scream to mean you're alive?

That voice, joyful and tinted with laughter—she rolled onto her side to see Conrad smiling at her. He no longer wore his dark cloak and clothes.

136

He wore a bright yellow tunic with ivory trim and trousers of gray. Half a dozen gold bangles hung off his wrists, and he wore several gold chains around his neck. He stood proudly, like he belonged in this godly house.

"Where are we?" Her voice came out hoarse, and her throat felt dry.

"Well," Conrad started, plopping down on the bed. "Do you remember meeting my friend?"

It took her a moment to remember. "Ezra Deacon is your friend?" she asked with no small amount of disbelief.

Conrad nodded. "It's a long story to explain, but I take it that you two have met?"

She nodded. She didn't feel like explaining that meeting to him. She didn't feel like explaining anything to anyone. She closed her eyes, and the rest of that night came back to her. The counterattack. The dark greenhouse. The bitter drink. The relief.

"What did he give me?" she asked.

"Ruby powder," he whispered.

"What is that?" She'd never heard of it before.

"It's one of the magic-infused illegal drugs that the Gray Elite fight hard to purge from the city," Conrad said. "It's made by magic and gives non-magicians a decent high, but in your case, it consumed the magic in your system and gave you a relatively smaller high."

"And Ezra had some?" She couldn't imagine Ezra, the general's son, the perfect Gray Elite soldier, breaking the law for her favor.

Conrad's smile widened. "Ezra has access to the confiscated stores, as well as a few magic dealers," he whispered. "And he did save your life, so I wouldn't question his methods or means too much."

She released a breath.

The door opened again, and this time, Ezra appeared at the bedside. He, too, had discarded his dark clothes for those of a noble. In his hands, he held a canteen. "I'm glad to see you're awake. I had a fear you'd not wake up at all. How do you feel?"

She groaned in response.

Ezra gave her a small smile. He gently jostled the canteen. "Time for another dose, I'd say. Fresh batch too."

Raven didn't ask where or when he had had the new batch of ruby powder made. Conrad helped her to sit up, and Ezra handed her the uncorked canteen. She took it in both hands. The metal felt smooth and cool, and the drink had a faint scent of flowers and that undeniably *red* scent. She lifted it to her lips and took several long drinks under Ezra's watchful eye. It tasted much the same as it had, only less bitter and more floral—and *red*.

She could feel the fever retreat with every drink, with every gulp that flooded down her throat and into her bones, her blood, her muscles.

Ezra pulled the canteen away, and she smiled at the boys. "It's working," she said.

Conrad nodded like he hadn't doubted it for a second. His eyes were looking at her but not at her—her magic, the fever. Ezra kept his stare on her, worried and intent.

"What happened, Raven?" Ezra sat down on the bed, corking the canteen. He set it on the bedside table and leaned forward onto his knees. "Is that even your real name?"

Conrad's dark brows shot upward.

"Yes," she said.

Ezra didn't look convinced. He looked...betrayed.

Guilt pulled her heart into her stomach. Sisters, she'd really made a mess for herself. She inhaled, unsure of what to tell him and what not to, of what Conrad knew and what he suspected. "Raven is my real name."

Conrad shifted. "I have a better idea. How about we discuss our secrets over lunch and a tasty beverage? Hmm? Breakfast has worn off."

Ezra took a moment to think about it, then nodded. "I'll send the order." He stood. "Raven, do you feel well enough to eat in the lounge?"

"There's a lounge?" She glanced to the doors where Conrad and Ezra had come from. "Where am I?"

"My family's estate," Ezra answered. "It's in the heart of Moorin, and it's the last place the automatons will look for you."

The Deacon Estate, General Deacon's home. She felt the color leave her face.

"My father isn't here," Ezra said, his voice quiet. "He is still in Lenhala. He won't be back for a while. *Someone* left the city in a state of chaos."

He meant her, she realized. Her face warmed but not from the fever.

Ezra met her gaze, his face serious. "Raven, did you try to kill my father?"

"No," she said without hesitation.

Ezra blinked, and relief replaced his worry.

"On the contrary, he tried to kill me. Twice." Her bravery returned, buffed by the ruby powder, and she added, "He was just mad that I got away."

Ezra chuckled. "Sounds like him." He motioned to the canteen on her nightstand. "You'll need to keep a regimen of ruby powder—a drink every hour or so, most likely." He glanced toward the door. "Stay in this room for right now. I don't want any of the servants to get suspicious. They know I have friends staying here, but I would rather them not see you up close. I'll come when the meal is ready."

"You've got wanted posters," Conrad added playfully. "They're not a bad rendering, though they make you look more vicious than you are."

Raven sighed and reclined back into the pillows. Wanted posters. Just what she needed.

"I'll see if I can't snag one for you," Conrad said.

Ezra cleared his throat in farewell, to give the order for lunch to his servants. He left, and Conrad released a sigh. He leaned back on the bed, propping himself up with his elbows.

"You're full of surprises, aren't you?" he said.

She sighed dramatically. The ruby powder made her feel significantly better. Was this how she felt before the fever? It didn't seem possible. "I remember when I wished for adventure. Now I wish I had a little bit less."

Conrad laughed, an easy rumble. "It does seem to happen that way, doesn't it?"

"How did you meet Ezra?"

He considered her for a moment. In the daylight flooding the room, his dark skin shone with golden tones. His coal-dark eyes glittered—thinking. "I'll trade you secrets," he said, grinning. "I'll tell you where I met him, if you tell me where *you* met him."

"In Lenhala," she said.

That part Conrad already knew, and he motioned for her to continue.

"You said *where*, not *how*."

He laughed, rolled his eyes, and said, "Correction, I'll tell you *how* I met him, if you tell me *how* you met him."

"Zander took me to the Summer Solstice Ball," she said. "I met Ezra there. Then, the next day, I was walking through a garden with a friend when a thief attacked. I defended myself and her and killed him. When the Gray Elite came to investigate, Ezra came with them. He brought me to his father's office, and because he knew his father would likely kill me, he gave me hints as to a secret way out, which worked. After that, I haven't seen him until now."

Conrad hummed. After a beat, he said, "I met him when I attempted to burgle him. He caught me but not before I found that he was trying to smuggle a few magicians out of the city. I offered him help in exchange for not turning me in; he accepted because he's the kind of soul to trust blindly. It worked in his favor, though."

She blinked. "Ezra smuggles magicians out of the city?"

Captain Ezra Deacon of the Gray Elite, son of General Deacon—a magician smuggler? Collaborating with a pirate?

Conrad's smile grew wider and a shade more wicked. "We help each other out now and then. We've become something shy of accomplices."

She laughed, the feeling foreign in her body, which had grown used to the constant burn. She ran a hand through her hair and then cringed at the oily feeling it left on her fingers. When had she last washed it?

"The bathroom is down the hall," Conrad said. "Second door on your left."

She nodded. Her stomach felt viciously empty, as empty as her scalp felt dirty. And yet she found herself in a cloud of carelessness. She glanced at the canteen of ruby powder on the nightstand. She could feel it working, dulling the fever into nonexistence, replacing it with something joyful, something bright and happy.

"I have a few things to take care of before this evening," Conrad said. "I will see you shortly for lunch. Do try to stay out of trouble."

"Only if you do," she said.

He winked, then left, leaving her alone in her strange new room.

She wiggled her arms and legs, no longer numbed and burning and useless. She easily pushed herself to the edge of the bed and set her bare feet on the floor. The floor was tile, alternating blue and white and gold, patterned in a lovely mosaic. Unlike the boys, she still wore her dark clothes, as soiled as her hair.

She took laps around the room to regain her balance. The ruby powder altered her balance, and it took a few moments to get used to the wobbly feeling. She meandered to the leaded-glass doors. She didn't open them. Beyond, the garden of the Deacon Estate formed a green square around the house, protecting it from the wide streets beyond. All around, similar estates grew like palaces and castles, some bigger and some smaller, but all grand. She spotted the heart of the city a short distance away, rising like needles toward the endless blue sky.

Would Ezra report her presence to Zander? Did they even know of each other's secrets? The thoughts passed through her mind quickly, and she pushed the worries aside. Compared to the fever that tore her apart, splintered her bones, and clawed at her skin, the high filled her with a sense of floating, carelessness, and peace. She preferred the high, despite the minor fluctuation in her balance.

She caught a whiff of human stink and grimy hair. Sisters, was that *her*? She tiptoed into the corridor. Ivory carpet softened her footsteps. The walls were pale wood and smooth white stone. Brass sconces dotted the walls, but no light flickered. The only light came from a window at the far end. Along with hers, she counted five sets of oak doors. All were closed. It gave the hall a lonely feeling.

The bathroom was a masterpiece of ivory and gold tile, deep purple walls, and pale wood accents. The center of the room held two wide sinks and a floor-to-ceiling mirror. Sisters, she looked awful! Grime darkened her hair and clumped the roots. On either side of the vanity was a pale wooden door that led into a separate toilet and shower. Brass pipes ran along the walls to the ivory fixtures. A narrow wicker cabinet held rolled towels and soaps.

She helped herself to the soaps, stripped off the dirty men's clothes, and stepped into the shower. It was a mosaic of gold and white tiles. She turned one of two matching brass knobs. The pipes creaked, a gush, and then cool water flowed from the showerhead and doused her. She played with the knobs until the water turned lukewarm. The soap smelled unlike anything she had used before, not floral, not sweet.

Only after she had scrubbed the grime and dirt from her skin and hair did she return to her room. She wore only a towel. She didn't feel like putting on her dirty clothes so soon. She had seen a wardrobe in the bedroom. She would look to see if she had any other options first. Sure enough, the wardrobe contained a few basic articles. She pulled a loose white cotton day dress over her head and tied the simple gray corset herself. She left her feet bare.

She meandered to the balcony doors and stared at the city beyond as she lazily braided her damp hair. Oh, how she had missed being clean! Her spirits had lifted tenfold.

The oak doors opened, and Conrad sauntered in. "Ezra had to step out. It will just be the two of us for lunch."

"I'm starved," she said and meant it. She meandered to the door, not minding her bare feet or state of dress, and Conrad didn't reprimand her.

They ate in a small, comfy lounge with purple walls and golden wainscoting. The heavy gray drapes over the leaded windows gave it a cozy, sleepy feel. The food wasn't anything special: sliced bread, soft cheese, fruit, and spiced nuts. As they ate, Raven talked Conrad into telling her one of his pirating stories, one where he wasn't yet a man but had a fierce thirst for the world.

"I thought I wouldn't return to the shore again," Conrad said dreamily, his hands moving with the story like ocean waves. He sighed and looked Raven in the eye, "But I was destined to return to Wayward Point, for I had already left a piece of my heart behind."

"The girl?" Raven asked, the girl whom he had loved, the girl who had left him behind for another, the girl who had broken his heart.

"Before her," Conrad said. Something calm came over his face. "It started bright and warm, but even then, when we met after that voyage, a part of me knew it wouldn't last. He was afraid of drowning, and I had a love of the sea."

"What happened?"

"We grew apart as people do," Conrad said, the longing in his voice turning bittersweet. "But my first love is the sea, and she always will be. He knows that." He took a drink of his tea and frowned, wishing it were something much stronger.

When Raven returned to her room, the fever had started to crawl back. She reached first for the ruby powder and took a large drink. At once, she realized her mistake. The sudden influx surged against the fever, making her dizzy. She corked the canteen and fell onto the bed, barely making it under the covers before it stole her into the darkness of a nap.

That night, Raven woke to a low rumble of thunder. She rolled her sluggish body onto her side, facing the balcony doors. Darkness pressed against the leaded-glass doors and the windows. The light in the room was dim—dark but unnaturally illuminated.

Raven fought to keep her eyes open; her eyelids were heavy. So tired. She leaned back into the silken sheets and let her eyes close.

A sigh, a creak—barely a sound against the gathering storm.

A breeze, she told herself.

A sigh, a creak—more than the breeze. Wood moving. Hinges giving.

She opened her eyes.

The doors stood open. The darkness beyond the doorway thickened, blacker than the night, undulating like stirred ink.

Wrong, her body screamed a heartbeat before her mind echoed, *wrong!*

Raven sat up. Every muscle, bone, and thread of her body protested. Sisters, what had happened to her? Why did she feel as though she had been beaten?

The storm rattled on the other side of the darkness. Those doors should be closed! Heart pounding, she tried to reason. *The wind*, she told herself. The wind had opened the doors. The darkness shifted, churning like fog, defying nature with every movement. It pressed against the windows. Tendrils of darkness searched the seams, the sill—for entry.

She tried to get up, but her legs had turned leaden, thick and useless. *Don't move.*

A voice caressed her mind, cold as winter's darkest night, fearless and vengeful. A terror like she had never known gripped her bones.

Through the darkness, something stepped—something a shade lighter than the darkness around it. A figure emerged from the darkness. As it moved, though, it became humanoid and male. He stepped over the threshold and into her room. He wore dark leathers and robes made for silent movement, for shadows. Belts of daggers crisscrossed his lean torso. A hood hid his face in shadow. Tendrils of darkness clung to his frame, slipping into the room with him.

Raven trembled. Without thinking, she grabbed for the silver candlestick from her bedside table and held it like a sword. The burned wick angled like a tiny hook.

143

He took a graceful, lethal step toward her. She lifted the candlestick higher.

He tilted his face to the side, lifting his chin, and the shadow over his face receded. He wore a dulled copper mask.

Do you think that will stop me?

Somehow she knew it wouldn't, but she didn't lower the candlestick. She wouldn't go down without a fight.

Don't you know who I am?

The mask, the predatory gait—she knew. The Revenant.

Yes, that's right.

She trembled. The candlestick shook. No one saw the Revenant without dying. Wraith. Assassin. Deadly.

The Revenant reached to his sides and withdrew two daggers, sharpened to deadly edges. He took a predator's step closer. Ready to end her. The Wraiths had sent him to kill her for ruining their plans, for causing the death of Caroline and the destruction of her cave. For the Wraiths to have found and sent the Revenant, they must have been furious—enough to want her dead.

The Revenant stalked toward her the way a cat corners a wounded mouse. His shoulders and knees bent for easy movement, his entire body lithe with controlled grace. He came within reach of the bed, and she couldn't bring her arms to move. He knocked the candlestick from her grip. The darkness grabbed it before it hit the floor, swallowing it whole—it never made a sound. The shadows trailing the Revenant swallowed the room, the tiles, the doors, the walls, the ceiling, edging closer.

The Revenant climbed onto the bed, daggers gleaming in unnatural light. She couldn't move. She started to beg, her words a tremor of pleas, but a thunderous crash sounded from the storm. The thunder shook the estate, the room, tearing apart the floor, the ceiling, the doors—the room shattered.

Raven jerked upward—awake.

She gasped for breath. Cold sweat covered her skin. Nothing pinned her. She had fallen asleep in her corset. With every moment, her heartbeat slowed. She released her white-knuckle grip on the sheets. Outside the closed leaded-glass doors, thunder rolled low and lazy just like it had in her dream. Lightning flashed several beats after.

On the other side of the doors, despite the storm, Moorin glowed. Streetlights and lanterns illuminated the towering heart of the city in gold and silver.

A dream.

It had been a dream.

No assassin had come for her; no unnatural darkness had unlocked the balcony doors. The Revenant hadn't been sent to kill her. Still, her heart hammered madly. She could still see the Revenant's violent stance in the balcony doors, his dark robes and copper mask.

She put a shaky hand over her heart. She hoped Engor was right in thinking the Revenant's silence meant he had been killed.

She pulled her knees up to her chest, content to sit and listen to the storm while her heart returned to normal.

With the rough awakening of her nightmare, Raven didn't at once notice the fever. It came back slowly but still too fast. It raged like it knew she had dampened it, and the resurgence made her heart spin and bones ache. A fraction of the terror she had felt in her dream returned, and she fumbled for the canteen of ruby powder. Her shaking hands fought with the cork, but after a desperate time, she won.

She took a long, generous drink. And then a second.

Thunder rolled. She took a third.

She set the canteen on the bedside table and sat up while the drug worked, calming the raging fire, dampening the violent magic. She brought her hand up to the centrum. Such a silly thing to have caused so much trouble. If she told Conrad and Ezra what it really was, what would they say?

Conrad would be thrilled at the story, at the secrecy. Ezra would frown. Would he want to tell his father about it? Would Conrad say to give it to the highest bidder?

No. She wouldn't tell them about the centrum. No one could know.

Thunder rolled. Lightning flashed a heartbeat sooner. The air smelled like rain, wet and warm and fresh. She struggled to free her limp self of the blankets. Her legs felt like wooden sticks and sand. With every step toward the balcony doors, the ruby powder worked its magic, freeing, soothing, lifting.

She threw open the balcony doors just as a clap of thunder shook the sky. The air was heavy with impending rain, thick with moisture; it sounded like a cool drink of water to her retreating fever. She half fell onto the balcony and latched her hands around the ivory railing.

The humidity sank through her dress, sticking the thin material to her skin. The lightning flashed through the thick bubbling clouds of dark gray and blues. To the far distance, on the other side of the city, lightning flashed continuously between the clouds, a stream of light over the horizon.

She could feel the rain coming. The magic under her skin, be it her own, the centrum's, or the ruby powder, yearned for it. Craved it. She waited on the balcony, watching the lightning come closer, closer, closer, until the thunder and the lightning clashed together. She could hear the rain smacking into the steel and copper and iron and glass, each drop crashing to the earth from the boiling sky, cooling the air, the ground, and everything in between.

The wall of rain surged over the city. The sound grew and grew, overwhelming all else. The lines of rain grew distinct. The rain hit the edge of the Deacon Estate as lightning flashed, making each drop glow bright as a tiny moon. The drops crashed onto the well-kept lawn, the flower beds, the marble walkways, the foundation, and the edge of the balcony.

The rain hit her skin like drops of ice, cooling the fever, quenching the burn, aiding the ruby powder. The first drops turned to steam on impact. Raven held her hands palm up, watching as the rain hit and vanished into vapor.

She lifted her chin to the rain as it became a downpour, soaking through her dress, soaking her to the bone, banishing the last of the fever. It soaked through her hair and pulled it down her shoulders and back. It reminded of her diving into the cool lagoon at the treehouse.

"That's a good way to find a cold," came Conrad's voice from behind her.

She turned. He stood in her room, just outside of where the rain pitter-pattered the tile. He still wore his fine clothes, and he regarded her with a mixture of curiosity and concern.

When she didn't answer, he tilted his head. His loose braids fell over his shoulder, the beads clinking together. "Raven?"

"The rain feels nice." She stretched her arms out on either side of her.

"I'm sure it does," Conrad said, motioning for her to come inside. "But, seeing as it's nearly two in the morning, come back inside before someone calls the Gray Elite about the crazy girl on the balcony."

She didn't want to. "Why don't you come out here?"

"Because I don't want to get wet," he said simply. He motioned again. "Come on, before you get sick."

She let the rain soak her a heartbeat longer, let out a dramatic sigh, and walked back into the bedroom. Her bare feet slapped against the tile.

Conrad shut the balcony doors, and once inside, her wetness became a hindrance to her movement.

"And you're leaving a mess," Conrad said with a mock sigh, head tilted at the puddle growing at her feet. "Wait here."

Conrad sauntered to the pale wooden armoire and rifled through the contents until he pulled out a simple robe of soft gray. He tossed it onto the bed. He held up his finger to her, vanished through the main door and returned a few moments later with a yellow towel as wide as a blanket.

He tossed the towel to her and turned his back while she disrobed and dried.

"Maybe you drank a little too much," he said. "No more than a sip at a time of your medicine."

"Yes, doctor," she said, her voice childish.

He laughed.

She grabbed the gray robe from the bed and slipped it on. Odd how standing in the rain had renewed her spirit. She took a quick swig of the ruby powder, a swig monitored by Conrad, and then collapsed back into the bed.

Had the bed always been this comfortable?

She never heard Conrad lock the balcony doors, gather her wet clothes, or let himself out. And this time, her dreams were pleasant.

They arrived in Moorin during the storm, after midnight but before dawn; Thalame couldn't tell. He'd never been the best at telling the time. He'd met a Wraith once who could spot the time of the day by the scent of the air.

The city lay quiet around them. Most of the automatons had been withdrawn into whatever hiding holes they went to when it rained. Only the most resilient ones marched up and down the streets, their copper and steel hulls blurred and dulled by the rain. Zander walked a step in front of him, hood up, stolen clothes soaked.

Lucky resounded in Thalame's mind. He didn't like *lucky*; he liked it better when he got through on his own skill, rather than luck, because luck was fickle.

The whole blasted trip into Gracita had been lucky. They had managed to stowaway on a cargo ship and somehow evaded the Gray Elite air patrol, and the Sisters must have been watching out for them when they slipped out at the docks in the bleakest hours of the night.

But they were here, and that was what mattered.

Zander cracked his head to one side, the movement agitated. He easily sidestepped into another alley; Thalame followed. He glanced down the alley they had been going down—the shadow of one of the few automatons loomed closer.

The rain came down a little harder. Making their way through the streets of Moorin came easier in the rain. The rain thickened the shadows and blanketed footsteps. People stayed inside unless they had to go out, and even then, they hurried with hoods over their heads or umbrellas blocking their view of the two darkly clad men fleeting from alley to alley. The heavy rain dissuaded the patrols from a chase should they be seen.

Thalame would've been lying if he said he hadn't dreaded this part. When Ivy had questioned him about it, he'd played tough. She hadn't bought it. She'd gotten that twitch in her upper lip, the one she got when she wanted to argue but didn't.

Zander led the way. Their directions to the inn were years old, but the odds of it having moved were slim. Zander led; Thalame watched his back. Just like the old days. Days long gone.

They paused to let a coach roll by. The automaton goat pulling it wore a poncho. The rain smacked against the slick material, sounding like a thousand needles hammering against steel. Thalame rolled his neck. Sisters, he could use a solid night of rest. He hadn't slept through the night in weeks.

The coach passed, and Zander darted across the street. Thalame followed on his heels. Neither made more than a whisper.

The alleys grew narrower. The streets became dirtier and less illuminated. The automations became fewer and far between. Finally, they found the Wooden Goblet, one of several cobbled-together buildings on one of many nameless side streets. Without losing his threatening gait, Zander marched through the front door. Thalame followed.

The tavern was empty, save for a girl arranging tankards over the counter. She wore simple clothes and a stained apron.

"Welcome," she said halfheartedly. She eyed the two of them with careful suspicion, taking in their stolen clothes in a few quick blinks. Her eyes shifted to the clock, likely taking note of the late hour. "Breakfast isn't for a while, but we have beds available. One room or two?"

Thalame started to speak—

Zander barked, "Where's Engor?"

Thalame closed his mouth. Still in a bad mood, then.

The girl looked Zander up and down without surprise. She knew who—and what—they were. She held Zander's gaze for a moment, then said, "He's in the kitchen." She nodded toward the wooden door that led behind the bar.

Zander took two steps toward the door when it opened, and the graying man Thalame barely remembered marched through.

"You got friends," said the girl.

Engor eyed the two of them with callused suspicion, his scowl deepening. He sighed through his nose and turned back into the kitchen. The kitchen doubled as a meeting room. Several maps had been sprawled out on an oak table. It smelled like a kitchen; a thousand dinners had soaked into the stone and the pots and pans hanging from the ceiling. Herbs were drying, tied by hemp from the ceiling. The kitchen was empty, save for the three of them, so Thalame tossed his wet hood back. Zander hesitated, then mirrored his actions. His wet hair flopped to his shoulders in scraggly strands.

"The wind rushes from the stars," said Thalame.

"The sea reaches for the sky," added Zander.

"And the stone carries us," finished Engor grimly. "Welcome to the Wooden Goblet, Wraiths. You're just in time. We're going to need all the hands we've got."

"What do you mean?" Thalame asked before Zander could growl at the man like he'd done at every other person they'd come across.

Engor leaned onto the table and let out a groan. The table groaned too.

"What happened?" Zander demanded.

"There was a raid," Engor said. He looked down at the map where they had placed a red X over a building. "Unexpected. It was a doctor's place. Killed a few magicians. We don't know what happened to the doctor. She's still unaccounted for. Gray Elite blew the whole clinic to rubble. We didn't have the time or people to combat it. We retaliated the next night, a silent raid on the patrol station closest to where the raid happened. Poisoned the water tank. If we're lucky, it will kill a handful and put the others out of work for a while. We also got a few magicians they'd detained."

"Good," said Zander. "And they're safe?"

Engor nodded. "As safe as magicians can be in this place." He frowned; the lines on his face seemed deeper. "But we've got another situation."

Thalame stood still as stone, keeping his face neutral. He didn't like Engor's tone, like it had been their fault.

"Such as?" Zander asked.

"Conrad showed up a few days ago with a sick girl with him, half dead from magic eating her alive," Engor said gravely. "We tried our best to do what we could for her, but the magic was too strong, unlike anything we'd ever seen. I was going to write a letter to Deikun about it after our counterattack, but when I got back afterward, they were both gone."

"What do you mean sick?" Thalame asked first, before Zander could jump on the question. He felt Zander look at him, felt the accusation and fear in it, but Thalame ignored it.

"Sick like a fever," Engor said, and Thalame bit back his own surprise.

Zander cursed.

"We painted runes with Wraith ink, but the magic ate through it like nothing I've seen before. It was ravaging, starving. Conrad was painting a new rune every hour."

"And they're gone?" Zander spat, leaning on the table. He looked livid at the news, his eyes feral and his face grimacing. With his damp hair, he looked like a madman.

150

"Gone," Engor confirmed, nodding.

Thalame let out a short sigh, and he dared to meet Zander's gaze. A silent message passed between the two long time friends. A silent agreement and shared suspicion. Thalame had more to say, but he didn't want to say anything more in front of Engor. Wraith or no, Thalame didn't know enough about the man to trust him.

Magical sickness. Thalame had pondered the idea, but Raven wasn't a magician. Unless she somehow contracted it when they were in Lenhala, and her non-magical blood reacted poorly to magical exposure. He had heard of those. She had grown up in a small town, Zander said, with little to no magical contact.

"Why did Conrad leave?" Thalame asked.

"Sisters only know," Engor said. "We left for the counterattack, and Conrad volunteered to stay behind with her. I thought he was being a nice guy for once, but when we got back and saw them both gone, no one had any idea. I've got a few of my people trying to track them down as we speak."

"What did this girl look like?" Zander asked, his voice angry but resigned; caution underlined his words.

Engor opened his mouth, but he never got the chance to speak. The backdoor to the kitchen opened, and two darkly clad figures walked inside. By the looks of the robes and leathers, they were Wraiths. They wore fewer daggers than Thalame or Zander did.

"Report," barked Engor.

"We found them," said one of the Wraiths, a female, her voice sharp as a razor's edge. She threw back her hood. She fixed her eyes on Zander and Thalame. "Who are they?"

"Friends," Engor said. "Extended family."

She nodded once, then she turned her full attention to Engor. "Like I said, we found them."

"Where?" Engor said.

Thalame felt Zander tense beside him, fighting the urge to clench his fist, every nerve in his body fighting to stay calm and composed. Thalame reached out and casually set a hand on his friend's shoulders. It took little effort to still the warring emotions, and Zander released a calming sigh. Zander glanced at Thalame, a silent *thank you* in his eyes.

To anyone else, it would have looked like Thalame had stopped him from speaking rudely when, in truth, Thalame had used his powers to calm him. Same endgame.

The girl with the sharp voice took a step toward Engor. "You'll never believe where they went," she said, dark glee shining in her eyes. She leaned forward and placed one of her fingertips on the map of the city.

Raven took a swig of ruby powder first thing the next morning. Sisters, what had gotten into her last night? Had she drunk too much of the potion? She remembered the stiffness of her fever and then the ecstasy of the rain. Thank the Sisters Conrad had come when he did, or she might have spent the rest of the night on the balcony.

The storm lingered, the clouds pale and gray. The rain was light and misty, the wind a gentle pressure against the walls and windows. Raven sat up in bed while the ruby powder worked on her fever, and when she felt better, she got up. She walked a lap around the stately room. Its sparse and clean style reminded her of the Gray Elite.

She hunted through the armoire and found only an extra set of bedclothes and a simple robe like the one she wore, only in white.

Footsteps sounded outside, boots, and then a gentle knock came to her door.

She paused, unsure of what to say. She saw the shadow of two feet standing on the other side. She cleared her throat. "Yes?"

Ezra let himself inside. He wore a fine housecoat with a stylized D over the heart. "I'm glad to see you're awake." He shifted a parcel in his hands as he looked between Raven and the open wardrobe. "I didn't have time to stock much, only the essentials, but I managed to procure you something else to wear in the meantime." He set the parcel on the bed.

"Thank you." Raven had never been overly sentimental, but the feeling overwhelmed her. "For everything you've done. You didn't have to help me, but you did. Twice now. I owe you a great deal."

Ezra nodded and tucked his hands into his pockets. He seemed as uncomfortable with her gratitude as she did.

She shut the wardrobe doors. "Why did you help?" she asked, her voice soft. "Not that I'm not grateful. I am, very much so."

"That is something I planned to discuss over breakfast." Ezra swallowed and glanced at the leaded-glass doors. "Which is why I came to see if you were awake. It's a casual meal, just the few of us."

His tone—he wasn't telling her something.

"The few of us?" she repeated.

Ezra nodded, still not meeting her gaze. "Conrad, you, myself, and maybe another, but I'm unsure if the fourth guest will be able to attend." He cleared his throat. "Breakfast will be in the lounge down the hall. It's not ready just yet. If you should need something else, let me or Conrad know."

"Thank you," she said.

How much would she owe Ezra by the end of her stay?

Ezra gave her a quick, polite bow and left. It wasn't until the door shut that she realized his words—she could ask him or Conrad for things she needed, meaning Conrad could walk freely around the house and outside it in order to fetch those things. She couldn't. She was to stay within these few rooms.

A prisoner. Again.

Irritation heated her blood and her cheeks. The fever surged past the effects of the ruby powder, only instead of a numbing, painful heat, she felt a pleasant rush—not unlike the sensation of falling.

Then she reminded herself that Conrad wasn't the most wanted person in two kingdoms. If she left, she might be recognized. Then she and Ezra would be in trouble. Ezra was right to keep her inside.

She inhaled, filling her lungs to capacity, and released her breath slowly. Then she unwrapped the parcel that Ezra had brought. Inside was a dress of blue and copper, and underthings. She didn't pause to consider if it would fit. It had been a gift, and she would make it work. She gathered the parcel and returned to the bathing room. One of the showers was in use; running water rattled through the pipes and smacked against tile. A male voice was humming a lively tune. She blushed, the heat traveling from the top of her head to her toes.

"I assume that's Raven," came Conrad's voice from the shower to her right.

"It's me," she said, her voice awkward and a pitch too high.

Conrad laughed. The sound rumbled against the water. "Don't worry, little bird. I don't bite—unless you ask, but even then I reserve my right to refuse. I have to be in the right mood for that."

Her blush heated even more. She shut herself in the other shower. It didn't bother her to share a bathing room. She had shared one with the other girls in Silver Glen and with the Dwellers. She'd never not shared a bathing room. She washed; all the while, Conrad continued to hum a tune that made her think of seaside shacks and the endless ocean, of mermaids and deserted islands.

Raven took her time washing, drying, and dressing. The dress Ezra had chosen was a simple sleeveless summer gown with bright blue silk skirts and corset bodice of copper. It fit as fine as anything. The silk around her legs felt like water woven into fabric. She returned to the vanity. Conrad—dressed in beige silk trousers and matching tunic—stood at the sink, running a fragrant oil over his braids.

She joined him at the sinks and found a comb in one of the drawers. She combed and tossed her damp hair over her shoulder.

Conrad extended his arm to her like a gentleman, and she threaded her arm through his. They walked into the hall and into the lounge, where Ezra stood by the windows, alone. The eyes of his reflection glanced toward them, then back outside.

With the storm, the windows let in only dreary light, and the chandelier had been lit. A dozen glass globes flickered with light, brightening the space.

On the round table, tea had been served—four cups set around the teapot. Four place settings had been arranged. Covered dishes lined the table, and Raven could smell bacon and ham and eggs; her mouth watered. She didn't even know how hungry she had been.

Conrad and Raven sat at the table, but neither moved. The settings, the room—it all felt so formal and stiff.

"Help yourself," Ezra said, eyes on something out of the window. "No need for excessive manners."

Conrad made himself a cup of tea, and after a moment, Raven followed his lead. She took several sips before Ezra joined them. He looked bothered. Raven glanced to the fourth place sitting. Did his nervousness have to do with the lack of the fourth guest?

Conrad lumped a large amount of everything onto his plate. Raven took nearly as much, eager to sate her wild hunger. Ezra sipped his tea and waited until they had filled their plates before adding small servings to his own. Raven didn't ask or question it; her hunger didn't allow space for her mind to think such thoughts. They began to eat, silently.

Ezra picked at his food. Conrad and Raven devoured theirs.

"I owe you an explanation, Raven," Ezra said after a while, a bit reluctantly, his fork pushing eggs around his plate. He met her gaze. "And I believe you owe me one as well."

The food in her mouth soured. She paused mid-chew, her throat suddenly tight. She forced her food down and took a large drink of tea. Beside her, Conrad's brows rose. Ezra held her gaze, patiently waiting.

She nodded, her face warming. "You're right."

"Oh," said Conrad, leaning onto the table, "I do love a good story. And I get two? The Sisters must not hate me after all."

Raven pushed the remaining food around her plate while Ezra and Conrad recounted their first meeting. Ezra, the strapping young Gray Elite eager to please his father, and Conrad, the Wraith-turned-pirate looking for an easy token. Either could have blown the whistle on the other. Ezra could have turned Conrad in for what he was—a magician. Conrad could have turned Ezra in for treason, for aiding magicians.

Their alliance had been sporadic at first but had grown steady in the past few years. Ezra kept his father off the map. Conrad helped the magicians once they crossed the border into Tinatun. They settled deeper into the kingdom, he told Raven, and pockets of magicians dotted the central parts of the kingdom.

"The Wraiths aren't the only ones capable of helping," Conrad added a bit darkly. "Despite what some people think, pirates aren't all murderous madmen."

Ezra's grimace softened. He looked like he had something else to say, but with Raven present, he held his tongue. Raven wondered if it had something to do with the boy Conrad had left to be a pirate.

"You don't help the Hawks?" Raven asked carefully, not wanting to throw suspicion onto herself.

Ezra shook his head. "I've had little contact with the Hawks," he admitted. "They're not the most...understanding—at least, not in my experience. They're more worried about starting a revolution than they are righting things."

Raven took a sip of her tea. Did he know about Zander?

"You have a look that wants to say something else," Conrad said, curious stare on Ezra.

Ezra frowned. "Why must you notice things?"

Conrad shrugged. "Observant men last longer."

Ezra released a heavy sigh. Keeping his eyes on his plate, he said, "I distrust the Hawks because they sent the Revenant to kill my mother."

Raven gasped. "Did she..."

"I saw it happen," Ezra said lowly.

Raven's breath caught in her throat.

Conrad's eyes widened, his humor gone. "You *saw* him?" Conrad asked, awestruck.

"I wasn't supposed to," Ezra said. "It was four years ago. My father had gone on a tirade, and I didn't want to be in his crosshairs. So I hid. Yes, I know, it was a moment of cowardice on my part. My mother came into the room after having argued with my father. She paused at the window, and I saw living shadows surging toward her. She didn't have time to scream before the shadows took her. I saw...a figure in the shadows. I closed my eyes, and when I opened them again, the shadows were gone, and my mother was dead."

Assassinated.

Raven remembered her dream, the living shadows thick enough to block out the light, that never stopped moving. How could she dream of someone she had never met? She had only heard the stories. Her mind invented them, she told herself, had invented the Revenant in her dream. Her nightmare. Thinking about it made her nearly sick.

"Why did he kill her?" Conrad asked. He had the grace not to be smirking.

"She was Gray Elite," Ezra said. "The real reason was never made clear, although I assume it had everything to do with my father. They tried to kill my father that same day, but that assassin failed. They've tried several times since, with no luck. The Hawks are determined to see me orphaned, it seems."

Heavy silence fell over the table. As if in sympathy, the thunder rolled.

Ezra released a sigh—even his sighs were dignified—and leaned back in his chair.

Conrad broke the silence, his perpetual grin breaking through the grimness. He looked between Ezra and Raven. "I hear that our little bird tried to assassinate your father," Conrad said, shaking his fork at Ezra.

"He framed me," Raven said.

"I believe you," Ezra said. The story of his mother had taken its toll; he looked exhausted. "I was there during this supposed assassination attempt, remember. I had a feeling he was planning something."

"You told me how to get off the balcony," Raven said. Which had saved her life.

Ezra chuckled. "I honestly didn't think you'd have to use it. I was worried. I hadn't slept since the ball, and then my father started this..." He rolled his hand through the air, gesticulating for words he couldn't find. "He has always been hungry for power, but it was like he had started to go mad. He would do anything to gain Regent Dunel's favor, and since Dunel despised the Hawks, and he thought you were involved with the Hawks, he

158

despised you. And you got the better of him, which he couldn't stand, and he had to make it look like he had been taken by surprise."

"I would like to say I planned it all," Raven said, "but I'm not nearly that conniving."

Ezra offered her a small smile that did not reach his eyes. It faded quickly. "It started about seven months ago. Suddenly, my father was agitated, angry, and shouting at everyone. I thought it had something to do with Zander's disappearance. My father was blaming the Hawks for it, saying they had killed him. His obsession with the Hawks grew into something unseemly."

Raven felt the color drain from her face—seven months ago, when Zander had stolen the centrum from the Hawks.

But...how had General Deacon known that? Raven dismissed that worry. She knew only a fraction of what had happened that night.

"Raven?"

She blinked; Ezra and Conrad were both looking at her. Both wore curiosity, though Ezra's mixed with worry, and Conrad's mixed with his special type of madness.

Ezra leaned onto the table. "Did it have something to do with Zander?" he whispered.

"I...don't know." She couldn't tell him about the centrum, and despite her assumptions, she didn't really know—so it wasn't a lie.

Ezra held her gaze for a long heartbeat, then he whispered, "I know about Altair's Augur."

Conrad dropped his fork and spat a curse that fell somewhere between a hiss and a laugh. He bent to retrieve his fork from the floor.

Raven's lack of surprise didn't faze Ezra. He held her gaze, and she knew that he knew.

"The senior staff of the Gray Elite have known about it for a while," Ezra explained. "To the rest of us, it was just a myth. Something to joke about. I started looking into the subject on my own, and I discovered that not only did the thing exist, but the Gray Elite had been actively seeking to rebuild it for years. And then the threats started. The Hawks had rebuilt it and claimed it was functional.

"So, the Hawks who wanted a revolution had Altair's Augur, but the Gray Elite wanted it too. They traded threats back and forth, each a little more menacing than the last. Then, the Hawks threatened to use the augur on the old palace, saying that seeing it in pieces was better than seeing the Gray Elite profane it." Ezra sighed and poured himself another cup of tea.

Raven held her hands under the table to hide how they trembled. She worked hard to keep her face calm.

"Zander was sent by the Hawks to kill my father," Ezra said. He spoke the words evenly, but his eyes told a different story—that his friend had been sent bothered him. "But my father caught him. I was in the next room. I overheard him tell Zander that he would spare him if he brought him the centrum of Altair's Augur." He ran a hand through his hair, leaving it a mess. Even ruffled, he looked regal. "And then Zander vanished."

Ezra's knowing, suspicious gaze fell on Raven. Conrad remained stone still, eyes wide and lips slightly parted—like a child waiting for the next part of the story.

She swallowed. She reached for her tea for something to do with her hands. In her shaky grip, tea sloshed over the sides. She set it down on the saucer with a sharp clank.

The silence thickened, awaiting her addition to the story.

"He stole it," Raven whispered.

Conrad's lips quirked into a pirate's grin. He approved.

Ezra held her gaze. The truth settled, and relief washed over his face. "My father was furious when he heard the news. He threw things, shouted at the servants, and beat one for serving his tea too hot. He took over the search for Zander, claiming it to be out of worry, but I knew the truth. He sent his men all over the country, but no one could find him."

"Both the Hawks and Gray Elite knew that the centrum had been taken," Raven said. To say the word out loud sent a prickle of dread along her skin.

"And the Hawks hired me to fetch it back," Conrad said. Understanding had washed the humor off his face. He knew the true value of what he'd stolen, what he had briefly held. He let out a grievous sigh. "This is why I'm not a fan of the city. So much squabbling and backstabbing."

"You didn't know what it was?" Ezra asked, brow raised.

"No," Conrad said, shaking his head. "The man who hired me gave me a rough description of Zander and of the item I was to retrieve. He conveniently left out his name."

"You didn't find that strange?"

"He offered me a hundred thousand marks, tokens, or piks. Said I could have any currency I wanted," Conrad said. "To a poor man like me, that kind of money could set me up for decades."

"You could have sold it for whatever price you wanted," Raven said.

160

Conrad groaned. "Hindsight has perfect vision, I know."

"Zander didn't tell me until he had to," she said.

"You knew?" Ezra asked, though it didn't come out as a surprise. He motioned to her, and said, "Seems like it's your turn to tell us a story."

The locket around her neck seared against her skin.

"Zander showed up in the village where I grew up." She could still see him, that first time she laid eyes on him: terrified, ragged, a refugee. "He told everyone he had escaped the capital. We welcomed him. We believed his story. He came to hide the centrum, I realize now. Then a thief snuck in while I was on watch." She glanced at Conrad, who wiggled his eyebrows. "And Zander and I went after him. We chased this thief nearly to Lenhala. Zander's brother showed up and took us into the city. We got mixed up in the Hawks and the Gray Elite, and that's when Zander told me about everything."

"Oh, tell the story of how you got sold in Wayward Point." Conrad waved his hands at her.

"You *what*?" Ezra said, frowning.

Raven half laughed. "I was in the woods, avoiding Zander, actually, and this automaton got me. Scavengers found me and sold me as a slave."

"To a fighting arena," Conrad added excitedly. "She turned her opponent to ash."

Ezra didn't look enthused.

Raven shrugged. In a few more breaths, she told him how Conrad had gotten her out. Conrad explained how the Wraiths helped her find a job onboard a small smuggler's ship.

"And then she got sick," Conrad added last.

"Where is the centrum now?" Ezra asked.

Raven paused. She pulled her lip between her teeth and averted her eyes from Ezra. What should she say? Did Ezra know she had given the empty box to his father? Had his father kept it from him?

"I had it," Raven said. The lie came smooth, "I don't anymore. Zander does. He wanted to hide it where no one would find it ever again."

"The bottom of the ocean is a good hiding place," Conrad said matter-of-factly. His tone came light, but his eyes stared hard at Raven. He glanced to the locket—her skin went clammy.

She waited for him to ask, to expose her, but he didn't. He sipped his tea.

Ezra considered her but didn't push the issue. "As long as it stays gone, it doesn't matter where it is." He leaned back and took a sip of tea. "I don't blame Zander for what he did. I would have done the same in his position. No one should have that kind of power. That's why the ancient people dismantled it. If I were regent, I would take the damn thing apart again and destroy the pieces. If the Hawks had their way, they would destroy Moorin. If the Gray Elite had their way, they would destroy Lenhala."

Just like they tried to do with magic, she thought bitterly. Raven pushed her cold eggs around on her plate. So much information to take in at once.

"The best we can do is continue to help magicians out of the Gray Elite's wrath until a better solution is found," said Ezra.

"Or until the world tears itself apart and the little things are no longer problems," Conrad said lightheartedly.

Ezra tipped his tea to Conrad.

Raven stared at her mostly empty plate. All this talk of Hawks and Gray Elites and Altair's Augur and its missing centrum—she thought she left it all behind when she left the Dwellers, but it had found her again.

Considering she held the centrum, she supposed she understood why.

The doors to the lounge opened. From where Raven sat, she couldn't see who had entered. Ezra and Conrad both could. Ezra quickly stood—a nervousness came over his features that made him look like a boy. His cheeks reddened, and his eyes brightened.

"I'm glad you were able to join us," Ezra said.

A sweet-sounding female voice laughed, gentle and beautiful. "You mentioned tea and biscuits. How could I say no to that? Are these your guests?"

Conrad watched the girl with interest, his coal eyes bright as stars.

Raven started to turn her head, but the fourth guest walked around the table and to the last place setting. Ezra eagerly pulled the chair out for her.

"Thank you," said the girl. She sat.

She looked to be around Raven's age, maybe a year or two older. She had olive skin and a healthy amount of weight on her slender frame. Her black hair shone like wet jet. She wore a simple, elegant summer dress of sky blue and yellow. She carried herself with regal intimidation and polite grace, her back straight, her neck poised. Her honey-hazel gaze settled on Raven, as watchful as a hawk's and gentle as a deer's.

Ezra cleared his throat. "This is Raven Thane and Conrad," he said, motioning to them in turn. "Friends of mine."

The girl kept her eyes on Raven.

162

"Raven, Conrad, this is Rosaria Whisehunt, Princess and rightful ruler of Rhynwier."

Raven gawked at Rosaria. *Princess* Rosaria. The very princess that the Dwellers were bent on rescuing, right here, in front of her, only an arm's length away, looking at her.

Rosaria lifted a well-groomed brow. She wore no makeup, though she looked achingly beautiful. Subtle bags darkened the skin under her eyes, the evidence of sleeplessness being her only imperfection.

"Are you all right?" asked Rosaria.

"I'm fine," Raven stammered. "I thought... You're here."

Rosaria blinked; then understanding washed across her face. "Ah, you thought me dead like the rest of the kingdom."

"I thought you imprisoned in the Tombs," Raven admitted.

Rosaria nodded. "I was, or I still am—technically speaking, of course."

Raven glanced around the room. "The Tombs do not uphold the horror the name suggests."

Rosaria smiled. "If only that were true." She glanced at Ezra, and a strange softness came over her face, soothing the subtle emotion that had been there before.

"My home," started Ezra, "like many of the old estates, is connected to a network of tunnels. They were once a way for military leaders to meet in secret, but I have been using them to sneak Rosaria into the estate."

"The estate is much roomier than a cell, and I assure you, the Tombs lives up to its name," Rosaria said, tipping her tea toward Raven.

"Dark, forbidding, and underground?" Conrad asked.

"All three of those," Rosaria said, nodding. A darkness came over her face, though she tried to speak lightly.

Ezra and Rosaria shared a long look, and the same softness came over his face that she wore on hers. Conrad winked at Raven.

"I am no more a prisoner here than I was in Lenhala," Rosaria said. She brought her attention back to Raven. "I am no closer to my throne. I am watched. No matter how many times I tell the Gray Elite I won't ask for the throne if they would just let me out. I'll become a citizen, I've said countless times, but still they refuse. You are from Rhynwier?"

"I am."

"I apologize for being useless and powerless." Rosaria's eyes softened with sadness and regret.

"It's not your fault," Raven said, and she meant it. "You didn't willingly give up your throne. They stole it."

That admission smoothed the crease in Rosaria's brow. "However, my time here and there has given me much time to think on how things should be, how I could change things. The only way from this mess is forward."

"Things change and will always be changing," Ezra said. "Power changes hands. Kingdoms shift, and borders shrink and expand."

"And this war between Gracita and Rhynwier will destroy us both in the end," Rosaria said grimly.

"Rosaria and I share many political views," Ezra said to Raven. "I didn't expect it, and neither did she. We started to talk more and more, and then I started sneaking her upstairs to the estate." He looked almost giddy. "Did Zander tell you about her?"

"Zander?" Rosaria focused on Raven. "Winchester? You know him?"

Raven nodded. "He mentioned you."

Rosaria's eyes brightened. "Is he well?"

Raven bit her lip. "I can't say. He was the last time I saw him." How long ago had that been? Two weeks? Three? "He blames himself for your capture."

The princess's eyes darkened with guilt. She took a deep breath and slumped in her chair. "Sisters...all that seems like ages ago. It wasn't his fault. Or, even if it was, I don't blame him. I convinced him to go out that night because I was feeling stuffy. He didn't want to go, but I talked him into it. I'm to blame, not him."

"Am I the only person who doesn't know this Zander fellow?" Conrad asked, brow cocked.

Raven ignored him and said to Rosaria, "Zander told me you grew up together."

The princess nodded, a faint smile curving her lips. "I grew up thinking my last name was Winchester. I was thirteen when his father told me the truth of my heritage. I went to bed in tears that night, and Zander snuck into my room to tell me that I'd always be his sister, and he would still beat up people for me if I asked him to."

Raven half laughed. That sounded like Zander.

Underneath it, she felt a pinch of jealousy.

"How did the princess end up here, I wonder?" Conrad asked.

"Well, I suppose it started after General Winchester told me who I was. Zander and I got swept away in the Hawks," Rosaria said. "I thought the idea of rebels taking back the city was thrilling at the time. I wanted to be queen as much as any little girl, but as I grew older, I realized that what I imagined was a game of dress up, and that being queen was no game. The Gray Elite caught rumors of my existence, and the Hawks treated me like a glass doll that would shatter if left unattended—it drove me mad. I convinced Zander to sneak out of the house with me, like we used to do before, and...we ended up separated, and I was captured by Gray Elite. They locked me in the palace for a while, and then they sent me to the Tombs several months ago. And now here I am."

Rosaria had a storyteller's smooth voice, one that drew the ear to her words, one that never hurried or hesitated. Even her words were regal, sharpened with cleverness and intelligence, softened with kindness and empathy. Both Ezra and Conrad were listening intently.

"Those were a few hard months for the city," Ezra added. "The Gray Elite and the Hawks were trading punches in broad daylight. Every day, back and forth." He cleared his throat. "But there is something else I wanted to ask you about," he said to Rosaria. "What do you know about magical sickness?"

Rosaria blinked. "Not much. Why? Is someone sick?" She glanced at Conrad, who pointed at Raven. Rosaria's brow furrowed. "You're sick? Magically sick?"

Raven hesitated, lip between her teeth.

Conrad leaned onto the table, and said, "She turned a pirate to ash."

Rosaria's eyes widened. "Ash?"

Raven retold her story to Rosaria, starting with the slavers. She didn't know why she told the princess so much or what compelled her to speak so freely. Conrad and Ezra already knew the story—something in Rosaria's eyes softened at the story and encouraged Raven to continue, no matter how foolish the story made her look. Rosaria listened, and just her expression made Raven feel as though she hadn't done everything wrong, as if the whole mess weren't her fault.

Finished, Raven slumped onto the table and reached for the teapot.

"I haven't heard of anything quite like that," Rosaria said. "I haven't heard of someone catching magic like a cold. Magic is..." She struggled for the right word. "...deeper than that. It's not just in the blood. It's in the spirit, the soul. It is a person."

"I don't understand it either," Raven said. She didn't want to think about the mess she had made: the magic, the fever, the Hawks, the Gray Elite—everything had been turned upside down several times, and now her head hurt when she tried to sort it all out.

166

Rosaria's eyes lingered on Raven. "What do you know of the folklore of magic?"

"Little," Raven admitted. "Only that the Sisters gifted magic to the people of Rhynwier a long time ago."

Rosaria nodded. "I remember hearing the stories from my nurse when I was little. Some scholars thought the Sisters gifted the magic; others thought humans stole it. Either way, it was my ancestors who either accepted the gift or stole it. They used the magic to unite the people and form the Kingdom of Rhynwier, named after Rhyn, the first king. As more children were born with the gift of magic, entire schools were built to teach them about the Sisters and how to use their magic.

"But somewhere, it began to change. Our neighbors did not have our magic, and they grew to hate and fear magicians. To prove that they did not need magic, they developed technology, including Altair's Augur. Altair himself studied magic, intent on learning it. He could not, and it made him bitter. He built the augur to be able to use magic."

At the mention, Raven's skin prickled.

Somewhere deep in her bones, she felt a spike of doubt. The story seemed to be lacking, but because she didn't understand the feeling, she didn't tell Rosaria about it.

"I don't know the stories that well," Rosaria said, her eyes going misty. "The Gray Elite slaughtered the scholars in their takeover, and the few who escaped were hunted down. An older scholar lived at Winchester House, and much of what I know came from him. He died not a month after I learned of my heritage."

Ezra took Rosaria's hand in his own—a small gesture, but it's effect on the princess was immediate. She brightened, smiled, and that softness returned to her features.

Raven understood. Rosaria's parents, the king and queen, had been murdered by the Gray Elite, assassinated. Their servants, the magic scholars, the magicians—anyone with magic had been purged from the city on that day. Books of magic and history had been burned. Entire libraries and schools were destroyed.

"And the Gray Elite did all of that," Raven said, "because they feared magic?"

"Fear gets the best of us," Conrad said. "Even grown, educated men."

"I admit," Ezra said, still holding onto Rosaria's hand, "I fear magic. I used to have nightmares about the Wraiths coming for me; my father told me stories of the assassins, shadow-men, he said. Looking back now, I know he wanted me to be afraid of them, to see the Hawks as monsters to be eradicated. Still, I didn't entirely believe him, then..."

"You mentioned you are on a routine of ruby powder," Rosaria said to Raven, breaking the tension.

She nodded. "It's helping considerably."

"I'm no scholar, but I would like to speak with you after breakfast about this magical fever of yours," said the princess.

"I would have to move around a few appointments, but I'm sure I could make room," Raven said. "Maybe if I move my hour of pacing after my hour of counting the floor tiles, I could make room."

Rosaria smiled. "I will be there."

After they finished breakfast, Raven sat with Rosaria on the floor of her room. The sunlight had broken through the stormy clouds, glowing bright gray and yellow through the balcony doors, brightening the floor around the two girls.

"This is an old trick." Rosaria held her hands between them, palms up. She motioned for Raven to do the same, their fingertips barely touching.

Raven felt a shift, barely there, like someone had opened a window in the room, allowing the air to move in a different direction, only *inside*. Rosaria wore deep concentration, her eyes focused on their hands, on the space between them. After a long moment of silence, Rosaria curled her fingers around Raven's.

The feeling came gradually, a subtle shift within her. It came from somewhere deep. The fever, she realized. It obeyed Rosaria's summons, coming gently toward the surface.

Rosaria's brow creased.

And the feeling subsided. Rosaria released her hands.

"What was that?" Raven asked.

The fever crept back to where it hid underneath the ruby powder.

"I summoned your magic," Rosaria said. At Raven's blank face, she added, "It is an old trick the magicians used to see if children were gifted. The scholars taught it to me when I was young. They knew who I was, even when I didn't. Later, Brigadier General Winchester told me it's part of being royal. He said I should know how to summon forth magic in others."

"You have magic," Raven said.

Rosaria nodded. "It's part of the royal bloodline, I was told. A king or queen is tied to the kingdom in ways we can't understand. We are connected to the magic, somehow. I've always thought that's why the Gray Elite needed me alive, because the kingdom and its magic need me."

"Then..." Raven looked down at her hands. "You summoned magic. From me. That means I do have magic?"

Rosaria nodded. "It is there. It responded, but it's not like magic I've felt before. It's tangled, wild, and...raw. It's not throughout your body; it's clustered. I've not felt anything like it before. It's different. It's..."

"Wrong?" Raven supplied.

"Unnatural," Rosaria whispered.

Raven's heart sank. She didn't see the difference in those words.

"Magic lives within the person, a force that compliments the magician in personality and heart," she explained. "This magic, your magic... It doesn't ebb and flow with you like it should. It's violent, aggressive. Did something happen while you were in Lenhala? Something strange? Did you come into contact with anything odd or unusual?"

If she took the centrum off, would the fever go away?

Rosaria studied her face, her hazel eyes penetrating. She stared, unblinking, for what felt like too long, until Raven thought her heart would burst out of her chest.

"Something did happen," Rosaria said softly, her voice velvet. She tilted her head and blinked once—deliberately. "It isn't just the magic that is tangled. You're tangled. You've been through a lot in a short amount of time. Change is hard on most people, and you've had a large dose."

Raven nodded. "That's an understatement."

"Tell me about it."

"Which part?"

"All of it."

Raven blinked at the princess. "All of it? I don't know where to start."

"The beginning."

Raven swallowed. She didn't even know if she could recount the entire disaster, but she knew where it started.

"I grew up in a small village to the far north of the kingdom," Raven said. "Nothing ever happened. I wanted out. I wanted adventure like those I'd read about. I wanted to see the rest of the world. I feared that I would live out my years in that place and die without ever stepping foot beyond it." She half laughed.

"You are a very long way from there now," Rosaria said, smiling.

"And I often wonder if I will ever see it again."

"Do you have family there?"

"My father and stepmother and my half-sister."

"Do you miss them?"

Raven hesitated to answer, and her own silence surprised her. She did miss them, but she did not miss being in Silver Glen. She wouldn't mind seeing them, if only to visit and then continue her adventure. She nodded. "Yes."

Rosaria's eyes drifted to Raven's throat, to the locket her dress did not hide.

"It was my mother's," Raven said, covering the simple locket with her hand. "It's the only thing I have of hers."

Rosaria gave her a small smile, one that understood loss. "I had hairpins that belonged to my mother. They were in my hair the day my parents were killed. Those hairpins were the only thing I had of that life, but I left them in the Winchester house. Speaking of, how did you and Zander meet?"

At the mention of his name, a different warmth surged under her skin. Raven told Rosaria what she had told Conrad and Ezra, how Zander had ended up in Silver Glen, pretending to be a refugee. "We went after the thief," Raven said, "who ended up being Conrad, but I didn't meet him until later." Raven told Rosaria everything—to get it all off her shoulders felt incredible.

Rosaria said nothing with words or by expression. She simply listened.

"And now all of this is happening," Raven said with a sigh. "Are the Hawks and Gray Elite really trying to start a war?"

Rosaria sighed before she answered. "From what I have gathered, tension is rising steadily on both sides. I'm afraid that a terrifying and costly end may be in sight."

Raven pulled her legs to her chest. War. "I sometimes wish I'd never left home. I wanted adventure, but... Sisters, I don't know much more I can handle."

A soft, motherly smile stretched across the princess's lips. It spoke of a deeper understanding that reminded Raven of her stepmother. "There was a saying inscribed on the wall of the royal library," Rosaria said. "It had always been there, written in the old language. The scholars translated it to say, 'Fate throws us where we need to go, not where we want to go, and sometimes we fail; sometimes we change the world.'"

"The old language?" Raven asked. Like the old god, the one the Gray Elite tried so hard to erase.

Rosaria nodded. Her peaceful expression turned into a grim one. "So much knowledge has been lost over the past one hundred years, and it scares me. How will we ever get it all back?" Her voice thinned. "There are books and scrolls scattered around the kingdom, kept safe by loyalists to the crown, but even if we could take back our kingdom, how would I be able to make that knowledge public again?"

The faint emotions traveled over Rosaria's fine features, fear and uncertainty. Solemn sincerity shaded her eyes. She worried over her kingdom's future, a future that she might not have a part in shaping. Her kingdom—Raven couldn't imagine the guilt she felt.

"Zander worries about you," Raven said, and Rosaria's eyes drifted back to her own. "He blames himself and wants to help you get out of here. He thinks you're being held prisoner."

"I am, but I don't see how freeing me would do anything other than upset the Gray Elite," she said, hugging herself. "And that isn't something the Hawks need to do. And it's not terrible here. I like it better here than in Lenhala."

"Is it because of Ezra?" Raven whispered, mischief on her tongue.

Rosaria smiled, a secret smile. "We have gotten along rather well." A spark appeared behind her eyes. "His visits have made these months in the Tombs much more pleasant and endurable. He sneaks me out like this now and then when his friends in the guard are on duty. That way, I won't be counted as missing."

Friends in the guard. Ezra had people in the Gray Elite, as did his father. The webs grew and grew.

"Do the servants not suspect?"

"Many of them are in the dark, along with the general," Rosaria said. "There are several secret entrances to the tunnels below, and one of them is in my room. That way, I can get out easily should the general or his men make a surprise visit. That hasn't happened, but I like to be prepared."

"Ezra must care about you a great deal to take that risk," Raven said. Should either of them get caught, both would face treason and Sisters knew what else.

Rosaria nodded. "Ezra has the bravery of ten men; he just doesn't know it. Don't tell him, because I don't want him to know. I like him better that way." A blush warmed her cheeks. "And now he's taken you in as a prisoner too. He tells me you're a wanted woman for attempting to assassinate the general. Don't worry, I don't believe a word that comes out of that horrid man's mouth, if he's a man at all and not some demon in human skin. I'll never understand where Ezra came from. But, if it comes down to it, the secret entrance to the tunnels is through the wardrobe in my room. There is a notch in the wood, on the upper right corner. Press it to release the false panel."

Raven quickly committed that to memory. "I hope it doesn't come to that."

"As do I." Rosaria stood and held a hand out for Raven. "Tell me, have you ever played chess?"

"A few times with my sister."

"Are you any good?"

"I can't say. My sister never took the game seriously. She let me win."

Rosaria smiled. "I love the game, but Ezra does the same to me. He lets me win. I know he does it, but still he continues. I have a set in my room. Come, let's play and give each other a real challenge."

Raven walked with the princess toward the doors, going over the rules in her mind. It had been a while since she had played chess, but the idea of not sitting alone in her room, waiting for her next hourly dose of ruby powder, sounded pleasant.

Raven was smoothing the clean linens over the bed when she heard the gentle rustle of a breath. She whirled around; her breath caught in her throat. A figure stood against the twilight of the balcony. The doors stood open, letting in the sprinkle of the fountain down below, the gentle chatter of a garden party an estate away.

The figure leaned casually against the doorframe, his lean body easy and his posture nonthreatening. The glow of twilight hid his face.

"Don't look so surprised, little bird," came Conrad's voice from the figure, and relief spread over her limbs. "There are few places in this city I can't get into. A locked door is no match for me."

"I will send word to the locksmith of his folly." She tossed the sheet over the bed a bit haphazardly. She didn't care if they were tucked in. She preferred them not.

Conrad chuckled and stepped into the room. She could hear the gentle tinkling of the beads in his braids. He shut the balcony doors behind him and locked them.

"Did you go out into the city?" Raven asked.

"I did." He offered no other explanation. "Your balcony was closer, and a few servants were clustered underneath mine. I thought I'd be cautious. Don't want to make the help think I'm breaking in."

"You are, technically."

He shrugged. "Details." He sauntered to the door, then paused. He leaned against the side of it like he had nowhere else in the world to be. The softening twilight glittered against the knives along his torso, attached to a thick leather belt. "It might be in poor taste, but I overheard you and the princess talking."

"Eavesdropping?"

He didn't deny it. "She said your magic was unnatural and clustered."

Raven busied herself with straightening the wrinkles in the sheet.

"Kind of like it's not supposed to be there. Kind of like your body isn't used to it being there, like it was thrust upon your body suddenly." His words were not cold, only curious.

Raven glanced up; Conrad's eyes were pinned on her locket. She put a hand over it, hiding it from his view.

"You have it, don't you?" he asked, his voice low and whispering, threatening but playful. His coal-dark eyes glinted.

She didn't answer.

"It's all right, little bird," Conrad said, pushing off the door. He turned to go. "I'd rather not dive headfirst into a war either. Your secret is safe with me; however," —he paused with his hand on the knob— "what happens when the ruby powder no longer works? Are you going to let it eat you alive until you're nothing but ash?"

"If it keeps the kingdom safe," she said.

"Then they will steal the stone from your ashes," he said darkly.

The sunlight had been fading imperceptibly, growing darker with every passing heartbeat, until she and Conrad stood in darkness. The lights flickered on in the garden, shining blue like light through ice.

She closed her hand around the locket. "Then, I suppose I won't care if there's a war."

He chuckled, his grin turning feline. "If that is the case, I'll take it first and hide it somewhere no man will ever find it."

"Better than Zander did?"

"Oh, much better," Conrad said. "I once visited an island full of lost things. It's where people go to forget things, and once an item is there, anyone looking for it will never be able to find it. However, if one isn't looking for anything, they find everything. Quite a mystery."

Raven had the thought to ask him where this island was but held her tongue. Conrad hesitated a moment more, then left himself into the hallway. His ghost-like footsteps trailed into the hall.

Raven finished making her bed, mind on the centrum and the augur and the island where things could be hidden forever.

It would be better for all if the centrum could be lost forever.

The storm had blown out, and without the clouds, Moorin lay beneath a sky of stars. The lights blanketed all but the brightest, but Thalame could imagine a sea of stars up there. He'd spent enough nights staring at the sky above the treehouse.

Sisters, he wished he was there now, with a cup of berry wine and Ivy's company. Maybe two cups of berry wine. Or three.

Thalame and Zander stood in full Wraith gear on the darkened edge of some fancy house. Engor called them estates, which in his opinion was just a fancy word for house—big houses but houses nonetheless.

The Deacon Estate stood proud among the oldest and grandest estates. It's garden sprawled and ended in an iron-spiked wall. Few rooms in the estate held light, not surprising for this time of night. According to Engor's spies, General Deacon was still in Lenhala. There should be few lights in his house, yet there were four rooms in use—in the guest wing.

Zander couldn't keep still. He clenched and unclenched his fists; he paced; he tapped his feet. Poor bloke. He'd barely said a word since they'd left the Wooden Goblet, other than muttering curses to no one and everyone. Thalame understood without having to touch him. He'd tried to calm the raging emotions, but Zander had shrugged off his hand.

"We don't have to do this," Thalame said quietly.

Zander didn't say anything. He didn't acknowledge that Thalame had spoken. He held his stare on the lit windows of the Deacon Estate.

They had told Engor they would look into Conrad and the girl's disappearance and reappearance at the Deacon Estate. Neither had implied they knew or suspected any more than what Engor did.

"Yes we do," Zander said, almost too quiet to hear. Fury painted his face. "If nothing else, we need answers."

Thalame understood; Zander wanted to know why she had snuck away, where she had gone, and how she ended up in Moorin—with Conrad, of all people. Blasted thief. In Thalame's opinion, the Wraiths should have strung him up as an example to anyone else feeling greedy.

Thalame had his suspicions. Had she found out that Zander wanted to send her home? Wanted to keep her safe at the treehouse? Girls were smart like that. And Conrad—Sisters only knew what that madman was scheming.

"She needs to be held accountable," Zander said. Thalame thought he spoke more to himself than to him. "She needs to explain why she's here, why she's *there*, and smacked for making herself so hard to get to."

Thalame didn't agree with the last one, not entirely. Though the girl had put a wrench in their plans, she'd kickstarted them at the same time. He'd known Zander for a long time. He'd like to think Zander wouldn't actually hurt her, not even after all she'd put him through with her disappearance, but if she had committed treason against the Wraiths? Thalame didn't know if Zander would follow through or not.

"Zander," Thalame said. "Do you think the general's people got to her first?"

"I don't know. It might be another of Conrad's games," Zander spat with distaste. "Malik warned us not to trust a word he said."

Thalame hesitated; he knew what he needed to say, what needed to be said before they set foot on the Deacon Estate. "Zander, if she has spilled any of our secrets, Hawk, Wraith, or Dweller—"

"Then she will receive the punishment fitting of that crime," Zander said, his voice flat, empty, emotionless. He lifted his chin. "The punishment for treason within the Wraiths is death. If she has betrayed us, then she deserves no less."

Thalame held his breath. Zander had wiped the emotion from his voice, his face, locking it up wherever he put it when he didn't want to feel it. His eyes blanked, cold as starlight.

"There's still a chance it's not her," Thalame said.

"I know," Zander said. "But who else could it be?"

"Anyone, really," Thalame said. "Do you want it to be her?"

"Yes and no," Zander said, emotion slipping back into his voice. "I want it to be her because that means she's alive. I don't want it to be her because I might have to kill her for treason."

And if Zander flinched, he would have to kill the girl. He hated the thought of it, but he knew that Zander never flinched, never missed.

And, the girl wasn't their only objective. Engor had given them another, one more pressing. Tonight, the Wraiths launched Project Demo, and everyone had to be on their toes. All across the city, Wraiths waited, prowled like Zander.

All they had to do was wait for the signal, and then the fun would begin. Fun for them, not for the Gray Elite. They would have a long, long night.

Ezra came to fetch Raven for tea. He did not take her to the lounge down the hall, but to another lounge in a different wing of the house. The lounge was larger, the circular table capable of sitting ten. Heavy blue drapes hung on either side of the windows. Sconces brightened the room in shades of pale yellow.

"It has the better view," Ezra explained, motioning to the window.

He was right. From the leaded-glass windows, she could see the sprawling gardens, dark for the night, and in the distance, the glittering heart of Moorin glowed like barely-contained sunlight, pale yellow and blue spilling from every window. The spires and towers looked like something from a dream, whimsical and beautiful and dangerous.

Rosaria already sat at the table, her ankles crossed, her shoulders straight. Even as a prisoner, she sat like a princess. Raven sat beside her and helped herself to a cup of tea—a sweet tea infused with fruit and herbs to rest both body and mind, Rosaria explained.

Ezra cleared his throat—two guards stood on either side of him. Raven blinked; had she walked right past them? She hadn't heard them enter the lounge. Both guards wore a Gray Elite uniform. They stood like soldiers, ready for action, armed with a pistol, a saber, and a crossbow. Neither looked older than Ezra.

"These are two of my trusted men," said Ezra. He introduced Warrant Officer Bertrand, the taller of the two, built like a wall. He had a full but trimmed sandy beard. Next to Bertrand, Warrant Officer James—the other guard—looked small, though he stood as tall as Ezra.

Both men gave respectful bows to Raven.

She stared blankly. Did they not know who she was? Who Rosaria was? Then she remembered Ezra's words. His men. Trusted men. Like the guards who reported Rosaria in her cell when she was not.

"This is Raven," Ezra said, motioning to her. "She is a guest of mine."

"Is it a pleasure to meet you, Miss," said Bertrand, his voice deep and strong.

"A pleasure, indeed," said James, his voice reedy and lyrical.

"Likewise," Raven said.

"Word on the street is I've invited my friends over for tea," Ezra said.

The two guards joined them at the table. Conrad remained absent. Ezra didn't mention him, so neither did Raven. Being the pirate that he was, he had likely gone snooping for loot in the city. With all these towering estates, she doubted he had to look far. Or he might have been busy with Wraith business. And she reminded herself that Conrad's business was his own, not hers.

Bertrand and James shared a casual and respectful greeting with Rosaria—they had met before.

Raven sipped her tea while Ezra told Rosaria about meetings he had attended that afternoon. One had been with Gray Elite; the other, with smugglers. Rosaria listened intently. Bertrand and James had been on patrol that afternoon. Not as exciting as a meeting with magician smugglers.

"Patrol is always boring," Bertrand told Raven. "Reported robberies, fights, drunken brawls, civil complaints, that sort of thing. The automatons handle the dangerous stuff. We get stuck with the paperwork."

James had gone to a suspected home invasion in a wealthier district, though he doubted the homeowner because Slenders had been patrolling, and nothing got past a Slender.

"Some people just crave the attention," said James. "They can't find something; they immediately call the patrol and cry burglary. I told the guy to question anyone else living in the house. He didn't like that suggestion."

"Oh, you mean suggest that they're idiots?" Bertrand said, laughing.

James began to tell another story of his patrol, and Ezra leaned toward Raven. He hid his mouth with his teacup. "You all right?" he whispered.

"Yes," she whispered back, hiding her mouth with her teacup as he did. "Where is our other friend? The one with sticky fingers?"

"He doesn't tell me where he goes," Ezra said. "He's always kept his agenda close to the chest, if he's got one at all. I wouldn't put it past him to make it up as he goes. He comes and goes, and as long as he doesn't cause a stir out there or bring a horde of angry patrollers to my door, I'm content."

The story came to an end, and Bertrand and Rosaria laughed. Ezra smiled, as did Raven, and she found her eyes flickering to the windows to see if a shadowy figure lurked beyond. She admired Conrad, his cunning, his fearlessness, his ambition. Without his assistance, she would still be fighting for her life in that pirate arena. If she hadn't been killed. If she hadn't escaped on her own.

The conversation flitted around with a casualness that Raven hadn't felt in a while. For the past couple weeks, it had been a constant sense of panic, of scheming, of rushing. This newfound peace—she liked it. The ruby powder helped too.

As it turned out, Ezra had an inner circle of Gray Elite like Bertrand and James who reported to him and occasionally brought him magicians or gave him their location. James worked in the emperor's office and gave Ezra access to high-tier reports and files. He had, more than once, hidden reports on magicians or added notes to deter the Gray Elite.

When she had first met Ezra, he hadn't seemed nearly so treasonous. She liked this other side of him. Beneath the regal stance and soldier's smile, he rebelled.

Raven didn't add much to the dwindling conversation. Between the tea and the ruby powder, her thoughts drifted like clouds, pretty and hard to grasp. Her body felt airy, her feelings indifferent.

Ezra and James were discussing a theater uptown that they had been using as a safehouse for magicians when a distant commotion sounded from somewhere in the house, a crash like something had fallen, something heavy.

The lounge fell silent. Ezra stood, as did Bertrand and James, each wearing a soldier's mask—ready for anything. Rosaria tensed.

"What was that?" Bertrand asked.

"I don't know." Ezra pushed his chair out and started toward the door. "I will find out. Escort our guests back to their rooms. Quickly."

Bertrand and James nodded. Ezra left, his steps quick, steady—the march of an officer.

Raven met Rosaria's eyes. Though the princess held herself calm, her eyes gave away her unease, and that unease matched Raven's. Neither knew what had happened. Had a servant dropped something or fallen? She hadn't seen servants, but Ezra had mentioned them, so they must have existed somewhere else in the vast house. Her gut, however, dismissed that logical answer.

Bertrand and James silently escorted Rosaria and Raven out of the lounge. Bertrand walked with Rosaria, and James walked closer to Raven. In the corridor, they headed in opposite directions. Raven glanced over her shoulder at the princess, who walked steady, despite the fear in her eyes. Raven tried to mimic her.

Why would Bertrand lead Rosaria the wrong way? Unless he planned on taking her a different route or, more likely, underground. They would be walking to the closest entrance to the Tunnels and returning her to her cell in the Tombs.

Which meant they suspected something other than a bumbling servant.

Raven's gut twisted—what did they think it was?

James turned through a narrow passage between corridors, a servant's passage, and he hastened down an unlit hall. Raven sped up to walk with him. His nerves did nothing for her own. Thunder boomed, but it sounded off. Too close, contained.

"What's that?" she whispered.

James didn't answer. He gripped the hilt of his saber.

They turned down a corridor that looked familiar. She and Ezra had walked through it on the way to the lounge. Not far from her room, where she could indulge in the sleepiness of the tea for the rest of the night, and—

"What?" James gasped and stopped.

It did not take long for her to see why.

Moonlight and city light glowed through the high windows that lined one side of the corridor, but something was very wrong. Raven stumbled forward as her eyes focused on that wrongness.

Moorin's white-light brightness had changed. During the time it had taken her to leave the lounge and walk into this corridor, dozens of fires raged across the city, red-orange and angry, consuming. She couldn't take her eyes off the flames, bright as daylight, red-hot, deadly. Moorin was burning.

The coolness of the window shocked her—she had unknowingly pressed her hands flat against the leaded glass; her nose was an inch from her wide-eyed reflection. Her breath fogged the glass.

"Miss?" came James's quiet command, an order, not a question.

She stepped back from the window, her breath a heartbeat behind. The fires had grown bigger, their plumes of black and gray smoke billowing out of control toward the stars. As they stood there, another burst of light came from another part of the city. The sound of it reached them seconds later—like contained thunder.

"An explosion," James breathed. "Sisters."

Sirens began to wail, a thousand undulating screams. Raven could almost hear the muffled screams of thousands and thousands of people, waking from their sleep to panic and chaos. She could imagine it, people rushing into the streets in their night clothes, unsure what to make of the smoke and fire, only to be rocked by another explosion, sending fear rushing as high as the smoke.

She gasped, feeling a mimicry of that fear.

Panic, fear, rage—it lined the smoky air, rising with the plumes, staining the night sky in shades of black, gray, and red, blanketing even the brightest of stars.

James's eyes searched the horizon. He spat a curse as realization turned his uncertainty into rage. "Sisters. Those are the patrol stations. The locations are right for them. They've blown them up!"

"But who would—" She stopped herself from finishing the question. She knew exactly who. The Wraiths. "Why would they do this?" Didn't they know how many innocent people would be caught in the middle?

"Revenge," James answered grimly.

She shook her head in disbelief.

"I know, but I will say this for the Wraiths. They're not careless. If I had to guess, they evacuated the homes around the explosions. I've heard they go in and tell the people to get out, and if they listen, they live, but if they refuse and remain, well then, Sisters had better be watching over them."

It made her feel only a little better.

"We need to move." James put his hand on her shoulder, guiding her away from the window. She allowed it. He was right.

She tore her attention from the burning city. The corridor had darkened. The tint of the flames and smoke dimmed the light, turning it smoky. With every step she took toward the other end, the smoky light dimmed; the corridor darkened.

And darkened.

And—*wrong*, something inside her screamed.

Raven looked to the high windows; they had gone dark, blackish. She couldn't see the fires or smoke or anything—a blackout. Her panic surged, and her heart raced, threatening to jump up her throat and out of her body.

James pulled his saber free. "What's this?" he gasped. He maintained a fierce countenance, but his voice shook.

Raven felt something, but her thoughts hit a wall. Blurred. She knew...something, had felt something before. Had she forgotten it? Something important. Something... It was an infuriating feeling. Had the ruby powder affected her memory?

And then, within the dimmed light, shadows jumped from the ceiling. Quiet and nimble as ghosts. One landed behind James; the other landed in front of Raven, blocking her view. It took less than a heartbeat for the shadow to become a figure. Dark robes and leathers and dark steel plating. They were Wraiths.

Wraiths. Her heart skipped a beat. The Wraith in front of her held his ground; he had his gloved fingers wrapped around the hilts of two daggers at his waist. James let out a war cry—and was abruptly silenced. He fell to the ground, blood seeping from a wound on his throat. His eyes went dark.

Dead.

And, like that, she stood between two masked Wraiths. James's killer advanced a step toward them but hesitated. James's killer wore a dark silver mask; the other wore a mask of dulled copper.

Raven trembled. They had been sent for her, hadn't they? They knew that she had gone to Ezra, and here they were, hunting her down. She had become a traitor, and these Wraiths had come to kill her for it.

She fumbled a step back. The Wraith in front of her didn't move; the second Wraith took another step closer.

She turned and ran. The closer Wraith grabbed her arm. She didn't hesitate; she balled her fist and slammed her knuckles into the Wraith's jaw. Her knuckles hit the edge of the copper mask, but she didn't feel the pain.

The Wraith spat a colorful curse, and his grip loosened. She yanked her hand out of his and ran.

She made it to the door—her fingertips brushed the handle.

Faster than lightning, tendrils of shadows slithered up from the floor and down from the ceiling, locking together like teeth across the door, locking her in. She wrenched her hand from the handle before the shadows covered it. She stumbled back but hadn't anywhere to go—black and blue shadows crawled up the walls faster than she could blink, slithering and converging. They surged underneath her, and all in the matter of a few seconds, the shadows submerged her, the corridor—everything. She stood encased in a tunnel—with the Wraith.

He stood at the other end of the shadow tomb. The shadows moved like light through water, constant and beautifully deadly, alternating shades of deepest black, blue, and gray.

Shadows, these shadows—she had seen them before. They had entered her dreams, haunted her for hours after waking.

And the mask, the copper mask.

The Revenant.

He stalked toward her with the grace of a seasoned killer, a predator ready to tear her throat out. Raven scrambled back until her back hit the smooth wall of the shadows. The shadows gave a little with her weight but held. She could feel the shadows moving, undulating, slithering, an oddly sizzling texture—magic, she realized. Powerful magic.

He came at her. She screamed but it did little; the sound itself seemed to be trapped inside with them, muffled and distant. She tried to strike him again, but he caught her wrist. In a few quick moves, he pinned her to the ground. He held her wrists on either side of her head, opening his robes and exposing his middle; daggers lined the leather belts strapped around his torso. He hadn't pulled any of them.

She squeezed her eyes shut. No. No. No. A gasp escaped her throat. A feeble plea for her life. She felt tears of panic and fear push against her eyes. If he hadn't drawn a knife, how did he plan on ending her? Crush her throat with his bare hands? Craft a dagger out of shadow? Force his shadows down her throat and tear her apart from the inside?

She shuddered. She tried to pull herself out of his grip, out from underneath him, but he wouldn't budge.

She stopped struggling.

The shadows made the smallest of sounds, like the muffled chitter of a thousand cicadas underwater. Was that what the underworld sounded like?

And breathing. Soft, agitated breath hitting the other side of the Revenant's mask.

Raven opened her eyes. The Revenant had lowered his head until he hovered a hand above hers. His copper mask had been carved with lines that curved around each other, never meeting, never crossing. It looked like a design from the Temple of the Three Sisters.

She slid her gaze along the copper and into the eyes of her killer, the only part of him visible. The Revenant met her gaze. He had sapphire eyes—her breath caught in her throat. Her heart skipped too many beats. Everything stopped.

She knew those eyes. She would know them anywhere.

Her breath tumbled out in a gasp, "Zander?" Her voice choked on the tears she had yet to cry.

He shuddered. Hot breath hit the other side of his mask. The shudder traveled down his arms and into her wrists, down his torso and into his legs.

"Zander," she repeated, a little louder. It was him. Zander had been sent to kill her by the Wraiths; Zander was the Revenant.

Zander's sapphire eyes searched hers, wide and disbelieving, caught between regret and relief. She couldn't hold it back. Her chest heaved, and tears began to fall—her fear and panic got the better of her.

He shuddered again, his breath heaving. He gasped—the shadows around him faltered, loosening their seams. Raven glimpsed the white of the walls between the tendrils. The second Wraith stood in the corridor, waiting. He made no move to intervene.

Zander shifted, releasing her arms, but he did not get up. He leaned forward onto his hands, one hand on either side of her head. His breaths came out strained, pained. It mirrored in his eyes.

Raven lifted her shaking hands to his mask. Her fingertips grazed the smooth metal, along the cheekbones, the carved edges, and to where it tied around his head. She pulled the leather ties and lifted the mask off his face.

Zander's bronze skin had gotten a few shades darker since she had last seen him. He had pulled the top half of his hair back, and the bottom half had grown out. She clutched his mask to her chest; the emotion in his eyes shifted to something she hadn't seen on him before—regret and joy mixed together.

She found the same emotions tangling inside of her. Joy at seeing Zander again, regret because of what she had likely caused.

"What are you doing here?" Zander whispered, his voice shaky, not at all like the arrogant cadence she remembered. He blinked; wetness smeared across his eyes, glistening along his lashes. "What did you tell them? How could you turn on us? Don't you realize what this means? The Wraiths think you've betrayed them to the Gray Elite, Raven." His voice shook on her name. "The punishment for betrayal is death."

He *had* come to kill her. On the Wraiths' orders. She had suspected it, but hearing his admission tore through her.

"Is that why you're here?" Her voice came out just as weak as his. She couldn't take her eyes off his. If she blinked, would he finish the job? All that time thinking she would never see him again. Even after all this time, her heart still jumped when he looked at her. "To finally be rid of me?"

Zander choked on a gasp.

He had. He had come here to kill her, nothing more. Suddenly, the relief at his presence and the fear at his magic turned to fiery rage. She gripped the mask hard enough that it shook; her knuckles turned white.

"That's what you came for?" she asked. "To get rid of me? Fine. Do it."

His eyes widened.

"Then you won't have to worry about me being a *hindrance* in all your plans."

"Raven—"

"You just want me gone!" She thrust the mask up and smacked it against his chest.

He yelped as the air rushed out of his lungs, but didn't relent.

She beat it against him. "You were going to leave me behind! You wanted to send me back to Silver Glen!" Tears started to roll down her cheeks. Furious that he had both caused her to cry and witnessed it, she beat the mask against him harder.

He didn't move.

"You didn't want me there. I was just a problem, a hindrance, an obstacle. A means! All you cared about was yourself and your princess, and she's not even in trouble!"

His brows came together at those words. Of course he would want to hear about Rosaria, his princess. All about his princess.

She beat the mask against his chest one last time and then threw it. It hit something, but she didn't look. The words had left her hollow. All her rage, gone. Ashes. She wiped the tears from her face.

Zander parted his lips, but rather than speaking, he winced. His shadows sputtered. He let out a gasp of a grunt, slumped onto one elbow, and the magic around them dissolved. His hot breath hit her ear, gasping.

"Raven—"

Raven put her hand on his shoulder, then shoved him hard. He fell off her and onto the floor, and she rose to her feet. She straightened her dress and smoothed her skirt while he fumbled to his feet.

The other Wraith leaned against the wall, his arms crossed. Another boy stood by him, wearing dark robes and leathers, not that much different from the Wraith's wear Zander wore. It took Raven a moment to realize that this third Wraith did not wear a mask; it was Conrad. At the sight of his familiar face, relief spread through her limbs. His braids were tucked underneath his hood, but his eyes shone with his casual mischief.

He looked very much like the stranger she had met at the arena.

Zander grumbled a curse under his breath while glaring at her and rubbing his chest. He took a shaky step, and as his eyes slid to the windows, exhaustion wiped any other emotion from his face. His magic, the rune—it took a heartbeat for Raven to realize he had used his magic, and the rune on his back likely burned. His steps evened out with each one he took, and he grabbed his copper mask from the floor.

The other Wraith laughed—she knew that laugh. Through the dark mask, familiar eyes met hers. Thalame.

"Long time, no see," said Thalame, his voice muffled by the mask. "Glad to see you're not automaton chum."

"Who're you?" Zander spat, pointing at Conrad with his mask. He swiftly attached it to his shoulder so that the face looked at Raven.

"Zander, this is Conrad," Thalame said before Raven could speak. "Conrad, this is Zander."

"Oh," Conrad said in exaggerated understanding, his eyes wider than they should have been. He looked Zander up and down. "You're the one everyone keeps talking about. Yes, you do look familiar. Hmm?" He tilted his head at Zander, studying him. "That is an interesting mask. I haven't seen many quite that color."

Zander shifted his shoulder. "And I'd prefer it stay that way," he said lowly.

"Gotcha," said Conrad, winking at Zander. "Wraith's honor or something like that, right?"

Conrad glanced at Raven, and something like sympathy and curiosity shone in his eyes. Zander glanced between the two of them, a crease between his brows. Raven saw the assumption in his eyes, and she made no assertion to correct him. Let him think whatever he wanted.

A beat of silence, and then Zander spat at Conrad, "What are you doing here? I didn't think you were a Wraith anymore."

Raven frowned at the bitterness in his tone, but Conrad let the comment roll off his shoulders. He sauntered a step forward. "I would love to stand here and trade insults, but we don't have that kind of time. The Gray Elite are searching the house."

Raven tensed; Zander spat a curse. Thalame didn't look surprised. Conrad must have already told him.

"And we need to get out before they find us," added Thalame. He closed the space between him and Raven and pulled a dagger from his side—he pressed the blade against Raven's throat.

Zander balled his fists and stared at the blade. Conrad scowled. Neither moved.

Thalame met her eye with a grim seriousness. "Have you betrayed us?"

"No," she said. As she spoke, her skin graced the sharp edge of the blade.

Thalame's expression didn't change. "Yet we find you here, a guest in the enemy's house, wearing clothes of the enemy."

"Ezra isn't the enemy," she said.

Thalame's eyes narrowed.

"I didn't tell him anything he didn't already know."

The dagger at her throat didn't scare her, though she knew it should have. Thalame's empty stare did. She turned her eyes to Zander, whose skin had turned a shade ashen.

"He knows more than you think he does," she said. "The Hawks, the Wraiths, the magicians. But he's not your enemy."

Conrad sighed dramatically. "She's right, but let's do this later. Like I said, we don't have—"

A blast shook the floor, the walls, and rattled the windows. A flurry of voices followed, shouting orders; booted feet thundered on the tile, then the carpet. They were on the floor below them.

"—time," Conrad added.

Thalame spat a colorful curse and pulled the blade away from Raven's throat. With deft fingers, the blade vanished back into its sheath.

"This way's a dead end," Zander spat, pointing to the end of the corridor where Raven had come from. "We'll have to hide and wait it out or fight."

"Neither of those sound promising," said Thalame.

Conrad glanced at Raven with a knowing glance. His eyebrows wiggled.

Her thoughts clicked together.

"Rosaria's room," Raven breathed.

All eyes turned to her. At the sound of the princess's name, Zander's eyes focused hard, and her anger flared. Ignoring it as best she could, she started toward the other end of the corridor, toward Rosaria's room.

Raven said calmly, "There's a passage that leads underground."

She walked down the corridor, Conrad on her heels. Thalame and Zander followed. Conrad fell into step beside her and slipped her an encouraging smirk. It annoyed her at first, but then she realized he had armed himself. She had nothing, only her ebony dagger, but she would fumble before she could get to it. If a Gray Elite squadron surprised them, she would need his daggers and his skill.

Raven led them to Rosaria's room, just a door down from her own. By the sounds, the Gray Elite had started their search of the floor. Her heart thumped like a drum, so loud she knew everyone had to hear it.

Rosaria's room was dark, though the blaze of Moorin glowed behind the gossamer curtains. It cast the room in a ghostly light. The room didn't look in use, aside from a few books stacked on the desk and the lingering perfume in the air.

Raven walked straight to the wardrobe, a carved masterpiece of oak. Little moons had been carved along the doors, repeating the moon's phases over and over. Raven pulled open the doors and pushed aside the simple linen and day dresses. She ran her hand along the upper right side until she found the notch; she pressed it. A series of clicks sounded from within the wall, gears connecting and turning, a belt clicking, unlocking—the back panel of the wardrobe swung out like a door to reveal a spiraling stone staircase. Pale orange lights hung from the walls in wide intervals, just enough to illuminate the edges of the steps.

"Would you look at that," came Thalame's nonplussed tone behind her.

Raven started to go first, but then Conrad set a hand on her elbow.

"Allow me," Conrad said, gently pulling her aside and stepping into the wardrobe, "considering I am armed and you are not."

She didn't argue. Conrad started down first, Thalame followed, and Raven moved next. She didn't want to have to stare at the back of Zander's head. His sure footsteps came after her, and she heard the panel slide close with the same clicking gears.

The pitiful light from above diminished with each click until the light from Rosaria's room vanished. She trailed one hand along the stone wall and held her dress away from her feet with the other; she did not want to trip. Zander walked a step behind her, closer than she thought he ought to, but she didn't complain. She wouldn't give him the satisfaction.

Several long moments passed in silence. The sounds of the Gray Elite faded; the sound of the chaos and fires diminished. A stale, muffled silence replaced it. Raven knew the feeling well—underground. She had lived seventeen years underground.

It didn't have the sense of comfort she thought it might. Instead, it felt stifling.

At last, they reached the end of the spiraling stairs. A hallway stretched out before them. Other tunnels connected to the hall, archways leading into near complete shadow. The lights buzzed, a muffled chittering that put Raven on edge. The pale orange lights left generous shadows between them.

Conrad paused at the bottom and gave her a smirk.

"Do you think Ezra made it out?" she asked.

"He has rank in the Gray Elite," Conrad said. "They wouldn't kill him on sight, especially in his own house like some common criminal. He is well liked by the people, and his murder would cause quite the stir."

"Why would the Gray Elite storm the estate?" Zander asked.

Conrad shrugged, gesturing to Raven and himself. "You knew we were there. It wouldn't be a stretch to assume Gray Elite spies figured it out or suspected it."

"They were looking for us?" Raven asked, voice dry.

"Most likely, they were looking for *you*," Conrad corrected.

Because of the centrum. She fought the urge to reach for the locket. She caught Zander's eye and turned her gaze away before he could say something, either out loud or silently.

That meant that if anything happened to Ezra, it would be her fault. Her fault for leading the Gray Elite to his door. Would General Deacon charge his own son with treason? She would like to think he wouldn't, but she remembered the coldness in his eyes when he had taken the iron box from her, like nothing else in the world mattered.

"Where are we?" Thalame asked, running his hand along the stone wall. "Please tell me it's not the sewer."

"Tunnels that run underneath the city," Conrad said. "They connect the upper crust Gray Elite to the secret places they feel the need to know about without the public knowing about them."

Zander grunted, a scowl on his face. The tunnels under Moorin likely reminded him of the sewers under Lenhala the Hawks had used. These smelled better, at least.

Thalame set his gaze on Raven. "You said Rosaria was in the house."

"She has a cell in the Tombs, but she goes up to the house," Raven said. Zander started to speak, but she added bitterly, "Yes, the tunnels lead into the Tombs."

Zander's lips came together. He looked like he wanted to say something else, but didn't. He swallowed. "Do you know the way?"

She shook her head.

"I do," Conrad said casually.

Raven raised a brow at him. He shrugged. Of course, being a pirate and a thief and a Wraith, she shouldn't be surprised that Conrad knew his way around the secret tunnels of Moorin or how to get to the high security prison.

"Why? Do you need to find a cozy cell for yourself?" Conrad asked Zander.

"We volunteered for the route that goes through the Tombs," Thalame said.

"Oh, risky," Conrad said.

"Volunteered for what?" Raven asked.

"Project Demo," Zander said, meeting her eye. "The Wraiths' plan to destroy an automaton factory, and—"

"I've heard about it," Raven interrupted.

Zander's lips pursed before he continued, "We volunteered for the route that goes through the Tombs. We had planned to go in through the entrance a few blocks from here after we'd dealt with you."

"Our plan was to rescue Rosaria and do our part for the Wraiths in one go," said Thalame.

"Ah," Conrad said. "Interestingly enough, we have similar goals. This way. Don't dally."

Conrad started down the long hall without further explanation. Raven started after him. Zander fell into step beside her, and Thalame a step behind. She didn't look at Zander. She didn't acknowledge his presence. They followed Conrad in silence down a side passage, down a flight of stone stairs, and into a long hall that looked similar to the other, except the lights had a yellowish cast, not orange.

No one said a word. Raven suspected that, like her, they were listening for footsteps. These tunnels would not be an ideal place to be ambushed by Gray Elite.

They came at last to the end. A picture of a dreary old general on a fat automaton horse had been mounted on the stone wall. Beside it, an iron panel held a lever. Conrad closed his fingers around the lever and pulled it down. A series of clicks and clanks sounded behind the painting, gears and cogs and belts churning to life. The painting swung inward.

Another secret door. How many more existed within the city?

The painting opened into a broom closet. A globe hung from the ceiling, sputtering pale yellow light over stacks of barrels, dusty crates, broken picture frames, toolboxes, brooms, and mops. A single door stood on the other side, made of plain iron.

Conrad walked toward it. He turned sideways and put his finger to his lips. He pressed his ear against the seam. He listened, an intensity took over his eyes, and then he stepped back and pulled the door open.

Artificial light flooded through the doorway, enough that Raven shielded her eyes. It took a few heartbeats for her eyes to adjust to the light. Blinking, she saw Conrad step through, followed by Zander. Thalame motioned for her to go next, and she did. Wraiths on all sides.

They stood in a hallway. The walls and ceiling were stone, painted white. One wall held nothing but stone. The other held equally spaced iron-barred doors. Pipes ran along the ceiling: some went to the lights; others never stopped. The lights buzzed incessantly. The gentle rumble of human moans and whispers gave Raven a chill. It smelled stale, unwashed bodies and sterile cleaning solution and starched linens.

A prison. The Tombs.

No sooner had the thought crossed her mind than a voice asked, "Raven?"

In the cell closest to the secret entrance, an olive skinned girl with dark hair appeared between the iron bars. Rosaria still wore her simple dress. Behind her, the commodities of her cell were above the average prisoner. She had a real bed, not a prison cot like the empty cell next to hers, and a red and gold rug on which sat a little table. A teapot sat there, a thin line of steam twisting into the air. A folding screen shielded a toilet and sink, decorated with an ocean scene, complete with pirate ships and sea dragons. A bookshelf stood just out of view, thick with colorful spines. A cushy chair sat beside it.

"Is something wrong?" Rosaria whispered. "What happened?"

"The Gray Elite stormed the house," Raven said. "We just barely made it out, thanks to you."

Rosaria gave her a small smile. Then her gaze slid from Raven to the three Wraiths. Her smile fell into a frown, and she took a step back from the door.

Zander appeared beside Raven at the door. "Ros? You're okay?"

Rosaria looked him up and down and studied his face. That she hadn't recognized him immediately gave Raven a burst of sadistic enjoyment. Rosaria's eyes widened. "Zander," she said in disbelief. "I'm fine, but what are you doing here?"

"We came to get you out," he said like it was obvious. He looked down at the sturdy iron lock. "Stand back." He stepped back and readied his hips; he would kick the lock.

"Don't," Rosaria warned. She rushed to the door and slapped her hand over the lock.

Zander gaped at her.

"A guard patrol will come through at any time to check on the prisoners, and if they see me gone or the door broken, they will sound the alarm. Something has happened up top, and it won't be the same guard as normal. The Tombs have a very strict kill-on-sight policy when it comes to prison breaks."

Raven caught her meaning—it wouldn't be Ezra's men coming to check on her.

Zander wanted to argue, but he gave in. "Fine, but I'm coming back for you. I promise."

Rosaria held his gaze, nodding.

Footsteps sounded from the far end—boots.

"That's the patrol," Rosaria whispered. "You need to go."

Zander hesitated.

"Go," she insisted. "I'll be fine. They have orders not to harm me."

The patrol came closer. By the muttering, they were not happy. Thalame put his hand on Zander's shoulder and guided him away. They skirted the end of the cellblock as the patrol came around the other.

"We're on the south end of the Tombs," Thalame said, urgency on every word. "We need to get to the north end with as little fuss as possible."

Zander's gaze settled on Raven, and she bristled—as if she would be the one to cause the fuss. She met his stare and glared back, daring him to say something. He didn't.

They started north. The prison was a grid pattern, long corridors of cellblocks, halls on either side, and meandering patrols. Sneaking past the patrols was easier than Raven thought it would be. With the panic stirred by the unknown chaos above, four extra sets of footsteps didn't stand out.

By the muttering she heard from the patrols, they were performing a routine inspection as per protocol during an emergency. They had to make sure all prisoners were where they were supposed to be. Rosaria had been right. If she had been discovered as missing, an alarm would have been raised. Sneaking would not have been an option.

They made it through twenty corridors without a problem. On the twenty-first corridor, as Raven sprinted across the corridor, a Gray Elite patrolman turned the far corner.

"What's that?" the patrol spat. He stomped down the corridor.

Zander cursed under his breath.

Conrad stood on the other side of the cellblock—if he crossed, the patrolman would see him.

"Show yourself," spat the Gray Elite. Several more boots joined the first. A gun cocked. A saber unsheathed. "This is your only warning before we fire."

Conrad met Raven's gaze, then winked. A mischievous smile stretched across his lips. He started to move, and once she realized his intention, her heart jumped into her throat. She started to protest, but Zander pulled her back.

Conrad leaned out from the corner. "Who? Me?" he asked innocently, pointing to himself.

"Stop!" The patrol ran toward him.

Laughing, Conrad ran back the other way, leading the patrol south.

Zander grabbed Raven's arm and yanked her north. She watched the patrol dash around the corner without looking at them. They chased Conrad down another cellblock.

Raven sucked in her breath. Conrad had bought them time.

"Come on," Zander said, pulling her forward. "Make it worth it."

Gunshots echoed down the corridor, and her chest tightened. She quickened her pace, following Thalame. With the distraction that Conrad had started, the patrols ran toward him, toward the south end, leaving the path to the north end clear.

A second gunshot, then a third. She didn't look back.

38

Thalame, Zander, and Raven paused for breath at the north end of the Tombs. Like the south end, it ended at a stone wall, painted a sterile white. Thalame started along the wall, and Raven followed. Her entire body shook. Her breath came in gasps. Her heart felt as though it had crumpled.

"He'll be fine," Zander whispered. He walked behind her. "He's survived our attempts to kill him; he'll survive a horde of Gray Elite."

Horde. She didn't like that word. The gunfire had stopped. She desperately wanted to believe Zander, believe that the silence wasn't because the target had been hit, but because the target had vanished.

Conrad had bought them time by luring the patrols away from them and where they needed to go. He had used himself as bait. If something happened to him...she couldn't take it. He had done so much to help her. If it hadn't been for him, she would have died long ago, either from being beaten to death in the arena or burning alive in her sleep.

Thalame led them into a workroom. An iron grate floor hid a mess of pipes and pumps, all hissing and gurgling. Pipes jutted up through the grate, dividing the room into sections, and joined pipes on the ceiling. Some pipes vanished into tanks and pumps as large as small houses; others vanished into the stone walls. The entire room rumbled, the sound blanketing their footsteps.

On the far side of the workroom, a worker stood with his back to them, watching a dashboard of dials and gauges. Thalame snuck up behind the worker, and in a blink, he had the man on the floor, unconscious. Thalame then led them to the far side of the room, to a series of four giant tanks behind a web of pipes. The smallest pipes were no bigger than her arm; the largest looked big enough for her to stand in.

"This is our way in." Thalame started to climb the web of pipes, moving quickly and efficiently, reminding Raven of a spider. He climbed to the top of the pipes and dropped onto the farthest tank.

"Through a pipe?" Raven asked.

"Yes," Zander said, jumping onto the pipes. He started to climb.

Thalame twisted the hatch on the tank, pulled it open, and dropped down inside. Raven sucked in her breath as he vanished. No splash followed.

"It's empty," Zander said, looking down at her. "The Wraiths were thorough in their planning. Come on."

Raven hesitated.

Zander raised a brow. "Unless you'd rather stay here and wait for someone to come by and ask why you're here?" The cadence of his voice, playful and arrogant, reminded her of Silver Glen, back when the world was wide and full of adventure, not ravaging fever magic and automatons. Zander's lips twitched into a smirk, curious and watchful.

She bit back an insult and started up the pipes—a feat in a dress. She climbed slow, and Zander matched her pace. He made it to the top a hand before she did.

Raven dropped onto the tank and glanced into the dark inside.

"Thalame's fine." Zander crouched by the hatch and jumped down. His boots landed on the bottom of the tank. He looked up at her, his sapphire eyes catching the light, as did the copper mask on his shoulder. "I'll catch you." He lifted his arms and motioned for her.

His words hit something deep, but she pushed it back down. Not now. Instead, she gathered her blue skirts, inhaled, and jumped. For a thrilling heartbeat, she felt nothing but air. Then Zander's strong hands caught her waist, softening her landing. For a moment, they stood so close, she could smell the sweat and leather and the sour scent of ale on his breath. She met his sapphire eyes, and the trembling in her stomach settled.

Crack—a glow appeared in Thalame's hands, glinting off the metals scattered Zander's torso. Raven jumped out of Zander's hands, breaking the small moment. She smoothed her skirt and cleared her throat. Thalame held a small clear cylinder with brass-capped ends. Inside, blue-green smoke swirled, glowing bright enough to see by.

"A new trick of Niall's," Thalame explained, twirling the cylinder through his fingers. "It's a reaction of something to something else. Don't ask me questions about it; I don't know the answers."

The blue-green glow illuminated the rusty inside of the water tank. Hundreds of pipes led off it. Thalame started toward the largest of the pipes, just wide enough for him to crouch inside it. The light moved with him, leaving the big tank in an inching darkness.

"We're crawling through that?" Raven asked, her distaste echoing off the tank.

Thalame chuckled but kept going. "It's not so bad." The pipe dampened his voice.

"Easy for you," Raven said, motioning at her skirts. "You're not wearing a dress."

"You're welcome to take it off," Zander said, smile stretching his lips.

At the sight of it, she realized how long it had been since she had seen it. Something tight loosened in her chest, and it was just like old times. "I wouldn't want to distract you," she said, gathering her skirts in preparation to follow Thalame and the fading light. "You need all the focus you can get."

Thalame laughed; Zander gave her a smirk.

She crouched into the pipe, her hair brushing the top. Zander crouched behind her. She moved slower than Thalame, but he didn't comment on it.

"You're helping them blow up the factory?" Raven whispered as casually as she could.

"Yeah," Zander said. "It's part of the oath we swore when we became Wraiths. We have to help each other against those who oppose magic, and help our fellow Wraiths. It's not worded like that, but that's the point. And, when we saw that one of the routes into the factory went through the Tombs, we took it without question."

"The Wraiths aren't going to help you rescue her?"

"We didn't mention it," Zander said. "The fewer who know, the better."

"Most people here don't know she's alive," added Thalame, "including most of the Gray Elite and the Wraiths."

Zander knew she lived because of the Hawks, and because he had grown up with her. Because he'd gotten her kidnapped.

"And it just happened that the Deacon Estate was on the way to the entrance of the Tombs," Zander added, his voice light but underlined with something darker.

"The Wraiths are concerned about Conrad and the sick girl vanishing," Thalame said. "We didn't ask, but we thought old Engor might be talking about you."

"We asked what she looked like," Zander said. She heard the desperation in his voice. "Description fit."

"And besides that, Conrad had been seen consorting with Ezra, a Gray Elite, and they assumed treason," Thalame said. "We were to investigate that too."

"Did you try to kill him too?" Raven asked, failing to hide the bitterness.

196

"Yes," said Thalame, a half laugh on the word. "But he caught on, told me the Gray Elite were coming and we needed to get out if we wanted to finish Project Demo without being dead."

"Rae," Zander asked, her name a breath. "What happened?"

"That's really too long of a story to explain in this setting," Raven said. "If we survive, I'll tell you about it."

"Okay." He started to say something else but stopped. He cleared his throat. "You met Rosaria?"

"I did," Raven said. "She's nice. I like her. Ezra has taken care of her since she's been here. I think they like each other."

Zander scoffed.

"What?" she asked. Did he not believe her? That old feeling burned through her chest, but she pushed it down. "Oh? Jealous that Ezra's been taking all her time?" It came out more bitter than she intended.

"No, I'm not jealous," Zander said quickly. A beat passed before he added, "Ezra is like a cousin to me. Why would I be upset that he wants to spend time with other people? I'd rather know more about you and Conrad. You two seem to be getting along."

His words were strained, and it brought a shameless smile to her face. Thankfully, he couldn't see it.

The pipe widened and ended at another tank similar to the other, ending their conversation. Raven straightened and stretched the tension out of her back and legs. Behind her, Zander did the same. Water lingered in the bottom, evidence that the tanks hadn't been emptied that long ago. It would seem the Wraiths had people on the inside, either to inform them when pipes would go dry or to make sure the pipes dried. Thalame stuck the glowing glass between his teeth and climbed up to the hatch. He hung off the sides like a spider and worked to open the hatch.

Zander stepped close to her, close enough that his breath warmed her cheek. He whispered, low enough for Thalame not to hear, "It's not like that between me and Ros. I'm not... She's not you." His voice came out husky and raw, and it sent a warm tingle up her spine.

She dared a glance at him; his eyes were soft, nothing like the killer's eyes she had looked into at the estate.

"Ros's like my sister," he said.

Thalame opened the hatch, bathing them all in in dull, artificial light. The sudden brightness startled her. Taking advantage of it, Zander leaned in and planted a kiss on Raven's cheek and then jumped up to follow Thalame out of the tank. For a moment, she stood alone in the tank's shadows. The kiss had turned her bones to lead, her blood to fire, and kindled the fever the ruby powder had dampened. Her mind replayed his words over and over until they sounded nothing like him and she doubted he had even said them.

Then Zander appeared in the hatch. He reached his hand down for her. Raven jumped and latched onto his hand, and he heaved her out. They were in a workroom similar to the one in the prison, only smaller. Tanks and pipes gurgled, hissed, and steamed, pumping water through and taking it back. In a short few heartbeats, Thalame and Zander knocked out the two workers, and hauled their unconscious bodies near the tank. Out of sight.

"Okay." Thalame threw his glowing glass back into the empty tank, where it smashed against the bottom. The smoky insides let out a sigh of release, then fell silent. "Here's the plan. We're making our way into the factory's basement. From there, we plant explosives—" he patted a small canvas bag hidden under his cloak "—set the timer, and get out as fast as we can. With luck, we can be on the surface with Rosaria before these things blow."

"We were all given a portion of compact explosive powder," Zander explained to Raven. "We set the timer for two hours. If all goes well, all the Wraiths will have planted theirs, and by the time they go off, we'll all be clear."

"What about anyone inside?" Raven asked.

"They should be evacuated," Thalame said. "The sources on the inside said the place would be empty tonight."

"We're all placing the explosives at different locations, so that the effect will be total and catastrophic," said Zander.

Raven blinked between them. "That's it? You're just going to plant explosives and get out?"

Thalame raised a brow.

"I expected something more...elaborate."

Thalame shrugged. "Sometimes the simple solution is the most effective. We're going for effect and result, nothing more."

"And, when one explosive goes off, it will ignite any close by," Zander said. "So it doesn't matter who gets there first."

Zander met her eye—he didn't like this plan either. She could think of too many things that might go wrong, too many people who might get hurt because of revenge on the Gray Elite.

"You wouldn't think it harsh if you witnessed the public executions the Gray Elite put on," Thalame said, scowling. "They hang magicians where all can see. It's south of the city and set up like a theater so everyone's got a good view. The Gray Elite have done more than enough damage to magicians and non-magic users in the pursuit of stomping out magic from the world."

Raven's stomach turned over. "I didn't know."

Thalame shrugged. "Sometimes, it's not even magicians they execute but people they just don't like and want to be rid of. Accuse someone of consorting with magic, and the Gray Elite storm in. Can't prove someone's not a magician as easily as you can prove they are."

She swallowed, feeling foolish.

"We're going to show them magic isn't something they can push around forever," Zander said, his voice firm. "If a few people get caught in the crossfire tonight, it will be nothing compared to the number of people the Gray Elite have killed."

"Okay." She summoned what courage she had left. She could feel the ruby powder wearing off; she should have taken a drink right after tea.

"We plant the explosives, we get out, we get Ros, and we all hightail it out of Gracita." Zander's eyes fell to the locket around her throat. "Do you still have it?"

She blinked, put a hand over the locket, and glanced at Thalame.

"He knows," Zander whispered. His voice fell. "He, Ivy, and Niall. I had to explain it after...you vanished."

Her stomach turned over with guilt. She wanted to correct him, *after I ran away*, but she didn't. "Yes," she said instead. "I have it."

Relief washed over his face. Thalame's gaze flickered to her locket, just once. Zander hadn't wanted to tell anyone about the centrum. The fewer who knew, the better. And she had forced him to confess to his friends.

"I'm sorry," she said before she could stop herself. "I didn't mean..."

"We'll talk about this over tea or rum," Thalame interrupted. "Later, when we're all alive and well. Right now, we've got a job to do, and I don't want to keep these explosives strapped to my chest any longer than I have to."

Raven nodded, shaking herself out of her guilt. "You're right," she said, voice stronger. "Lead the way."

Thalame started through the workroom. The iron grate floor held them above a tangled web of metal pipes, much like the other room. Everything hissed and steamed at the joints. If Ivy were here, she would have been able to rig one of her steam traps and blow the factory up in minutes.

They started up an iron-grated stairwell, through a dingy hall with ghastly orange globes for lights, and through a series of halls and iron doors—all underground, all stale and muffled. Finally, Thalame took them through a door and into a vast room filled with thousands of pipes of different metals and sizes, tanks of varying shape and use.

"The subbasement," Thalame whispered.

Raven gawked as they walked. The subbasement of the factory seemed to go on for several city blocks. Pipes vanished into the ceiling and ran into bigger pipes and pumps and tanks. On every side, machines rumbled and pumped and gurgled and clanked. Giant machinery, belts and arms, rotating and humming—the purpose for most impossible to guess. The air stank of grease, oil, and the tang of metal. She followed Thalame, hoping he had a better sense of direction in this place than she did. Hundreds of glass globes illuminated the basement in pale yellow. Every other globe had been turned off, leaving puddles of shadows between each one.

Thalame led them to an iron-grated stairwell and into the basement, a less jumbled version of the subbasement. The pipes seemed to be more organized, most running from the subbasement, and fewer tanks. Narrow, horizontal windows lined the top of the basement wall, letting in light from the street level.

They moved through the basement, and halfway around a thicket of copper pipes, a vicious, unearthly *crack* sounded above. Raven gasped, ducking involuntarily. Neither Zander nor Thalame jumped. Through the narrow windows, a blinding white flash lit up the night. Sparks surged through the globes and the wires connecting them together—the lights burst. Globes shattered, raining glass onto the iron floor. Luckily, they had been standing between two globes.

The factory fell into darkness. Faint emergency lights, spaced farther apart, remained on, shading the basement in a dangerous shade of red-orange. The machines rumbled and then halted, and all at once, the basement felt like a tomb. Too dark, too quiet.

"That's the signal," Thalame said.

"For what?" Raven whispered. A retreat?

"Gretchen's shut off the main power by shorting the factory's circuits," Zander explained. "Her magic is lightning."

For less than a heartbeat, Raven wondered what it felt like to command lightning.

"We're on a timer now," Thalame said, picking up the pace. "We've got to get to the boiler before it's up."

Thalame made barely a sound as he moved, darting between the machines. He navigated a path away from the main aisle that ran through the basement, away from the emergency lights, leaving a shadow of himself for Raven to follow. Zander stayed behind her, no matter how slow she moved up and under and over the obstacles that Thalame seemed to have phased through.

She wiggled between two pipes, hands on the floor, and slithered out the other side. She took a brief moment to see if Zander had the same trouble she did—he did—when she caught movement—a humanoid figure, no more than a shadow, walking along the aisle parallel to them.

Zander crawled between the pipes and stood beside her.

"I thought you said the workers weren't here?" she whispered, eyes on where the figure had been.

"They shouldn't be," Zander said. "And when the emergency lights kick on, that means they have to head to the surface. Anyone left inside will leave."

Raven hadn't taken her eyes off the sliver of the aisle. Zander frowned and followed her line of sight.

"I saw someone," she said.

"Hopefully, they were heading out." Zander gave her a little push.

"Keep moving," Thalame whispered, just far enough ahead for them to still hear him. "No time for stragglers."

Someone leaving, Raven told herself. She followed Thalame through the machinery, Zander on her heels, but she kept one eye on the aisle. More than once, she thought she saw someone move. They were not in a hurry. It made the hair on the back of her neck stand.

And, worse yet, she felt the ruby powder's effects fading even more. The fever crept upward from wherever it slept.

She caught up with Thalame—no, Thalame had stopped. He held up his hand to them for silence.

"Is someone there?" asked a voice, human and not human at all. The cadence came too melodic, too calm.

Raven's heart skipped several beats, and she reached out to a pipe to steady herself.

"Shit," Zander spat, his whispered voice as panicked as she felt.

Footsteps sounded in the aisle, soft and even. Then, ahead of them, walking across a smaller aisle toward the main one, came the pale red glow of an automaton's searching eyes. The glow came closer, the beams growing brighter, sweeping across the aisle, looking.

The automaton appeared between two thick pipes. It paused.

None of them moved. Raven dared not even breathe.

The automaton had the shape of a man, its sleek metal body formed nearly perfectly, the metallic skin a sickening beige. It wore no clothes, but it didn't need them. The skin over its legs and middle was smooth like metal, seemingly seamless, and it had *ears*. In the shadow, Raven couldn't see its face but didn't think she wanted to.

"I detect magic within the vicinity," said the automaton man, the voice in the same calm, melodic tone.

Zander's breath came out in slow, strained puffs. Thalame breathed the same.

Slowly, the automaton's pale red eyes started to look their way. If it saw all of them, the mission would be lost. Raven bit her lip. It detected magic. Thalame and Zander had runes tattooed on their backs to hide their magic from detection. The automaton could only be detecting her surfacing magic as the ruby powder wore off. And if she ran, it would follow her. Not them.

Foolish, stupid, and desperate.

She thought of Conrad, how he had led the Gray Elite patrols away so they would have a chance to succeed. He had thought of them, not himself.

She had to think of them too.

She knew what she had to do. As the pale red lights inched closer, she darted to the side of the passage. The beams followed her movement.

"Halt," said the automaton.

"Raven," Zander hissed.

She crawled underneath a set of pipes and toward the main aisle. Her feet hit the iron floor with force enough to signal her presence to the automaton. She stood, bathed in the red-orange glow of an emergency light.

The automaton came around the corner, slim body moving with mechanical pace, unlike a human. Its pale red beams found her immediately.

In the red-orange of the emergency light, she could see its face. It wore a human's face like a mask, its skin waxy and dull.

"Halt, civilian. This is a restricted area," said the automaton. Its waxy lips didn't move. A high-pitched whirl of machinery sounded, and then its eyes turned blood red. "Magic detected."

She ran. The automaton ran after her, its sculpted legs carrying it just as fast as hers. It wouldn't tire. It would outrun her. She dashed around a corner and grabbed hold of a wire shelving unit, yanked as hard as she could while running, and sent it and the dozens of tools and toolboxes clattering to the floor. The unit itself lodged across the aisle.

She didn't look back. She didn't stop to look where she ran. She didn't slow down or pause. Half a dozen automatons joined the pursuit, their eyes going from pale red to blood red, their metal feet thundering against the iron-grated floor.

"Magic detected," chorused around her, in time with, "Intruder alert."

What would they do if they caught her? She didn't dwell on the thought. Maybe Ezra would get to her before the Gray Elite hanged her. Or would she be sent straight to General Deacon?

She ran around a corner and down a narrow aisle. Right into the path of a waiting automaton man. She tried to stop but couldn't. She careened into its chest, and with the automaton's human-sized legs and human-sized balance, they both crashed into the floor. Raven landed on top; the metal did not give as flesh would. Rather than a heartbeat, gears churned, and steam hissed with its chest.

Its pale red eyes turned blood red. As she scrambled to her feet, a cold metal hand fastened around her arm and yanked her to her feet. It held her arm high, forcing her to stand on her tiptoes. Blood red eyes surrounded her, bathing her in their light.

"Magic detained," said the automaton.

Detained. She did not like the sound of that word.

As it pulled her arm a little higher, stretching her in ways she shouldn't be stretched, a shadow jumped from the ceiling. Dark robes and leather and steel and a dark silver mask—a Wraith. The Wraith landed on the automaton's shoulders and, with a deft movement, slid a dagger into the automaton's waxy neck. The eyes sputtered.

The Wraith let out a cackle of laughter—a feminine crackle—and with a sickening twist, she popped the automaton's head off its shoulders. Steam hissed out in a shoot, wires sparked, and a tiny gear rattled from the broken neck to the floor. Its arm fell, releasing Raven's.

The Wraith jumped from the automaton as it began to fall and landed on another before it could move. A second head popped off as the first automaton crashed into the floor with a thud.

"Move!" shouted a second Wraith. He joined the other in popping heads, and Raven didn't stay to watch. She listened and ran.

Wraiths descended from the shadows, and head after head smacked the iron floor. More humanoid automatons appeared, but they gave Raven little mind; they ran to the fight. Raven ran and ran and ran until she couldn't breathe, then collapsed to her hands and knees, gasping for breath. Underneath her skin, the fever crawled. It picked at her bones, warming and tearing and searing.

It stole the very breath from her throat.

Not here, not now.

If the fever came back and took her, she would be a dead girl.

Raven slowly caught her breath. It did not want to be caught. The fever kept it at bay, just outside of her reach.

"Raven?" Zander appeared at her side, eyes wide with worry. Several daggers from his belts were missing. "What was that? You could have gotten yourself killed." He wasn't yelling. He sounded afraid.

She didn't have the breath to tell him she had done it to give them more time. He didn't ask. He closed his fingers around her arms and hoisted her back to her feet.

"Thalame?" she managed to ask.

"Probably in the fight," he said. He looked over his shoulder. The fight continued. Knives and heads and blood red eyes. Metal on metal, yelps and grunts and shouts.

As he spoke, an automaton darted out from a side path, one of its arms missing. Its blood-red eyes sputtered but found them. Zander hurled a dagger at the automaton. The dagger sank into the slit of the automaton's mouth, and as it reeled backward, Zander jumped. He grabbed the hilt of the dagger, twisted, and with another dagger, popped the automaton's head from its shoulders.

Another automaton appeared, and a Wraith appeared from above and took it down.

Raven turned and ran. Zander followed.

"There wasn't supposed to be anyone down here," Zander said between breaths. "We didn't know about the security automatons."

"What now?"

"We go ahead with the plan," Zander said. "This only complicates things. The Gray Elite will know without a doubt that it was the Wraiths. They might be on the way right now."

Zander slid around a corner and pulled her with him, and they ran down a narrow side aisle. She imagined the sirens, running throughout the night, and the people. First the explosions and fires, now the factory. Zander guided her through countless aisles, away from the fight. How many Wraiths would die tonight because of her? She had tried to help, had wanted to help, even by putting herself in danger, and she had only made it worse.

"That's the boiler," Zander said, breathless.

It was hard to miss. The boiler was a massive tank that stretched from the ceiling of the basement to the floor of the subbasment. Metal railings circled it. Water gurgled and rushed through the hundreds of pipes that led into the tank. The pipes ran through the ceiling, through the floor, and every which way. A raised platform before the boiler held numerous dials that measured temperature and pressure. The needles on each twitched continuously. Smaller tanks surrounded the bottom of the boiler, catching runoff and holding any surplus.

Raven circled the boiler. She didn't see any explosives.

"Shit," spat Zander, kicking a nearby pipe out of frustration. He'd noticed the lack of explosives too.

No one had arrived, because they had all rushed to help her.

"I'm sorry," Raven breathed. "It's my fault."

Zander didn't jump to argue, and she knew it was true. She doubled over, shame heating what the fever hadn't already. She released a pitiful sigh of frustration. Again, she had messed up their plans. First the princess, now the factory.

Maybe the fever should eat her alive.

And it felt like it might.

Zander turned around, unsheathing two daggers in a single deft twist of his body.

An automaton approached. "Unauthorized personnel. Magic detected. Emergency Protocol Initiated." The automaton raised its hand, palm first. Its fingers stretched, moving backward to reveal the metallic insides. The barrel of a pistol emerged from its shifting palm.

Raven sucked in a breath, and in a flash of black and gray and blue, Zander moved. He jumped faster than the gun fired, smothering the automaton in shadows. The gun fired; the bullet tore through the shadows—not without resistance—and landed in a nearby tank. The shadows dissolved. The automaton's head hit the floor; the body followed.

"Scrap metal," Zander muttered. He kicked the automaton's head.

Raven turned her attention back to the boiler. She circled it, then walked up to the platform. The dials remained constant. Her blurry reflection looked back at her from the largest dial.

"What now?" she asked, more to herself than anyone else.

Zander climbed the few steps to the platform, a dagger in each hand, not unlike her dream version of his assassin self, the Revenant. The sounds of fighting hadn't died down. It had attracted more attention, more automatons.

206

"Sisters," Zander breathed, leaning on the railing. "This isn't working. We need to get out of here while we can, before the Gray Elite storm the place and we're all dead."

One of the larger pipes creaked. The water within the boiler gurgled, hot water surging up and pushing steam through the factory and cold water surging back into the boiler. Water that ran through the entire plant. Through every floor, every sink and toilet. Between the floors, the walls, the ceilings.

Ivy would have done something clever by now to have the whole thing explode.

And Raven knew what she could do.

The fever had returned. The magic had returned—the automaton had detected it in her. The magic that had turned a man to ash in the blink of an eye. The magic that boiled under her skin like fire.

A strange calm came over her. She focused, searched for the fever, and pressed her hands flat against the steel of the boiler. She felt the water inside, felt the energy of it, felt it feeding the boiler—gushing through pipes like the veins of a creature. And she had her hands on the heart, the source of its life.

"Raven?" Zander asked, but she barely heard him. He took a step closer. His hand touched her shoulder. "We need to go."

"No," she said, firmly. "Let me do this."

He hesitated but pulled his hand back—as if burned. Did he feel the fever?

She called on the fever, urged it to her command, and it listened. She pushed the fever into the boiler, into the water. At first, nothing happened. Then, the temperature gauge began to shift toward the red side. Higher and higher it twitched. Beside it, the pressure gauge did the same.

A warning bell sounded on the boiler, a pitiful bell compared to the war raging between the pipes.

"Sisters," Zander gasped. He stepped closer to Raven, daggers at the ready. "Keep doing whatever you're doing. I've got your back."

She fed her fever into the boiler, into the water. The steel under her hands warmed considerably, but the heat didn't burn her. The water overheated, the steam too much for the pipes, overloading the machines it ran. Above them, all around them, pipes began to groan, whine, and creak.

More. More. More.

She forced her magic into the pipes in the subbasement. The subbasement filled with the creaking, clanking, and banging of pipes as the pressure rose faster than the machines could handle. The first pipe burst. Steam hissed from the break, and water splattered onto the subbasement floor. A second burst, and then a third. Boiling water poured from the broken pipes, and steam thickened the air with heavy humidity. One after another, the pipes in the subbasement burst.

Raven stumbled backward. Her fever remained, but it had been sated, just as it had been with the pirate. A dizzy spell knocked her into the railing.

Zander appeared at her side. "How?" he gasped, looking between her and the boiler with wide eyes.

Her breath came in gasps, and he didn't push her to answer.

They didn't have the time. Water poured into the subbasement. Already, the water reached the first step of the stairs, and the steam made the air horridly heavy. Sweat stuck her dress to her skin, and it sank into her scalp. Zander pulled her away from the boiler and into the basement. The air was less heavy, but the steam was seeping through the vents. As they ran, water gurgled unpleasantly in the walls, and several machines had flashing red lights.

"This way!" Zander slid around a corner.

How he knew his way around, she didn't have time to question. They had known their way in, and it made sense for them to have an escape route planned.

An automaton man tried to stop them, but Thalame appeared from nowhere, digging a dagger into the machine's neck, twisting, and throwing its head into the rising water. He had a split lip, and a Wraith who followed him had a black eye. Sweat glistened on their faces. Water splashed under the floor, rising far too quickly for comfort. Thalame and the other Wraith joined the dash for the exit. They reached the stairwell just as the steaming water splashed over the top stair of those leading down into the subbasement. Pieces of machines and forgotten tools floated in the rising tide.

"The others?" Raven gasped as she made it to the main floor, a step behind Zander. He had paused to look behind him.

"There's a dozen ways out of the basement," Zander said. "They'll get out."

"I don't know what you did," Thalame said to Raven, chuckling. "But I'm glad you did it. You used Ivy's trick, eh?"

Raven winked at him. She didn't feel able to explain what she had done. Not now, at least.

"Let's move!" said the other Wraith. He kicked open the stairwell doors and they ran onto the factory floor. An alarm wailed, and red lights flashed. Through the tall windows that lined the main floor, the city still burned in shades of frightening orange and red. Shadows darted from doors across the room, jumping to lose sections of the windows, climbing up the massive machinery to skylights, and fading into nothing at all—Wraiths escaping.

"Come on," Zander said, urging her forward. He took her hand, and they ran toward the closest door.

From behind them, a door crashed open. A man shouted, "Pull the emergency vents before it ruins the whole batch!"

Thalame and the other Wraith threw their combined weight against the doors. The lock cracked and burst, and the doors swung out. They ran out into the smoke-stained night. Behind them came a dangerous *creak, creak, creak*, and then—*crash*. Something heavy fell from somewhere high and smashed something else.

They had destroyed the automaton factory. Not the smoothest mission, but a success.

Moorin was in chaos.

Smoke covered the sky, and not even the brightest stars shone through. The smoke drifted upward, fast from some fires and slow from others, clouding over the city like fog. The fires reflected off the smoke, making it seem as though the sky itself burned. The smell—Raven coughed as it racked against her throat—smoke, fear, ash, and dust.

The street outside the factory was crowded with worried Gray Elite and panicked civilians, and no one noticed Zander, Raven, and Thalame slip out. Too much fire, too much smoke, too many people shouting and yelling and crying. Too much distraction. Fires raged from the patrol stations, and the factory creaked and groaned like it might collapse at any moment.

Thalame and Zander slowed, making their way through the wide-eyed crowd. So many people stood on the streets, watching, waiting for the next fire, the next explosion. It didn't take long to realize why; streets had been shut down, and the blocks surrounding the burning patrol stations had been evacuated. People in sleeping gowns, dressing robes, and slippers clung to one another, children sobbed, and they all looked terrified.

Raven's stomach squeezed. How many people had been hurt? The Wraiths had evacuated the people they could, but what about their homes? Their possessions? True, their lives mattered more, but to lose everything—she hated the thought.

A part of her thought it justice. The Gracitans had caused her kingdom nothing but suffering and loss for one hundred years: killed thousands of magicians. Destroyed history. Erased culture. They deserved it...didn't they?

Raven shook her head. She wouldn't think about that. Not right now. They had to get out of this mess first. Then she could wallow all she wanted.

She kept her eyes on Zander's back. Thalame walked a step in front of him. The farther they went from the factory, the less chaotic the streets. Thalame led them from the chaos, and it took a few streets for her to realize they were winding back to the Deacon Estate.

For Rosaria.

Even though she knew it shouldn't, a twinge of jealousy stung her chest. *Stupid*, she thought. She cared for Rosaria too. She wanted Rosaria to come back with them.

Thalame led the way through the crowded street without trouble. Too many people stood around, looking lost and helpless, begging the Gray Elite for help, complaining about not being able to go home, asking for help looking for loved ones. The Gray Elite were far too busy handling the fires, the factory, and the chaos of people to pay attention to the two Wraiths and a wanted girl slipping between shadows.

Getting to the Deacon Estate proved easy. Thalame and Zander took Raven through the unlocked gate near the servants' door, through the empty kitchens, and through a series of servant passages to the floor where they had ambushed her. The lights had been extinguished, leaving the corridors in shadow.

"That guard," whispered Thalame to Raven. He glanced over his shoulder at her. "Did you know him?"

It took her a heartbeat to realize he meant James, the Gray Elite who had been charged with escorting her back to her rooms. The Gray Elite whom Thalame had killed. Her stomach somersaulted; she hadn't thought of him since. His body had vanished from the corridor.

"I knew only his name," Raven said. "I met him at tea."

Thalame grunted, and they fell again into silence.

Raven led them first to her room, intent on another drink of ruby powder. Since she had steamed the factory, the fever felt slaked. It hadn't vanished, and with every heartbeat, she felt it gather, growing. She pushed open the door to her room but stumbled to a halt on the threshold.

Her room had been trashed: the blankets on the bed, thrown off; the mattress, upturned; the wardrobe, strung about; the ruby powder, gone.

"It's been searched," Thalame said, toeing one of the silken sheets on the floor.

"They were looking for something," Zander confirmed, eyes drifting to her locket.

Raven put a hand to her locket. Looking for her or it?

"No time to dwell on it," said Thalame.

Rosaria's room had been searched too. The clothes were strung over the floor, the curtains had been rifled, and the drawers of the desk had been pulled out and emptied. An inkwell, turned on its side, slowly leaked from its corked top. A puddle of black stained the tile and the wooden handle of a pen unlucky enough to have fallen into the ink's grasp. The wardrobe had been emptied, but the secret door hadn't been opened.

They slipped into the tunnels through the hidden panel and started toward the Tombs. It took Thalame a few tries to recount the path Conrad had taken them on, but they finally came to the portrait and the broom closet on the other side. Thalame listened at the seam of the door. After a pause, he led them into the Tombs. Thalame and Zander walked with cat-like steps; Raven's footsteps echoed.

Like the factory, the main lights had gone out. The stone halls were lit with the same red-orange emergency lights, spaced to leave each cell in a ghostly glow. The inmates howled and laughed at the chaos.

Rosaria met them at the door, panic-stricken. She had tied her black hair into a braid and pulled a cardigan over her dress. The red-orange light striped her cell. A series of lumps under the blankets on her bed mimicked a human body, and for a moment, Raven felt sickened. Then she realized—a decoy to buy them time.

"What happened?" asked the princess.

"No time," Zander said.

He stepped back to kick open the cell door, but Rosaria held up her hand. She pulled a simple iron key from her pocket. She easily slipped her small hand through the bars and stuck the key into the lock. With a gentle turn of her wrist, the door unlocked, and she stepped out of her cell. She locked it back and tucked the key into her pocket.

"I have my own key," Rosaria whispered. She winked at Raven, and the last remaining ill-will she felt toward the princess vanished.

Raven took a step back toward the secret door, to find their way back up through the Deacon Estate, and get out of Moorin, when a whisper of a voice drifted from somewhere else in the Tombs—a voice she knew. A voice that hammered in her chest with its mischievous familiarity.

Thalame opened the broom closet's door, and Raven took off down the hall. Zander hissed her name, but she didn't stop. She careened around the end of the cell block and into the next.

And there, leaning casually against the bars of one of the cells, stood a tall, lean young man with dark skin and dark braids nearly to his waist. He looked ghastly and full of shadows in the red-orange light, but that intimidating illusion vanished when his eyes met hers and his lips spread into a wide grin.

"Conrad," she breathed, starting toward him. He was alive!

"Look who's alive after all," he said, his tone light and playful. He turned his attention to the cell he stood beside. "This is the girl I told you about."

Raven came to a stop just outside the cell, leaving a little more than arm's reach between her and it. A tall, slender woman stood within the cell. The harsh light aged her, but at second glance, she didn't look older than forty. Unwashed brown hair hung past her shoulders. She wore the uniform of the Tombs, brown trousers and shirt. Her eyes appeared dark in the light, though the shadows couldn't mask the cleverness within them. The prisoner took Raven in from head to toe with an objective appraisal.

"Hmm," said the woman. "I'm glad to see she's dressed for tea, not adventure." She spoke in a lighthearted, authoritative tone.

Raven blushed; the stranger's words felt like a scolding. "I wasn't prepared for adventure," Raven said, glancing down at her blue silk skirt. It had been torn, stained, and soaked with only Sisters knew what.

"One should always be prepared for adventure," said the woman. She had a mild accent that Raven couldn't place.

Footsteps approached from the other end, quick and quiet.

"Raven? What are you doing?" came Zander's voice. He stopped a hand's distance from her. His eyes fell onto Conrad, then the woman.

"Raven, this is Captain Bailey Luckett," said Conrad, as if Zander hadn't appeared. "She's a friend of mine."

"Captain Luckett," Raven repeated. The captain Warren had told Malik about, a retired Wraith, Conrad's friend—and the pieces clicked together. Captain Luckett was a pirate captain, *his* captain. She looked a bit ragged and worn around the edges, but she looked far too clever to be lumped in with the typical pirate scum, as did Conrad.

"I found her. Now all I've got to do is get her out," Conrad said. "Gather any master keys on your travels through the Tombs?"

Zander said something under his breath that Raven didn't wish to repeat. No, she didn't have any keys, but she did have a solution. She stepped up to the bars and set her hands on the lock of Luckett's cell. Conrad raised a brow, and once he realized her plan, he took a large step back. Luckett looked at Conrad with a raised brow, then mirrored his step back.

Raven pushed her fever into the lock. The metal warmed, warmed, warmed, and started to soften. A little more.

"What are—" Luckett started to ask.

The lock melted like hot clay and landed on the floor in a red-hot pile of goo.

"Sisters," Conrad and Zander breathed in unison. Zander looked worried; Conrad looked thrilled.

"Sisters, indeed," said Captain Luckett, mouth tilted in a smirk. She carefully touched the bars of her cell, testing for heat, and finding them suitable for touch, pushed the door open. Luckett stepped out, skipped over the goo, and then looked at Raven. "I like you, kid."

Conrad and Luckett started the other way.

"We've got a way out," Raven said.

"Don't worry," said Luckett, throwing a smirk at Raven over her shoulder. She walked like a captain too, sure of her every step. "We've got one too."

"Come on." Zander pulled her away from the cell. "Before a patrol wanders through and finds the door melted."

Zander pulled Raven by the hand, and they slipped into the broom closet to find Thalame and Rosaria waiting inside. Thalame pulled the hidden lever, the painting swung open, and they clamored through.

"Want to explain how you did that?" Zander asked her as they started down the stone corridor.

"What did you do?" Thalame asked.

She told them, and neither Thalame nor Rosaria looked surprised.

"But...how?" Zander gawked at her hands.

"I don't know." She put her hand up to the locket. His eyes followed. She knew now that the centrum had somehow infected her, and she had somehow used it, but she hadn't the slightest idea of *how* or *why*.

"When we have time to sit and talk," Rosaria said, "we will."

Spoken like a queen. No one objected or disagreed. Raven didn't feel like talking or trying to think about the locket or the centrum or her strange new powers. Right now, they had to slip out of Moorin while the chaos distracted the Gray Elite.

None of them spoke on the way back to Rosaria's room. It looked as disheveled as it had the last time. The fiery light of the city hadn't diminished, and it bathed the room in a sickly glow. However, the Deacon Estate was quiet, and they took this moment to take a collective breath.

Zander muttered a curse and bent over, hands on his knees. Thalame slumped against the wall. Rosaria took a lap of the room, taking in the damage. Her stare lingered on the spilled ink, her face not betraying any emotion or thought. She held her shoulders back, her chin up, proud but thoughtful.

"What now?" Thalame asked. "Should we stay here a while? Might be the safest place in the city night now. Right under the Gray Elite's nose. They've already searched it so they might not come back for a while."

Zander shook his head. "No," he said, looking toward the windows. The fiery light cast his face in grimness. "We need to get out of here while the city's a mess. Besides, the Gray Elite have shown their true thoughts on Ezra. They don't trust him if they searched his house like this."

"For all we know, the general could have ordered it," Thalame added.

Zander agreed.

Raven thought about suggesting they wait for Ezra. He could give them a good plan of escape, a sneaky way out of the city, but a twinge of fear held her lips closed. The fever swirled under her skin, ever present, waiting for the time to strike.

"The Gray Elite would not have searched this house without the general's approval or knowledge," Rosaria said, her voice calm. "They've not bothered Ezra in these six months, so something has changed." Rosaria's eyes drifted to Raven, knowing.

Raven felt Zander and Thalame look at her too. They all knew.

"I suppose we all know what that was," she muttered, but in the quiet of the room, she might as well have shouted. The Gray Elite were looking for her. They had stormed the Deacon Estate for her, trashed the rooms looking for her.

Whatever fate Ezra found, it would be her doing. Raven met Rosaria's stare again, but the princess didn't smile or offer encouragement, as though she knew it too.

"And if the general gets word that I am gone, he might come back to the house," Rosaria said.

"We need to leave soon," Raven added, and Rosaria nodded.

"Ros," Zander started, but she held up her hand.

"Later," she said. "When we're not in danger."

Zander gazed at Raven—he had more he wanted to say, but Rosaria was right. Now was not the time. He stood between Raven and Rosaria, looking a bit lost between them, two bits of his world that had found each other without him. Raven felt a bit delighted that she had a connection with the princess that he didn't. Shameful thoughts, but her thoughts regardless.

"We could go back to the inn," Zander suggested. "Engor's got connections to get magicians out of the city. We could use him."

"The Gray Elite will be looking at the Wraiths," Thalame said. "They know that we attacked the factory and are smart enough to assume that we also attacked the patrol stations. The Gray Elite will be unorganized but no less ruthless."

"And the air docks are likely shut down," Zander said. "That eliminates the sky."

"Don's," Rosaria said.

The other three looked at her.

"Who?" asked Raven.

"Don's place," Rosaria said. Something dangerously like hope brightened her face. "Ezra told me about it. It's a pub he told me to go to if I ever needed to get out of the city. He said to ask for the barkeep's special and say that Ezra sent me."

Thalame and Zander glanced at each other. Neither had heard of Don or his place, but they wouldn't question Rosaria.

"Sounds as good a plan as any," said Thalame. "Do you know the way?"

"No, but I know the address," Rosaria said. "He told me in case I ever had to escape." She rattled off the address.

"That's not far," Thalame said, glancing toward the windows. "We'd be out of the city just after dawn."

Before they set out for Don's Place, they washed the grit and grime off their faces and hands and brushed it off their clothes as best they could. Zander and Thalame found summer cloaks in a spare bedroom, and Rosaria pulled cloaks for herself and Raven from the pile of discarded clothes in her room. They returned to the tunnels, following Rosaria as she melodically recalled Ezra's instructions on how to navigate the tunnels; she had turned it into a sort of song. Rosaria did not have a singer's voice, but if her song got them out of the tunnels, Raven didn't care.

At last, they came to a dull iron ladder. It took them into an alley between two shops, both closed for the night. They had put distance between themselves and the old estates, as well as between them and the burning city center. The chaos sounded farther away, and the smoke and fire glowed in the distance. The air still smelled of smoke.

Rosaria took Raven's arm in her own, two casual girls walking to destress from the horrors of the night or to look for someone lost. They trotted out of the alley, the boys behind, into the darkened street.

They had entered a shopping district. To Raven's horror, looters and thieves were having their way along the street, smashing storefronts and grabbing whatever they could. Some seemed to only be in it for the smashing and breaking. Rosaria held on tighter to Raven's arm and led them away from the worst of the looting.

It all made Raven's stomach turn. Chaos on every side.

And she felt the fever clawing at her insides, feeding off her panic and fear.

They continued on their way, avoiding looters and the few automaton patrollers who remained beyond the city center. Gunfire peppered the air, both nearby and distantly. Had all the Wraiths made it clear?

How many people would be dead once the sun rose? How much of it would be her fault? If she had never gotten on that airship, if she had stayed in Wayward Point—if she had stayed in the treehouse—how much of this would not have happened?

A part of her didn't want to know the answer, and another part didn't care. She could hear her stepmother's voice: *What's done is done.* Raven banished all thoughts other than survival from her mind. Later, as Rosaria had said. Right now, she wanted to get out. She did not want to be anywhere near Moorin when the sun rose.

Don's Place glowed on a street corner, brassy doors facing either street, with glass globes burning inside despite the hour and chaos. Through the windows, Raven spotted maybe a dozen or so patrons sitting around the dark tables. Most were drinking, but no one looked happy. She could feel the tension in the air, the panic, the fear.

A man stood just outside the doors, hands in his jacket, cigarette between his teeth. He stared blankly down the street, but as they approached, his dulled eyes sharpened on them. Exhaustion pulled his face down, aging him ten years. He took a puff on his cigarette, making the end glow bright red-orange.

The red-orange of the emergency lights, of alert, of panic.

Rosaria's hand tightened on Raven's. *Wrong*, she seemed to say.

And within the same heartbeat, the wrongness became clear. From the alley behind Don's, a dozen Gray Elite swarmed onto the street, pistols drawn. They came from an alley across the street, and then one adjacent—blocking them in.

Rosaria sucked in a breath as the word tumbled from Raven's lips, "Cornered."

"They were waiting for us," Rosaria breathed.

The guns were cocked in disharmony.

"Halt," shouted a voice through the silence.

Raven suppressed a shudder. The Gray Elite had been waiting for them at Don's. They knew they would come here. Someone had told them, tipped them off. Her fear for Ezra's life had churned her stomach; her doubt of his loyalty burned. Either he had told them willingly, or they had forced it out of him. Neither settled well.

Thalame let out a low, quick whistle. A warning. Raven followed his line of sight, and her heart fell. Gray Elite lined the rooftops all around them, guns and crossbows aimed.

They had come prepared.

A spotlight flared to life, bathing the four of them in harsh white light. Another joined it, and another. Three spotlights marked their location, shrinking the shadows to puddles beneath their feet.

"Do not move," shouted a Gray Elite from the street. "You are under arrest by order of the Gray Elite. Do not resist, or we will open fire."

The Gray Elite on the street began to creep toward them.

"You got the cover?" Thalame asked lowly.

Zander let out a quick sigh, and in the blink of an eye, shadows rose like walls around them, the tendrils tightening together and curving over them. Bullets peppered the shadows, but none made it in. They made the softest ding against the shadows, dozens of them, like water against hot iron. Zander gritted his teeth like he felt every single one.

"Zander?" Raven asked.

"I'm fine," he spat back, his voice strained with concentration.

"Start moving," Thalame commanded. "He'll follow."

"Where?" Raven asked. "We are surrounded."

"Don's?" Rosaria asked. "We can still get away. We get in and block the tunnel after us. It will give us time."

"And if the Gray Elite get in?" Raven asked.

"We can fight better if they're coming at us one at a time," Thalame said, his voice strained. "Now move. I don't know how much longer Zander can—"

"Just go!" Zander growled.

They started to move toward Don's. The shadow globe moved with them, undulating as it rolled around them. It reminded her of a bubble moving through water. The spotlights hit the sides, dancing across the thinner shadows. Footsteps thundered on the other side. Gray Elite were coming closer.

"They're blocking us," Zander said.

"I got it," Thalame said immediately. He drew two daggers from his person and handed one to Raven and the other to Rosaria. He drew two more for himself.

The shadows widened, and then in the blink of an eye, swallowed the Gray Elite in their way. The shock of being inside the shadows gave them a disadvantage. Thalame attacked in a fluid motion; Zander's shadows smacked and distracted. Rosaria disarmed and took down a Gray Elite. It all happened so fast. One of the Gray Elite came at Raven, and as a tendril of shadow smacked his head to the side, her dagger found a place in the Gray Elite's neck.

Another came at her. Raven didn't think, didn't hesitate, only acted.

And just like that, the Gray Elite patrol was dead. Three. She had killed three Gray Elite. Their bodies lay bleeding at her feet. She grabbed the pistol from the closest, cocked it, like she had seen Zander do a hundred times with Birdie.

Shouting came from outside the shadows, commands, orders, warnings. The sound moved through the shadows like water, turning distorted and heavy.

"What now?" Raven asked, breathless. "We're just drawing attention to ourselves."

Zander winced. His shoulders flinched inward. Pain, she realized, from the rune that burned when he used his magic. As if reading her thoughts, he grunted; a part of their shadow globe dissolved, but Zander flexed another tendril in its place.

Rosaria opened her mouth, but a massive roar of an airship's engine stopped her words cold. The engine crackled and hissed. Machinery cranked and clanked, and something hit the street with a thunderous bang, shaking the stone under their feet—something large. An engine roared to life, gears smashing against one another, cogs groaning, belts whining, steam hissing—louder than she had ever heard them. It sounded as loud as an airship, only bigger and meaner and closer.

In her mind, she saw an army of automatons, red eyes glaring brighter than the city on fire.

"Sisters," Zander gasped. He reached out with his hand, and the shadows parted enough for them to see the commotion.

Raven gasped, but she wasn't the only one.

It was not an army of automatons, but just one. A massive automaton. It crouched on the ground, its arms and legs folded together. The Gray Elite transporter that had dropped it onto the street was flying into the smoky night. The automaton rumbled and clicked. Steam hissed from its shoulders and hips and back, and its limbs began to unfurl. Creaking and hissing, it rose to a height of forty feet.

Gleaming red eyes focused on the shadow orb. It started toward them. As it moved, thunderous and heavy gears crashed together, clicking and clanking in a dangerous, mechanical harmony. It had feet the size of small houses, and each footstep cracked the pavement. The brass and copper and steel plates left few vulnerable spots, and the steam from its shoulders shot twenty feet into the air.

Zander tightened his shadows. He and Thalame readied themselves, daggers in each hand. Sweat ran down Zander's temple, and exhaustion muddied his stare.

"Zander," Raven started. "You can't fight that thing. Look at it! It's a death sentence."

He grimaced at her. He knew. He would still fight.

Panic, hot and slippery, worked its way into every limb, every thought. She shook her head. Her grip on Thalame's dagger shook. Her aim with the pistol wavered.

They should escape, give themselves up, anything other than fight that monster. But if they gave themselves up, they would surely face execution. All of them, magicians. If the Gray Elite didn't shoot them on sight first.

No, their odds were not good.

Surrounded on every side. Guns aimed at them. A colossus coming for them.

Raven pulled back a sob. She didn't want to die, especially not like this, cornered and exposed and vulnerable and helpless.

Are you helpless?

The voice spoke as clear as it ever had. She glanced to see if anyone else had heard it—no one had. The voice felt as close as if the speaker stood beside her and yet closer still and yet from nowhere.

The thunderous automaton came closer. It raised its balled fists. Zander spat a curse and tightened his shadows. A whirl sounded—something struck the top of the shadow orb. Zander screamed, the shadows flashed, and then the entire orb shattered like glass. Zander collapsed onto his hands and knees, panting.

And they were fully exposed, but the bullets did not fly.

The Gray Elite watched from the sidewalks and rooftops—watching the colossus.

The colossus straightened. On the bottom of its closed first was a glowing rune. As it retracted, the glow faded.

"That's a disrupting rune," Thalame spat. He crouched beside Zander and set a hand on his shoulder. "You all right, mate?"

Zander spat a curse and wobbled to his feet. He pulled two daggers from his waist, and he and Thalame jumped into the fight.

At first, the size of the colossus worked against it. The boys dashed between its legs, around its ankles, looking for a way up to the neck—the most obvious place for a weakness, like in most automatons. Every time they found a foothold, the colossus would shake its leg or swat them off, or one of the Gray Elite would shoot at them.

The colossus was too fast for them, the metal too slick, too thick to pierce. With every passing heartbeat, Raven felt something tug at her stomach, not panic, not fear, but a knowing. A nudge.

You are not helpless.

Zander had made it to the colossus's waist, his dagger between his teeth, when the top half swiveled. Zander lost his grip and started to fall; the colossus swatted at him, but rather than hit him with the flat palm of its hand, as the hand moved, the fingers extended. From the index finger of the colossus, a sword slid out.

Raven screamed the same moment that Zander's painful cry pierced the air—the sword had gone through his upper arm. The colossus thrust toward the ground, pinning Zander to the pavement. A beat passed, then the colossus yanked the sword free.

Zander's blood, fresh and bright and red, splattered the ground at Raven's feet.

See what it did? It shouldn't exist. Erase it.

Zander whimpered, and the sound shattered something in Raven's chest. She ran to him, regardless of the Gray Elite, of the colossus, regardless of his blood spilling out too fast. She collapsed beside him, his name on her lips. His arm had been cut through, nearly severed. The bones were crushed, splintered, the muscles torn, and everything else in the way had been obliterated. Pain paled his face to a deathly white.

All else went quiet. The wet thwack of his body hitting the ground sounded again and again in her mind.

Zander. His trembling body at her knees. His limp arm and paling hand. His blood, soaking into the knees of her dress and hem of her cloak.

All she knew was Zander and the automaton monster that had hurt him, that would hurt them all.

You're not helpless.

The fever, the panic, the fear—it became white hot fury. She felt it in her hands, in her blood, in her body—the magic that had boiled the water in the factory, that had melted the lock, that had turned a man to ash.

Do it.

She knew what to do.

She stood.

The colossus loomed over her, bloodied sword still protruding from his finger. Despite Thalame's efforts, he hadn't done any damage. He stood on the other side, shaking his head at her. He said something, but she didn't hear him.

The automaton lifted its sword to finish the job.

"No," Raven said to the colossus. She stepped over Zander, stood in front of him, his blood wet and warm on her clothes.

The colossus's red eyes refocused on her, nearly blinding her, but she didn't need to see.

"Raven," Zander hissed, her name a gasp on his pain-laced breath.

The colossus retracted the sword and started to reach for her with both of its hands. To capture, not to kill.

It never touched her.

The colossus's red eyes flickered. Its gears jerked. Its engine sputtered. It straightened, its movements slowed, jerky. An alarm rang from within its metal body, the high-pitched warning bells muffled by the steel plating.

Raven did not let her focus fade. She had more, and she would give more.

A Gray Elite officer shouted commands, and as his words met the air, blue-white flame erupted around the colossus, bright as daylight, blinding the officers, stunning the civilians who had gathered at the commotion. Screams echoed, panicked and fearful and trembling.

They should be afraid.

Raven felt the flames consume the colossus, melting the metal gears and cogs and belts and screws and plates, turning them to liquid, to gas, to nothing at all. The water in the machine's innards boiled and burst and evaporated; the gears malfunctioned and sputtered against each other; the brass and bronze and steel armor bled into the others.

She felt it consume everything, burning it out of existence.

Raven released her hold over what remained of the automaton. The fever—the magic, her magic—returned to her without fuss, sated with the burning. As it returned to her, she stumbled backward; a wave of dizziness and nausea hit her hard, and she collapsed to her knees. She tried hard not to empty her stomach.

Where the colossus had stood, a pile of molten white-hot goo remained. The pavement it touched hissed and steamed.

She had done it.

She had tried to turn it to ash, not goo, but she supposed she would accept that. Maybe metal didn't become ash.

Pride filled her, not entirely her own, but the magic's too.

She heaved a breath, unaware of having held it. With it, the heat of the colossus flooded her lungs.

"Raven?" came Rosaria's uncertain voice.

The street came back into focus. People in their robes and housecoats gawked and stared and pointed from alleys and side streets. The bewildered Gray Elite looked too, wide-eyed, open-mouthed, and unsure. It didn't last long. The Gray Elite quickly recovered from the shock and reorganized themselves. Those on the street began to close ranks around her.

She could... No, her magic dwindled with the use. She couldn't do anything. Even if she could, she couldn't burn these people. They were people, not machines.

Her stomach upheaved, and she bent over on her hands and knees. The pavement beneath her palms was hot, but the heat didn't hurt her. Her stomach turned over. She squeezed her eyes shut.

Feet on the pavement. Scrambling. Gray Elite shouting orders.

The world shifted under her hands, and she felt the cold, clamminess of unconsciousness slithering across her skin and through her mind.

The Gray Elite would certainly kill them now.

The worst of the feeling subsided. The pavement blurred between her fingers. Gray Elite boots came into her view, dirty with dust and debris. A strong stench of smoke wafted with the soldiers.

She took a breath, unready to meet whatever fate the Gray Elite had for her.

A second pair of boots appeared. Orders were spat, but as the words met the air, a roar sounded in the sky. An engine—and then dozens of them—roared above them. The two officers stumbled backward, eyes on the sky.

Raven managed to look up, craning her neck and stretching her dizziness to do so. Airships raced through the smoky sky and toward the city, faster than any other airship she had seen. The buzzing of the engine chittered like bugs, like wasps.

The airship flew closer. Rockets screamed through the air with a piercing howl, spitting sparks from the ends. The rockets exploded over the crowd with an otherworldly bang, spitting too-bright colors in every direction in a dazzling display of light. A few pistols shot, but the sound of the rockets' swallowed the sound of the bullets.

Hands grabbed Raven's shoulders and hoisted her to her feet. The world wobbled. She didn't have the energy to resist.

"Let's go," came Rosaria's strong voice. The voice of a queen giving an order.

Raven fell against the princess, and Rosaria lifted Raven's arm over her shoulder. Raven blinked at the scene as it unfolded; Thalame lifted Zander's limp body from the street, pulling his good arm over his shoulders. Zander's limp arm hung awkwardly as his side, dripping blood. Ladders dangled from above, and Rosaria pulled Raven onto the closest one.

"Hold on," Rosaria breathed in Raven's ear.

She folded her arms around the wooden rung. Rosaria did too, keeping Raven between her arms, securing her body with her own. Thalame did the same to Zander, only he strung a belt between Zander and the ladder.

"*Go!*" Rosaria screamed.

An airship whirled, the high-pitched screech deafening, and then a second airship joined it. The ladders lifted them away from the ground, flying higher and higher. Raven glanced up—the ladders were attached to smaller airships. Two ships carried the four of them away while a small army of them blasted the air with light and sound—a distraction. The airships moved in a chaotic pattern, organized but frenzied.

Raven rested her head against the rung of the ladder. She didn't have the mind to question this rescue. The vibrations of the airship carried through her hands and into her head. It took all of her failing concentration to hold on.

The airship carried them away from Moorin, away from the automaton and the Gray Elite, away from the smoking patrol stations and collapsing factory. They flew higher and higher, through the clouds, through the smoke, and to a massive airship waiting on the other side.

What little breath Raven had vanished at the sight.

The engines purred like thunder. The balloons were painted gold and white, flecked with stars of blue and silver. A promenade deck shone like crimson. On this side of the clouds, the first rays of dawn highlighted the edges of the airship with liquid gold. The hull was shaped like a boat, the bow pointed, the stern curved, and masts held up rigging between the balloons and steam vents.

Raven tried to count the decks, but they moved too fast and her mind moved too slow. But she didn't need an exact number to know they approached not just an airship, but a sky city.

The smaller airships flew underneath the sky city, to air docks tucked safety underneath. Her attention wobbled and darkened as their airship did not fly underneath but hovered over an extended platform. Rosaria and a stranger helped Raven down from the ladder.

Between her unsteady feet, through the iron lattice floor, she could see the clouds below them. The clouds swirled where the airships had punched through. The dawn glowed against the clouds in shades of lavender.

Several strangers helped Thalame with Zander. They lifted his unconscious body between them. Blood dripped from his arm.

All the commotion formed a buzzing in her head. Too much.

"Hey there, little bird," came a familiar voice. Conrad appeared beside her. The pale morning light caught the gold beads in his hair. He tilted his head at her. "Welcome to the *Orion*. Looks like someone else needs a medic."

Rosaria said something, but Raven didn't hear her. The world closed in, darkening the corners of her vision, tunneling. She put her head into her hands.

The *Orion*—a sky city.

With that thought, with the gold and white sails unfurling with snaps and whips, with the sunlight waxing into daylight, Raven's world faded to black.

Raven came to in a room of plain oak walls. A brass lantern hung from the ceiling, gently swaying. Dividers of white linen and oak blocked two sides of her view. It smelled clean, coldly so. Every heartbeat, every blink, brought her closer to reality.

A hospital or a clinic. She sat up, despite her achy body. She was in a narrow corridor lined on both sides with cots, each divided by folding screens of stark white linen. A figure lay sleeping in the cot across from her, an arm thrown over his face.

It took a long moment to adjust; exhaustion tugged on her shoulder blades, urging her to return to the cot, to the warm blankets, to the pillow.

She rubbed her face. What had happened?

And then she remembered.

Moorin. The patrol stations, the Wraiths, the factory, and the colossus automaton she had reduced to glowing goo. She drew up her legs and rested her head on her knees. She had been exhausted after turning that pirate to ash too.

Magic. She hadn't believed it at first, but now she did. She had magic, like it or not.

The hospital ward sounded with the moans of several patients and snores of others still. After a long moment of gathering herself, she pushed her feet toward the floor. Someone had taken the time to remove her filthy dress. She wore instead a simple gown of off-white that ended above her knees. Her boots sat on the floor beside the bed, and a cloak had been thrown over the foot of the bed.

At the commotion of her movement, a man appeared around the partition. He wore a short-sleeve off-white shirt and brown trousers. His small satchel held clean bandages, pills, and bottles. A tattoo of a cat stretched up his right arm.

"There you are," he said kindly in a Tinatunian accent. His golden brown face stretched into a welcoming, friendly smile. "How are you feeling?"

She groaned. Like she had been dropped from the airship and picked back up.

"That's expected," he said. "I'm Corin. I run the hospital ward, particularly the magicians. I hear you had quite the expenditure on the ground. Melted a whole building of an automaton." He pulled a green bottle out of his satchel. "Drink this. You'll feel much better."

She took the bottle and held it against her lips. It tasted cool and refreshing. Only after it ran down her throat did she think that it might have been wise to ask before drinking. She drank all of it, the few gulps the bottle held.

"What was that?" she asked, handing him back the bottle.

"Rejuvenation Potion," he said. "It's a blessing for magicians. Takes away that bite of running on empty."

Raven nodded. She didn't feel like asking questions or listening to an explanation of how it worked. She could feel the potion working, warming through her bones, waking her up, bringing a small amount of energy back to her body. She moved her arms and legs about. While the potion did not erase her sluggishness, she no longer felt as though she might collapse.

Corin watched her with a knowing smile. "Better?" he asked.

"Better," she said. Then, her heart squeezed. "What about the others? My friends. Zander, what about Zander? His arm—"

"Slow down," he said, holding a long-fingered hand in front of him. "They are all fine. Well, they're all alive."

She choked on that word.

His smile flickered into a frown of sympathy. "Can you stand? I'll take you to see them. They've been asking about you every hour."

"Zander—"

"We will see him first," he said, his words calming and soothing. "But let's make sure you're capable before we head out anywhere."

Corin moved to the bedside, arms waiting to catch her in case she fell. Raven worked her way to the edge of the bed, set her bare feet on the floor, and stood. The world wobbled once, then righted itself. She quickly slipped on her boots and the cloak. Corin led her down the corridor.

She could feel the gentle movement of the sky city, the vibration through the shined metal floor and the rosewood walls, humming and buzzing. The engines rumbled, a distant but constant roar. It thrilled her to be in a sky city, enough that a part of her hadn't yet accepted its reality. She wanted nothing more in that moment than to see Zander and make sure he had made it.

They came to the end of the corridor. Double doors led to the hall outside, to the rest of the airship, and four single doors led into the intensive care rooms. Two were occupied. Through the clouded glass, the first patient was a stranger, but the second—Raven caught her breath in her throat. She knew the dark hair, the bronze skin.

Corin let her into the room.

Zander's chest steadily rose and fell. He lived. A tube and a mask pumped air into and out of his lungs. They had removed his bloodied clothes; a linen blanket covered him from his ankles to his navel. Bandages lined his chest, thickest around his left shoulder. His left arm was gone. Nothing but a stump remained.

228

Raven stood at the bedside. His right arm lay exposed, unmoving. She gripped the bedsheet hard enough to turn her knuckles white. His arm—he had lost his arm. Tears gathered in her eyes. It felt like her fault. She should've been the one lying there, missing a piece, not him. She had been the stupid girl alone in the woods that day.

She hung her head. She didn't want Corin to see her shame and guilt.

Standing there, she heard the faint rumble of engines, the creak and groan of metal and leather and wood, the hissing of steam. An airship. A sky city. A dream realized. She would give it all up to make Zander whole again.

"The blade went completely through," said Corin. "Amputation was our only choice. It severed the nerves."

Raven bit her lip as the first tear slipped out of her eye. It drew a wet line down her face.

"But," said Corin, stepping into her view. He stood on Zander's left side. "We have other options now that the arm is gone. Mechanics. An automaton replacement."

She blinked at him. "A mechanical arm?"

He nodded. "It's not a new idea. But, this is something we will talk to him about when he wakes up."

When, not *if*.

Raven swallowed what tears she hadn't yet cried and braced herself. Zander would wake up; the medic said so. She looked down at Zander's still face. Her life had been a constant of ups and downs and unknowns since she had left that day with Zander on what she had thought would be her only adventure—that felt like a lifetime ago.

"There's a room set up for you," said Corin. "When you're ready, I can call someone to take you there."

Raven took a long look at Zander. Would he blame her for his missing arm? Would he agree to a mechanical replacement? She would have to wait for him to wake up. She took a deep breath, gave Zander's warm hand a squeeze, and let go.

A young boy led Raven out of the hospital and through a maze of hallways and staircases; she tried to keep her bearings, but within a few turns, she felt lost. The hospital was in the lower deck, said the boy. The lower deck looked like it had been cobbled together from a dozen other ships: some metal, some wood, some with curved doors, some with rectangular doors. Finally, he led her up a spiral staircase of iron lattice and into a corridor of rosewood paneling, shined brass grating, and polished steel—the upper deck.

The upper deck looked as romantic and beautiful as Raven had imagined airships being, only with a bit of pirate flare that she found quite endearing. He led her up a wide staircase and into an identical corridor to the one below. Rosewood doors lined the corridor, equally spaced. Each had a creature emblazoned on the wood in gold. He led her to the lion's door.

He knocked.

"Enter," came Rosaria's voice, and Raven's heart jumped into her throat as the boy opened the door. Raven stepped over the threshold, and her eyes at once fell on the princess. A relieved smile stretched over Rosaria's lips as she pulled Raven into an embrace. "Thank the Sisters."

Beyond Rosaria, the little room held the necessities. Not unlike an inn, only much nicer. Two beds were stacked on one side, fastened to the wall to keep them from toppling. One corner held a wash basin; the other held a small wardrobe and bookshelf.

"I can handle her from here," Rosaria told the boy, and he bowed and left without another word. Rosaria closed the door and let out a sigh of contentment. "I rather like the crew here. I feared at first they would be pirates and no good, but they have been beyond accommodating and pleasant."

Raven washed up and changed into clean, simple clothes—trousers, blouse, and plain corset with minimal boning. Though she could nap, she wanted to see the others first. Rosaria didn't object. She hooked her arm with Raven's and led the way to a lounge a floor above with a gorgeous view of the blue afternoon sky. Clouds floated in the distance, fluffy and unmoving as mountains, while wispy clouds raced by.

Thalame, Conrad, and a few others she didn't know sat around an oval rosewood table. Leather-padded chairs circled it. Three teapots had been scattered along it, none matching, set into a swiveling stand that moved with the ship so that the teapot remained steady. Cups hung off the stands, each a different pattern and color.

She met Thalame's eyes; he looked utterly exhausted, but he tipped his head to her in silent greeting.

Captain Luckett sat at the head of the table, looking like a pirate queen in her ornate chair. She slung one leg over the arm of her chair and sat with her arm draped over the other. Her brown hair had been washed, untangled, and braided back. Her drab prison clothes had been replaced with dark trousers, black leather boots, a beige blouse and dark blue corset, and a red coat with gleaming brass buttons and black trim—every bit a captain.

"There she is," said Luckett, motioning to Raven. In the light, her eyes appeared light brown but no less clever. "I hoped I would get the chance to thank you for getting me out of the Tombs and for giving me the chance to show off my new fleet to the Gray Elite. Those bastards won't be forgetting that defeat anytime soon." She laughed, and the hearty sound filled the room. She motioned to the empty chair to her left. "Sit."

Rosaria slipped her arm from Raven's and sat beside Conrad, who watched the exchange with curious eyes. Raven made her way to the captain's side, every pair of eyes in the room on her. She sat, and her gaze fell on the young man sitting across from her, on the captain's right. It took a moment to place his brown eyes and skin and assortment of rings.

Malik.

"Glad to see you're alive," said Malik, leaning in his chair like he had somewhere else he would rather be.

Raven made herself a cup of tea while the conversations along the table resumed. Luckett and Malik returned to a conversation of what in the ship had been repaired while she had been away, how many of the crew had died or left, anyone new who had joined, engine room gossip, and what news of the empire since they had made their dramatic escape.

She gathered that their majority of losses had been on the Gracitan side of the fight, while the rebels—as Malik called them—got away relatively unscathed.

According to Malik's gossip, more than just Wraiths had taken the opportunity to rebel against the Gray Elite.

Raven listened halfheartedly. Something about Luckett bugged her. She had dark brown hair and light brown eyes with streaks of gold like lightning. She and Malik shared several facial features—the straight nose, the shape of the lips, their ears—too many similarities for coincidence. They had to be related. Mother and son, if Raven had to guess. By Malik's beige-brown skin, his father had been Tinatunian.

"I hear my medics think your friend might be a good fit for one of their mechanical limbs," Luckett said to Raven.

One of—so there were others? Raven swallowed a large gulp of tea. "I suppose so."

"It's not as scary as it sounds," Malik explained. "Corin has a mechanical leg."

Raven blinked. "I hadn't noticed."

Malik nodded, confirming his point. "It's hard to notice when you're not looking."

Tea time passed casually, and as the others trickled out, Luckett invited Raven to come with her—by her tone, it was not a suggestion. Luckett sauntered beside Raven at a leisurely pace; Malik walked a step behind. Luckett led Raven through a verbal tour of the *Orion*: the engines, tanks, uppers and lowers, the barracks, the village, the cargo hold, the bridge. Raven hadn't the mind to keep track of all the jargon. It sounded familiar from her books, but she didn't want to admit that to Luckett.

Luckett led Raven into a room with cushy chairs and a beautiful rosewood desk and matching high-backed chair—the captain's office. One wall was entirely glass and held a fantastic view of the bridge. Raven approached the window. Down on the bridge, the pilot stood at the helm. To the right of the pilot, the navigation stations boasted more maps than Raven had ever seen, charts and more compasses than she thought necessary, even for a large ship. To the left of the pilot was a station packed with speaking tubes, dials, and gauges. It looked like the bridge from the *Marianne*, only larger and more complex.

At the bow, a glass front showed a marvelous view of the sky as the *Orion* parted the clouds around it.

"She's a beauty," said Luckett with a sigh. She sauntered to a mass of speaking tubes behind her desk. She flipped one open and said into it, "How are we doing, Bear?"

"Steady on course, Captain," said a hoarse female voice.

"That's what I like to hear," said Luckett, and she closed the speaking tube.

232

Down on the bridge, Raven spotted the woman called Bear—she manned the station of speaking tubes and gauges. She did not look like a bear, nor did her hoarse voice suit her small frame and tidy bun of dark hair.

The wall behind Luckett's desk held the largest map Raven had ever seen. It showed Gracita, Rhynwier, and Tinatun, but also the expanse of ocean on either side, and a large landmass on the far western side, an ocean away. Raven gravitated toward it without realizing it.

"Where is this?" Raven asked.

"That is known as the Untamed Lands," Luckett said. "It's a wild kingdom with nature as its ruler. Some say that dragons lurk in the dense jungles and wide desserts and that ghosts haunt the ruins of the people who came long before us."

"Have you been there?"

"Only once." Luckett came to stand beside Raven. She put her finger on the eastern side of the Untamed Lands, on a gulf surrounded by jungle. "Spent a week trying to navigate the coast, but it's like the land itself doesn't want you there. We would make maps, and then the land would change on us, and our maps were useless."

Raven's stomach turned over, but not in fear. It sounded like an adventure from a book.

"But I asked you here to speak about something different than the Untamed Land's impossibilities." Luckett sat in her captain's chair.

Raven walked back around the desk, only then realizing how she might have been disrespectful by going to the map. Luckett's map. One thing she knew for certain—do not disrespect the captain. She laced her hands together. Luckett and Malik both eyed her as though they had never met her before.

"Is there something in particular you require of me?" Raven asked, her voice reflecting her unease.

Luckett continued to study her.

Raven added, "I thank you for your timely rescue. We would have been dead if not for you and your crew."

"Do you still have the locket?" Malik asked.

Raven blinked at him but nodded. She put a hand to the chain around her neck and pulled it out of her blouse. Did Malik know about the centrum too? Thalame and the rest of the Dwellers did, and Conrad had figured it out on his own. She didn't think it extreme for Malik to have discovered it.

It didn't matter; she wouldn't let them have it either. She wouldn't let anyone use the centrum like she had done. She would keep it safe.

Luckett's eyes fell on the locket, and her gaze shifted into something between disbelief and remorse. She blinked, and dampness smothered her lashes. She brought a hand to her mouth, but it didn't hide her discomfort.

"Is something wrong?" Raven asked.

"You got that from your mother," Luckett said. Not a question.

"I did. It's all I have of her. She died when I was little."

"She died?" Luckett asked, eyebrows raised. The mistiness of her eyes cleared, and she fixed her piercing gaze on Raven. "*That's* what your father told you?" She scoffed.

Raven started at Luckett's insensitivity, but then her words clicked. "How did you know my father told me?"

Luckett sauntered around the desk and stopped in front of Raven. She took the locket in one hand and ran her thumb over the engraved gold. "I won this locket in a game of dice when I was twelve years old," Luckett said. "I cheated, but that's not the point. I carried it with me always until I met Samuel."

The implication smacked the breath from Raven's throat. Her words came out weak, "You gave it to him?"

"Not to him," Luckett said. "But to our daughter."

Raven took a closer look at Luckett, her light brown eyes, her peachy skin, her heart-shaped face. All thoughts ceased. Luckett cupped Raven's cheek and tilted her face up. Raven's heart trembled over and over—her *mother.*

"You look like me at your age," Luckett said. The mistiness returned to her eyes. "My mother's name was Raven. When I had to name a baby girl, that's the first name I thought of."

Raven couldn't speak, couldn't breathe. She had imagined her mother a hundred different ways, but never had she been a pirate captain of a sky city. Reality had always come at the end of any daydreams involving her mother, reminding her that her mother was dead.

But she wasn't.

As it sank in, Raven found her voice. She murmured, "What happened?"

"Samuel was a mechanic; I was a navigator. One thing led to another, and then I was pregnant. The war was raging, and the world was in a state of change and uncertainty. He insisted we go back to that little town of his to get away from the world for a while," Luckett said, her touch ginger on

Raven's chin. "I agreed because few captains want a pregnant girl working. You were born, and I couldn't sit still. Samuel settled well, but I hated it. I couldn't live underground. The walls felt like they were pushing in on me. I wasn't old yet, and I couldn't stand the slow life of retirement, not when I had so many years of my life yet." Luckett blinked, and the moisture along her eyelashes thickened. "When my baby girl was old enough to drink cow's milk, I left. Samuel refused to let me take my girl with me. He stayed on the ground; I returned to the sky."

"You left me," Raven managed to say. The weight of those words hit Luckett as hard as the realization hit Raven. She flinched as though struck.

"I wanted to take you with me," said Luckett, her voice thinning. "But your father refused me. He knew I lived dangerously, and he said I wouldn't be able to take care of a baby like he would, and I wouldn't find a nursemaid who would love her like he would. He seemed to think I'd let her wander right off the edge of the ship." She tried to laugh, but it faded. "He...made a good argument, and I...I left you with him."

Malik shifted. Raven glanced at him; he looked guilty.

"You knew about this?" Raven asked him.

Malik averted his gaze and nodded. "Your locket gave it away," he said quietly. "I remember playing with it when I was little. I knew where it had gone. When I saw it with you, and you said your mother gave it to you, I knew who you were."

"Malik is your brother," Luckett said. "Half-brother, but a brother still."

"Did you leave his father too?" Raven asked. The words left her mouth with a bitterness.

Luckett sighed through her nose. "Yes, but it's a different story. Malik's father was a nice man for a while, but underneath his handsome face was a violent drunk. He hit me once, and I didn't give him another chance. I took Malik with me because I knew I could raise him better."

Raven wiggled her locket out of Luckett's grasp and fell into one of the cushy chairs. She leaned forward, elbows on her knees. Her mother, alive and well, a captain of an airship. If she had known, she might have left Silver Glen sooner. Her father had known, and he had withheld the information from her all these years.

So much information, so many thoughts, rattling without course.

"And it seems you've inherited my sense of adventure," Luckett said with a sigh. She leaned against her rosewood desk. "I'm not sure if it's a blessing or a curse. Could be either. Runs in the family, I'm told. I had an uncle who sailed to the Untamed Lands and never returned. Who knows; he might be living in the wild out there."

Raven inhaled, held it, and slowly released it. So many secrets. So much, so fast. She met Luckett's gaze; it had softened.

"I guess I can't be that mad at you," Raven said to her mother. "You did rescue us, after all."

"You broke me out of prison," Luckett added. She tipped her head toward Raven. "Conrad's been telling me all about you. Really riled up the Gray Elite in Lenhala, and now we've nearly burned Moorin to the ground. The Gray Elite will be after blood this time—yours, to be specific—especially after that automaton meltdown." She let out a low whistle. "Magic also runs in the family." She motioned between her and Malik. "Likely another thing you picked up from me."

"You were a Wraith," Raven breathed as she remembered.

Luckett nodded. She closed her fist tight and then unfurled her fingers like a flower blooming. Something dark as midnight hovered in the air above her palm. It wiggled like water but thicker.

"What is that?" Raven said, pushing herself into the chair.

"Ink," Luckett said. "Stains like a bitch, though it helped me be one hell of a mapmaker."

"It's the same ink that we use to tattoo the runes," Malik added.

Luckett turned her hand over. The ink spilled out her hand and onto a piece of parchment. Rather than go everywhere like regular ink would have, it listened to Luckett's silent command and painted a rune onto the paper, perfect lines and curves, the rune the Wraiths tattooed on themselves, the rune Conrad had painted on her.

Raven glanced at the map behind the desk. It had been drawn with ink, the lines too perfect to have been brushed or stenciled, Luckett's map.

Luckett awaited Raven's response, but she didn't give her one. Raven didn't feel like explaining the mess of her magic to Luckett or Malik. She flattened her hands against her trousers, letting the heat from her palms soak into her thighs.

"Another time," Luckett said, her voice soft. She stood and sauntered to the map behind her desk, hands folded behind her back. When she spoke, she spoke with the strength of a captain. "We head north for now, away from Moorin. The news will spread, and the Gray Elite will be furious and hungry for revenge. They will be on the hunt. They might even see this as a declaration of war. It's hard to tell from this distance. We'll have to wait and see what happens. I've got ears on the ground in Moorin and Lenhala. Either way, we are getting out of the line of fire."

Raven nodded. War. At least Altair's Augur couldn't be activated, not without the centrum.

Luckett promised a hearty dinner, and Malik offered to walk Raven back to her cabin.

"Would you like a proper tour of the ship?" Malik asked.

"Not right now," Raven said. She didn't feel like walking. She wanted to lie down for a while and rest. Until dinner, or maybe until dinner the following day. She didn't know.

They paused outside her door. No one else stood in the corridor.

"It's okay," Malik said softly. He laced his graceful fingers together in front of him. "Do you want something to drink to take the edge off?"

She considered it but shook her head. She met his eyes. "I've never had a brother before."

"I've never had a sister." He gave her a sympathetic smile. "We will both be learning something new."

He hesitated, then drew Raven into an awkward hug, a man not used to hugging anyone. With an equally awkward parting, he left and she let herself into the room. Rosaria hadn't returned, leaving the room empty. Raven took a steadying breath—she'd had so few moments alone to think. She took off her boots and corset and meandered to the bunk beds. A few dark hairs clung to the bottom bunk's pillow, so Raven climbed to the top. A cloth panel hung along the side of the bed to prevent her from rolling out or being thrown should the ship tilt. The cloth was faded blue and stitched with clouds and stars.

Raven flopped onto her back and released an exhausted breath.

Before she slept, she had to see for herself—she pulled her locket from under her shirt and then unhooked it. She lifted it off her skin and held it up. She pressed her nails into the seam, and the mechanism gave—her heart stopped and tumbled into the back of her ribcage.

The glowing red centrum was gone. In its place was a clear crystal. Raven dumped the crystal into her palm. Cool to the touch.

Empty.

Then she knew without a doubt that her suspicions had been right. The iron box had kept the centrum contained and safe. Her locket had not. The centrum had slowly seeped through the metal and into her, infecting her with the fever. She had survived the fever, she had conquered it, and she had won the centrum's magic.

She returned the empty crystal to her locket and snapped it shut. She would explain herself to Zander and Thalame and the others. Later.

A strange calm came over her, one she hadn't felt in months. Without the centrum to keep safe, to hide and guard, she didn't have anything to lose in telling them about it. With the centrum gone, Altair's Augur could never be used. She had inadvertently prevented it.

She had stopped the worst from happening.

She tucked the locket under her pillow and reclined. The bed was soft, the blanket was warm, and she fell into a dreamless, peaceful sleep, unlike she'd had in months.

Raven woke to Rosaria's head peeking over the side of the bunk. Raven blinked rapidly to clear the intoxicating drowsiness from her eyes.

"Zander's awake," Rosaria said. "He's asking for you."

Raven bolted up and fumbled down the ladder. She quickly laced up her corset and pulled on her boots and ran into the corridor. Rosaria ran with her to the hospital and into the intensive care room. Zander was sitting up in bed, reclining on a mound of pillows, his sapphire eyes glassy but open. They fell at once onto Raven, and a sleepy smile stretched over his face. Fresh bandages wrapped his shoulder and his left arm's stump.

He lifted his right hand for her, and she grabbed it with both of hers. He tugged without force, trying to pull her closer. He hadn't the strength.

"I'm sorry," she said, collapsing into the chair beside the bed. She clutched his hand tighter. She pressed the back of his hand against her forehead. "I'm sorry."

"For what?" he asked. He spoke slow and sleepy.

"For everything," she said, her voice a plea. She met his eyes, her own wet with tears. "For running away, for getting caught, for messing up your plans over and over. I thought...I thought you didn't want me there. And now I..." She glanced at the stump of his arm. "I'm sorry for what happened to you."

"It's not your fault, Rae." Her nickname on his lips sent a wild surge down her spine. She wanted to curl up beside him on the hospital bed. "You didn't stab me. If not for you, that thing would have finished me off."

"If not for me, that thing wouldn't have hurt you in the first place," she said lowly, a mirror of what he had said to her not that long ago.

Zander frowned. "No. I shouldn't have tried to keep you safe like that. I was doing the opposite of what I wanted. I thought...I thought you'd be

238

safer if you stayed, so I could focus on the mission instead of worrying about you. I didn't want anything to happen to you. I should have just told you. I thought I'd get another chance when it was all over. And then you were gone...just gone." His sapphire eyes searched hers. "I looked for you. I didn't know what to do. I looked and looked, but you were gone."

She blinked. Warm tears smothered her eyelashes, and one traitorous tear trailed down her cheek.

"I should never have let you out of my sight," he whispered. "Not even for a second. No matter what."

"Zander," she started, but didn't know how to say what she wanted to say.

"I love you," he said. The words came out shaky, but they struck through her.

She gaped at him, sure she misheard.

"I love you," he said again, softer.

Raven gripped his hand tighter; her own shook. Everything inside of her seemed to have stopped at his words. She tried to form her own, but her throat refused to cooperate.

"I have for a while," he whispered. "I didn't know how to tell you. I thought..." He sighed, and a sad smile came over his face. "I asked your father for your hand, you know."

"You did *what?*" Raven's brows shot up, and her voice croaked.

"He said no," Zander said, smile widening. "He said he didn't trust me enough, and if I wanted his daughter, I had best prove myself. He said to ask again in a year. I'm sure this will count against me."

Raven laughed, and it unclogged whatever had closed her throat. She couldn't imagine Zander asking that of her father, but she could imagine her father resisting the urge to punch Zander. And her father's behavior in regards to Zander, the glances in her direction, looks exchanged with her stepmother, the odd look when Raven mentioned him—it made more sense.

"That's why I wanted you to come with me," he said. "I thought I would find the time to tell you."

She returned his sleepy smile. "If you had said those words to me at any other point than right now, I might have hit you."

"Ah," he said. "The invalid thing works for you, huh?"

She blushed but laughed. She leaned toward him and kissed him. Her lips met the soft wax of balm. She lingered a breath above his lips.

"Again," he whispered.

She leaned away. He pouted.

"You will get another one when you're better," she promised.

"I will hold you to that."

"You better."

He grinned, and that old arrogant mischief shone in his eyes. She brushed his dark hair out of his face. He would need a haircut too. The bottom half of his hair had grown out and gave him a shaggy look that she didn't like.

"What do you think about an automaton arm?" she said.

Zander's smile widened. "I told them I'd do it."

Her eyes widened.

"I can already picture it." He looked to where his left arm should have been. "Brass and steel, strong enough to shatter bones and deflect bullets and blades."

Raven smiled. Zander would get better. He would get a mechanical replacement for the arm that he had lost. The panic in the city would die down. She would explain her story to the others. They no longer needed to keep the centrum safe, and maybe she and Zander could join her mother in the skies, away from the Gray Elite, the automatons, the Hawks, the Wraiths, and everything else. They could find their own adventure in another part of the world, maybe Tinatun or the Untamed Lands or find somewhere entirely new.

She had no plan, and the world felt wide open for the first time in a long while.

General Oliver Deacon hated flying. He liked the convenience of flying, but he preferred his boots on solid ground.

His private airship had landed in Lenhala in the middle of the afternoon, and among the dozens of other airships coming and going from the docks, no one paid him any mind. He kept his face calm on the way to the house, but once past the servants and staff and safely in his study, he let his fury show.

Bested again by wicked magicians.

Wicked as sin, the lot of them. Mistakes of nature. They thought themselves gods among men, but he would prove no such thing existed.

But how was he supposed to know the Wraiths were planning an assault on the Gray Elite the same night he had planned to slip into the city unnoticed? His spies had seen the girl at his house—his own damn house—but by the time he had arrived, the city had been burning, sirens had been wailing, and the streets had been clogged with panicked masses and looters. The air docks had been shut down, and he'd had no choice but to return to Lenhala.

Someone among the workers at his estate had hidden the girl and her friend there, in a wing rarely used, right under his son's nose. He'd already reprimanded the boy for being narrow-sighted. It didn't matter; he would discover the traitor, even if he had to torture his entire staff to death. No one played him for a fool and lived. He knew from experience that someone would crack. He just had to keep pressing.

But it would have to wait.

Deacon sighed through his nose. No sense in worrying about it now. The girl had fled—on an airship, no less. Tracking her down again wouldn't be easy, but it could wait until she showed her face again. He had more important things to worry about.

Like a meeting he didn't want to be late for.

Deacon walked to the far side of his study, one shadowed by monstrous bookshelves. He pulled a heavy tome, pulling the lever hidden inside, and the far bookshelf swung open. A lantern waited just inside the passage. The small flame within the dusty globe flickered brighter and brighter as he made his way down the winding iron staircase. The door shut automatically after a few moments, though he paused to make sure it closed completely. He didn't want any snooping servants to find it again.

The stairs led deep into the hillside. It had originally been a bunker, an ancient meeting room used by the dead king and his generals before the Gray Elite had taken it over. Deacon had made a few minor adjustments, but overall, he had found the secret bunker a marvel for discreet meetings and uninterrupted naps. He paused at the large oak table in the center of the room to make sure nothing had been moved since he had last been inside. Seeing that nothing had, he started toward an iron door on the far side—one of his minor adjustments.

The door led down a stone hall with no lighting other than the lantern he held. The stone had been carved with magic. The smooth walls and ceiling and floor showed no signs of tools. It irked him that magic could simply bypass the tools of humanity.

The hall led into a cavernous chamber far below Lenhala and directly underneath the old palace. Another door led up into the palace's library, but Deacon kept that door locked at all times. He didn't want some Gray Elite to wander down and find his treasure. The room was an ancient structure of glass-smooth stone walls with decorative arches around the domed ceiling. It had come from a kingdom before Rhynwier, in the days of rampant and unchecked magic, a time of utter chaos.

And, as per their meeting agreement, the chamber had a single occupant. He stood on the far side, mostly in shadow. He had brought a lantern too, but it burned low. He drank from a short glass of amber. His dark suit blended in with the shadows around him.

"How is Moorin?" asked the man.

"The devastation is remarkable," Deacon said lightheartedly. "The Wraiths planned their attack well, striking hard to distract, and then striking harder. They've done enough damage that Moorin will be feeling it for years, maybe decades."

"They acted out of desperation," the other man drawled.

Deacon shrugged and waved away the talk. He walked to the table and set his lantern down. Maps of Moorin, Lenhala, and cities in between littered the table. He put a hand on his lower back and stretched. Blasted airship seats.

"I hear some are calling this a declaration of war," said the man, his tone lazy and bored. "I hear that the Gray Elite's prototype automaton was *melted.*"

Deacon snorted his answer. His spies had brought him the news, fear wide in their eyes. He wished he had seen it, but he was glad he hadn't. Magic like that shouldn't exist. "I can't comment on that nonsense," he said. "Regardless, Gracita would still be victorious in war."

"Not if you can't see your enemy," said the man. "The Wraiths are everywhere and nowhere. They have support throughout the kingdom."

Deacon grunted. He hated the entire idea of there being a society of magicians out there, consorting on all the wicked things they could do with their magic, the evil they could create.

The man in the shadows chuckled, a sinister sound that grated on Deacon's ears, like he had planned the whole thing from start to finish, right under Deacon's nose. "I think this is a prime time to test our project," the other man said darkly. "Remind any lingering rebels who is in charge and who is not."

"I agree," said Deacon.

Both men turned their attention to the structure that took up the majority of the chamber, a monstrous network of obsidian pillars, crystal veins, and limestone. It took up the space of a large house, reaching nearly to the top of the cavern. Altair's Augur. Horrible, mysterious, and beautiful.

The two men walked side by side to the platform that served as the control panel for the device. The user stood on an obsidian platform, before a limestone ring. Inside the ring were alternating crystal and obsidian spikes, leaving enough room between their points for the centrum.

Standing beside the augur, Deacon felt small, and he loved the feeling of having control over such a thing. Godly, even. No one knew how it worked, only that it did. The magical laws and logic that the device followed went beyond what anyone knew; even the dead scholars hadn't a clue of its workings. Deacon had read every book those fools had had on magic before tossing them into the fire, but he found nothing on how the machine worked, only that it existed. It didn't matter. The machine worked, and that was good enough for him.

Like Altair, Deacon didn't need magic to be powerful. Magic would bow to him.

Deacon reached into his suit jacket and retrieved the little iron box—the centrum. At the touch of smooth metal against his fingers, his heart skipped a beat. He restrained himself. Not too eager. He held the little box on his palm, offered it toward the other man, and asked, "Would you like to do the honors, Brigadier General Winchester?"

General Winchester gave him a small, lazy smile as he took the little box. "It would be my pleasure."

Deacon stood still while Winchester stepped up to the limestone ring, his shined shoes clicking against the stone, the lantern light sliding down his slicked-back hair. His sapphire eyes glittered in anticipation, despite his calm face.

This way, he could say without lying that Winchester had started the augur. His hands were clean.

Winchester set the box in the middle of the limestone ring. It hung there between the spikes without touching any of them, another feat of lost technology. Winchester placed his hand on the limestone pad underneath, and a gentle hum started. It sounded like a thousand children humming the same note, and it gave Deacon a horrible sense of being watched. The humming grew louder and louder as the device woke.

The crystals began to glow a faint yellow, then a glorious orange, and finally a violent red. A pulse surged through the crystal, toward the centrum. The energy would surge into the centrum, where it would be magnified tenfold, and from there, it would surge up the obsidian covered crystal tower of the device and into the Gray Elite watchtower, the tallest point in Lenhala, where the blast could be aimed and fired.

Right now, the canon was aimed at a small town east of Lenhala, a known hideout of magicians fleeing into Tinatun. That little town and its traitorous sheep farmers would be the first to see the true power of the Gray Elite.

Deacon felt a shiver in the bottom of his stomach just thinking about it.

Altair's Augur hummed louder and louder, the ancient magic working, and then—all at once, it silenced. The red magic flowed into the centrum and stopped.

Neither Winchester nor Deacon moved. Both looked at the centrum. Winchester removed his hand, and before he could try it again, Deacon pushed him aside. He put his own hand on the panel. The device whirled to life, humming and humming, glowing brighter and brighter. The red light surged into the centrum once again—and again stopped dead.

"Something is wrong," Winchester spat.

Deacon stared at his hand, then at the box. The box. The box. The box! He grabbed it and forced a dagger into the seam of it, wrenching the iron open.

The box was empty.

Deacon swore. That's why that little harlot had given it up so easily. She knew. She had taken it out before he could. She had tricked him, fooled him. Again.

"Well," Winchester said calmly, though his eyes burned. "This complicates things."

Deacon set the empty box on the table. "Yes, it does." The empty box. The melted automaton. A wicked smile stretched his lips. "But don't worry, old friend. I know exactly how to get it back."

About the Author

Beatrice B. Morgan lives in southern Illinois. When she isn't reading or writing, she is most likely playing a video game. She is a night owl, caffeine addict, yoga enthusiast, dog person, hopeless romantic, optimist, and shameless Ravenclaw.

Follow her online:

bbmorgan.com
Twitter: @BBMorgan_W
Facebook: @BBMorganBooks

STARS AND BONES:
Thief in the Castle

The notorious Juniper Thimble is destined for execution. Caught stealing the king's crown—in addition to her long list of crimes—she has only one way out. Juniper must survive the biggest, most deadly con of her life, commissioned by the king himself. Disguised as the crown prince's lover, she is forced to protect him with her life...literally. Guarded by a surly squire, relentlessly attacked by demons, and surrounded by mysteriously disappearing servants, Juniper must dispatch the threat to the prince's life before they find out who she really is.

books2read.com/thiefinthecastle

Authors 4 Authors Publishing

A publishing company for authors, run by authors, blending the best of traditional and independent publishing

We specialize in speculative fiction: science fiction, fantasy, paranormal, and romance. Get lost in another world!

Check out our collection at https://books2read.com/rl/a4a
or visit Authors4AuthorsPublishing.com/books

For updates, scan the QR code or visit our website to join our semi-monthly newsletter!

Want more heart-pounding YA? We recommend:

FYR

by Lisa Borne Graves

At seventeen, Toury arrives in Fyr, where magic is power, a prince's love is deadly, and female autonomy is a dream. Formerly a loner and burden to her adoptive parents, she ruins her chances of a fresh start by offending an ogler who just happens to be the prince.

Alex, the Prince of Fyr, is no novice when it comes to pressure. He has to face his father's ailing health, the expectation to marry soon, and the hidden necromancers trying to take over the realm by exploiting his dark curse. At least there's hope in a cheeky savior, but Earth girls aren't so easy.

books2read.com/fyr